Si
is pr

COLBY AGENCY

Back to the Beginning

**Colby Agency —
For the most private
investigations!**

DEBRA WEBB

was born in Alabama, USA, to parents who taught her that anything is possible if you want it badly enough. When her husband joined the military, they moved to Germany, and Debra became a secretary in the commanding general's office. By 1985 they were back in the States, and with the support of her husband and two beautiful daughters, Debra took up writing full-time and in 1998 her dream of writing for Silhouette came true. You can write to Debra with your comments at PO Box 64, Huntland, Tennessee 37345, USA, or visit her website at www. debrawebb.com to find out exciting news about her next book

Debra Webb

COLBY AGENCY:
Back to the Beginning

Safe by His Side
&
The Bodyguard's Baby

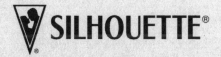
SILHOUETTE®

*First published in Great Britain 2005
Silhouette Books, Eton House, 18-24 Paradise Road,
Richmond, Surrey TW9 1SR*

COLBY AGENCY: BACK TO THE BEGINNING
© Harlequin Books S.A. 2005

Safe by His Side © Debra Webb 2000
The Bodyguard's Baby © Debra Webb 2001

ISBN 0 373 60295 2

. *161-0805*

*Printed and bound in Spain
by Litografia Rosés S.A., Barcelona*

Safe by His Side
by
Debra Webb

Dear Reader,

It is with great pleasure that I offer for your
reading enjoyment my first ever Silhouette
Intrigue, *Safe by His Side*. Raine and Kate are
two very special characters who will take you on
a journey of spine-tingling danger and edge-
of-your-seat suspense. Their story begins in the
Great Smoky Mountains of Tennessee, my home
state.

Jack Raine is the kind of enigmatic hero whose
mystery every woman yearns to unravel. Kate
Robertson is just the woman for the job, but
a case of amnesia makes the task a bit tricky.
Raine will do whatever it takes to protect Kate
from the threat that follows him, but there's no
way he can protect his heart from the woman
who may very well prove to be his enemy.

Safe by His Side was the first of my Colby
Agency stories. The Colby Agency is the best
in the business, and so are the men and women
who make up its ranks.

Please let me know how you're enjoying the
Colby stories. You may write to me at PO Box
64, Huntland, Tennessee, 37345, USA.

Enjoy!

Debra Webb

Many thanks to an outstanding guide, Lee Lewis, for his superior knowledge of Smoky Mountain trails, and to a terrific friend and expert drawer of maps, JoAnn Reynolds.

A special thanks to Natashya Wilson, a wonderful editor, for believing in my work and giving me this opportunity.

This book is dedicated to the man who helped make all my dreams come true— my wonderful husband, Nonie.

Prologue

"Failure in this assignment is almost a given," Victoria Colby told the investigator sitting on the other side of the immense oak desk that had once belonged to her late husband, James. "And should you choose to accept it, your life will be in constant danger—perhaps from more than one source," she added cautiously.

"I understand," Katherine Robertson replied.

Victoria eyed the young woman with more than skepticism—uncertainty...maybe.

Did she really understand?

Victoria wasn't so sure that she understood, herself. This was the most sensitive assignment the Colby Agency had undertaken in the ten years since she had assumed the helm. She'd been reluctant to take charge at first, but the small Chicago-based private investigations firm her husband had operated for the final years of his life had been near and dear to his heart. So Victoria had worked hard to make the agency the best in the business. It was the one thing she could still hold on to and feel close to James.

She passed a thin manila folder with a red "Top Secret" cover sheet on the front to the eager investigator, who immediately opened it to review the meager contents.

"Who does Jack Raine work for?" Katherine asked, glancing up only briefly.

"He used to work solely for the CIA, but four years ago he shrugged off the brass and became a contract agent. Since that time, he's worked for them all—NSA, DEA, CIA. He'd been under deep cover for the FBI for seventeen months when things went sour. The story is that he left the son of a prominent mob leader named Ballatore dead and an extraordinary sum of money missing."

"He turned?" Katherine looked from Victoria to the folder and back in disbelief. "A guy with a record like this?"

Victoria nodded slowly. She could hardly believe it herself. Jack Raine's work history might be restricted reading—which meant no significant details were available for their perusal—but his reputation was spotless, not to mention unparalleled. The man had every commendation his government could give him. Somehow, between the known and the unknown, things just didn't add up—at least, not for Raine's longtime friend Lucas Camp. Lucas had asked Victoria to take this assignment as a personal favor. Raymond Cuddahy, Lucas's boss and the new director of Special Operations, didn't like the idea of a civilian agency's involvement. He had, however, given his consent—eventually, and off the record.

Like Raine, Lucas had worked for the government in one capacity or another for most of his adult life. He had recruited Raine into the CIA and was probably the only man alive who'd had an up-close-and-personal relationship with the elusive Jack Raine. Both men now worked, in different roles, for a highly covert special operations unit created to provide support when all else failed.

Lucas had shared a cage with Victoria's husband as a prisoner of war during Vietnam. The two men had helped each other to survive. And Lucas had been a key factor in Victoria's own survival in this cutthroat business after her husband's death. Had it not been for Lucas, the Colby

Agency might have gone under long ago rather than becoming the elite organization it was today.

Victoria owed the man.

"It's your job to find out if he's turned." Victoria leaned forward and propped her elbows on her desk. She laced her fingers and rested her chin atop them. "And to bring him in, either way."

Without responding, Katherine turned her attention back to the file in her hands and frowned.

Victoria noted again what a lovely young woman Katherine was. She had only been with the agency for one year. At twenty-five, she still lacked the life experience Victoria usually preferred in her investigators, but Katherine was an especially quick study. Her looks were definitely deceiving. She had a model-perfect build, with long dark hair and even darker eyes. But beneath that pretty exterior lay the wit and intelligence of an excellent tracker. Instinct and guts—that's what had gotten Katherine noticed in recent months.

Victoria couldn't help wondering why such a beautiful young woman didn't seem to have much of a social life. Of course, the world was different now than it had been when Victoria was twenty-five. She studied the woman seated across from her. Perhaps Miss Robertson had the right idea, she mused. *Career first and foremost—and then maybe a husband and family later.* Those had been Katherine Robertson's exact words in her interview thirteen months ago, and she'd been true to her word. She concentrated on work with a determination Victoria seldom saw in a person her age.

"How did the Colby Agency end up with an assignment like this?" Katherine asked, breaking into Victoria's thoughts. "This case has federal jurisdiction written all over it."

"For six months Raine's own people have been unsuccessful in their attempts to bring him in. It's difficult to capture a man who, for all intents and purposes, doesn't exist. That—'' Victoria gestured toward the folder Katherine held ''—is all there is on Jack Raine. Each time his whereabouts have been locked on to, he's managed to slip through their fingers.

''Unfortunately, Raine knows too much about too many things to simply write him off. If he's turned, the government needs to know so they can defuse the situation. If he hasn't, then he needs protection. Ballatore wants him dead.''

Katherine examined the one and only photograph the file contained of her target. ''Well, if he's a criminal, he's certainly a handsome one,'' she said without looking up.

''He is that,'' Victoria agreed. With sky-blue eyes and sandy blond hair, Jack Raine was a breathtaking, lean and rugged six foot two. Victoria never doubted for one minute the other reputation Lucas had warned her followed Raine—lady-killer. But, beneath those devastatingly good looks, the man was a highly trained soldier, specializing in death and deception.

''Why me?'' Katherine looked up, her surprise at being handed such an important assignment evident.

Victoria sighed. This was the part that bothered her most. ''Raine is an infiltrator—the best in the business. He's spent the past twelve years of his life living on the edge, getting in and out of places no one else could. He's good, maybe too good. *If* you can find him, the extrication will be extremely risky. I have reason to believe that he's playing some sort of game—dropping clues like bread crumbs. It's more than possible that the few times he has been located were intentional. We might not get so lucky this time.''

Victoria paused a beat before she continued. ''To answer your question as to why you were selected for this assignment, you're a woman, and you're young and beautiful. That will get you closer than anyone else in our agency. The fact that you don't have a great deal of field experience will probably keep you alive.''

Katherine arched a dark eyebrow. ''How do you figure that?''

''If Jack Raine suspects for one second that you're tracking him, he won't take the time to find out which side sent you.''

''Oh.'' Katherine dropped her gaze to the folder in her lap and studied it for a moment. ''I see.''

Victoria straightened and leveled a serious gaze on the Colby Agency's newest investigator. ''I'll understand completely if you choose to decline. I'd never ask one of my people to take a job they didn't feel comfortable with.'' She drew in a heavy breath and added, ''I have to admit, Katherine, this one worries me, but you're our best shot at getting close to this guy.'' And Lucas is depending on me, she didn't add.

As Victoria had anticipated, Katherine met her gaze with a determined one of her own and, without the slightest hint of misgivings, asked, ''When do I start?''

IGNORING THE DRIZZLING November rain that dampened her hair and chilled her to the bone, Katherine tossed the one duffel bag she'd allowed herself into her rented car. She checked her small shoulder bag once more to confirm that a full prescription of her heart medication was there. She shook the small bottle of pills and smiled. She was definitely ready. Her little secret would be safe as long as she took her medicine and steered clear of an in-depth physical examination until she had proven herself. Then it wouldn't matter, the agency would keep her anyway. She had worked too hard for this opportunity to lose it because she couldn't measure up to someone else's perception of acceptable physical condition.

Finding Jack Raine hadn't been as difficult as she'd imagined it would be. It had taken her only two weeks to pinpoint his location based on the latest information Lucas had given her. It seemed almost too easy. She wondered if Jack planned it that way. Did he savor the chase?

Catch me if you can?

She shook her head at the thought of the kind of man who would get his jollies that way. What purpose could it possibly serve for him to yank around the very system for which he had once worked? Something just wasn't right. Katherine had that feeling—the one her father called cop's instincts. Except she wasn't a cop. She had failed the required physical. The same type required by the Colby Agency for investigators. But Katherine had already been employed by the agency as a researcher, so she had delayed the appointment after her promotion. Now all she had to do was prove herself. Then the results of the physical wouldn't matter.

After arriving in Gatlinburg the afternoon before, Katherine had checked into a hotel. Within a few hours of her arrival she had located Raine's residence and done a little advance scouting.

His place was the typical Smoky Mountain retreat, a rustic rental cabin that probably had a fabulous view of the surrounding mountains and valleys. The place sat a good two miles off the blacktop in a particularly remote area.

The rendezvous point and estimated time of arrival had been arranged with Nick. All was go.

Katherine slid behind the wheel of the green Ford Taurus and checked her reflection in the mirror. She swiped the raindrops from her face and immediately banished the flicker of uncertainty she caught in her eyes. This was her big chance—she wasn't about to blow it by getting cold feet.

"You can do this, Robertson," she whispered sternly.

Despite her dislike of the reasons she'd been chosen for the assignment, she intended to make the best of it. She might be young and she might be new, but she was a damn good investigator and tracker. And she intended to prove that her physical limitations wouldn't hold her back.

Nick didn't approve. And her father would likely blow a fuse when he found out. But by then it would be a done deal and they would both see.

She could do this.

She would do it.

Katherine started the engine, set the transmission to Reverse and put her plan in motion.

Thirty minutes later, the drizzle and the fog making the curvy mountain road even more treacherous, Katherine neared her destination. She quickly reviewed her strategy one last time, then took three slow deep breaths to calm her racing heart. She assured herself once more that she could do this.

Katherine spotted the sudden movement on the highway in front of her too late. She slammed on the brakes and swerved hard to the right. She felt the wheels lock. Heard the squeal of tires.

And then everything went black.

Chapter One

Jack Raine jerked his front door open and stared down at the drenched woman standing on his deck. The freezing precipitation had gone from bad to worse in the last hour, and she appeared to have gotten the worst end of it. He had lived in this remote location for over a month without a visitor and he damn sure didn't want one now. This wasn't the sort of place that attracted door-to-door salespeople or that a passerby merely stumbled onto.

"If you're lucky," he said roughly, "you're lost."

The woman drew back a step at his brusque tone. "I'm…I had an accident," she stammered.

"Accident? Let's see some ID," he demanded. He would never understand why anyone would be out on a crappy morning like this. In the mountains, days like these weren't fit for man or beast. And whoever his visitor was, she certainly didn't fit either category. She didn't even have on a coat. "Where the hell's your coat?"

"What?" The woman stared up at him as if his question made no sense at all.

For the first time, Raine noted the dazed look in her dark eyes. Her arms were wrapped around her waist, and she swayed slightly before she caught herself. With one trembling hand she pushed long, dark strands of hair from her face. Rivulets of water slid down her pale cheeks. A blast of cold November wind whipped across the deck. She shivered. And damned if her teeth didn't chatter as well.

Raine swore under his breath and yanked her inside. This was the last thing he needed. He slammed the door and stared down at the trembling female with complete irritation and utter distrust. She was dripping wet from head to toe.

"I—I just need to use your phone," she said weakly. Her frail attempt to free herself from his grasp only served to send her swaying backward. When he steadied her, she almost wilted in his arms.

"Whoa," Raine said, concerned. "You need to get out of those wet clothes and warmed up before you do anything else."

"The phone…I just need to use the phone," she whispered before she closed her eyes and sagged against his chest.

Instantly he felt the wet and cold invade the warmth of his dry clothes. Raine blew out a breath of frustration and did the only thing he could—he picked her up and carried her to the bathroom. He had to get this lady warmed up fast. As cold as she was, shock and hypothermia represented definite threats. Concern overrode his usual self-preservation instincts.

He settled her on the closed lid of the toilet and watched for a moment to ensure that she wasn't going to fall over. She shivered uncontrollably. He crouched in front of her and removed her hiking boots and rolled off her socks. She sat there, seemingly unaware of his movements.

Raine opened the shower door and twisted the hot-water valve to wide open. Once the water was steaming, he adjusted it to a bearable but still plenty hot temperature.

"Okay, lady, let's see if we can't get your body temperature headed in the right direction," he muttered more to himself than to her. If she heard him, she didn't react.

Raine pulled the dazed woman to a standing position and then helped her into the shower. When the hot water hit her she gasped, shuddered violently and sagged against the translucent glass wall. Before Raine could catch her, she slumped to the tile floor, the water spraying directly on her face.

"Damn," he growled. He reached inside and tried to pull her to her feet, she only whimpered and huddled more deeply into a fetal position. Muttering expletives, Raine stepped into the cubicle and pulled her to her feet, then wished to hell he had turned off the water first. Too late now. Besides, she needed the heat a lot more than he needed comfort.

"You have to get out of these clothes," he told her. Liquid heat pelted his skin through his flannel shirt.

She lifted her hands to her blouse and worked on a button, her movements stiff and awkward. Raine swore under his breath. At this rate, she'd never get her clothes off. Raising her body temperature was top priority. He had hoped to allow her some privacy during the process. But if she couldn't do it, he'd just have to do it for her.

What the hell? He'd undressed plenty of women in the past. He pushed her hands away and deftly began to release the remaining buttons.

She jerked back and stared up at him. He could see that it took her a while to bring him into focus. "What are you doing?" she asked weakly and clutched at his hands. Her pupils were unevenly dilated.

He cursed through clenched teeth.

Concussion.

She had a damn concussion. Why hadn't he noticed that before? He knew the signs. Her left temple was bruised. Gingerly he touched the discolored spot. She winced and drew away but not before he felt the size of the lump that had formed there.

"We need to take the rest of your clothes off. We have to get you warm and into something dry," he said as he resumed the unbuttoning process. To his relief, her hands fell away and she made no further protest.

"Thank you," she said softly, her breath whispering across his downturned face.

Raine tightened his jaw. He wouldn't say she was welcome—because she wasn't. He didn't want her here... didn't need her here. But he couldn't just let her die out in the cold any more than he could neglect an injured animal. He looked at the woman silently watching his fingers undo the final button of her blouse and wondered if he was making a big mistake.

He peeled the wet blouse down her arms and pitched it to the bathroom floor. Steam billowed around them and sweat beaded on his forehead as he reached for the hem of her undershirt. She automatically lifted her arms and closed her eyes. When he pulled the undershirt over her shoulders and then her head, he tensed. The scrap of cotton slipped from his fingers and joined her blouse on the wet tile floor.

Raine's gaze riveted to her naked breasts. Not particularly large breasts, but they were nicely rounded and the rosy tips tilted slightly upward. He had the sudden, insane urge to draw one into his mouth and taste it.

She shivered and he forced his gaze back to her face only to find her watching him from beneath half-closed lids. Her lips parted and for one instant Raine allowed himself to want her, but then she whispered, "I'm so cold."

Raine turned his back and silently cursed himself for the bastard he was. "You can do the rest," he said harshly. Surely she could get her jeans off. Hell, she probably could have gotten the blouse off if he'd given her time. Perverted SOB, he cursed himself once more.

What the hell had gotten into him? It hadn't been that long since he'd had a woman. Ogling an injured female was about as low as a man could go. A muscle in his tense jaw jumped when he heard her small sounds of frustration and fatigue as she struggled with the wet jeans. Raine clenched his fists and ignored the urge to turn around and look at her. The spray of hot water on his chest did nothing to calm his mounting tension or the hard-on he had acquired in the last sixty seconds.

He flinched when she touched his rigid shoulder. "I can't do it," she said wearily.

Raine licked his lips and swallowed tightly. This was damn ridiculous. He'd seen more than his share of naked women, what the hell was the big deal with this one?

He turned around slowly and met her pleading gaze with an annoyed glare.

"I'm sorry," she managed to say weakly before collapsing against the shower wall.

Raine set his jaw so hard he thought his teeth would crack. He grasped the waistband on either side of her slender hips and tried without success to peel the material down as he'd done with the blouse, but the tight-fitting jeans wouldn't cooperate. He sucked in a deep breath and did what he knew he had to. Raine pushed his hands inside and worked the material, panties included, down over her icy skin.

She was lucky to be alive. The last time he'd touched skin this cold, it had belonged to a dead man.

As chilled as her body was, his was getting more heated by the moment. His groin tightened painfully when his hands moved over the swell of her hips and glided down several inches of thigh. He straightened, held her firmly by the waist, placed his bare foot between her legs and pushed the jeans and skimpy panties down to her ankles.

He immediately averted his gaze from the triangle of dark curls between her thighs.

He almost groaned. He'd been in these woods longer than he'd realized.

She braced both hands against his chest while she struggled to kick her feet free of the soggy material.

"Thank you," she murmured on a frail breath when she'd finally freed herself. She squeezed her eyes shut and swayed back against the wall.

Raine kicked the jeans to one side. "No sweat," he lied.

He knew the hot water wouldn't hold out much longer, so he stripped off his own shirt, pulled her against him and turned her back to the hot spray. She sucked in a sharp breath and clung to him helplessly. He bit the inside of his jaw to stifle the groan that rose in his throat at the feel of her firm breasts pressed into his chest.

Damn, this woman was going to kill him and she didn't even have a weapon.

They stood in the steamy shower until the water began to cool and her shivers had subsided. Raine held her steady with one arm while he turned off the water. He guided her out and helped her dry. He focused intently on the job rather than the peach-colored skin flushed from the hot shower.

He used another towel to squeeze her long, thick hair dry. Neither spoke during the drying process. Raine refused to acknowledge how good her made-for-loving body looked. Curvy and firm, yet soft. Tall, but not too tall, with long, shapely legs. Chestnut-brown hair and dark chocolate eyes—eyes that would surely darken even more with passion.

When her hair was as dry as it was going to get without a blow-dryer, Raine wrapped a clean towel around her and tucked the corner beneath her arm. He quickly dried his chest and arms and tossed his towel to the floor, then swiped his wet feet.

She gazed up at him with those dark, shimmering eyes, a ghost of a smile touched her lips. "I feel much warmer now."

Before he could respond, her knees buckled and Raine barely caught her before she hit the floor. He drew her into his arms and carried her into the bedroom. After depositing her on the bed, he rummaged through the chest of drawers until he came up with a bulky sweatshirt. It would fit more like a dress on her, but it would have to do. Besides, he decided, beggars couldn't be choosers. He looked at his unwelcome visitor as he retraced his steps to the bed. At the moment she didn't look as if she cared about much one way or another.

"Hold up your arms," he ordered. She obeyed and Raine immediately regretted his command. With her arms extended above her head, the towel fell away from her upper body, giving him another good look at her perfect breasts.

Raine shoved the sweatshirt sleeves onto her arms and then pushed the neck opening over her head with a bit more force than was necessary. She winced as the material slid down her face.

"Dammit," he muttered. He'd hurt her, and all because he couldn't prevent his body's reaction to hers. Raine stepped to the side of the bed and drew back the covers. When he had readjusted the irritating bulge in his wet pants, he walked back to the foot of the bed and lifted the woman into his arms. She pressed her cheek to his chest and closed her eyes. He frowned when his heart skipped a beat or two at the feel of her soft cheek against his skin. What the hell was wrong with him? He didn't usually get so worked up over a blasted female.

Raine placed her in the middle of the bed and covered

her with every blanket and quilt he could find. He stalked into the great room, fingered the thermostat to a higher setting, then placed several logs on the fire. He stoked the blaze until he was satisfied that it wouldn't go out for a while. Then he trudged back to the bedroom and adjusted the blinds to let in the warm glow from the sun that had finally broken through the thick clouds hanging in the sky. The rain had stopped.

The newscast had said that the temperature would reach a pleasant forty degrees today, if the clouds cleared. Raine blew out a disgusted breath and turned back to the bed.

There was no telling how far his mystery guest had walked before she had stumbled upon his place. Raine had picked this particular cabin because of its seclusion. With the high volume of tourists floating in and out of Gatlinburg, his was just another face in the crowd on the rare occasions that he went into town. The last thing he had expected way out here was company.

As soon as he was sure the woman was out for the count, he'd put on dry clothes and take a ride to check out her vehicle. There would likely be some form of identification in her car. He wanted to verify her accident story as well, for his own peace of mind. She certainly seemed harmless enough, but Raine hadn't survived this long by letting his guard down—even for a beautiful woman in distress.

If she had merely had an accident and showed up at his door for help, she had nothing to worry about. He'd keep an eye on her and rouse her every couple of hours just to be safe. When she awoke, he would drive her into town and drop her off at the emergency room. He had enough medical training to know she would probably be fine, but medical attention wouldn't hurt.

If *anything* at all appeared suspicious about her ID or the means by which she had arrived at his door, she wouldn't need medical attention—she'd need an undertaker.

HER EYES OPENED and she blinked to focus. She stared at the white ceiling for a long time before it occurred to her to try to move. Her head ached and felt oddly heavy. She licked her lips. Her mouth was as dry as sandpaper and she could hardly swallow.

On her left, sunlight poured into the room from a large window, spreading its golden glow across deep green carpet. The bright light hurt her eyes, but at the same time felt good against her face. She was tired and it was quiet. Maybe she should just go back to sleep, she thought, her eyes closing of their own accord.

"How's your head?"

She snapped her eyes open and jerked her attention to the right, toward the deep male voice. Every aching muscle in her body tensed, and her head screamed in protest of the sudden move.

He sat in a chair a few feet away, watching her. She blinked and then frowned. Did she know this man? He looked vaguely familiar. She inspected his features more closely. Blond hair, light blue eyes. His face was lean and angular, exceptionally handsome. He seemed tall, but it was hard to tell with him sitting down. Still, she couldn't put a name with his face. What had he asked her? Her head...yes...*how was her head?*

"It..." She cleared her rusty voice and tried again. "It hurts."

"My guess is that you have a concussion. You probably need to see a doctor. I'll take you into town to the hospital."

He didn't sound as if he relished the idea. She wondered if this man had some reason to dislike her. She pushed up into a sitting position and the room spun wildly for a sickening moment. Her stomach roiled. She groaned and rested her head in her hands.

"Where am I?" she asked in a thready whisper.

"Don't you know?"

She thought about that for a while, but no matter how hard she tried to form an answer she couldn't. She had no idea where she was. She shook her head and immediately regretted it.

"Your license says Virginia. Is that where you're from?"

Virginia? Was she from Virginia? She should know where she was from. If her license said so, then she must be. "Yes," she finally told him for lack of a better answer.

He didn't speak again for a while, but his intense gaze never left her. His close scrutiny made her uneasy. "Who are you?" she ventured hesitantly.

"What's *your* name?" he asked, ignoring her question.

"What?" That was a ridiculous question. He'd seen her license, he should know her name without asking. She scanned the room once more. Besides, why would she be in a strange man's bedroom? He must know who she was. He had to be playing a joke of some sort. Well, she didn't want to play. Her head ached.

"Tell me your name," he repeated sternly.

She opened her mouth to speak, but nothing came. She frowned and snapped it closed. Her name…what was her name? She had to know her own name. Panic slid through her veins.

Everyone knows their name.

She threw the covers back and stood too quickly, only to plop back onto the bed. As soon as the dizziness had passed, she stood again, a bit more slowly this time "I have to go," she announced as calmly as she could. She concentrated on putting one foot in front of the other. She had to get out of here. Away from this man. Away from his questions.

"Your name is Denise."

She silently tested the name as she took another step toward the door. *Denise*. It didn't ring a bell, but if that's what her license said... "Yes, that's it."

He snagged her arm and pulled her around to face him. He shook his head and swore, an ugly four-letter word. "Then why does your driver's license say Kate?"

How had he moved up behind her so quickly, so quietly? Why was he holding her arm so tight? "I...I don't know," she stammered, her voice faltered as fear mushroomed inside her.

He pulled something from his pocket and placed it in her hand. A driver's license. "That's you." He pointed to the picture. "Kate Roberts."

She stared at the picture, concentrating. Was that her? She suddenly realized that she didn't know what she looked like. Hysteria bubbled up in her throat. How could she not know what she looked like? She jerked free of his grasp and half ran, half stumbled to the dresser. She peered at her reflection in the mirror.

Terror gripped her. She didn't recognize the face staring back at her. She moistened her lips and swallowed tightly. She looked at the reflection again, mentally inventorying the details. Dark hair and eyes, pale skin. She looked at the picture on the driver's license once more. It was the same face. Kate Roberts, she read. *Kate*. That sounded right.

"Your clothes should be dry by now. When you're dressed, I'll take you to the hospital." He started toward the door.

"Wait," she called after him. When he faced her, she asked, "Why don't I know my name? Is there something wrong with me?" The panic tightened like a steel band around her chest now. She braced her left hand against the dresser for support. The license dropped from her slack hold as her right hand fluttered to her throat where her breath had caught.

He hesitated, seeming uncertain of how to answer. "You were in a car accident. It looks as if you hit a deer. I think maybe you bumped your head pretty hard." He shrugged. "They'll be able to help you at the hospital."

She released the breath she'd been holding as she watched him disappear. She turned all the way around in the large bedroom then. Absolutely nothing looked familiar. She noticed the bathroom door open and walked slowly in that direction. At least she knew she had to relieve herself, that was something.

After she'd taken care of necessary business, she picked up a comb from the vanity and fought with the tangles in her hair. She stared at her reflection. "Kate," she whispered. She looked like a Kate—didn't she?

When she was satisfied with the state of her hair, Kate walked sluggishly back into the bedroom. She found that if she didn't move too quickly, the dizziness didn't overwhelm her. The man stood quietly waiting for her. He'd piled jeans, panties, T-shirt, socks, shoes and a wrinkled blouse on the bed.

"The sooner you're dressed the sooner you'll get the medical attention you need."

"Thank you," she murmured. Kate moved to the bed and inspected the stack of clothing. Were these the kind of things she liked to wear? She had no idea.

Kate heard the door close and she looked around to find herself alone. She pulled off the huge sweatshirt and tossed it on the bed. After donning the panties, socks and jeans, she pulled on the T-shirt. Kate reached for the wrinkled blouse, but thought better of it. She'd just keep the warm sweatshirt. She sat on the edge of the bed and tugged on the high-top boots.

Kate picked up the driver's license and tucked it into the pocket of her stiff jeans. She looked at herself again in the mirror and summoned her courage. A doctor would know why she couldn't remember who she was. Everything would be fine just as soon as she got to the hospital.

Kate firmed her resolve and went in search of the man who had promised to take her to help. She found him in the great room warming by the fire. He'd already pulled on his coat. He stepped to the sofa and picked up a parka and a small purse. "These were in your car."

Kate accepted the items and draped the long, narrow strap of the purse over her shoulder, then pulled on the tan-colored coat. The sweatshirt hit the tops of her thighs, the coat only came to her waist. What a fashion statement, Kate mused. But at the moment, she truly didn't care. Remembering the license, she stored it in the purse.

"Do you know what these are?" he asked, holding out what appeared to be an unlabeled prescription bottle for her inspection.

Kate took the bottle and twisted off the cap. She peered at the small blue pills it contained, then shrugged as she recapped it. "Are they mine?" She met his watchful gaze. Why did he look at her like that?

"They were in your purse, so I would assume they belong to you." He plucked the bottle from her hand and jammed it into his coat pocket. "There was a duffel bag in the trunk, I've already put it in my Jeep. Are you ready?"

"I'm ready," she told him, somehow as anxious to be away from him as he appeared to want to relieve himself of her. Though she didn't quite feel threatened, something about him made her uneasy.

Katherine followed the man out into the cold sunshine.

It looked to be late afternoon. The sun hovered just above the tops of the evergreen trees surrounding the cabin and the small clearing. A gravel driveway veered down the slope and off into the woods. Did she know this place? Had she been here before? With him? Her gaze darted to the handsome stranger who appeared to be her reluctant savior.

He reached to open the door of his Jeep, but hesitated. He cocked his head and listened, his gaze narrowed. "Damn," he muttered and quickly shoved her against the closed door.

"What's wrong?" she asked, frowning at the throb in her head generated by his sudden move. Then she heard it too. The distinct sound of gravel crunching beneath tires.

He spouted another curse and then turned to her, his gaze fierce. "Listen to me, Kate," he said harshly. "If that's who I think it is, we're in deep sh—"

"I don't understand," she broke in, fear snaking around her chest and squeezing like a boa constrictor.

"Listen," he growled, giving her a little shake. "They won't hesitate to kill both of us, do you understand *that?*"

Kate nodded, ignoring the intense ache it caused. She couldn't breathe…she couldn't think. Kill them both? What was he talking about? Why would anyone want to kill her?

Call in…

The phrase flitted through her mind. What did it mean? Oh, God. What was happening? Her panic was complete now, fueled by her inability to comprehend the situation. She shuddered against it. Closed her eyes to make it go away.

His hands were under her sweatshirt, probing the waistband of her jeans. Kate snapped her eyes open. "What are you doing?" she cried, tears burning behind her lids.

"Kate, you're our only chance at surviving this little

party." He captured her gaze with his, and the sheer determination there forced her to pay attention. "This—" he shoved something hard and cold that she somehow recognized immediately as a gun into her waistband. She instinctively recoiled, but he caught her by the waist and held her still "—is our only chance." His cold blue gaze pierced hers. The feel of his roughened palm against her bare skin felt strangely soothing. "Just listen to me, and when the time comes, do what I tell you—don't hesitate—just do it no matter what it is. Can you do that?"

Before Kate could respond, a car skidded to a halt right beside them. Two men jumped out of the black sedan, big, ugly guns in hand.

Oh, God. They were going to die. And Kate didn't even know why. How had she gotten in the middle of all this? She lifted her gaze to the man standing beside her. What had this man done to deserve to be hunted down like this? Wary and uncertain as to how to react, she aimed her attention at the two men stalking purposely toward them.

"Well, well, Danny, looks as if we've found our man," the larger of the two men said with a sneer. He waved his gun and added tauntingly, "And it looks as if he's got the little woman with him, too."

The man beside her shifted his body closer to hers. "She's just a lay I picked up in town last night."

Instinctively, Kate started to refute his words, but before she could speak, the goon with the gun moved closer.

Vinny grabbed her purse from beneath her jacket and looked inside, fishing out her license. "She looks a little worse for wear." He winked at Kate and shoved license and purse back at her. "What'd you do, Rick, ride her all night?"

Rick... His name was Rick. Kate looked at the man standing next to her and tested the name. She frowned. He didn't really look like a Rick. But what did she know?

"Maybe she's still got a little fun left in her." The goon moved closer, snagging Kate's chin in his beefy hand.

Kate gasped. Rick pushed between them. "Don't touch her," he warned in a voice so deadly it sent shivers skipping down her spine.

"You ain't in no position to be giving orders, Ricky boy. Pat him down, Danny," he directed the other goon.

Rick stood stone-still while the man named Danny frisked him. The whole scene took on a surreal quality. It suddenly occurred to Kate that this was just like in the movies. Two big guys in black suits arrived in a black sedan carrying scary black guns and...*she was going to die.*

The urge to vomit burned at the back of her throat. Kate fought the impulse. She felt certain that such a move would not endear her to these men. If they thought she was sick they might just shoot her on the spot.

"That's it, Vinny," Danny announced as he handed the other man a gun that looked very much like the one they both carried.

Rick had been carrying that gun. Kate suddenly recalled that she, too, carried a gun. Did it look like that? She tried not to breathe too deeply now, remembering the cold steel object tucked into her jeans. Her head throbbed insistently.

"How the mighty hath fallen," Vinny sneered, the words filled with sheer hatred. He stepped closer, until he was toe to toe with Rick. Vinny stood there for a long moment and stared before he spat in Rick's face.

"You don't deserve to live another minute. If I didn't have strict orders to take you to Dillon, I'd kill you myself, right now." Vinny's mouth twisted in anger. "But the old man, he wants you to look him in the eye and tell him what you did. Otherwise I would do you right here."

Rick rubbed his hand over his face to rid himself of the man's spittle, then cocked his blond head. "What's stopping you, Vinny? I won't tell if you don't," he said in a patronizing tone.

"Shut up, you piece of crap," Vinny bellowed as he shoved the tip of his gun barrel under Rick's chin. "I might forget orders for once."

Kate's heart almost shuddered to a stop then, but Rick only laughed derisively. "Don't kid yourself, Vinny, you're a made guy all the way down to your Gucci loafers. You don't take a piss without orders."

"Get in the frigging car." Vinny shoved Rick in the direction of the sedan.

Rick pulled Kate close to his side. She didn't have time to decide if being near him was a relief or not. Gun barrels stuck in their backs, Kate and Rick were ushered forward.

"You, up front," Vinny said, and propelled Kate toward Danny.

Danny half dragged her to the passenger side of the car and pushed her inside. Kate glanced at Rick in the back seat. She wondered if he had a plan. She hoped he had a plan. Was the gun in her waistband part of that plan?

Once Danny slid behind the wheel, they headed down the sloping driveway. Kate took one last look around her in hopes of remembering something, anything, but nothing came.

She studied the driver. He appeared young and almost innocent upon first inspection, early twenties maybe, but he looked as mean as a junkyard dog on closer examination. She listened to the heated conversation between the two men in back. Rick—the name still felt strange— goaded the other man unnecessarily, in Kate's opinion. It looked as if he intended to get them both killed long before they reached a destination.

"How does it feel to know you slept with a killer?"

Kate jerked her head up and stared at the driver, Danny, who'd directed the question at her. "What?"

"Didn't he tell you?" he quizzed with a widening grin. "Rick's a cold-blooded killer. There's no telling how many men he's killed. Hundreds, I'd guess."

Kate moved her head slowly from side to side in denial of his words. Why was he telling her this? She didn't want to hear it.

"Well, it's true." He shot her a sidelong smirk. "But he's going to pay now."

Could she possibly believe anything this man told her? Who were these people? She closed her eyes. Maybe he was only taunting her, trying to scare her. He didn't need to do that, she was already scared to death. God, her head hurt.

Call in...

The words skittered across her mind again. What did they mean? *Call who?*

"Too bad you had to be in the wrong place at the wrong time, baby," Vinny said as he kicked the back of Kate's seat.

"Kate's a lifesaver," Rick remarked wryly. "She gave me a second chance."

"A second chance at coming, maybe," Vinny scoffed. "Kate?"

Kate tensed at the sound of Rick's voice when he said her name. The tiny hairs on the back of her neck stood on end. Something was about to happen.

"Remember what I told you, Kate. You're my only chance," Rick said slowly. "*Our* only chance."

"Shut your frigging mouth," Vinny commanded. Kate heard the grunt that followed a hollow thud, knowing that Rick had just been whacked across the abdomen by the goon in the back seat.

Kate's head swam. What was she supposed to do? How could she save them? She could feel the cold steel jabbing into her pelvis. What did he want her to do?

And suddenly she knew.

Slowly, while keeping a close watch on the driver, she eased her right hand across her thigh and under her sweatshirt. With a swiftness that shocked even her, she drew the gun and expertly pointed it at the driver's head. She even held it with both hands just as she'd seen in the movies.

"Stop the car," she commanded in a voice she hardly recognized.

"What the hell?" Danny shouted, almost losing control of the speeding car.

"Give me that gun, bitch, or I'll blow your man's head off!" Vinny barked.

"Squeeze the trigger, Kate," Rick ordered coolly.

Kate looked from Rick to the man driving the car. Was he insane? She couldn't do that? How could she do that?

"Gimme the gun!" Vinny roared, pressing the barrel of his own gun hard into Rick's temple.

Kate's eyes darted back and forth between the men. What was she supposed to do? Everyone was yelling at once. Danny shot her quick, nervous glances, his knuckles white as he clutched the wheel. Vinny screamed vulgarities alternately at her and Rick. The car careened faster and faster down the winding mountain road, yet the events inside the vehicle seemed to lapse into slow motion.

"Squeeze the damn trigger, Kate! Now!"

The car suddenly swerved, Kate squeezed, the gun fired and all hell broke loose. She could hear the muffled curses and grunts of pain as Rick and Vinny wrestled for control of the gun. Danny struggled with the steering wheel, trying to pull the car out of its tailspin. A slim shaft of sunlight poured in through the small hole the bullet had made in the car's roof. Kate peered at the perfect circle in total amazement and then at the man fighting the inertia pulling the car round and round.

As if she had done this sort of thing all her life, Kate

pressed the barrel of the gun to the driver's perspiring temple and said, "Stop the damn car or I'll blow your head off."

When the car skidded to a sideways stop in the middle of the road, Danny immediately stuck his hands up in the air. *Just like in the movies,* Kate thought again, a faint smile tugging at her trembling lips.

"Put your weapon on the floor and kick it under the seat, then get out of the car."

It was Rick's voice. He had Vinny's gun now.

"You heard him," Kate told Danny, her aim still level with his forehead. God, this was amazing. Had she done this before?

The two goons got out. Rick marched them to the edge of the blacktop. Kate followed behind him, her gun hanging at her side from a hand that had long since gone limp with aftereffects.

Rick cocked his head to one side, lifted his weapon and took aim. "Now run!"

"Hey, man, we can work this out—" Vinny began nervously.

"Run!" Rick roared.

"You're not going to kill them?" Kate shrieked.

Gunfire erupted and Kate gasped. She squeezed her eyes shut and dropped to her knees on the cold, hard pavement. *Oh, God.* She clamped her hand over her mouth to prevent the scream that twisted her throat. She didn't want to see this. Didn't want to be a part of it. Had no idea how she had gotten involved in it.

"Let's go."

Kate forced her eyes open, expecting to see two dead bodies lying in the ditch

No one…no bodies.

She looked up at Rick. "I thought you shot them," she croaked.

He grinned, a dangerous yet ridiculously sexy widening of his lips. Kate shivered at the insane turn her thoughts had suddenly taken.

"Who says I didn't?" He grabbed her arm and pulled her to her feet.

Kate stood on shaky legs and stole another glance at the thick woods beyond the ditch. She still saw no bodies. She settled her gaze back on the face of the man guiding her back to the car. Savior or crucifier, she wondered.

"What do we do now?" she asked, her voice thin.

He opened the car door. One eyebrow quirked when he swung that intense blue gaze back on hers. He lifted the weapon from her loose grip and said, "We get the hell out of Dodge."

Chapter Two

Raine mentally reviewed every move he had made in the last four weeks as he drove like a bat out of hell down the steep mountain road. How had Ballatore's hired guns found him? He hadn't made a single mistake—he never did. The two times he had been found by Lucas's men in the last six months were intentional. Allowing only a glimpse, he had wanted Lucas to know that he was alive. The man deserved that, if nothing else. Raine couldn't quite bring himself to believe that Lucas was the leak who had blown his cover and almost gotten him killed.

But it was definitely someone in Lucas's organization. Raine knew that for certain now. He had called Lucas's private voice mail only three days ago and left the number to a downtown Gatlinburg pay phone. The information had to have filtered down to Ballatore—there was no other way the old man could have known to look here for Raine. But how many were involved in working Raine's case? Cuddahy, Lucas's boss, for sure, and at least three other special ops agents. Raine would have to find a way to narrow down that tight little group. But right now he had to concentrate on not getting caught.

Raine groaned when a stab of pain knifed through his gut. Vinny hadn't broken anything, but he had damn sure given Raine something to remember him by.

Steering the car onto Highway 321, Raine decided his best course of action would be to get out of Gatlinburg in a hurry. He would worry about dumping the car and picking up another means of transportation farther down the road. It would take Vinny and his sidekick a while to walk down to civilization. Not much traffic found its way to where he had left them. And even if someone did come along, no way would they pick up two strange men—especially a couple of guys who looked like refugees from Alcatraz.

He should have killed them, but he hadn't. *She* had distracted him. He glanced at the woman clinging to the passenger-side door. He never allowed anyone to distract him. Raine could analyze that bit of irony later.

He estimated he had about two hours before a new and much more intense search began. Maybe he'd get lucky and Vinny would get lost in the woods and freeze before finding help. "Scumbags," Raine muttered.

"You…you were going to drop me off at the emergency room."

Raine snapped his head in the direction of the small, hesitant voice. She trembled beneath his irritated glare. He forced his gaze back to the road and the ever-increasing traffic as they headed south on 441 and into Gatlinburg proper.

What was he going to do with her? If he let her go, *they* would find her and kill her. A professional never left loose ends. If he took her with him, she could easily be caught in the crossfire and wind up dead anyway. Raine set his jaw and considered his options. He didn't owe this woman a damn thing, but if she ended up wearing a toe tag it would be his fault.

He released a frustrated breath. Kate Roberts was an innocent bystander in his world of death and mayhem and Jack Raine didn't off innocents—directly or indirectly. She was his responsibility now whether he liked it or not, and he sure didn't like it. If he kept Kate with him, she had a chance of surviving, slim though it might be.

Slim? Who the hell was he kidding? *Anorexic* would be a more accurate description. Raine knew the odds of his being able to evade capture much longer without doing a permanent disappearing act. And they weren't good, especially now.

But he had to find that leak. To do that, he couldn't afford to get caught—at least not yet.

Raine no longer owed the government anything, but he did owe it to the other men, like himself, who put their lives on the line for that government. Contract agents were especially vulnerable since the very agencies that hired them denied them when an assignment went south. If a leak existed at a high enough level to have access to Raine's assignments, then no one was safe.

He snatched another glimpse of the woman in the passenger seat. Kate would just have to come along for the ride until he could tuck her away someplace safe.

"I'm afraid there's been a change of plans," he told her. He might as well get this over with. No point in keeping her in the dark.

"What do you mean?" she asked, her eyebrows knitted with concern. Her hands twisted together in her lap, her face looked pale and drawn.

She was scared to death, Raine decided after giving her another sidelong glance. "It would be a mistake for me to leave you behind. These people don't like loose ends and you're definitely a loose end."

"I don't understand." The pitch of Kate's voice rose steadily. "You said I needed medical attention...I don't understand," she repeated.

Raine cursed under his breath when he saw tears slip down her cheeks. He had no tolerance for crying females.

What the hell had he done to deserve this? Raine swallowed the hard, bitter answer that climbed into his throat. He knew what he'd done. He'd sold his soul a long time ago and now he was going to pay for it, in the form of a weepy female amnesiac.

A tiny sound, almost a sob broke loose from Kate, jerking Raine from his reverie. "There are a lot more guys like Vinny after me—a helluva lot more—if any of them get their hands on you, medical attention won't do you any good." He shot her a fierce glare. "That's just the way it is, so shut up and let me think."

Raine focused his full attention on the road before him. The next town with transportation possibilities was his destination. He had to get somewhere—anywhere—as fast he could without taking a chance on speeding and drawing attention to himself. He couldn't allow any distractions, not Kate's whining or his own uneasiness. He had to concentrate on driving. He didn't have time to waste. This sedan would soon be a heavy liability.

KATE'S MIND RACED like an out-of-control roller coaster. She had to do something. This man, Rick, wasn't going to drop her off at the hospital as he'd promised. She should have known better than to trust him. Of course, her options had been limited. He certainly seemed considerably less threatening than the other two goons she'd met today. He was definitely the lesser of the evils.

But would he drag her along with him and get her killed? Kate might not remember her life, but she instinctively knew she wouldn't have a death wish if she did. She shot the man driving an assessing glance. And this guy certainly had himself some unsavory enemies. Kate had to think of something…something that would provide her with an avenue of escape.

If she could get away from this man, she could call the

police and tell them everything. The police would get her to a doctor who could help her to regain her memory.

The harshness of that reality slammed into her with such force that it sucked the air right out of Kate's lungs. She didn't just not know her name—she didn't know anything. Where she was from, what she did for a living, whether she had any family. Nothing…she knew nothing.

"Oh, God," Kate muttered. Panic clawed at her throat, making her want to scream despite the knowledge that it would do her no good. Her heart pounded in her chest and her head ached unmercifully. She had to get out of here. A definitive click of the power door lock told her that he knew exactly what she was thinking.

Kate refused to look at him, afraid she'd give away her swiftly deteriorating condition. She had to calm down and think of a plan.

Any kind of plan.

Call in.

The words shook her with their intensity. That inner voice louder now, demanding action.

Call in, she repeated silently. "555–4911," she mumbled involuntarily. The numbers spilled from her mouth as naturally as breathing.

"What?" he demanded, his eyebrows crunched in irritation.

"I have to use the phone!" Kate blurted. "I have to…call in," she added more slowly.

"What the hell are you mumbling about?" he growled, glaring at her as he stopped for a traffic light.

"Rick, I have to—"

"Don't call me that," he warned.

Kate blinked, confused. "But those other men called you that."

"And look where it got them."

Kate stifled a gasp. Was he trying to shock her?

He chuckled and turned his attention back to the busy street. "You," he said, tossing her an unreadable look, "can call me Raine."

Fear trickled through Kate. *Raine.* She swallowed tightly. *Your life will be in constant danger.* Words, images, sensations crashed through her consciousness. Kate trembled with the effort of maintaining her composure under the mental assault. This man was dangerous. She didn't know how she knew, she just knew. And every moment she spent with him put her in danger. *Constant danger.*

She had to get away from him. "Please," she began in an unsteady voice. "You have to let me find a telephone."

"I don't have to let you do anything," he told her flatly, without ever taking his eyes from the road. "Besides, who will you call? You don't even remember who you are. Remember?" he taunted irritably.

"I...I remembered a number. I think maybe it's my mother's. Maybe she lives here and I was visiting her when I had my accident. I need to let her know that I'm okay," she pleaded with all the vulnerability and femininity she could muster. Kate had no idea if she even had a living mother, but neither did he.

"No." The single word was cold and emotionless.

Anger shot through her, but Kate tamped down the emotion. She had to approach Mr. Hardass with something a little different. Like an actress given her cue, Kate burst into tears. "Oh, please. You have to let me call. Maybe if I can hear her voice it will help bring my memory back. Please," she pleaded.

Raine ignored her completely.

Kate moved on to plan B: she sobbed relentlessly. The occasional peek she dared take in his direction reassured her that she was winning the battle. Raine literally squirmed in his seat. She kept the theatrics going at a steady pace.

Hey, she thought, maybe I'm an actress.

"All right, all right. Just shut up, for Christ's sake." He plowed his hand through his hair. "One phone call and then I don't want to hear another peep from you."

"Thank you," Kate murmured humbly. She stared out at the passing landscape and gave herself a mental pat on the back. She allowed her tears to dry slowly, swiping her eyes occasionally for added effect. Kate was certain that this man was smarter than most; it would be better not to regain her composure too quickly. No point in risking his finding out that she had pushed his buttons to get what she wanted.

Maybe she was a psychologist, she mused, biting her lower lip to prevent a tiny smile.

A large visitors' center came into view up ahead on the right. Kate felt her hopes rising. Somehow she'd find a way to ditch him there. She could easily get lost in the crowd. Raine passed the center and her hopes plummeted.

"Why didn't you stop? You said I could have one phone call."

"Too crowded," he told her, keeping his gaze fixed straight ahead. "The fewer people who see us the better."

Kate huffed an indignant sound and crossed her arms over her chest. She leaned back in the seat and forced herself to relax. She had no choice but to acquiesce to his authority—she was, after all, his hostage. Kate frowned at the thought, but it was unfortunately accurate. For all intents and purposes she was the hostage of this Raine character.

He's the best in the business. The words echoed inside her aching skull. She glanced at the man driving and considered again if somehow she did know him. The best in the business of what? she wondered.

A strong profile defined the angular features of his handsome face. His forehead and nose were prominent, but not too much so. A strong chin and chiseled jaw finished out the lean lines. He wore his thick, sandy hair a little too long. And those eyes. Kate closed her own eyes and summoned the image of those stormy blue eyes. Among his many assets, including a strong, muscular body, Raine's eyes were definitely the most appealing. His personality, unquestionably the least.

Kate opened her eyes wide. What had gotten into her? There wasn't the first thing appealing about the man! He was hell-bent on getting her killed, and besides, her interest in him was purely professional.

Kate started. Her heart rate accelerated. *Professional.* She did know this man. Then why didn't he know her? Vivid images of her naked breasts pressed against his bare chest flashed through her mind. Him removing her clothes...his strong arms wrapped firmly around her. *In the shower.* Oh, God, they'd showered together—naked.

Oh, God. Raine had told the truth. She wasn't an actress or a psychologist. She was a bought-and-paid-for whore! Oh, God. Kate closed her eyes and willed the tears to retreat. Every fiber of her being rejected the idea. But what else could those snatches of memory mean?

Raine slowed the car and took a hard right. Kate blinked rapidly to clear her blurred vision. He parked the car in a slot in a large, vacant parking lot. As had been the case when she'd stepped out of his cabin that afternoon, they were surrounded by dense woods. Nothing looked even remotely familiar.

A large painted sign read Alum Cave Bluff Hiking Trail.

Kate didn't realize Raine had gotten out of the car until he opened her door. "Get a move on," he ordered in a military tone.

Kate dropped her feet to the pavement and pushed herself up and out of the car only to be slapped in the face by a cold blast of wind. She sucked in a sharp breath of frigid air and shivered. The only thing that kept her convinced that she hadn't died and gone to hell was the arctic chill of this damn place. At least it wasn't raining. She glanced around the unfamiliar area. In fact, it looked as if it hadn't rained here at all.

Raine ushered her toward a pay phone that looked strangely out of place in the deserted parking lot surrounded by trees. He picked up the receiver and listened for a dial tone.

"Okay," he said roughly. "You've got one minute and don't say anything you'll regret." He pulled some change from his pocket and thrust it at her, then leaned against one side of the open blue canopy that served as the telephone's protection against the elements.

Kate nodded mutely. She accepted the change and receiver and tried to pretend that he wasn't so close, but no way could she completely block out his powerful masculine presence. His scent, leather and something vaguely citrus, invaded her senses, making her feel even more disoriented.

She deposited the coins, then reached a shaky hand toward the numbers on the face of the telephone. Call in, she silently repeated to herself over and over. No matter how often she said it, the numbers she'd remembered so clearly only minutes ago would not resurface. Kate licked her lips nervously and stabbed a string of meaningless numbers, stopping after the seventh one. She quickly replaced the receiver in its cradle, the change rattled into the coin return.

Now... she had to think of something now!

"It...was busy," she stammered. "May I try again?" She bit her lower lip and prayed he wouldn't realize what she'd done.

Raine straightened and she almost gasped. He glared at her impatiently. "So try again. I don't want to be here all night.'' His gaze darted from her to the entrance of the parking lot and back several times while she dropped the coins in and redialed.

It was during one of those split seconds when he looked away that Kate propelled herself into action. She brought her right knee up into Raine's crotch as hard as she could. She nailed him square between the legs with all her might.

A wounded, animal-like grunt sounded from deep in his throat. Surprise flashed through his blue eyes and then he was on his knees on the ground. Instinct absorbed all thought, Kate dropped the receiver and ran as fast as she could toward the trail disappearing into the woods.

Kate pushed forward trying to stay off the main trail. Branches and undergrowth slapped at her arms and legs.

Faster! She had to run faster or he would catch her. Thick old growth and trees forced her to return to the main trail. She ran as rapidly as she could, despite the fact that her legs felt like rubber and her head throbbed as though it might explode any minute.

Tripping and clutching at anything in her path for support, she didn't look back. She couldn't stop. Run! She had to run!

Kate's lungs felt ready to burst. Her chest hurt. She gasped for air, but she couldn't stop. She had to keep going.

What was that sound?

Louder…it got louder with every step she took. Her heart hammered in her chest, her blood roared in her ears.

Water. It was only the river running alongside the trail.

Run, Kate, run. She pushed forward a little faster. Her entire body stung now from a lack of oxygen, but the desire for survival spurred her on.

What was that?

Kate shifted to look back, lost her balance and tumbled to the ground. It took a few moments for her mind to catch up with her sprawling body. Kate jerked herself up and turned around, fully expecting to find Raine towering over her.

There was no one or nothing there.

Kate shook herself, trying to shrug off the prickling feelings. She had to keep moving.

She moved swiftly but cautiously across a footbridge that was nothing more than a fallen tree with the top side hewn down flat. A primitive handrail provided support. After crossing the footbridge, she walked up the massive stone steps of a natural-rock formation. Under different circumstances, the formation might have captured her attention, but not now.

Right now she had to move as quickly as she could.

The steps took Kate through the huge rock and back to the trail. There was still no sound behind her. She smiled to herself. Undoubtedly Raine was still on the ground curled into a fetal position holding his pride and joy. She'd really nailed him good. He'd be in serious pain for a while yet.

Or maybe, she considered hopefully, he had decided going after her would be too much trouble and had already taken off in the car. Could she be that lucky?

Just to be sure the coast was still clear, Kate glanced over her shoulder once more as she started to run again. At first the sight of Raine moving swiftly toward her didn't register in her brain—then suddenly it did.

He was only a few yards behind her. Kate lunged up the trail's steadily climbing grade as fast as her weak body could take her. She couldn't let him catch her.

Faster! She had to move faster!

The trail made a sudden left. Kate veered a bit too sharply and lost her balance. Raine's powerful arms closed around her and they both tumbled to the ground.

They skidded to a grinding halt in the rocks and dirt.

Kate struggled to free herself, but Raine pinned her to the ground with his full body weight.

"Let me go!" she yelled vehemently as she managed to grab a handful of his sandy hair.

A string of curses exploded from his mouth when he jerked her hand out of his hair. His eyes blazed like fire. He clenched his jaw so hard a muscle jumped furiously in his cheek as he immobilized her completely beneath his strong body.

Kate could do nothing now. The run and subsequent struggle had drained her already weak body.

For several seconds, neither moved or spoke. The only sound was the wind shifting through the trees and their ragged breathing. He felt hard and heavy on top of her. She watched his nostrils flare and that same muscle tic in his jaw. His mouth looked hard and grim. When their gazes collided, he tightened his hold on her wrists to a bruising intensity. For one fleeting instant sexual awareness sparked between them, strong and hot. Then it was gone, replaced by fury.

"Let me go," Kate demanded once she'd caught her breath. Fear zipped through her at the possibility of what lay in store for her. He was really angry. A number of unpleasant scenarios flitted across her mind.

"I ought to do just that," he growled as his blue gaze burned into hers. Kate could see the depth of the barely checked rage there. "You're nothing but a pain in the ass—more trouble than you're worth. I should just leave you for the cleanup team. That would put us both out of our misery."

"I don't know what you're talking about," Kate managed to say with the last bit of strength she could muster. "I want you to let me go." Her entire body trembled as much from weakness as from fear of the man crushing her into the ground.

"You just don't get it, do you?" His tone was cold and impatient, his piercing gaze ruthless. "They've seen you with me. You're marked…history…dead meat." With a frustrated exhale and a pained groan, Raine pushed himself up, pulling Kate up in the process.

Kate watched in confused disbelief as he dusted himself off and shoved the hair from his face. It pleased her immensely when Raine's face paled slightly and his hand went to his stomach as a wave of nausea obviously hit him.

"Why should I believe you?" Kate crossed her arms defiantly over her chest. She was covered with dirt and her hair was a mess, but she didn't care. She only wanted to get away from this man…this killer. Danny's words replayed in her head. *There's no telling how many men he's killed.* Kate backed up a step. "I…I don't believe anything you say," she stammered.

"You know, I really don't give a damn whether you believe me or not. If you think those guys we left back there weren't for real, then maybe you've lost more than your memory."

Kate tried to decide what to think. How could she know what was real and what was not—who she could trust and who she couldn't? She didn't even know who she was! Completely overwhelmed and scared out of her mind, she broke down and cried, real, soul-shattering sobs. She couldn't take any more, she was truly at the end of her emotional rope.

"Don't start that again." Raine ran both hands through his hair and shifted uneasily.

"What am I supposed to do?" Kate gasped out between sobs. "You got me into this mess."

Raine blew out a long breath, his eyes softened just a little as he took the step she'd retreated. "I know I got you into this mess." He looked away for a moment before continuing. "You have to understand that as long as you're with me and I'm breathing, I'll keep you safe. But if you pull another stupid stunt—" Anger flared in his eyes again. "You could get us both killed."

Kate's knees went weak. He was right. She had no idea what was going on. She didn't stand a chance without him. "Are you still going to take me with you?"

With a resigned sigh, he replied, "Yes." His eyes locked with hers. "I just hope I don't die regretting it."

Relief flooded Kate at his response. She didn't understand the situation, but she felt certain he did. She would just have to trust him to straighten things out.

"Thank you." She swiped at her tears. "I promise I'll do whatever you say from now on. You won't regret it."

"I already do." Raine turned and headed back in the direction of the parking lot.

Kate combed her fingers through her mussed hair and let out a weary breath. Relief rushed through her, calming her frazzled nerves. She dusted the dirt from her clothes and started out after her less than saintly savior.

Raine stopped abruptly and turned around. He grabbed Kate by the shoulders and squeezed hard. His expression was stone cold as he stared into her eyes for a seemingly endless moment before he spoke. "But, I swear, if you do anything else that pisses me off, I'll kill you myself." With that said, he released her, turned and stalked away.

Judging by the look in his eyes, Kate had no doubt that he meant exactly what he'd said. She hugged herself tightly for a moment and watched his angry retreat.

He was crazy. He had to be. But, she was hopelessly at his mercy. Those other men were killers. It would take a killer to protect her from them, if everything he said was true. Kate had no alternative but to follow him and do whatever he told her.

And she did, still feeling dazed and brushing the dirt from her rumpled attire.

The last of the sun's warmth showered down on them through the opening canopy of tree branches as they neared the parking area. Kate noticed that her breath fogged the cold air. She wondered, as she marched behind Raine like a prisoner being led to her execution, where in the world they were. She had no idea even what state they were in.

Without warning, Raine stopped and Kate smacked into his wide back. He motioned for her to keep quiet as he stepped closer to the edge of the woods and surveyed the parking lot.

Kate peeked around him. A uniformed man was inspecting their car—the car they'd left in the parking lot, she amended. It wasn't really theirs, it belonged to the two goons. After the man in uniform circled the vehicle, he returned to his truck and spoke into his radio mike. He wasn't a policeman. Kate strained to make out the markings on the truck.

A park ranger.

So they must be…she suddenly made out the rest of the words: Great Smoky Mountains, Gatlinburg, Tennessee. A ranger! He could help them. If only… She looked at Raine.

"Damn." Raine pulled back from his viewing position. He glanced at Kate and then frowned. "Don't even think about it."

"What's he doing?" she asked innocently, as if she had no idea what he'd insinuated. How could he know that she'd had the overwhelming urge to scream her head off?

"He's running the plates." He swore. "They're strict about abandoned vehicles around here. Let's get moving." Raine turned and headed back up the trail.

"Where are you going? We can't go that way," Kate exclaimed in a stage whisper. She flung her arms heavenward in mute frustration and then muttered heatedly, "There's nothing back there but trees and mountains." Kate stood her ground. She wasn't about to go back into those woods, not when a perfectly good car waited in the parking lot. If Raine didn't want to talk to the ranger, all they had to do was wait. He would leave eventually.

Raine glared at her impatiently. "The guys who are after us will be monitoring reports made by the local authorities, especially the report of an abandoned car with a bullet hole in the roof. Not to mention a couple of loaded nine millimeters under the seat. When that ranger ran those plates he gave them our exact location. They'll be here soon, you can bet on it."

"Don't you mean the guys who are after *you?*" Kate set her hands on her hips and glared back at him, all memory of the promise she'd made gone.

"Same difference. You're either going or you're staying. I'm going." Raine stalked off, leaving her to decide for herself.

"But the ranger could help us!" Kate called after him, still clinging to the hope that she might separate herself from this whole nasty mess.

"Dream on," he called back without stopping.

Kate rolled her eyes and sighed in exasperation. What was she supposed to do? Run to that park ranger and risk being turned over to the *other* bad guys, or follow a man who could very well be a deranged killer himself?

One thing was certain, Raine could have killed her already if that had been his intent, but he hadn't. He had, in fact, done everything he could to protect her. She hadn't forgotten how he'd stepped between her and Vinny.

Maybe Raine was a good guy. Instinct told her to go with the known rather than the unknown. But could she trust her instincts? She didn't even know who she was, how could she know whether to trust her judgment?

Still less than convinced, Kate headed in the direction into which Raine had already disappeared.

Chapter Three

Crossing the primitive footbridge again, Kate reminded herself that following Raine was her only logical option. Besides, even if she had decided to make a mad dash for the park ranger, Raine could easily have stopped her. She watched his strong, confident strides. He moved with more fluid grace than a man his height and size had any right to. And quietly as well. Hardly any sound at all accompanied his steps.

Raine.

Kate concentrated with all her might to grasp that fleeting hint of recognition that flitted through her consciousness each time she looked into those piercing blue eyes or considered his name. She just couldn't quite latch on to it. She knew him, yet he was a total stranger.

Maybe in another life? *Right, Kate, you can't even remember this life.*

Kate shook off the mental frustration and climbed the steps that would take her back through the large, unique rock formation. She paused to admire the natural beauty of the awesome rocks. She smoothed her hand over the cold, rough surface, tracing the imprints time and the elements had left forever embedded.

Maybe, Kate thought with a smile, she was a geologist.

"You're wasting daylight."

Startled by the sharpness of his voice cutting through the silence, Kate snatched her hand back like a child caught reaching into the cookie jar.

He stood some ten yards away, as still as the stone she'd been admiring, hands on hips, glaring at her. Damned if he didn't make a hell of a picture when he was angry, she suddenly thought. Tight jeans encased muscular thighs and a worn leather bomber jacket filled to capacity covered his broad shoulders.

He glanced up at the sky and then directed his scowl back at Kate. "The sky's clear, it's going to get really cold tonight. Unless you plan to sleep under the stars, you'd better get a move on. I won't stop to remind you again," he added before he turned and continued.

Kate had the sudden, almost overwhelming urge to click her heels and salute. God, he would make a great drill sergeant. She quickly scanned the vast, blue sky. It looked much bigger somehow from here. There wasn't a cloud to be seen. He could be right, Kate supposed. Obviously she wasn't a meteorologist. She didn't know one cloud from another, or what their absence meant in regards to their current circumstances. She shrugged and forced her weak, wobbly legs into gear. She'd have to hurry to catch up or risk being left behind.

The trail climbed steadily upward. Kate was a little winded by the time she got within conversational distance of Raine. Not that he would be interested in conversation—he'd made that point quite clear. Her chest still ached, but she attributed the discomfort to fear. This man, she glowered at her leader, scared her. His friends—no, make that his enemies—scared her.

The trail took a hard right, which brought them into an area of total and unexpected devastation— a raw, open gash in the side of the mountain. Kate was taken aback by the stark contrast to only moments before.

There was absolutely nothing growing—no trees, no bushes, no nothing. The large expanse looked like the aftermath of a savage hurricane. Massive boulders lay scattered like marbles. Huge trees had been tossed about like toothpicks. In the distance, trees, logs, mud and rocks lay piled at least fifty feet high, a decaying monument to whatever had taken place to wreak such destruction.

Raine trudged on relentlessly, taking little note of their surroundings. Kate had been so engrossed in the unnatural phenomenon that she'd fallen way behind again. True to his word, Raine didn't appear concerned about whether she kept up or not. Pushing herself to move faster, Kate soon caught up with him.

"What caused all that? It looks like an artillery battle was fought here." She took one final look back over her shoulder at the naked area. In some stretches the earth had been scraped down to the bedrock. How could that spot look as if it had been hit by a holocaust and everything around it still appear so lovely and tranquil?

"A flash flood." Raine stopped and looked back as if he'd only just noticed his surroundings. He stared at the devastation for a long moment.

Just when Kate was sure he didn't intend to say anything else, he continued. "They say a monster storm hit, dumping massive amounts of water in a matter of minutes. Cresting at—" he shrugged "—more than twenty feet, it was like a highland tidal wave surging through and taking with it everything in its path."

Kate looked around warily. "That doesn't happen on a regular basis around here, does it?"

One corner of his mouth lifted in a half smile. "You don't have anything to worry about as long as you don't stand in one place too long," he said, and then pushed off, heading ever upward toward wherever the hell they were going.

Kate didn't find his little jab amusing. She heaved a frustrated breath and obediently trudged after him. In her efforts to keep up with his long legs, she tripped over every exposed root and loose rock in the trail. She glared at his broad back. Raine seemed to know exactly where to place each step. His self-assuredness frustrated her all the more. Just once she'd like to see him lose his footing or trip over one of nature's obstacles, she mused as she kicked another rock out of her path.

Kate shivered in her parka. The sun was dropping slowly but surely behind the mountains in the distance, taking its waning warmth with it. Orange and purple streaks slanted across the sky behind the slope of majestic trees that gave way to the valley below. The view was breathtaking. Though Kate felt sure she had heard of the Smoky Mountains, somehow she knew she'd never before seen a view like this one.

An occasional squirrel scampered into the open, gave Kate a curious look and then disappeared back into the forest. Birds went about their business, flying overhead or squawking from their perch on a nearby tree limb. Kate didn't readily recognize any of the varieties. She obviously wasn't a bird-watcher.

Raine, on the other hand, seemed to know his way around this place. How did he know so much about the mountains? she wondered. Had he always lived around here? For that matter, what did she really know about him at this point?

Nothing.

Except that he was dangerous, she reminded herself. She had no idea where they were headed, either. She was cold and achy. Dusk had descended upon them. And she was starving.

She had a right to know where he was leading her, didn't she?

Damn straight, she did.

Kate stamped off after him. "Excuse me!" she shouted to his back.

As she had anticipated, he ignored her.

Her anger brought with it a burst of energy, Kate broke into a dead run. "I said, excuse me," she repeated when she skidded to a halt right beside him.

He paused, turned to her and lifted one eyebrow, a look of bored amusement on his too-handsome face. "I'd be more careful where I stand if I were you," he warned. He inclined his head toward her side of the trail.

Kate glared at him for half a beat before looking in the direction he'd indicated. Her eyes widened in fear when she realized she stood on the edge of a precipice. Instinctively, Kate flung herself at Raine. His arms went instantly around her as her feet shifted in the loose dirt and rocks that scattered over the edge.

"Holy cow," she muttered as she clung to his jacket. His arms felt strong and reassuring around her. "I didn't even see it."

Raine set her away from him and on solid ground. "You should be more careful," he said smugly, giving her an amused look.

"Thanks for the warning," she retorted, her heart still thundering painfully in her chest. She called him every vile name she could think of under her breath.

Raine reached out and grasped a heavy wire cable that had been strung alongside the trail for some sixty or seventy feet. "Hold on tight and watch your step," he called back to her.

Kate uttered a nasty four-letter word, one she didn't even realize she knew until it rolled off her tongue.

Raine didn't have to tell her twice to be careful. She held on to the cable with both hands as she cautiously edged forward. She took one hesitant look at the drop-off and cringed. It plunged a good hundred feet down. If a person survived the rolling, tumbling fall, climbing back up would be a real problem. Kate felt fairly certain that Raine wouldn't be interested in helping her climb back up.

To her surprise, he waited for her on the other side of the drop-off. When Kate made it to his position, she wrinkled her nose and asked, "What's that smell?" The deep woodsy scent was gone, replaced by some sort of chemical odor. She couldn't quite identify it, almost a metal smell.

"Alum Cave Bluff. The rain and subsequent slides bring out the metallic odor," he told her flatly. He offered no further explanation, just turned and continued forward.

Kate stuck our her tongue at his broad back, but followed obediently. A regular Mr. Personality, she fumed.

The trail grew steadily steeper as the ground beneath her feet became more powdery and less rocky. Her close encounter with the precipice had caused her to forget the demand for information she had intended to make. She still didn't know where they were headed.

The trail led them underneath the overhang of a bluff. The interesting terrain momentarily distracted Kate as she squinted to make out the formations. The natural beauty of the rocks and landscape grew more and more difficult to see as darkness closed in around them.

"Watch out for the icicles."

Kate shifted her gaze from the rock wall to him. He pointed skyward and then moved swiftly beyond the craggy overhang.

"Icicles?" Kate frowned. What icicles? She looked up just in time to see a rather large one drop like a heavy dagger. The ice crashed to the ground a mere three or four feet in front of her. No further explanation required, she thought as she hurried past the overhang.

Raine had already resumed his trek upward. Kate plodded after him. They passed two more drop-off areas. She held her breath past both—each time seemed worse than the last with nothing more than moonlight to guide them.

Kate was freezing now. As she peered into the dense black forest, she wondered how long it would take to find a person's body in this environment. A body out in the middle of nowhere like this probably wouldn't be found until spring and by then it would have been something's lunch. She shivered at the thought.

Bears. She suddenly wondered if there were bears in these woods. She opened her mouth to ask, but then snapped it shut. She wouldn't give him the pleasure of knowing her concerns.

Lost in thought, Kate looked up to find that she'd almost run into Raine again. He stood waiting near a particularly steep area. The trail inclined so sharply that log steps had been embedded in the mountainside to assist with the climb. Raine took the steps two at a time. Kate swallowed tightly. If he could do it, she could do it. By the time she reached the top her heart fluttered wildly, but she had done it.

Before long the trail leveled out somewhat and Kate's breathing finally returned to normal. She hoped they would get to their destination soon, her feet and ankles were aching. Her head joined in the symphony of pain and her chest felt oddly tight.

The trees grew dense, almost blocking out the moonlight and making their trek even more precarious. Fraser firs soared high into the sky like giant Christmas trees. The crisp evergreen scent teased Kate's senses. She smiled and wondered if there were evergreens where she came from.

Virginia. Raine had said she was from Virginia. Virginia had evergreens, didn't it?

Her next step sent her feet in opposite directions. *Ice,* she realized too late. A shriek escaped her lips at the same time that her feet skated out from under her.

Raine's arms encircled her waist, catching her a split second before her bottom slammed against the hard dirt. He steadied her on her feet, but kept his arms wrapped tightly around her.

"I guess I'm not an ice skater," Kate whispered hoarsely.

"Guess not," he said, his warm breath feathered across her mouth. His ice-blue gaze seemed to capture the sparse moonlight and do strange things with it. Kate found herself mesmerized by his eyes, his nearness. She couldn't move or take a breath, she could only hold on to that worn-soft bomber jacket and absorb the heat emanating from his powerful body. Her mouth traitorously yearned for the taste of his, her fingers tightened on fistsful of leather.

"We're almost there," he said finally, breaking the charged silence. Raine dropped his arms, turned and strode off into the darkness.

Kate's legs moved of their own volition. She was too stunned to do anything but operate on autopilot. She blew out a long, slow puff of air that fogged against the cold night.

Get a grip, Kate. It was nothing. Just exhaustion, hunger and the play of moonlight.

A sign welcoming hikers to LeConte Lodge came into view. Kate silently thanked God for some form of civilization. She hoped this was their intended destination. Rustic though it might be, she added when they entered the clearing and the unobstructed light of the moon gave her a better look.

Several cabins, maybe a dozen or so of varying sizes, dotted the clearing. Not a single light pierced the night. It wasn't that late, someone should still be up.

The trail wound to the right of the lodge compound and disappeared into the blackness. A welcome center of sorts stood at the entrance. To Kate's distress, rather than enter the compound, Raine stayed with the trail.

"We're not staying here?" Kate hastened her pace to catch up with him again.

"The lodge is closed for the winter. There's no one here except maybe a caretaker, and we can't chance him seeing us."

"So, what are we going to do?" she asked, almost afraid of the answer.

Without bothering to respond, Raine took a sudden left through the knee-deep weeds and headed in the direction of a small cabin at the very back of the compound.

Kate followed, relieved to be heading toward shelter. She waded through the thick dead-for-the-winter grass. Sharp, prickling pain brought the sudden awareness that the grass was accompanied by saw briars, which pulled at her jeans and the skin underneath.

Raine made it to the cabin well before Kate. She watched him survey the door and windows—deciding on the best method of breaking and entering, she realized. By the time she made her way to the cabin, Raine was already inside.

The single room held one narrow bed, a kerosene lamp sitting on a table, two chairs and a small kerosene heater. The floor and walls were rough, unpainted wood, as best Kate could tell.

Rustic had been an understatement. Primitive was a much more apt description. But at least it would provide shelter from the cold wind and damp ground. She appraised the narrow bed once more. Anything was better than sleeping on the ice-cold ground.

But where would Raine sleep? she wondered absently.

Kate shivered. Shelter or no, it was still cold. She took the few steps that separated her from the bed and sat down with a satisfied sigh.

Dear God, it felt wonderful just to sit. Kate closed her eyes and succumbed to the exhaustion she'd been holding at bay. She pulled a scratchy wool blanket up around her and relaxed more deeply into the thin mattress. She licked her lips and imagined strawberry lip balm and almond oil hand lotion. That would feel so good about now, she thought with another sigh.

"Stay put," Raine ordered.

Kate opened her heavy lids to look up at him. He stood in front of the door, blocking the dim light the moon provided.

"If I have to run you down, you'll be the one doing the regretting."

"Where are you going?" Kate asked. He didn't have to worry, she didn't plan to move, much less run.

"If we're lucky, there'll be some canned food left in the dining cabin."

"Okay," Kate muttered, but Raine had already vanished from view. He left the door open, for the light, she supposed. The constant sound of the wind rustling through the treetops lulled her toward sleep as the cloak of moonlight and nocturnal silence folded around her.

WHEN RAINE RETURNED to the cabin with his booty, Kate was fast asleep. He set the cans of beans and franks and the bottled water he had found on the table, along with a couple of spoons.

He thought about just letting her sleep. She'd been nothing but a pain in the ass the entire trek up the mountain. But he knew she hadn't eaten anything, at least not since early morning, and he wasn't comfortable with her sleeping too much in the first twenty-four hours since her accident. Eating was a necessity. She'd need her strength to make the rest of this hellacious trip.

With a frustrated sound that was more groan than sigh,

Raine walked over to the bed and shook Kate. "Kate, you need to eat." He shook her again. "Wake up."

Kate's eyes popped open, she sat bolt upright, quickly scanned the room and then assessed him. "What?" she eventually asked.

Raine frowned. Most people didn't wake and immediately take stock of their surroundings. She peered up at him with those dark, chocolate eyes. Maybe he'd startled her.

"I found some food. You need to eat," he told her firmly.

Kate seemed to consider his words then said, "Okay." Still shrouded in the blanket she had found on the cot, she struggled to her feet and followed him to the table. After claiming one of the two chairs, she watched as he popped the tops from two cans and passed one to her.

"What is it?" she asked, trying to read the label in the almost complete darkness.

"Beans and franks."

"Ugh. I hate beans and franks," she complained.

Raine paused, spoon halfway to his mouth. "How do you know if you like them or not?"

Kate paused, frowning at the stuff inside the can she held. "I don't know. I just know."

"Eat it anyway," he ordered, then nudged the water in her direction. "And drink. You'll need lots of energy tomorrow."

She met his gaze across the table. "What happens tomorrow?"

"More of today," he said flatly.

"Oh, God," she groaned.

Reluctantly she drank from the water bottle then poked a spoonful of the beans and franks into her mouth and chewed. She shivered when she swallowed. Raine didn't know if it was from the cold or the cuisine. He bit back a grin and opened a second can. Food equaled survival, and the sooner Ms. Roberts learned that, the better off they'd both be.

"Have another," Raine teased when she'd at last finished her can.

"No, thank you," she said with another shiver.

"I'll just save the rest for tomorrow," he taunted.

"Great," Kate muttered as she stumbled back to the bed. She plunked down on one end, leaned against the iron railing and hugged the blanket around herself. "I'm not moving until the sun comes up and sheds some warmth on this cold, godforsaken mountain," she mumbled from beneath the blanket.

Raine didn't say anything. No point in bursting her bubble, he decided. She'd find out soon enough that his day started well before dawn, and on this trip they followed his schedule.

He sat down on the other end of the bed and leaned against the iron headboard. He watched her for a long while, wondering about this woman of mystery. Raine had particularly good night vision and his eyes had long since adjusted to the lack of light.

He ran through his mental notes regarding his inadvertent hostage. She didn't wear any rings, so he assumed that meant she didn't have a husband somewhere searching frantically for her. Her hands were soft and her nails well manicured, indicating a white-collar job of some sort. Her clothing sported designer labels, as did her pricey hiking boots. Whatever she did, she got paid well.

Judging by her vocabulary, she appeared well educated. As her strength returned so did her confidence. She seemed in good physical condition considering her injuries. If the transformation thus far was any indication, she tended toward bossiness.

Raine didn't know a lot about amnesia except that it could be temporary and usually returned sporadically.

"What?" she snapped from behind the blanket. All that remained visible were her eyes and that cloud of dark, silky hair.

Raine realized then that he had been staring at her for some time. She'd caught him. "I was just thinking that it's going to get a hell of a lot colder before this night is over and we'll need to do whatever we have to in order to survive."

She jerked the cover down from her face, her eyebrows veed in confusion. "What do you mean?" she asked warily.

"I mean, we'll need to share that one blanket." He lifted one shoulder in a careless shrug. "Or we could use it in shifts," he suggested.

She stared at him, aghast. "You must be kidding. I'm freezing!" She shook her head. "If you were a gentleman you wouldn't even have made such a suggestion."

"I'm glad that's settled," he said dryly. Raine cocked his head and eyed her with blatant amusement. "Just to prove I'm not completely uncouth, I will be happy to share my body heat with you if you're willing to share the blanket."

"*Pleeease,*" she cried in disgust.

"All you have to do is come over here and cuddle up with me. Nothing more." He pulled his jacket open wide and smiled invitingly. "It's a known fact that sharing body heat has saved many a poor soul from freezing to death. Between our jackets, that blanket, and whatever body heat we can work up, I'm sure we'll stay nice and toasty."

"I'd rather freeze."

"Suit yourself." Raine grinned and pulled his coat back around him. He crossed his arms over his chest, exaggerated a shiver and watched her struggle with her conscience.

"Can't you light that kerosene heater or the lamp?"

How refreshing, he thought. He hadn't spent time with anyone who had a real conscience in ages.

"Sorry, I don't smoke, so I don't carry a lighter."

"Well, don't...don't you know how to rub two sticks together or something?"

"I hate to lower your perception of me any further," Raine said, his smile widening into another grin. "But I was never a Boy Scout."

Kate sat up and sighed loudly. "All right."

"All right what?" he baited.

She glared at him. "We'll share the blanket." She made room for him beside her. "But don't get any ideas, because I'm fully trained in self-defense," she added sullenly.

Raine stood, moved to the other end of the bed and then lowered himself next to her. "How do you know you're fully trained?" he whispered near her ear.

"I don't, but you should," she said pointedly. Kate relinquished part of the blanket and turned her back to him.

Raine winced at the memory of her knee in his groin. She'd definitely knocked him on his can. Maybe...hell, all women knew where a man's weakest points were.

He'd gotten what he wanted anyway. He grinned as he snuggled in behind her, spoon fashion. She inched her body as far away from his as possible without falling off the edge.

Raine breathed deeply of her womanly scent. A hint of whatever shampoo she'd last used still lingered in her hair. "Mmm, you smell nice," he murmured.

She jabbed him in the gut with her elbow. Raine grunted from the unexpected blow to the already sore spot. "Hold your breath," she said icily.

Not a masochist at heart, Raine lay perfectly still until he heard the gentle, rhythmic breathing that indicated she had fallen into a deep sleep. Keeping warm on a night like this wasn't going to be easy. He slid his arm around her waist and pulled her body against his. Some concessions were necessary.

Despite the stomach-churning blow she'd delivered to his groin earlier that day, and then the sucker punch he'd gotten only minutes ago, he hardened like a rock in record time. Damn, he would never get any sleep like this. Between her neediness and soft body, he was completely and painfully aroused. Raine had worked with women plenty of times in the past and never had he lost his perspective like this.

His professional ethics had gone out the window practically from the moment he'd opened his door and found her standing there in the falling rain. Kate Roberts threatened even his most deeply entrenched habits of self-preservation.

Raine had always been a loner, taking care of no one but himself. What was so different about this woman? He had thought of little else but her all day. Never before had he felt such a need to take care of another person. Never before had he wanted a woman so much.

Nevers weren't supposed to happen to him.

It couldn't be just the circumstances. He'd been in a race for his life hundreds of times before. The odds had certainly been stacked against him numerous times in the past. Even the fact that he didn't know all the players in the game wasn't so unusual for his line of work.

But something was definitely different this time.

Kate was the difference.

Or maybe he was just getting old and soft…

…or stupid.

Chapter Four

Raine woke as the first faint glimmer of light streaked the sky with color. His backside felt half-frozen, but his front was warm and fully aroused. The ache he still felt from Kate's knee had not prevented his almost constant state of arousal since climbing into bed with her.

He was sprawled half across her body, his arms wrapped tightly around her waist, hers draped around his neck. Their legs were tangled, with his thigh resting snugly between hers. His arousal pressed into her soft belly. There was no way he could move that wouldn't cause unbearable friction between them, and possibly send him out of control. He didn't trust himself even to breathe. He felt damn close to embarrassing himself at the moment.

There had to be a way out of this. Raine had built his reputation on his ability to get in and out of death-dealing situations. Disentangling himself from one female should be a piece of cake.

Finally, he had to breathe. His chest expanded from the depth of the breath. Kate stirred beneath him and Raine gritted his teeth.

Each time he'd woken her during the night, she had burrowed closer to him. Now, she stretched languidly and tightened her hold around his neck, then arched against his thigh. Sweat popped out on his forehead. When she kissed his throat, he closed his eyes and bit his tongue to stifle the groan. Kate practically purred beneath him, planting soft, sweet kisses from the base of his throat all the way to his chin.

He couldn't take it any longer. The groan escaped, loud and gut-wrenching. He felt ready to explode. If she arched against him once more, his self-control would be history.

Kate tensed. Raine didn't have to look to know her eyes had opened, the earsplitting shriek that escaped her lips clued him in well before her hands pressed against his chest in an effort to shove him off.

"Give me a minute to—"

Kate cut him off as she arched her entire body like a bow and propelled him over the edge of the bed, her in tow. His back thudded against the wooden floor. A loud *ummph* escaped him as the wind whooshed out of his lungs from the weight of her body slamming into his.

"You sleazy bastard," she shouted angrily as she scrambled to free herself from the twisted blanket and his arms and legs. "How could you take advantage of me while I was sleeping?"

"Hold on just a damn minute!" he rasped. Raine grabbed her shoulders and held her still. "I didn't do anything. You were the one kissing me."

She huffed. "You must be insane! I did no such thing." She struggled against his hold, her every move grinding the heat between her thighs into his arousal. Suddenly she stopped fighting him. Kate's eyes widened in horror when she realized she was sitting astride his hips.

Kicking and tripping and cursing, she freed herself and stumbled to her feet.

If Raine hadn't been so painfully aroused he would have laughed at the whole situation. As it was, there wasn't a single thing funny about it.

Raine got to his feet and stormed out the door into the

cold. He felt immensely thankful for the bitter wind whipping around him. He needed a long walk and some relief.

KATE SHOVED her hair back from her face and hugged her parka around her. "Jerk," she muttered as Raine disappeared from sight. She grimaced at the pain shooting through her body. Yesterday's adventures had left their mark in the memory of every muscle. Her head felt foggy and achy.

Why had he gotten up before the sun? It couldn't be more than thirty degrees outside. Kate picked up the tangled wool blanket and cocooned herself in it, then plunked back down on the bed. Raine could do whatever he wanted, but she wasn't going anywhere until the sun rose above the treetops. She snuggled into the scratchy cover and closed her eyes. Just five minutes more of sleep and she would be good to go. Five little minutes...

"Wake up. It's time to go."

Kate's eyes shot open and she came instantly to attention. She tamped down her automatic reaction of fight or flight as she recognized Raine towering over her in the dim predawn light, a scowl on his face. "What?" she grumbled.

"It's time to go," he repeated impatiently.

"But it's not even daylight yet, why do we have to go now? It's still freezing outside." Literally, Kate didn't add as she hugged the blanket closer.

That annoying tic began in his angular jaw. Even in the shadowy light she could see his scowl deepen. "Because," he said slowly, drawing out the word, "it's over twenty miles to Cherokee, and if we don't make it today, we'll be spending tonight under the stars. There may not have been any heat in this cabin last night, but it was a hell of a lot better than spending the night out in the open."

"Twenty miles?" Kate echoed. Nothing he'd said after

that mattered at the moment. "You expect me to walk twenty miles—*today?*" He was insane. The man couldn't possibly mean *twenty miles*. Her muscles told her in no uncertain terms that walking twenty miles was not something she wanted to do anytime soon. Twenty miles, right.

"Give or take a couple," he said flippantly.

Kate stared at him in disbelief. "You're serious." It was a statement, not a question. Instinct told Kate that this man wasn't a kidder.

He crossed his arms over his chest and angled his head toward his right shoulder. The same way he'd done when he had taken aim at those two men yesterday. A shiver skated over Kate's skin.

"Dead serious," he told her.

Kate swallowed. "What would be the harm in waiting until daylight?"

"In case you've forgotten," he said, emphasizing the last word, "there are people after us who want us dead."

"You mean who want *you* dead," Kate clarified sarcastically.

Raine exhaled loudly. "We had this discussion yesterday." He cocked one sandy eyebrow. "Or have you *forgotten* that, too?"

"You're not funny." Kate shot him a reproachful glare. Her efforts only sent one corner of his mouth upward in a half smile.

"I wasn't trying to be. Now let's go."

Reluctantly, Kate stood. "I still don't see the need to hurry. We're in the middle of nowhere. What fool would look for us here?"

Raine slowly paced the room, scanning each square foot. "If we're lucky, no one. Hopefully, they'll assume that we picked up some other means of transportation. I don't think they would expect us to take this route, but I don't plan to stick around and find out."

Kate unzipped her parka and pulled the small purse she had forgotten she was wearing back around to her side. Small though it might be, it probably accounted for at least one tender spot on her back. She had been so tired last night that she hadn't thought to take it off. Raine's strong arms and muscular body accounted for numerous other discomforts. Some Kate didn't want to consider, like the hot ache deep inside her. She shivered and rezipped her parka, then tightened the blanket around her shoulders. She needed all the help she could get staying warm and shielding herself from *him*.

When Raine completed his survey of the room, he bent over and began to put the bed back in order.

"What are you doing?" Kate asked, puzzled by his actions. She wouldn't have taken him for a neat-freak.

"I'm making sure things are left the way we found them. So we don't leave a trail."

Kate frowned. He certainly seemed to think of everything. She wasn't complaining on that score though, the view from her position was pretty good. Faded jeans strained against his tight butt as he bent over the bed. His bomber jacket covered his back and shoulders, but she already knew exactly what that broad torso looked like. Kate concentrated hard on his long, muscled physique and tried to recall exactly how he had looked naked. A ripple of awareness made her shiver again as she closed her eyes and allowed the images to flood her mind. Tanned skin stretched taut over ridges and planes of hard muscle. Heat rushed through Kate as her breathing grew shallow and rapid.

If she had to be stranded in the wilderness, this was definitely the man to be stuck with. He was rugged, handsome, strong...*he was a killer*. What the hell was she thinking? Kate forced her eyes open to face the reality of her predicament. Raine stood right in front of her, studying her closely. Those piercing sky-blue eyes made her heart skip a beat.

"Are you all right?" he asked, a hint of concern tinging his low, husky baritone.

"Fine. I'm fine." Kate retreated a step and stumbled on the blanket hanging around her feet.

Raine advanced the step she had retreated and tugged the blanket from around her. "I don't think you'll need this." He folded the blanket and draped it across the foot of the bed just as she had found it.

Kate pushed her hands through her hair, careful of the tender spot on her scalp, and tried to smile, but her efforts fell far short of her goal.

"Let's go." He flicked one last glance at her before striding out the door.

Drawing in a fortifying breath, Kate followed him into the biting cold. She hesitated at the corner of the cabin. "Wait," she said suddenly. Already a half-dozen yards ahead of her, Raine stopped and turned around. "I need to...do something," she stammered, heat rising in her cheeks.

He adjusted the collar of his jacket higher around his neck. "So do it."

"I...I can't do it here." Kate shifted with growing discomfort. Obviously she hadn't been awake enough until just this moment to realize she had to go—bad. Or maybe it was the cold. Whatever it was, she had to go now.

He nodded toward the cabin. "Go around to the other side and make it fast. We're wasting time." All signs of concern had vanished. The cold, emotionless man who had mocked death when it came in the form of two armed goons was back.

Not wanting to be left behind, Kate hurried through the knee-deep grass and briars. The dead blades crunched beneath her hiking boots.

After finding a spot that represented the least possible threat to her bare bottom, Kate took care of business. She checked her purse for anything useful, like lip balm. Nothing but a hairbrush, her driver's license, and a wallet that contained a few small bills. Knowing his lack of patience, she quickly rejoined Raine. He might be cold and emotionless, but he was all she had. She met his impatient gaze and produced a smile.

"You're ready now?" he asked archly.

"Do I have a choice?"

"I knew I would regret this." His tone matched the implacable expression on his face. Raine turned and strode toward the trail they had abandoned the night before.

Kate followed quietly. She focused on trying to remember how she had ended up in this man's company. He had said something about a car accident. Her head ached from the concussion she had received, according to Raine, in that accident. But Kate didn't really remember anything before waking up in his bed. Fleeting snatches of memory about his naked body and their being in the shower together were about all she could recall. Except those sensations of knowledge that plagued her from time to time. She frowned. She would experience a sudden feeling or sense of knowing, but not quite a memory.

Kate sighed. Surely it was only a matter of time before her full memory returned, with or without medical attention. Wasn't that the way it happened in the movies? How would she know? she mused bitterly. Who was to say that the flashes of insight she experienced weren't scenes from movies? They could be fragments of her life just as easily. Maybe she was some sort of spy or cop or something, she thought, laughing bitterly at herself. Whatever she was, Kate decided reluctantly, she had definitely been hanging around with the wrong crowd.

The trail climbed steadily for a short distance before

they reached the crest and began the descent. Kate felt immensely grateful for the downward trek. She took care to watch for icy patches this time. Before long she even got the hang of stepping over the many hazards of the rocky trail. She felt immensely more coordinated today, and not as weak.

Raine waited for Kate at each of the slide areas. He warned her to stay away from the edge and to move slowly since there were no cables to hold on to this time. He stuck to her like glue as she braved the more precarious areas. Kate didn't bother to thank him since he didn't seem in the conversational mood. A hundred questions flitted through her mind, but she didn't vocalize them, either. She had a bad feeling she wouldn't like the answers. What were the old sayings? *Ignorance is bliss. What you don't know won't hurt you.* Kate hoped like hell that at least one would prove true.

Each time Raine took her hand and helped her across a particularly hazardous spot, a tingle zipped through her. Kate didn't really understand her physical reaction to the man. Did they know each other intimately as she feared? Did they have a history? If they did, he wasn't telling. Raine was the kind of man who probably had women falling at his feet all the time. For a man like him, she was most likely nothing more than another roll in the hay. Too bad she didn't remember the roll. She shook herself mentally.

Kate clenched and unclenched her fists against the numbing cold. She glanced down at her coat and for the first time realized she had pockets. Stuffing her hands inside the protective material, Kate also discovered gloves. An appreciative smile spread across her cold, stiff lips. She tugged the gloves out to slip them on and something fluttered to the ground. Kate frowned as she reached for the small object. *Matches.* A small book of matches. The kind people in bars always wrote their telephone numbers on and then gave to a prospective date. The cover was plain white, no advertisement. Kate opened it. No telephone number was scrawled inside. Why would she have matches? Did she smoke? If she had known she had matches in her pocket, Raine could have lit that kerosene heater in the cabin.

''What's the holdup?''

Raine's steely voice jerked Kate from her reverie. She stuffed the matchbook back into her pocket and hurried to catch up with him. She could mull over the mysterious matches later. Right now she had to follow her fearless leader.

Like a big orange ball of fire, the sun finally rose above the treetops in the east and bathed the beautiful mountains in a golden glow. Its warmth melted away the thick blue mist that had enveloped the majestic trees that covered the landscape around them. Kate stopped and held her face to the sun, allowing its kiss to warm her. When she opened her eyes once more, she viewed the solitude and serenity of her surroundings with renewed interest. This was surely the most beautiful place she had ever seen. She sensed it in the deepest recesses of her soul.

A distant *whop-whop-whop* sound suddenly cut through the serene fabric of the morning, the cacophony wholly out of place in the beautifully untamed environment.

Raine had already turned toward the sound, his searching gaze roaming the treetops.

''What's that?'' she asked. Dread filled her midsection, followed swiftly by fear. Kate knew instantly that whatever it was, it wasn't good.

''Trouble,'' he told her, his voice low.

Kate tried to rally her intellect. To determine exactly the source of the sound or what he meant by that one word, but she couldn't. She could only stand there, frozen with the fear of the unknown.

The bad guys. It had to be the bad guys. She could feel her forehead wrinkle with worry. Was it the bad guys? Or was *he,* she turned her attention to Raine, the real bad guy? *He's good, maybe too good.* The words sifted through the empty sieve of her mind. Kate's frown deepened. How could she know that? Good at what?

"It's a copter, they're looking for us at the lodge," he said mechanically. "We have to move faster, Kate."

He was beside her now. She hadn't even realized he had moved. Kate blinked rapidly, trying simultaneously to focus on him and the whirlwind of emotions churning inside her. Raine took her hand, wrapping his long fingers around hers and urging her forward.

"We have to hurry," he repeated grimly.

She didn't ask any other questions and he offered no further explanations. Kate simply allowed him to pull her along behind him. Raine moved with lightning speed and absolute silence. Kate stumbled frequently, but he always caught her. Soon the sound of the helicopter's blades cutting through the air faded entirely. Kate focused intently on the task of keeping up once Raine had released her hand.

Faster and faster they moved down the trail as it followed the contour of the mountain. Kate didn't know exactly how long they had been running, but surely the danger had passed. Raine continued to push forward anyway. She needed to slow down, but forced herself to keep his pace. If he could do it, she reminded herself, she could do it.

Just when Kate thought she might collapse, the unmistakable sound came again, blades beating through the frigid air. Kate turned to look out over the valley. Fear slithered up her spine. Without warning, Raine pulled her into the thick underbrush.

"Don't move," he whispered against the shell of her ear.

Kate nodded, too breathless to speak. She forced herself to ignore the feel of his hard body beneath her backside. He held her in his lap, his arms firm around her as if he feared she might suddenly make a run for it.

Her eyes widened and the breath vaporized in her lungs when the helicopter rose above the cliff and hovered over the trail on which they had been running only moments before. Kate turned into the protection of Raine's embrace. His powerful arms tightened around her, and for reasons she could not comprehend, she felt safe, no matter that the helicopter veered ever closer.

The wind whipped around them. Branches slapped at their bodies. The thunderous sound of the propeller echoed through Kate's body, making her heart pound harder. She closed her eyes and pressed her face into the curve of Raine's neck. She inhaled the scent of leather and man and took comfort in the promise he had made to protect her.

What felt like a lifetime later, the sound once more faded into the distance. Kate lifted her gaze to find Raine watching her. Something about the way he looked at her unsettled her, yet drew her. She couldn't look away. His gaze dropped to her lips, and her breath stalled in her chest. Just when she felt sure he intended to kiss her, he reached up and tucked a tendril of hair behind her ear. Slowly, gently, he traced the bruise on her temple. Desire, unbidden yet hot and insistent, raced through her veins.

"Raine," she murmured.

That steady blue gaze returned to hers. Kate moistened her lips, suddenly as afraid he might just kiss her after all as she was that he wouldn't, and asked, "Do you think they're gone for good this time?"

"Maybe…probably." The low, raspy sound of his voice sent goose bumps skittering across her skin.

"What do we do now?" Kate wasn't sure how much longer she could bear the unmistakable sexual tension sizzling between them. She wanted to fight it, to push him away as she had earlier. But she simply could not bring herself to move. She felt safe by his side. Safe from the men chasing them. Safe from the bitter cold. *Safe*.

His warm breath whispered across her lips as he exhaled. "We stay put until we're sure they're gone."

She hadn't noticed just how full and well shaped his lips were until now. Their movement as he spoke mesmerized her. The heat of his body tempted her to burrow more deeply into him.

"Kate."

She forced her gaze upward, away from those lips. "Yes." He was closer now, she felt sure of it.

Long fingers curled around her neck and pulled her closer—so close that their lips almost touched. Almost.

The faint sound of propeller blades jerked Raine's attention skyward. Kate followed his gaze. "Are they coming back?"

Raine listened intently a moment longer. "No, they're headed back toward the lodge." He got to his feet, pulling Kate up as he went. "Let's get moving."

Still unsettled by the intensity of that near kiss, Kate followed the man who had promised to keep her safe from the bad guys.

But who would keep her safe from Raine?

FOR HOURS they continued the downward trek that took them through several shallow streams. Using rocks and fallen tree limbs, Raine helped Kate keep her shoes and feet dry and to avoid icy patches. It was definitely too cold to get wet. From time to time, he offered her a drink from the water bottle he carried.

Kate had accused him last night of not being a gentleman. This morning she'd had to eat her words. He was proving more of a gentleman than she would ever have imagined.

And Raine had been wrong this morning, as well, when he'd said that there hadn't been any heat in the cabin last night. Not to mention the nuclear meltdown that occurred while they hid from the helicopter. Kate's skin still burned from the feel of his strong body against hers. Even through the layers of clothing, she'd felt the strength of him and the power he emanated. She shivered at the recollection.

Focus, Kate. This wasn't the time to fantasize about a man who might be more killer than hero. Thankfully they hadn't heard the helicopter anymore. With the thick canopy of trees overhead she doubted they could be seen from the air at this point even if their pursuers decided to come back. Kate didn't know if she had ever been chased by killers before or not, but it wasn't an experience she wanted to repeat anytime soon.

Kate shuddered when she imagined the sound of barking dogs behind them. How could she remember all these scenarios from movies—if that's what they were—when she couldn't remember anything about her own life? Maybe she was a writer or director or film critic?

That's rich, Kate. If that were the case, what the hell would you be doing in the middle of nowhere following James Bond? Kate had to laugh at herself then; she was pathetic.

She wondered briefly what god she had antagonized to deserve this fate. Whatever she had done in life to bring this penance, Kate prayed she would eventually remember it so she could be sure never to do it again.

Your life will be in constant danger—perhaps from more

than one source. Kate jerked to a stop as the words slammed into her mind. She swallowed the fear rising in her throat. Why couldn't she remember what those words meant? Or who'd said them?

Kate pushed aside the haunting questions and forced herself forward. She had to keep up. It would all come back, eventually. It had to.

They reached an intersection of sorts and Raine took the left fork, announcing that it was the Appalachian Trail. Kate wasn't sure if she had known anything about the Appalachian Trail before today, but she'd had her fill now. The trail seemed more like a ditch at times. Heavily eroded, it was even rockier than the previous terrain they had plodded over. Fir, spruce and birch trees surrounded them on both sides as they continued their downward descent. The only views were of trees and sparse patches of sky.

She scanned the now-familiar landscape and sighed. They had walked for hours with no sign of anything in the distance but trees. For the first time since they had started their journey, Kate wondered if Raine really knew where he was going.

A large, treeless outcropping came into sight. A huge rock jutted up the side of the mountain. It looked oddly out of place, as if someone had lifted it from some faraway spot and deposited it here as a conversation piece. Kate surveyed the strange sight. The trail wound right in front of the large, naturally misplaced rock. Raine again warned Kate not to veer off the trail. His concern was needless—she had no intention of getting more than a few feet from him. The possibility of getting lost or running into Raine's "friends" again tormented her thoughts. Not to mention the possibility of being attacked by a bear.

Lions and tigers and bears. The Wizard of Oz. This time she knew the memory was a movie. She even remembered the name of it. Bears? Kate wondered again if there were bears in these woods. She opened her mouth to ask, but thought better of it. If there were no bears here, Raine would laugh at her stupidity, and if there were bears, he would think her afraid. Besides, any self-respecting bear would be hibernating this time of year, she reminded herself. Kate dismissed the worry as one she could definitely do without.

Raine took a hard right, leaving the Appalachian Trail behind. If this man did not know where he was going, they were in serious trouble. Kate could not have found her way back to the lodge if her life depended on it—at this point she truly hoped it didn't. According to Raine, this part of the trail was rarely used. It continued downward, becoming weedy and even rockier. It soon opened up into a wider, somewhat grassy area. Kate was so exhausted by then that she hardly noticed the lovely mountain views around them. She stored away the glimpses of nature's beauty in its purest form for later consideration. Much later, when she had her life back and wasn't running for it.

The mountains jutted toward the sky on either side of them now as they moved steadily downward. Kate trudged on, numb and beyond exhausted. Snags of old chestnut trees stood on either side of the trail, haunting remnants of times past.

Raine moved forward, seemingly oblivious to anything and everything except advancing toward their destination. Wherever the hell that was. He hadn't uttered more than a sentence or two in hours.

Kate didn't have a watch, so she had no idea how long they had been walking. But her body was telling her that it had been a very long time and that she needed to rest.

No way would she even ask him to slow down. If the bad guys caught up with them, it was not going to be her fault.

RAINE STOPPED at the creek and waited for Kate to catch up with him. She dragged at this point. He had known this journey would be tough on her and he felt bad that it was even worse than he had anticipated. She was young and certainly fit, but the head injury and overall battering she had taken in the accident had left her in a weakened condition. But they had to keep moving.

When she came alongside him, Raine gave her a moment to catch her breath before he spoke. "We'll take a breather now."

Kate dropped on the old bench next to the No Camping sign, the first indication of civilization they had seen since leaving the lodge. They hadn't covered as much ground as he would have preferred, but they could still make up for lost time. Raine scanned the valley around them. They had the worst of the journey behind them, but there was still a ways to go.

He pulled a can of beans and a spoon out of each pocket and handed one of each to Kate.

"Gee, thanks," she said wryly. "You certainly know how to treat a girl right."

Raine allowed her a near smile as he pulled the top from his can. She'd been a real trouper most of the time, the rest of the time she had been a pain in the ass. Though he couldn't help respecting her adaptability, he couldn't make himself trust her. Too many years of not trusting anyone but himself, he supposed. He wasn't about to change now. But that didn't change the fact that he wanted her. And that was an unacceptable complication.

He shifted his gaze to Kate. Even with the dark crescents of fatigue beneath her eyes and the unnaturally pale quality of her face, she was still a hell of a looker. The memory of the shapely body that lay beneath that thick parka had permanently etched itself on the backs of his lids. Every time Raine closed his eyes, he could see her naked, the water from the shower sluicing over her toned body and the steam rising around them as he held her close against his own bare skin. Remembering the feel of her firm breasts against his chest made his groin tighten.

Raine shook off the images and forced himself to swallow the rest of his food. His only intention toward Kate Roberts was to keep her alive until he could get her someplace safe. She was an innocent bystander in all this, and he intended to make sure that she survived this close encounter with the game of life and death. But even Kate's safety remained secondary to his mission. He had to stay focused on his goal: to find Dillon and the mole in Lucas's organization. Even if that turned out to be Lucas himself. Every fiber of Raine's being resisted that possibility.

Raine clenched his jaw against the rage that boiled inside him at the mere thought of Dillon. Dillon would die, and the mole would be tried for treason if he didn't die first. Raine hadn't decided if he would let the bastard live or not. This game would be just like any other, he would play the hand dealt him. He glanced at Kate. She represented a wild card. Raine hadn't decided yet if she would make his hand or break it. Time would tell, and time was his enemy. He retrieved the half-empty water bottle and passed it to Kate, then drank the rest when she finished. They'd have to make it to a source of food and water tonight.

After they had eaten and Raine had buried their cans and spoons, they resumed their journey. Darkness descended as rapidly as the temperature. Raine felt a rush of relief once they emerged into Smokemont campground. The place amounted to nothing more than vacant open spaces for campsites, cold fire rings and a scattering of trees of varying sizes. A paved road circled the grounds. The last tourist had left more than a month ago. Raine had grown up in a nearby community, and there wasn't much about this area that he didn't know.

"What now?" Kate asked, exhaustion evident in her tone.

"Seven miles to Cherokee." Raine didn't look at her, but he heard her little gasp of disbelief.

"But it's dark already."

"Don't think about it, just keep walking. It looks like rain." With growing dread, he scanned the thickening cloud cover. The temperature hadn't dropped low enough for sleet or snow, but precipitation appeared inevitable. And as long as they were moving, Raine could keep his mind off the woman. He needed to be physically exhausted before he spent another night in her company.

An hour later they reached the highway. Raine headed in the direction of Cherokee. The long, black road lay before them like a dark, endless river. The wind had gotten stronger, determined to blow up a storm.

"How far now?" Kate asked wearily.

She hadn't complained at all during the past hour, but Raine knew she had struggled to keep up. He had pushed hard, he knew, and now she was paying the price. Damn, he'd done nothing but screw up since meeting her.

"Not far," he assured her. He would flag down the first vehicle that passed if he had to use his Beretta to get the driver's attention. It was obvious now that Kate couldn't make it much farther, and carrying her would only slow them down. "We'll be there soon."

"Thank God," Kate muttered. "I hope I never get another assignment like this one."

Chapter Five

"What did you say?"

Kate didn't know whether it was the stone-cold blue eyes that glittered at her through the darkness or his bruising grip on her left forearm, but uneasiness stole over her. She'd said something wrong—something Raine didn't like.

"Wh-what are you talking about?" A fist of fear squeezed in her chest.

"You said," he replied tightly, "you hoped you never got another assignment like this." He stepped closer, his size and strength bearing down on her now. "What did you mean by that?"

Kate held her ground—she couldn't have moved if she had wanted to. Her weak and exhausted body had gone limp with absolute fear. She stared into the icy depths of his arctic gaze and said the only thing she knew to say, "I don't know what I meant." Straining with the effort, she swallowed. "I didn't realize I had said it until you repeated it to me." That same gaze that had singed her with heat only a few hours ago now chilled her to the bone.

Kate knew one thing for certain, she would never forget the hard, unflinching expression on his chiseled features. If he felt anything—anger, disbelief, sympathy—neither his face nor his eyes showed any hint whatsoever of what might be going on inside his head. His piercing blue gaze bored into hers, searching, analyzing.

The noose of uncertainty tightened around her neck.

Call in filtered through her haze of fear.

Headlights seemed to come out of nowhere, the flash of light flickering across Kate's face, breaking the charged moment. Raine glanced over his right shoulder at the approaching vehicle before settling his gaze back on hers.

"I'm telling the truth, Raine," she said quickly, in a last-ditch effort to convince him. "I don't know why I said that. Maybe I'm a reporter or something. I just don't know." She released the breath she'd been holding and then added, "You'll...you'll have to trust me on this."

"There's only one person I trust, Kate, and that's me." He turned toward the twin beams of light steadily growing larger, extended his arm and stuck out his thumb in the universal gesture indicating that he wanted a ride. He cut Kate a sidelong look. "But, if it makes you feel any better, I do believe you."

Kate closed her eyes and uttered a silent thanks. He believed her. That's all that mattered at the moment. *If Jack Raine suspects for one second...* Kate's eyes snapped open at the sound of the voice echoing inside her head. *Suspects what?* And how the hell did she know his first name was Jack? Had one of the goons from yesterday called him Jack? She replayed the words over and over, but the answers would not come. What did that warning mean? Who did the voice belong to?

"Is it safe to be hitching a ride?" she suddenly heard herself ask. Kate didn't know if she was cautious by nature, but the thought that their pursuers might be driving down this same road made her uneasy. Not to mention the voices inside her head, and the man standing next to her. Come to think of it, Kate decided, she had a number of things to be uneasy about.

"Not driving something that sounds like that," Raine said impatiently.

An old pickup truck that was surely built before the invention of mufflers lurched to a stop in front of them. Raine opened the passenger-side door and leaned into the vehicle. Kate listened as he asked the driver about a ride to Cherokee. The old truck didn't look as if it would make it another mile much less all the way to Cherokee, but anything was better than walking in the frigid darkness with a storm threatening.

The man mercifully agreed to give them a lift. Raine stepped aside for Kate to climb in first. She eased onto the worn bench seat, the sensation of warmth inside the cab almost making her light-headed. Even the musty odor of stale tobacco and something resembling oil couldn't detract from Kate's appreciation of a ride. The heat blasting from the heater far outweighed all other unpleasantness.

Kate glanced at the driver as he struggled to grind into first gear. The old man eyed her with more interest than curiosity, his mostly toothless grin and scraggly beard doing nothing for his weathered face. Kate moved closer to Raine, putting as much distance between her and the leering old man as possible.

As if sensing her discomfort, Raine slid his arm around her shoulders and pulled her possessively against him. She was thankful for his strong presence as the truck jerked into forward motion. Kate had watched Raine in action. There was no doubt in her mind that he could handle whatever this strange man attempted.

Despite her misgivings about the driver, Kate leaned her weary head against Raine's solid shoulder. At the moment she didn't care if the man turned out to be Jack the Ripper, as long as she could rest for just a little while. Raine had promised to keep her safe and she had to trust him, even if he didn't trust her.

She still couldn't figure out why she would have used the word *assignment,* or why he had reacted so fiercely to it. Why would she hope never to get another *assignment* like this one? Wait a minute, did prostitutes consider their johns assignments? Kate shuddered at the thought. It had to be something else, she wouldn't allow herself to believe that distasteful possibility. Maybe she was a reporter and somehow she had latched on to Raine's story. Or, maybe she knew Ballatore's story. Kate tensed.

Ballatore. Who the hell was Ballatore? Had Raine used that name? Or had one of the goons who'd tried to kill them mentioned it? Kate closed her eyes and forced the questions away. She didn't know how she knew that name. She didn't know why she called this an assignment. She didn't know what her relationship with Raine amounted to. She didn't know why she didn't know.

God, she was so tired. Kate snuggled closer to Raine, and his arm tightened around her. He would keep her safe and that's all that mattered right now.

FIFTEEN MINUTES LATER, they were in the middle of Cherokee. The town was one long strip nestled between the soaring mountains. Neon signs flashed, advertising typical tourist-trap junk. Casinos, restaurants, motels, and other tacky, run-down buildings dotted the main street through the small town.

"That service station on the right will be fine," Raine told the driver. His voice sounded harsh after the long silence during the ride.

Without question, the old man pulled into the parking lot. Raine thanked him, opened the door and got out. Kate scooted across the seat and hurried out behind him. When her feet hit the ground, her legs felt rubbery beneath her. The cold night air seemed more brutal after the warmth of the truck.

"What now?" Kate asked, watching Raine as he surveyed the street in both directions. "A motel, I hope," she added when he didn't answer right away. "Or a restaurant, I'm starved."

"Not yet," he told her, his attention still focused on the mixture of gaudy and dilapidated businesses lining the long street.

"What then?" Kate hated the slight whine she heard in her voice. Every muscle in her body screamed in protest of taking another step; a dull ache had settled inside her head, or maybe it had been there all along but the task of keeping up with Raine had distracted her from the pain. Her chest still felt tight. She needed to eat—anything but beans and franks. And she was thirsty again, she suddenly realized.

"We need transportation out of here," he said as he started down the dimly lit street toward the busier end of town.

Kate flung argument after argument against her mental sounding board, but she trudged after Raine without protest. She had followed him this far, no point in changing her strategy now, no matter how much she wanted to check into a hotel and sleep for days. If he wanted to keep moving, she certainly didn't have a better plan. He obviously had some sort of plan, and any kind of plan was better than none.

Raine wandered through the casino parking lot, looking over each vehicle as if he was about to purchase one. Kate shivered. The cold night air had consumed the last of the warmth her body had managed to build up during their ride to Cherokee. Kate wrapped her arms around herself. She would walk until she dropped. Raine had to be tired, too. If he could keep moving, so could she.

Finally Raine opened the driver's-side door of an old

Chevy sedan. After surveying the interior, he looked across the top of the car at Kate and said, "Get in."

"What?" She frowned at his curt demand.

"Get in, dammit."

Kate felt her eyes go round in genuine horror. "You're going to steal this car!" she hissed, glancing around to see if anyone was watching them. A thief! The man was a thief as well as a killer. She shook her head slowly from side to side in disbelief. He was crazy. *She* was crazy for tagging along with him.

"Get your butt in the car!" Raine commanded. He shot her a look that would have spurred a dead man into action.

Kate jerked the door open and plunked down onto the seat. Maybe his plan wasn't so great after all, she decided. Stealing! And she was an accessory. Grand theft auto, wasn't that a felony? Kate yanked at the obviously never-before-used seat belt. It wouldn't budge. She pulled harder. By God, she might be forced to ride in a stolen vehicle, but at least she would ride safely. The engine suddenly roared to life.

Kate's startled gaze bumped into Raine's. "How'd you do that so fast?"

One of those rare, breath-stealing smiles spread across his lips. "Trade secret." He winked, then leaned across Kate to reach the seat belt.

A tiny curl of awareness coiled inside her as she watched Raine pull the belt over her lap and snap the buckle into place. Kate had certainly been this close to him before, but there was something different this time. His protective gesture, that was it. Just like when he'd stepped between her and Vinny, and when the helicopter had come back he had pulled her to safety. She hadn't asked for his help with the seat belt, he had simply taken the initiative, as if her safety was important to him. As if she mattered in all this madness.

''Thank you,'' she murmured, sounding too breathless.

Still leaning across her, Raine paused. His gaze lingered on her mouth for a moment. Neon lights flashed and flickered, filling the car with a mixture of garish light and eerie shadow. When his gaze lifted to hers, the lean, hungry look in his eyes twisted that little curl of desire until heat funneled just beneath Kate's belly button.

Raine abruptly banished the hunger in his eyes and straightened. He put the car in Reverse and muttered, ''You're welcome.'' Without another look in her direction, he backed the car out of its slot and pulled out of the parking lot.

Kate rubbed her hands up and down her arms as if she could warm herself by sheer determination. She relaxed against the cloth seat and tried to forget the needy look she had seen in Raine's eyes. She knew it wasn't right, but she couldn't help thinking of the way she had felt when she woke that morning in his arms, tingly and warm all over. Although she had been fighting mad with him for having responded sexually to her, she was more angry at herself for her own body's traitorous reaction. And then in the woods. She had wanted him to kiss her, and he would have if they hadn't been interrupted. On some level it pleased Kate to know that he felt the pull of desire too.

Maybe he was a bad guy, but he had some good points all the same. Especially, she thought with a little smile, those amazing blue eyes. She could imagine how really touching him and losing complete control would feel.

Stop it, Kate! She bit her lip. She couldn't think that way. *There's no telling how many men he's killed,* Danny's words rang out inside her head. Jack Raine was a killer.

...this one worries me. That other voice echoed right behind Danny's. Kate squeezed her eyes shut and tried to place the voice that haunted her. It was a woman. Someone

she trusted. That's all she knew. But who? Her mother? A sister? *Who?*

Kate sighed and stared into the darkness beyond the headlights. Was her past so awful that she couldn't bear to remember it? Or was it her that was so unmemorable?

The beam of the headlights moved over a road sign up ahead that read Bryson City 10 Miles.

"Bryson City, is that where we're going?" Kate turned to Raine, hoping he would choose to gift her with a straight answer. "What's in Bryson City?"

"That's where we're headed. Bryson City has public transportation." Raine didn't look at her, and, if his tone gave any indication, he wasn't interested in conversing. As usual.

Too tired to care, Kate leaned against the door and watched the first fat drops of rain splat against the windshield. The heater had finally kicked in, filling the car with its warmth. Soon the pelting against the glass grew steadier, turning the highway in front of them into a long line of black ink. The desolate road stretched out before them, taking Kate away from a past she didn't recall and into a future she understood nothing about. Her mind felt as empty and desolate as the highway. She shivered again, but this time it had nothing to do with the cold.

The hypnotic swish of the wipers lulled Kate toward sleep. Her lids felt so heavy…she needed to sleep…to rest her aching muscles and ease the tightness in her chest. She finally closed her eyes and welcomed the heavy blanket of inner darkness.

KATE SAT UP with a start as she felt the tires leave the pavement and bump over uneven ground. She glanced at Raine to see if he had fallen asleep at the wheel. He was wide awake and braking the car to a stop.

"Where are we?" Kate peered through the dark and

drizzle in an effort to get her bearings. She saw trees but couldn't make out anything else.

"We walk from here." Raine opened his door and got out of the car.

It took a few moments for his words to register, then Kate realized he intended that they walk in the rain. "But it's raining," she protested when he opened her door.

He reached inside and unbuckled her seat belt, then glared at her. "No kidding."

Kate sat there, stunned. She wasn't about to leave another perfectly good automobile. Especially a nice warm one. He was definitely crazy—worse than crazy. He was…he was… Kate couldn't think of a fitting description at the moment, but whatever it was, he was it.

"Get out of the car," he ordered, giving her one final threatening stare. His breath fanned across her face. A muscle twitched in his tense jaw. The dim interior light cast his stony features in shadows and angles that enhanced the impatient scowl on his handsome face. She couldn't possibly win in this battle of wills. Raine had no intention of giving one centimeter.

Kate exhaled in frustration. One corner of his mouth lifted the tiniest fraction—he'd won and he knew it. Raine straightened and waited for her to get out. Kate silently recited every swearword she could remember, twice. With equal measures reluctance and anger, she forced herself out of the nice warm car, then slammed the door. Raine had the grace not to allow that smile to completely form as he adjusted the collar of his leather jacket. Without another word, he strode toward what Kate recognized as the highway they had left behind. Raine had pulled the car onto a dead-end side road just far enough that it would be hidden from view.

Cursing under her breath, Kate struggled to unzip the thick collar of her parka and pull out the hood. By the time she had the hood pulled over her head, her hair was already damp. She shivered as the icy liquid slid down the collar of her sweatshirt and absorbed into the T-shirt beneath. Seething inside, she flung a few expletives at Raine's broad back. As usual, he ignored her.

Once they were on the pavement, Kate could see that Bryson City lay only half a mile or so away. At least they wouldn't be walking for long. It dawned on Kate then that Raine had abandoned the vehicle because it was stolen. Tucked in the cluster of trees, it would be days or weeks before the car would be found. The man left as few clues as possible. By the time the car was found and traced back to them, they would be long gone. He seemed to think of everything to cover his tracks. Maybe he was crazy. Yeah, right—crazy like a fox. Kate supposed that he had done the right thing, even if she was getting all wet. They hadn't come this far just to get caught because he made a stupid mistake.

He's managed to slip through their fingers. Kate frowned. That voice. She knew that voice. But what did the words mean? She looked at the man she struggled to keep pace with. *Him?* Whose fingers had he slipped through? The police? The other bad guys? Kate shoved her gloved hands deeper into her pockets and sighed. She had to remember. Every instinct told her that her life depended on remembering.

But she was too tired now to think about it anymore. She shuddered as the wind whipped the icy droplets against her face. God, how she hated to be cold. As if on cue, her stomach rumbled. She hated to be hungry, too.

When they reached civilization, Raine used a pay phone at a service station. Kate had no idea who or where he called. She was too wet and too cold even to wonder. She shivered almost uncontrollably now. The only thing on her mind at this point was getting somewhere warm and dry. She didn't care if she ate, only that she got warm.

After the brief call, she followed Raine to a seedy-looking motel on the edge of town. She wondered vaguely how he managed to keep from shivering as she did.

Because he's a machine, that's how. He doesn't have any feelings, she added decidedly. Jack Raine, if that was his full name, was a cold, heartless *killing* machine. Kate shuddered at the thought. Then she remembered the way he could make her feel with just the right look. Maybe he wasn't *all* machine.

Kate could only guess what her financial standing might be, but somehow she knew that this place—she scanned the shabby room once more—was beneath the usual for her. The term "motel" had been used very loosely, in her opinion.

"There's only one bed," she said, suddenly noticing among the decrepit furnishings the one bed, slightly wider than the last one they had shared, but singular nonetheless.

"This was the only room available. You heard the manager say so yourself. So put a lid on it and get in the shower. We have to get out of these wet clothes." Raine cut her a look that dared her to argue with him. He dropped his coat onto a chair behind him and quickly moved his hands down his shirtfront, releasing button after button with stiff, clumsy fingers.

"What are you doing?" Kate retreated a step only to bump into the lone bed.

"The same thing you're going to do, if I have to help you do it." His hard-edged tone and the implacable expression on his face reinforced his words.

When Kate hesitated, he added, "Don't worry, I'm too tired to be dangerous."

At that same instant he peeled his shirt off his shoulders, revealing more than Kate needed to see right now. Her mouth went incredibly dry. He walked into what was obviously the bathroom and, came out wiping his awesome chest with a towel, wordlessly offering her the first shower. He might be tired, but somehow she doubted the other. She decided right then and there that it would be safe to assume that Raine was definitely dangerous, even in his sleep.

Kate hurriedly unzipped her parka, shouldered out of it and dropped it to the floor next to the bed. Without sparing Raine a glance, she walked past him and locked herself in the minuscule bathroom. She stared at the still-unfamiliar reflection in the mirror. Her dark hair was wet and disheveled. The smudges under her eyes looked black against her pale skin. She was a mess. Shivering to the point that her teeth chattered, Kate quickly stripped off her wet clothes and stepped into the shower with the water as hot as she could tolerate it.

After unwrapping a new bar of soap, she closed her eyes and allowed the heat to relax her sore, stiff muscles. The wonderful sensation of liquid warmth was almost enough to make her forget about food. *Almost,* Kate thought as she rubbed the soap into a lather. She hoped they wouldn't have to wait for their clothes to dry to get something to eat. She was starved.

Since their pathetic excuse for lodgings didn't offer amenities such as shampoo, Kate had no choice but to wash her hair with the bar soap. She worked the lather into her hair, then she moved to her shoulders and arms, and on to her breasts. The steam rose around her, filling the tiny room with moist heat. Kate's breathing became slow and shallow as vivid memories of her shower with Raine reeled through her tired mind like images from a hot, steamy movie.

His broad, muscular chest and strong arms. Hands that were both gentle and comforting as he'd held her in his arms, warming her with his own body heat. Kate vaguely remembered him drying her skin and then carrying her to his bed. She braced her hands against the dingy, tiled wall when the terrifying events of yesterday and today replayed before her eyes. Raine stepping between her and Vinny, the out-of-control car ride, the loud, echoing sound of gunfire, the helicopter, and then the long trek across the mountain.

Just when she had decided once and for all what a bad guy Raine was, he did something like putting his arm around her in the truck, protecting her when she felt uneasy. Buckling her seat belt when she couldn't. And now, letting her shower first. Nothing about him fit one particular mold. And absolutely nothing about him could ever possibly be considered less than dangerous.

Then there was the intense desire she had seen in his eyes this morning and the lean, hungry look she'd noticed there tonight. Maybe he wanted to be nice to her in return for sex. Her eyes popped open and she pushed the water and hair back from her face. After all, they were pretty much joined at the hip for the duration of this little adventure. And he hadn't exactly said that they hadn't done it already. Surely if she had slept with a hunk like Raine, she would remember. Kate shivered involuntarily despite the hot water warming her skin.

Maybe the intense awareness between them was simply hormones. Or, maybe the man was flat out horny. Kate shivered at the thought of Raine's naked body moving over hers. Banishing the images, she turned off the water, pushed the curtain aside and stepped out of the tub. She pulled a clean, rough terry-cloth towel from the stack on the back on the commode. Kate hugged the towel to her breasts as she leaned forward and swiped the fog from the mirror. Would a man like Raine consider her attractive? she wondered.

She bit her lower lip and studied the reflection staring back at her. She was attractive, she supposed. Kate turned her head slightly and inspected the ugly bruise on her left temple. It had turned an unflattering shade of reddish purple. She lowered the towel from her breasts and scrutinized them as well. They weren't large, but, she decided as she surveyed her nude body, they did seem properly proportioned to the rest of her. Her waist was slim, her hips flared a bit, and her legs were long and toned.

All in all, Kate felt reasonably satisfied with what she saw. Now, if only she could remember the past and the personality that went with the body.

Raine pounded on the closed door, startling Kate. Her heart thudded out her panic at the possibility that they had been found already. Were the bad guys here? Raine pounded on the door again. Instantly Kate covered herself with the towel as if he might see her through the door.

"What's the holdup?" he demanded impatiently.

Kate pressed a hand to her throat. Thank God. He only wanted his turn. She blew a breath out slowly and licked her lips nervously. "Just a minute," she yelled back.

Quickly, she dried and wrapped a clean towel around herself. She retrieved the brush from her purse and hastily tugged it through her hair. Kate gathered her wet clothes and took another deep breath before she opened the door. He waited, blocking her exit, irritation etched in his features.

"Hang your clothes over by the heating unit. I've turned it on high so they'll dry faster." Raine had already undressed, leaving nothing but the towel draped precariously around his narrow hips.

Kate kept her gaze above his waist as she waited for him to step out of her way. The scattering of hair on his chest was blond too, she noticed, and it looked gold against his skin. Several thin, jagged lines drew her attention.

Scars, she realized. Before she could ask about them, he stepped aside.

Kate hurried past him. She couldn't look him in the eye, not after the thoughts she'd had in the shower. God, she must be insane, fantasizing about a man who was a thief as well as a killer. And a kidnapper if she added the fact that he had dragged her, unwilling, into this nightmare. She draped her clothes over the heating unit next to his and valiantly fought the impulse to turn around. Kate knew he was watching her, she could feel his gaze on her body.

She straightened, swallowed hard, then turned to face him. He stood at the closet with the door open. "I'll need you to wait in here while I shower."

Anger unfurled inside Kate. "You're kidding," she suggested, giving him an opportunity to retain his current status as a gentleman in her opinion.

"I never kid," he deadpanned. "I can't trust you not to make a run for it." He opened the door wider and motioned for her to step inside. "I won't be long."

Raine slipped down Kate's opinion poll several notches, all the way back to jerk, in fact. She recognized the futility in arguing with him, so she squared her shoulders and stamped across the room. Kate paused at his side and shrugged. "Why not? I've been subjected to numerous other indignities since making your acquaintance." She stepped into the tiny, dark closet and kept her back turned until he closed the door.

Kate huffed a disgusted breath. Of all the amenities for a dump like this to have—a real closet. She stood stone still in the middle of the unadvertised and unusual feature and mused over the irony of it all.

RAINE EXHALED in disgust as he closed the door and jammed a straight chair securely under the knob. He didn't exactly feel good about locking Kate in the closet, but he couldn't risk her running. And, though she appeared harmless enough, there was something about her that ate at him. He knew better than to get involved with Kate. She was an unknown factor...a risk. Swallowing back that ridiculous guilt he felt every time he so much as raised his voice to the woman, he entered the bathroom, leaving the door open so he could keep an eye on the closet door.

Raine stepped into the hot spray of water and closed his eyes. He pressed his forehead against the tiled wall and allowed the hot water to sluice over his tired muscles. He relaxed a moment longer before making short work of washing and rinsing. He didn't want to leave Kate stuck in the closet for too long. She might beat on the door or scream at the top of her lungs. Raine had quickly learned that Kate was almost as unpredictable as he was. And that was a helluva scary thought. Especially since he still didn't know much about her.

Except that he wanted her—wanted her bad. Raine swore. He was a fool. A damn fool. He'd had the hots for the woman practically since the moment he'd laid eyes on her. She was just so bloody vulnerable. And beautiful, with an innocence that tugged at something deep inside him. Raine had spent so much time in the company of scum, he had forgotten that there were still truly innocent people in the world. Kate struck him as one of those. There was something undeniably attractive about that part of her. Something that drew him like a moth to flame.

And he would probably get burned...or worse.

He was a fool all right.

After drying off, Raine secured a towel around his waist and hurried to remove the chair and open the closet door. Kate didn't look at him as she stepped out of her two-foot-by-four-foot prison. The towel effectively covered her slender body, but fully displayed those long, shapely legs. Need punched him in the gut again as he watched her walk straight to the bed and burrow between the sheets. Raine shook his head in self-disgust at how easily she could make him feel like a heel.

And want her even more. This woman was going to get him killed. Raine scrubbed his hand over his face and then through his hair. He had spent more than a dozen years facing death and dealing it out as well. For the first time in his life, he felt unprepared for the situation. He could look a target in the eye when that target took his last breath and feel little remorse, but every time Raine looked Kate in the eye something moved, twisted inside him.

This was bad, real bad.

Get a grip, Jack old boy, before you get yourself killed. He swallowed. Kate Roberts was just a woman. He only felt protective because she couldn't remember who she was or where she came from. That was all.

Yeah, right. Raine jammed his hands at his waist. Kate's memory loss was the least of their problems at the moment. Being with him was likely going to cost this pretty lady her life, that's what bothered him. But he couldn't chance leaving her behind at this point. Even if she turned out to be the enemy.

Shrugging off the thought, Raine walked to the bedside table and pulled the telephone book from the drawer. He was tired. He would be able to deal with all this better tomorrow.

"What kind of pizza do you like?" he asked as he thumbed through the Yellow Pages for a restaurant that delivered.

"I don't care," she said, her voice muffled by the cover. "I'm not going to eat with you and I'm not going to talk to you." Kate kept her back turned, refusing to look at him.

"I'm devastated," he muttered, then reached for the telephone and called in an order. How in the hell had he gotten himself into this situation? It wasn't bad enough that Ballatore's men were after him, even his own people had jumped on the bandwagon. The mole's doing, no doubt. And, as if that weren't trouble aplenty, he had to be saddled with—he glared at Kate's back—a helpless and annoying female who pushed all his buttons.

He was definitely screwed.

Raine had always known that he was going to hell for his multitude of sins, he just thought he'd die first. Not once had anyone ever warned him that when he got his it would come in the form of a high-priority assignment gone sour and a woman who turned him inside out.

Kate continued her silent treatment even after the pizza and drinks arrived. The smell alone was enough to make Raine salivate. He sat down in one of the two chairs flanking the small table and propped his feet on the end of the bed. Kate continued to face the wall while Raine ate his fill. He commented frequently on the delicious ingredients and the thick crust, but she ignored him completely. He knew she needed to eat, but he couldn't make her if she didn't want to. Damn, the woman irritated the hell out of him.

Finished, Raine stood, scratched his chest and stretched his arms over his head. He was tired. He made himself comfortable on the side of the bed next to Kate's back. She immediately wiggled to the edge, as far away from him as possible. Then, as soon as he had gotten situated just right and turned on the news, she edged off the bed on the other side and went to the table. He frowned. What the hell was she doing now?

Kate plopped into one of the chairs, picked up a large slice of pizza, and closed her eyes as she savored the taste.

"I thought you were on a hunger strike."

She took a gulp of soda, then flashed him a look. "I

didn't say I wasn't going to eat, I said I wasn't going to eat with you.''

Raine suppressed the grin that tugged at his lips. Kate had no intention of allowing him to get the better of her. He was beginning to wonder if maybe she was going to get the better of him. Kate Roberts had gotten deeper under his skin in the last thirty-six hours than anyone had in his adult life. It wasn't just the physical attraction either, and that was stronger than any he had experienced. It was the way she could turn his resolve to mush or make his insides twist just by looking at him. The sound of her voice made him want her.

Raine didn't want to want her. Somehow he had to get this crazy need back under control. He forced his gaze from her towel-clad body. Looking at all the silky skin revealed by her lack of clothing wasn't going to help.

Raine scanned the television channels for a while. As usual, nothing caught his interest. Eventually Kate got back into bed. Perched on the far edge, she kept her back to him. Still bored and restless, he allowed his gaze to linger on Kate's bare shoulders. His groin tightened. Damn, he had to get this woman out of his system. Disgusted with himself, Raine ran through the channels once more.

But how could he not think about her when he was stuck with her at least for a few more days?

Fear. She was definitely afraid of him on some level. That was the ticket. If he could keep her afraid of him, then she would never let him too close. That was the answer. Raine pushed the power button on the remote, turning the television off. He settled farther down into the bed without getting under the covers. No way was he going to chance coming in contact with her bare skin. That would be a big mistake.

And tomorrow he would concentrate on fear and intimidation, his specialties. Sweet little Kate would never know what hit her. She would keep her distance then. Raine felt a smile pull at his lips as he drifted into much-needed sleep.

RAINE WOKE at 6:00 a.m. His left arm was draped over Kate's breasts, his face buried in the curve of her neck. His left hand had tangled in her soft hair. Even the smell of cheap soap couldn't mask her womanly scent. He could feel the heat of her body all along the front of his. It would be so easy to tug the sheet down, ease his body over hers and take what he wanted. Would she resist after he used his lips and hands to persuade her? He didn't think so. Raine had seen desire in her eyes more than once. She wanted him, too. Maybe not as much as he wanted her, but the need was there.

Raine rubbed a strand of dark, silky hair between his thumb and forefinger. So soft, so sweet. He doubted that Kate had had much experience with men—especially men like him. His whole body tightened at the thought of how hot and snug she would be. He wanted to taste her, to bury himself inside her. To forget for just a little while.

Raine set his jaw hard. He allowed himself one last deep draw of her scent before he moved away from her enticing body. That line of thinking would get them both killed. He had to keep his mind on business. Disgusted with his intense state of arousal, Raine picked up his jeans and shirt and headed for the bathroom. He'd give Kate a few more minutes to sleep. She had tossed and turned a lot during the night. He wondered what demons chased her. She seemed entirely too young and innocent to have any significant demons, but looks could be deceiving, as he well knew.

Maybe she wasn't what she seemed at all. Maybe, she was bait—sexy, beautiful bait. Raine tensed. He hadn't considered that particular possibility until now. He stared at his reflection in the bathroom mirror. It wouldn't be the first time a woman had been used that way to trap him.

"You're a fool," he told his doubting reflection. He had already lost his perspective entirely when it came to Kate Roberts.

That was a mistake, a big mistake.

After he had dressed, Raine picked up Kate's clothes and sat down on the side of the bed. He turned on the lamp and looked at her closely. The sheet and towel had slipped down, revealing one firm breast, but that wasn't what caught his eye. She was even paler than she had been the day before. The bruise on her temple looked a nasty shade of red. Her rose-colored lips weren't quite as rosy as before and the dark circles under her eyes were much darker.

Something was wrong, but they had to put more miles behind them before they stopped for any length of time. Still, Raine had an uneasy feeling about the way she looked. He glanced at his watch. Six-fifteen. They had to get moving.

"Kate, wake up." Raine shook her gently. "Kate, you need to get up and get dressed."

She sat bolt upright, pulling the sheet over her as she went. She surveyed the room, her searching gaze instantly alert. Raine frowned. This was the second time he had noticed that waking reaction. He eyed her suspiciously. This kind of response definitely warred with his instincts about her. Whatever Kate had to hide was lost to her as well, and that provided Raine with a safety net of sorts. But what about when she remembered? He would deal with that when and if the situation presented itself.

"What now?" she asked, shoving long silky strands of hair behind her ears.

"Get dressed. We have to get moving." Raine pushed

up off the bed and crossed the room. He stared out the window while he waited for Kate to get ready. One way or another he would refocus his perspective, especially where she was concerned.

After a full ten minutes in the bathroom, she finally pulled on her coat and announced that she was good to go.

Though the sun was shining, the early-morning air cut straight to the bone. It was a damn good thing they didn't have to do any mountain climbing today. Raine glanced back at Kate, who had fallen behind. He frowned again. She didn't look as if she'd make it the few blocks they had to go. He waited for her to catch up before continuing.

Kate didn't ask any questions or make any comments when he led her into the bus station and used a clean credit card to purchase two tickets for New York City. She sat quietly and obediently. Another indication that something wasn't quite right.

When they boarded the bus, Raine ushered Kate to an empty seat in the back. Still, she didn't protest.

She sat next to the window, staring into the distance. Raine relaxed into the seat and closed his eyes. He hadn't ridden a bus in a long time; now he remembered why. Noisy, uncomfortable and smelly, just to name a few of the less pleasant points. But, it was a means to an end. His pursuers wouldn't expect him to take a bus.

"Why are we going to New York?"

Raine cracked one eye open and looked at his traveling companion. "I thought you were giving me the silent treatment?"

"Never mind," she muttered, then turned back to the window.

That damn guilt again. Raine cursed himself for feeling it. "I have a command performance in New York," he said quietly, irritated that he felt compelled to give her an explanation. "An old friend wants the pleasure of my company so badly that he's willing to kill for it."

Friend? Raine almost laughed out loud at his misnomer. He didn't have any friends in the true sense of the word, least of all the man he had most recently betrayed. Raine forced the image of Sal Ballatore from his mind. They were enemies, nothing more.

Kate turned back to him, her eyes wide with uncertainty and the slightest hint of fear. Raine knew that he had to pursue that avenue if he was ever going to keep his sanity. He'd been in this business too long to screw up because he couldn't control his lust for a woman.

"Have you really killed hundreds of men?" she asked in a tentative voice.

Raine smiled at the question. Where in the hell had she heard something like that? Danny, maybe. He leaned a bit closer and pulled his most intimidating face. "Do you really want me to answer that question?"

She swallowed tightly. Her voice trembled a little when she answered, but she kept her gaze locked with his. "Yes."

Raine lifted one shoulder in a careless shrug. "I don't know. I never really kept count. It's probably a fairly accurate estimate. But there is one inaccuracy." Raine leaned even closer, crowding her. "They weren't all men, some were women."

Kate drew back as far as possible against the window. She tried without success to mask the stark fear that stole across her features. "Are you...do you kill people for money? Is that what you do?"

Raine laughed softly. His answer had evoked just the response he had hoped for, but he really hadn't expected the second question. "No. I don't kill people for the money, *exactly.*"

She sucked in a sharp breath, licked her lips and then

hit him with another one. "Then why do you…kill people, exactly?"

Raine forced the smile to fade from his lips and turned up the intimidation a notch. "If I told you the answer to that, then I'd have to kill you, too."

Chapter Six

He was only joking, Kate told herself for the one hundredth time that day. She had asked a stupid question and she'd gotten a stupid answer. Kate twisted in her seat and stared out the window into the blackness.

The day had stretched into a lifetime. Kate's head still ached, but not as much as the day before. The pain and weakness in her muscles had grown undeniably worse. Maybe she wasn't accustomed to such a rigorous physical workout. Mountain climbing obviously wasn't her forte. Whatever the case, Kate felt exhausted and limp, as if her bones had melted, leaving her incapable of the slightest exertion. Even after a night's rest and the endless morning sitting on a bus, she still didn't feel refreshed. If she had ever been this tired before, she didn't care to remember that particular event.

She had hoped that with the dawning and passing of a new day, more memories would surface as well, but they hadn't. Raine had remained distant, in his own little world. He had spoken to her only once the entire day and that was to inquire whether she wanted to eat during one of the extended layovers. They had eaten in silence at a fast-food restaurant next to the bus station.

Kate passed the afternoon away watching the landscape go by and mulling over the few snatches of memory she could recall. The words and warnings didn't make any sense. The voice—the woman's voice—seemed familiar, yet no name or face emerged from the gray haze that hid her past. The phrase "call in" stirred the most emotion for her. The words seemed deeply entrenched, like a lesson gone over many times. On an elemental level Kate knew that she needed to follow that instinct the moment she remembered the number again.

Eventually the day had turned once more to night, and darkness enshrouded them. Kate relaxed back into her seat and, with the gentle rocking of the large silver bus, drifted toward sleep. Just before sleep took her, the thought occurred to Kate that she had yet to catch Raine in even a nap. Vaguely she wondered if he slept at all. Of course not, she decided as she gave in to her body's need to shut down, machines don't need to sleep.

THE GENTLE, rhythmic rocking had stopped.

Abruptly, Kate jerked awake. Raine was telling her to get moving. The other passengers had lined up single file down the long center aisle to wait their turn to exit the bus. Ignoring her body's protest, Kate pushed out of the seat and followed Raine off the bus and into the all but empty station. A handful of travel-weary people waited for their connections or for a loved one to pick them up. Kate scanned the sleep-deprived faces and wished she was like them—on her way home.

Home. Where was home? she wondered.

Virginia. Her driver's license had been issued in Virginia. Maybe that was home.

"What time is it?" Kate asked, then shoved her hands into her pockets and huddled into her parka as they exited the building. The night air seemed colder than it had been in Bryson City. They were traveling north, so that would make sense. "What time is it?" she repeated, increasing her pace to keep up with Raine's long strides on the uphill trek. The landscape seemed hilly, as if the city was carved into the side of a mountain, but nothing Kate saw clicked any recognition. In fact, she had seen about all the mountainous territory she cared to see in this lifetime.

"One thirty-five," he said without slowing down.

The bus had stopped so many times, with a couple lengthy layovers, there was no way Kate could gauge the distance they had traveled in time. She surveyed the sleeping town Raine seemed determined to cross on foot and came to one conclusion very quickly—they definitely weren't in New York City. She had been to New York. She didn't remember when or how, but she had been there. Kate remembered the skyscrapers, the traffic at all hours of the night. This wasn't the Big Apple.

Raine walked up the dark, quiet sidewalk as if he had a specific destination in mind. The long bus ride had made Kate's overworked muscles stiff and lethargic. She grimaced with each step she took. She hoped like hell that Raine didn't intend to walk from wherever they were to New York. If so, she was out.

"Where are we?" Kate forced herself to maintain his pace so he couldn't ignore her question.

"You don't recognize it?" He stopped, and leveled his penetrating blue gaze on her.

Kate's feet stopped before the rest of her did. When she had steadied herself, she hesitated before answering. Was this a trick question? Should she know this city? She looked around again, taking in the one- and two-story buildings and an array of storefronts. Nothing at all looked familiar. "No," she finally admitted.

"Charlottesville, Virginia," he told her.

Raine watched her reaction carefully. Kate struggled to keep her face clear of emotion. Virginia. That was supposed to be home, but nothing about this place felt like home. Panic swept through her, a cold, harsh reminder that she had lost her past. Lost herself.

Suck it up, girl. Don't let him get to you. Just because you lived in Virginia doesn't mean you've ever been to this particular town. "I thought we were going to New York," she reminded. Good move. Turn the tables on him. Make him squirm for a change.

He looked away then. "There's something I have to do first."

Without further explanation, Raine resumed his journey to God only knows where. Kate had little choice but to follow. After all, she had practically no money, no memory, no nothing. She could only stick to him and hope it was the right thing to do.

After crossing two more streets, they entered the dimly lit cobblestone entrance of a large hotel. Now this, she acknowledged thankfully, was a hotel. The well-kept exterior beckoned to the weary traveler. The lobby looked warm and welcoming.

Fortunately there were plenty of rooms, so Kate was able to have a separate bed. The moment they entered the room, she dropped her coat to the floor, kicked off her shoes and sprawled out on her big soft bed—the one farthest from the door, per Raine's insistence. Kate closed her eyes and sighed. She had died and gone to heaven. Now, if only she never had to move again. Well, just one last move, she told herself as she tugged the spread over her body. Kate burrowed into the thick cover and relaxed completely. She didn't care what other amenities the room might have.

She didn't open her eyes again, but she could hear Raine moving around the room. Kate didn't care what he did as long as he left her alone. She was so very tired, even breathing seemed an effort. The aroma of coffee brewing couldn't even rouse her. Tomorrow she would worry about trying to find home. If Virginia was home, surely she could find her way from here. All she had to do was give Raine the slip and hide from the bad guys who were after him. Simple enough.

Kate sleepily moaned her disbelief. Giving Raine the slip wouldn't be quite so easy. He didn't miss a single detail. Sometimes she wondered if he could read her mind. What a strange man. A paradox.

A cold-blooded killer. Kate shuddered and hugged the spread more closely. Danny had said that Raine had killed hundreds of men, and Raine hadn't bothered to deny it. In fact, he seemed rather proud of it, unremorseful. But something inside her—intuition maybe—kept telling her to trust him. She had no idea if she could really trust him or not, but one thing remained certain—Raine could have killed her long ago had that been his intent. He had taken care of her so far. She would just have to go with the flow. What else could she do?

FOUR A.M. The lighted display shone brightly in the darkness. What had awakened her? Kate strained to listen. Thunder exploded and lightning flashed across the darkness. It was storming outside, she realized with relief. She squinted at Raine's empty bed. Where was he? The next flash of lightning answered her question. Raine stood at the window staring out at the storm.

Kate disentangled herself from the covers and slid out of bed. She padded across the room to stand next to him. "What's wrong?" she asked as she rubbed her eyes to clear them. The brooding silhouette he made against the dim glow of neon and violent displays of nature's fury made her shiver.

"Nothing. Go back to sleep." He didn't spare her a glance, but continued his relentless gaze into the stormy night.

Lightning streaked across the sky again, followed closely by two more brilliant flashes, giving Kate a heart-stumbling view of Raine's bare chest and unsnapped jeans. Her eyes followed the golden trail of wispy chest hair until it disappeared into the half-zipped fly of his jeans. Desire coiled, sending a spear of heat through her middle. She blinked when the darkness returned as suddenly as it had vanished. Had she been openly gaping at the man's body? Yes, she had. Kate couldn't bring herself to meet the gaze she felt analyzing her. No doubt he had also noted her preoccupation with his bare torso.

Kate pushed a handful of hair away from her face and wet her lips. She had to say something—she couldn't just stand there like an idiot. The next flash of light brightened the entire room and the clap of thunder boomed so loud that Kate jerked, then staggered in its wake.

Raine grabbed her by the shoulders and steadied her. There was nothing tender about his grasp. He held her too tightly and too close, willing her to look at him.

"I'm okay," she managed to say, though her body denied her words by trembling uncontrollably. She couldn't look at him. Part of her wanted desperately to touch him, but another part—a much wiser part—wanted to pull away, to run. "I'm okay," she told him again when he didn't immediately release her.

"Somehow I doubt that," he said, his words blunt, his voice low and husky. The sound shivered over her nerve endings, both terrifying and tantalizing.

"Look at me," he ordered, cupping her face and forcing her gaze upward.

Kate looked at his mouth first, that full tempting mouth that was almost too beautiful to belong to a man. Two days' worth of golden-brown stubble covered his jaw, lending a definite roguish quality. Finally, reluctantly, Kate met that piercing gaze. Ice blue, with an underlying fierceness that drew her and pushed her away at the same time.

He caressed her cheek with the pad of his thumb, all the while his eyes weaved a sensual spell of their own. "Are you afraid, Kate?"

"Yes." The one word came out breathless, a mere whisper. A thought spoken.

"Tell me what you're afraid of," he commanded.

Kate swallowed. It was difficult to think clearly with him so close and his eyes so…so intent on her. "I'm afraid those men will find us."

His thumb slid over her lower lip, Kate shivered. "You're not afraid of me?"

Wariness had stolen into his intent gaze. Kate nodded, once. "A little," she admitted. "But you said you would keep me safe, and I believe you." She bit her lower lip to erase the sensation of his touch.

He made a small sound of satisfaction in his throat. "What is it about me that puts fear in you, Kate?" She stiffened when he lowered his head and pressed his lips to her cheek in a lingering kiss. "Is it my infamous reputation?" His fingers curled around her nape, tangled in her hair and pulled her head back while he planted a line of slow, steamy kisses down her throat. Kate shuddered when need erupted inside her.

"Or maybe—" Raine traced a path back to her ear with the tip of his tongue, leaving a trail of gooseflesh "—you're afraid of how I make you feel."

Kate's breath stilled in her lungs. Even the storm seemed to quiet for one long, electrifying moment.

He hummed a knowing sound against the shell of her ear. "So that's it." He nipped her earlobe with his teeth. Kate gasped. Her heart thundered in her ears, drowning out the renewed sounds of the storm raging outside.

"Sweet little Kate doesn't want to admit that she lusts after a killer."

Instinctively she flattened her palms against his chest and pushed. "Stop," she said in a shaky voice. "I want you to stop."

Raine's grasp on the handful of hair at her nape tightened, keeping her from turning away when he drew back to look into her eyes. His arm snaked around her waist and pulled her closer, until their bodies touched intimately. Kate's pulse reacted to the intense desire she saw in his eyes and the feel of him against her. He was aroused. She sucked in a sharp breath. He smiled. An insanely sexy, irritatingly confident gesture that affected only one side of his mouth.

"You're sure you want me to stop?" He pressed his hand into the small of her back, forcing her to mold to his unmistakably male contours.

Kate squirmed, but suppressed the urge to arch against the hard ridge straining into her belly. "Yes," she murmured, though yes was far from her thoughts. She wanted him to take her. She wanted to feel him inside her. God, how could she want him?

Instantly, Raine's hold relaxed, but he didn't release her completely. "All right," he rasped. "I just have to do one thing first."

Kate's gaze collided with Raine's a heartbeat before his mouth captured hers. Unlike his gruff words, his lips were soft, his siege tender. He tasted like coffee and something else, something dark and mysterious. A staggering swell of desire surged through her, making her dizzy with want. Without thought, Kate's hands slid over his muscled chest and her arms twined around his neck.

No, she didn't want him to stop. Kate tiptoed, pressing her body more intimately against his. She didn't ever want him to stop. Raine's answering groan set off a series of shock waves deep inside her, the pulsating aftershocks weakening her knees. His tongue pushed inside her mouth, hot and demanding. Kate moaned her acceptance as he explored, retreated, and thrust again.

His hand was under her sweatshirt, beneath her T-shirt, seeking, caressing. Each brush of his callused palm over her bare skin sent spasms of desire to her core. And then he had her breast in his hand; his thumb grazed her nipple, and it puckered and her feminine muscles clenched. Raine kissed her harder, commanding her body with complete mastery.

You're a woman... you're young and beautiful. That will get you closer than anyone else... The words exploded inside Kate's head. This was a mistake. She had to make him stop. Kate struggled to push Raine away. To stop his sensual assault. He broke the kiss and stared down at her, his breath ragged, his eyes glazed.

"I can't do this," she gasped, fighting for her next breath. She needed to get away from him. Kate pushed harder, trying to put some space between their heated bodies.

"It's all right," he assured her. "I'll stop." He took his time removing his hand from beneath her shirt, allowing his palm to glide slowly down her rib cage. Kate stood stock-still, afraid to move at all for fear of throwing herself back into his arms.

He lifted that hand, still warm from clutching her breast, and traced the outline of her cheek. "But next time I won't." He leaned closer, filling the tiny distance she had managed to put between them. "Next time I'll be so deep inside you that you won't know where you end and I begin." He dropped one final kiss on her cheek, his lips lingering there as he said, "Be careful what you let yourself lust after, Kate, you might just get it." Then he straightened and resumed his distant stare into the night.

Anger shot through Kate's veins, pushing strength into her boneless limbs. "You bastard! I didn't want that!" Her hands tightened into fists at her sides.

Raine leaned against the window frame and shot her a look over one broad shoulder. "Oh, you wanted it all right. Maybe you didn't *want* to want it, but you wanted it just the same."

Kate had no idea if she tended to be short-tempered under normal circumstances, but these circumstances were anything but normal. And her hold on her temper wasn't just short, it was nonexistent. Her breath came in ragged spurts. "You started it! You kissed me!"

Raine faced her then, and crossed his arms over his mile-wide chest. "You don't have to justify what happened, Kate. Many women have fantasized at one time or another about having wild, hot sex with a bad boy, especially one on the run. Why should you be any different?"

Raine manacled her wrist before her palm connected with his jaw. He shook his head slowly from side to side. "You don't want to do that," he said in a low, warning tone.

Kate jerked her arm from his hold and took a step back, out of his reach. "Don't touch me again."

Lightning flashed, giving Kate a good look at his face. He didn't smile, but she didn't miss the gleam of triumph in his eyes. Somehow he considered himself the winner in what had just taken place. The winner in what respect she didn't know. If she was smart, she wouldn't want to know.

Kate whirled away from him and strode back to her bed. She didn't want to look at him. She didn't want to talk to him. And she sure as hell didn't want to want him. Sliding beneath the covers, she squeezed her eyes shut and willed herself to sleep.

THE SOUND OF WATER spraying woke Kate from a drugging sleep. She forced her eyes to obey her brain's command to open, but it proved a difficult task. A thin ray of sunlight sliced through the dark room from the crack where the drapes met. On the bedside table, the clock's display read 10:00 a.m. Sitting up, Kate stretched and groaned with satisfaction at finally feeling rested.

Raine. Images from their early-morning kiss flooded her mind. She shivered and pulled the covers up around her. She scanned the semidark room. Where was he? The sound of water invaded her consciousness again and Kate realized he was in the shower.

In the shower—and she wasn't locked in the closet. Obviously he had given up on her waking anytime soon and decided to shower on the assumption that she would sleep through it.

Call in... The words raced through her mind, sending a rush of adrenaline through her veins. Call in. She had to call in. Numbers spilled into her head: 312–555–4911.

"Call 312–555–4911," she repeated aloud. Kate threw back the covers and dropped her feet to the floor. She stared at the telephone for all of three seconds before she turned the base to face her. Kate listened for Raine; he was still in the shower. She quickly read the instructions for making a collect call. She didn't want any charges to be added to the room.

Kate swallowed the lump of fear rising in her throat and dialed the appropriate numbers. When the operator asked for her name, she had to whisper Kate Roberts twice before the woman understood her. Finally the call was connected. One ring sounded across the line, then another.

"Hello."

Kate frowned at the strangely familiar male voice. She listened as the operator asked if he would accept a collect call from Kate Roberts. The man agreed without hesitation.

"Kate? It's Nick, honey. Are you all right?"

She couldn't put a face with the voice, but no warning bells went off inside her head, so Kate took that as a good sign. "I'm all right," she replied tightly.

"We've been worried sick about you. Why haven't you called in before now?"

Kate shivered. How could this man know her and she not know him?

"Kate, are you there?" Concern colored his voice.

Kate blinked. "I'm here," she said softly.

"Aunt Vicky needs to speak to you. She's been beside herself for *two days*."

Two days. Did that mean something? The man emphasized those words. Should they mean something to her? Kate creased her forehead in concentration. And who was *Aunt Vicky*?

"Kate, if you're safe that's our main concern. But..." He paused. Then, "Did you reach your destination? Was it everything you had anticipated?"

The water shut off in the bathroom. "I have to go," Kate muttered distractedly.

"Wait, please wait. I need you to stay on the line a *little* longer. Vicky needs to speak with you about your missed appointment. Don't hang up."

Kate glanced from the bathroom door to the telephone. If he caught her on the phone, what would he do? Should she tell him she had remembered this number?

"Kate? Are you still there?"

Kate stared at the handset. The voice...it was her. The woman's voice she always heard in her head.

"Kate, it's Aunt Vicky, are you all right, dear?"

The toilet flushed. Fear gripped Kate's heart. "I have to go." She quietly replaced the receiver in the cradle before the woman on the other end could respond, then pushed the phone back to its original position on the table.

Kate stood just as Raine stepped out of the bathroom.

Quickly, she stretched and then brushed the hair back from her eyes. ''Thanks for letting me sleep late,'' she said, trying her level best to keep the fear from manifesting itself in her voice. Those same old warnings kept echoing inside her head. *If he suspects for one second...*

Raine didn't say a word. He simply stood there, showered and dressed, and scrutinized her from head to toe. The thickening beard on his chiseled features made his presence even more fear-inspiring. When he at last seemed to be satisfied with the results of his visual inspection, he spoke, ''You needed the rest. As soon as you're ready, we have things to do today.''

Kate only nodded and hurried past him to the bathroom. Once inside, she closed the door and sagged against it. *Aunt Vicky. We've been worried sick. Two days. Was it everything you anticipated? Missed appointment?* Kate closed her eyes and willed the voices away. She couldn't think about that right now. None of it made sense anyway. And she could never let Raine suspect that she had made that call. *He won't take the time to find out which side sent you.* Which side of what? she demanded. No answer came.

Kate opened her eyes. She could do this. She had to do this.

RAINE UNLOCKED the door to their hotel room and entered first. The room faced the rear parking lot—not the usually requested view, but he preferred direct access to the outside. He set the packages containing their purchases on the table. A late-afternoon storm had kicked up, rivaling last night's. Raine didn't allow himself to waste any time dwelling on the kiss he had stolen from Kate. To say it had moved him would be a vast understatement. He didn't like the way she made him feel, but his actions were a means to an end. Kate had kept her distance all day. She didn't let him get close and that was what Raine had wanted.

Want really didn't have anything to do with it, he amended. He *needed* the distance. He had to keep his head on straight or they would both wind up on ice. Raine swallowed hard as he checked inside the closet. He didn't want to die himself, but the thought of Kate lying lifeless on the ground with a bullet through her head appealed to him even less. He wouldn't let anything happen to her. *And if she proves to be your enemy, what then?* Raine ignored his own warning.

When he was sure the room was clear, he motioned for Kate to come inside. She sighed and pushed from the door frame she had leaned against. The day had taken its toll on her. She dropped her coat onto the bed and curled around one fluffy pillow, then closed her eyes.

Raine frowned. The impression that something was wrong with her still niggled at his conscience. He pulled off his coat and tossed it across the bed. Maybe she needed some sort of special diet or vitamins. But he didn't have time to worry about that at the moment. Right now he had to consider the information Lucas had given him. Such as it was.

He shoved his hand through his hair and paced the length of the room. He hadn't wanted to make that call, but being saddled with Kate had left him little choice. Raine hoped like hell he hadn't made a mistake. He desperately needed Lucas to keep the various government agencies off his back for just a little while. Of course, putting the feds on Raine's trail wouldn't have been Lucas's idea anyway. That order had to have come from Cuddahy, the director of Special Ops. He was relatively new to the organization and intent on making a big name for himself. Raine didn't know much about the man, but he had the reputation of being a "by-the-book bastard."

Raine slowly turned and retraced his steps. He hadn't given Lucas their location and he'd made sure that he hadn't stayed on the line long enough for a trace. That's why he had made several different calls, and always from a different location. Kate hadn't complained about all the walking, but she had later protested the shopping.

He had bought new clothes and necessities for her as well as himself. Raine expelled a weary breath. He had to admit that Kate was the first woman he'd ever had to coerce into shopping. She hadn't wanted to do anything but come back to the room.

New clothes, dining at a nice restaurant, none of it appealed to her, as it would have to most women. She was tired, she'd said. Raine scrutinized her pale features. Maybe she had some sort of health problem. The bruise on her temple looked much better. But overall she seemed weaker now than when she'd first staggered into his cabin from the cold.

Raine suddenly remembered the unmarked bottle of pills he'd found in her purse that first day. The medication she hadn't recognized. He retrieved the bottle from his coat pocket and peered through the colored plastic at the small blue pills. Maybe this was the key to what was going on with Kate. He glanced at her still form and made a decision. If he had remembered the pills earlier, he could have done this today, but he hadn't given them a thought since the day he'd shoved them into his pocket.

Now he would just have to go out again and locate a pharmacist still open at 6:00 p.m. to find out what the bottle contained. Raine clenched his jaw and strode over to her bed.

"Kate." He shook her gently. His frown deepened when he noticed the sheen of perspiration on her face. He brushed the back of his hand across her forehead. Her skin was cool and clammy. "Damn," he muttered. She was definitely sick. Raine shook her again. "Kate, wake up."

Kate opened her eyes and stared vacantly at him. "What?" she murmured.

"We have to go out again. There's something I need to check."

She shrugged off his hand and turned back into her pillow. "No way. I'm exhausted. You go without me."

Raine blew out a puff of air. "No can do, Kate. Where I go, you go."

She rolled to her back and glared at him. "You don't have to worry, I won't run away. I don't have the energy to do anything but lie here. Just go and leave me alone."

Raine considered that possibility for about two seconds. As easy as it would be to do, he knew better. Kate might not take off on him, but he couldn't take the chance.

"Sorry, but I can't do that. Now get up."

Raine straightened as Kate struggled to her feet. When she had steadied herself, she planted her hands firmly on her hips and glared at him. "It's pouring down out there, I'm not going with you." She lifted her chin defiantly. "And you can't make me."

Raine bit back a grin. At least she still had some fight left in her. "I think you know better than that, but if you'll promise to behave yourself I'll let you stay."

"I swear," Kate said quickly. "I'll be an absolute angel."

"And you won't make a sound?"

She nodded adamantly. "Not a peep."

Raine shrugged. "Okay, suit yourself." He took the eight steps necessary to reach the closet and opened the bifold doors. "I'll let you out the moment I get back."

Kate's mouth gaped in disbelief. She glared at him, crossed her arms over her chest and said, "No."

"That's not an option. You either come with me—" he

gestured toward the closet "—or you stay in here until I get back."

Kate marched across the room, muttering things he couldn't and didn't want to understand. She stepped into the close quarters and whirled around to give Raine what could only be called the evil eye.

That grin he'd been holding back broke loose. "If looks could kill," he suggested.

"Don't give me any ideas," she retorted.

Raine reached out and took her chin in his hand. "Now that's not very sporting of you, Kate. Where's your gratitude for the man who saved your life more than once?"

Kate turned away from his touch, refusing to look him in the eye. That intense, protective feeling overwhelmed him again. Along with it came desire so strong that it shook him like nothing else ever had.

Every instinct told Raine to walk away from this lady and never look back, but he couldn't. He just couldn't. He brushed his knuckles down her soft cheek. "I won't let anything happen to you, Kate." Again she drew away. "I'll be back as soon as I can," he told her, then closed the door. Since he couldn't prop a chair under the knob as he'd done before, Raine slid his belt off and looped it around the side-by-side identical knobs. He tightened the cinch he'd made and checked its hold. That would do, he decided. This way he didn't have to worry about her making any unauthorized calls or slipping out.

Raine jerked on his coat and cursed himself all the way out. He locked the door and double-checked it. What a fool he was. Letting a damn female get to him like this. He'd thought if he scared her off, he'd be safe from the relentless physical attraction. All he had managed to do was strengthen this insane need to protect her.

He was a fool. If he kept going at this rate, he'd be a dead fool very soon.

KATE STAMPED her foot and blew out an indignant breath when she heard Raine shut and lock the door. She called him every bad name she could think of and a few she made up as she went. If he hadn't locked her up like an ugly stepchild, she could have called that number again. She still hadn't remembered anything else and she felt like death warmed over, but she'd been hoping to get the chance to call again.

Damn Jack Raine. Maybe she would be better off trying to get away from him. All she had to do was make herself scarce until all this whatever was over. She frowned. But how would she know when it was over? And what if something happened to Raine?

Kate gave herself a mental kick. She didn't care what happened to him. She shifted and took a deep breath. Well, maybe she cared a little—but not a lot.

The door to the room opened. Kate stilled. Was he back already? He fumbled around in the room for several minutes. Had he forgotten something?

Yeah, by God. He had forgotten she was locked in the damn closet. Kate balled her fists at her sides and glared at the slits of light angling upward through the louvered door in front of her. ''Raine, what are you doing? Let me out of this closet this instant!'' She muttered a couple more of those inventive expletives as she waited for him to obey her demand.

She heard him at the closet door then. Three seconds later the doors folded open. ''It's about—'' Kate's outrage died a swift and total death as she stared into the eyes of a stranger.

Chapter Seven

Raine cursed himself a dozen times over as he walked across the hotel parking lot. He had known this would be a mistake, and he'd been right. He should have left Kate Roberts at the hospital emergency room back in Gatlinburg as he'd originally planned. But he hadn't. He'd foolishly thought he could protect her. His need to play protector may very well have put her in even more danger. Raine blew out a breath and slowed a moment to stare at the bottle of pills clutched in his hand.

Inderal. Most common usage: heart conditions.

The pharmacist had said that the medication in the bottle could be prescribed for a number of ailments ranging from migraines to serious heart problems. And, if the patient was taking it for a heart condition and suddenly stopped, the result could prove life-threatening.

Raine swore again as he double-timed around the corner and down the stretch of sidewalk that led to their room. The pharmacist had also given Raine the name of a doctor who ran a clinic in his home just outside town. The doctor had gone into semiretirement some years ago and didn't carry much of a patient load these days, so he should be available. Of course, at 7:00 p.m. it was well past office hours, but Raine didn't intend to let that stop him. He needed to know if there was something wrong with Kate's heart. And there was only one way to confirm or rule out the possibility. He needed a doctor to examine her.

Raine swallowed hard when he considered the trip they had made on foot. Kate had held up pretty well, but he knew that the journey had been tough on her. He cursed himself again for being a stupid bastard. He should have taken her waxy complexion and complaints about being tired a little more seriously. But this was all new to him. He'd never really had to take care of anyone but himself. The flip side to what he had just learned was that he now had little reason to suspect Kate of having an ulterior motive for showing up at his door. No one in this business would send in an unreliable player—not in a game this serious. And a medical condition, especially one involving the heart, would definitely be a risk.

Raine paused at the door to their room. He took a long, deep breath and, key in hand, reached for the knob, then frowned when the door swung inward at his touch. He'd locked the door, no question about it. Raine reached beneath his jacket, drew his Beretta and automatically released the safety.

Cautiously he entered the room, his gaze swept from left to right and then shot back to the open closet doors.

Kate was gone.

He didn't have to step over to the closet and look inside. He didn't have to check the bathroom or look under the bed. He felt the answer in his gut. Emptiness echoed deafeningly in the room.

She was gone.

Adrenaline surged, sending his senses into a higher state of alert. Tension vibrated through every muscle as he crossed to the closet and checked the belt he had used to secure the doors. The belt had been loosened and removed, then tossed aside.

Someone had let Kate out. There were no obvious signs

of a struggle, he noted as he slid his belt back into the loops of his jeans. Raine inhaled deeply and considered the possibilities. If Kate had decided to scream her head off and a passerby heard the cries for help, it was feasible that the hotel manager had been alerted. Raine glanced again at the open door to the room. If that were the case then the police would have been notified by now. But the parking lot remained dark and quiet. Maybe he had jumped to the conclusion that she was innocent too soon. Maybe she was involved. She had shown up rather conveniently at his cabin. Raine shook his head. Her injuries were real, her amnesia was real. The medication, he touched the pocket containing the prescription bottle, was real. She couldn't be involved. Could she?

A cold chill skated down Raine's spine as he contemplated the only other alternative.

Dillon.

The shrill ring of the telephone sliced through the silence. Raine jerked around to glare at the infernal instrument. It rang again. He didn't take the time to wonder who would be calling, because he already knew.

Raine retraced his path, kicked the door to the room shut and strode to the table between the two beds. He waited two more rings, then snatched up the receiver. "Yeah." Raine kept his voice low and steady. There would be no hint of the degree of tension he felt for Dillon to enjoy.

No one else would play it out this way.

"Hello, Raine. Long time no see."

The hair on the back of Raine's neck bristled at the sardonic sound of Dillon's voice. The Puerto Rican roots he'd inherited from his mother still surfaced in the lingering accent Dillon had worked hard to lose. The image of the face that went with the voice filled Raine's head, taking his senses to another level of tension.

"Not long enough," Raine replied as he dropped onto

the bed and leaned against the headboard. He planted his left foot on the floor and pulled his right knee up to brace his firing arm. He kept the closed door sighted, just in case Dillon's henchmen showed up for seconds. "Can't say that I've missed you," Raine added when the silence on the other end stretched too long for comfort.

"Have you missed Kate?"

A trickle of fear managed to slip past Raine's brutal hold on his emotions, his heart rate increased to accommodate the uncharacteristic sensation. Raine swallowed the scathing response that formed in his mouth. Dillon already knew too much, no point giving away just how badly Raine wanted to keep Kate safe.

"She's quite a pretty lady," Dillon continued, his tone slick and coolly menacing. "Such beautiful dark eyes. I can't imagine why anyone, even you, Raine, would let such a lovely creature out of your sight. Whatever possessed you to lock her in the closet? Have you finally happened upon one you can't handle?"

Anger flooded Raine, drowning that tiny glimmer of fear. "What do you want, Dillon?"

"Why, I thought you knew." He chuckled, a harsh, emotionless sound. "I want you, Raine. Are you willing to trade yourself for this sweet young thing?" A frightened shriek from Kate punctuated Dillon's question.

It took Raine two full seconds, but he cleared his mind, banished all emotions. "Don't yank my chain, Dillon, just give me the details." Raine wished he could reach through the telephone and strangle the ruthless son of a bitch on the other end, but that would have to wait. Right now he had to focus on playing out this sick little game.

"There's a quaint place on Route 29 called Chances. Meet me there at midnight. I've reserved the proverbial room in the back."

A resounding click ended the conversation. Raine

dropped the receiver back into the cradle. He should have killed Dillon months ago. The world would certainly be a better place without him. Raine couldn't bear the thought of Dillon touching Kate, but it was Dillon's specialty that worried him the most.

Juan Roberto Dillon specialized in killing. He was one of Sal Ballatore's right-hand men and he had no qualms about taking human life. Race, sex, age or circumstances never entered the picture. Dillon enjoyed killing. The only thing he liked more was the hunt. And that's what tonight was all about.

Raine replayed every move he had made in the last seventy-two hours and could find no mistake. He didn't know how Dillon had found him. No way Lucas could have traced Raine's call. But somehow he'd been found. Dillon could just as easily have stormed the room and taken them both, but he hadn't. He had waited until Raine was out and taken Kate.

Dillon wanted to play. He liked the thrill of the chase, the sudden twists of fate. Everything was a game to him. Raine gritted his teeth against the rage that rose in his throat. This whole business was just one big walk around the Monopoly board to Dillon. Toss the dice and see where the game takes you. In the end, the player with the most money, and still breathing, wins.

The man was a real opportunist too. Rather than going to Ballatore after discovering Raine's true identity, Dillon had seized the opportunity for another, more self-serving purpose.

Raine allowed the vivid images to reel through his mind, his heart pounding harder with each passing frame of memory. Raine, Dillon and Michael, Sal's son, had picked up two million dollars in cash from a major cocaine distributor working for Ballatore. They had done it together numerous times before, but this time was different.

After the exchange went down, the three of them were alone in the warehouse. Vinny and Danny had waited in the car like always. Dillon was slapping Michael on the back one minute and praising his ability to close a deal, then putting a bullet through the kid's head the next.

Dillon had then turned to a stunned Raine and said, "I know who you are and why you're here." He'd pressed the barrel of his Ruger against Raine's forehead. "The only thing I don't understand," he continued with a sadistic smile, "is why *you* killed Mr. Ballatore's son."

The momentary distraction of Danny entering the warehouse was all that had kept Raine from winding up on the cold, hard concrete floor next to Michael with blood pooling around his shattered skull. Raine had barely escaped with his life, but he had managed to snag the briefcase containing the money on his way. It was his only security, and he'd hidden it safely away.

When a mob-ordered hit went down or a play for power took place, it rarely happened without warning. The one thing that could be counted on in this business was murmurings in the ranks or, at the very least, a gut instinct that something was about to go down. Raine had not once anticipated Dillon's move.

He had gone over and over every minute of the seventeen months he had worked with Dillon and found nothing to indicate that such a hit was in the plan. Raine had come to the conclusion that it hadn't been planned. Dillon had somehow learned who Raine was and used the information for an opportunity to kill his boss's only son and make himself two million dollars richer in the process. And, by simultaneously eliminating Michael and placing the blame on Raine, Dillon had put himself in the position of second in command to the grieving father. The perfect move—swift and efficient. Too bad for Dillon that Raine had escaped with the money.

Every perfect plan had its flaw. Raine hadn't played along and died for Dillon. Of course, when Dillon told his version of the story, Ballatore had ordered Raine found and brought to him personally for punishment. Then the feds had joined the party and decided Raine had turned. All in all, Raine had been left between a rock and a hard place.

But he'd been in tight spots before.

His plan was simple—he'd use the money as bait to entice Dillon. Dillon was a greedy bastard, he would want the money back. If Raine's plan worked, the mole who had blown his cover would eventually make a move to tie up his loose ends—including Dillon. So Raine had had to act fast. Luring Dillon would be easy, staying alive when the good guys as well as the bad guys were after him was a little more complicated. If Raine was lucky, Lucas would keep the feds distracted. Then Raine could concentrate on the old man. Ballatore wanted him brought in alive, but Dillon would try everything in his power to prevent that from happening. Dillon wanted Raine dead.

Dead men tell no tales.

And Kate…

Well, Raine scrubbed a hand over his bearded chin, Kate was still a wild card at this point. But he would soon know whose side she stood on.

KATE COMMANDED her trembling body to still as she watched the man named Dillon end the conversation with Raine. Her chest ached with fear and her heart fluttered like a butterfly trapped in her rib cage.

"Well, Kate, it looks as though everything is going to work out perfectly," Dillon announced to her, his voice dark and evil, his thin lips sliding into a sinister smile.

Kate swallowed the fear and blinked furiously at the moisture burning behind her lids. She lifted her chin and glared at the man who had forced her from the hotel at gunpoint. "He won't come. Raine won't trade himself for me. He hardly knows me," she said, surprised at the strength and challenge left in her voice. "He'll be long gone before midnight."

The idea that Raine would walk purposely into his own death trap to rescue her was absurd. What did Dillon take him for? A fool? Kate didn't know much about Raine, or fully trust him for that matter, but the one thing she felt certain of was that he was nobody's fool.

At least Dillon's proposition had given her a few more hours to live. Kate wasn't kidding herself. This was bad. Very bad. Raine had been right, at least about this much. These guys were killers and they intended to kill both of them. She should never have made that call. Kate had no proof of her suspicions, but instinct told her that it had been a mistake. A mistake that had brought the devil himself sweeping down on her like a hawk after a frightened field mouse.

Kate surveyed the private room Dillon had bribed the bartender into renting him for the night. It was small, maybe twelve by fourteen. Kate supposed the Thursday-night guys used the place for poker games or small private parties. The decorating enhanced the doom and gloom of her circumstances—circa early seventies with dark paneling, shag carpet and a wagon-wheel chandelier. A round table with eight chairs sat in the middle of the room, and a smaller one sat against the far wall. The only color to break the monotony was a large, rather garish, framed print of huge blue and gold flowers.

Country music blared from the jukebox on the other side of the paper-thin wall that separated her from the crowd of patrons drinking beer and having a grand old time. No one out there would pay any attention to the events taking place in the back room tonight.

Kate swallowed the fear and panic bubbling in her throat. Tonight there would be no poker or party. Tonight people were going to die and, unfortunately, she appeared to be one of the unlucky candidates.

Kate's gaze flitted back to Dillon's. His sick smile widened into a grin at the fear she knew he saw in her eyes. He wore his long black hair in a ponytail, giving a clean, unobscured view of his sharp hawklike features. High cheekbones dipped into hollows on either side of his thin lips. A straight blade of a nose, and a dark ledge of eyebrows that hovered over beady eyes. Excitement sparkled in those black depths as he watched Kate's chest rise and fall too rapidly.

The bastard got his kicks from watching his prey squirm. A jolt of anger shot through Kate and she suddenly wished for a weapon. A Glock nine millimeter, her weapon of choice. That would put a nice, clean little hole smack in the middle of his forehead, while taking off a large portion of the back of his skull.

Kate started. Her attention instantly focused inward. How did she know all that? Why would she have a favorite gun? She had never killed anyone, had she? She shuddered at the thought.

"Oh, he'll come," Dillon said, drawing her attention back to him. "You see, Kate—" He leaned back in his chair and rubbed his Ruger against his jaw. Kate flinched. Why would she recognize the brand of gun he carried? "Unfortunately for him, Raine fancies himself a good guy. It goes against his nature for the innocent to suffer." Dillon licked his thin lips as he screwed a silencer onto his weapon. With blatant challenge, he placed it on the table in front of him and crossed his arms over his chest. "It's his way of justifying what he does the rest of the time. My stealing you away and forcing him to come to me is an insult he'll have to answer."

Kate's gaze moved from Dillon's to the table, then back. She balled her fists in her lap and gauged the distance between her and the gun, between Dillon and the gun. Behind her, Danny and Vinny paced like caged lions. Even if she could get her hands on the gun before Dillon, which was highly unlikely, she would never be able to shoot all three of them before one of them shot her. Kate relaxed her rigid muscles and eased out a ragged breath. A bead of sweat trickled between her breasts.

Dillon smiled knowingly. He leaned forward, grabbed Kate's wrist and jerked her close. "You know," he whispered harshly, his lips brushing her temple, making her shiver uncontrollably, "I love this stuff." He pressed her trembling hand to his crotch, his arousal proving his statement.

Kate choked out a shriek and jerked free of his grasp. Dillon laughed at her, his eyes twinkling with the insanity that no doubt drove him. Vinny and Danny teetered like bullies in the schoolyard, backing up their leader with sound effects.

Kate closed her eyes against the sound, and against the image of Dillon, the personification of evil. Ice slid through her veins, immobilizing her body with cold, solid fear. If Raine showed up to rescue her, he would die. If he didn't, she would die. Kate opened her eyes and stared at the man in front of her. Who was she kidding? She was dead either way.

RAINE HAD KNOWN that Chances would be a dive in every sense of the word—cheap and disreputable. The place was definitely in keeping with Dillon's taste for the underbelly of life. Raine slid from behind the wheel of the Thunderbird he had "borrowed" and smiled at the one thing that didn't quite fit: country music. The sound wafted into the dimly lit, quiet parking lot. Neon lights flashed from the front of the building, advertising Budweiser and Miller beer.

Dillon hated country music. In fact, he hated most anything that had its roots below the Mason-Dixon Line. Raine had seen him kill a man simply because his Southern drawl grated on Dillon's nerves. Sick bastard.

Raine adjusted his jacket and then the all-but-worthless handgun he'd tucked up his right sleeve. He despised .22's, but finding the weapon—loaded and ready—stashed in the glovebox of the stolen car had been a stroke of luck. Satisfied with his unexpected contingency, he checked his watch: 12:05. Dillon would be pissed. He hated to wait. The move would throw him off balance, make him more likely to make mistakes. Raine needed whatever edge he could find to save Kate and get them both away alive. He checked the position of the .22 automatic once more and headed for the door.

He stepped into the crowded, smoky bar and took a moment to survey his surroundings. The bar extended the length of the room on one side. Only one bartender appeared to be on duty. Two waitresses skirted the tables filling the rest of the place. The crowd consisted of mostly men and no one seemed to pay Raine any mind, with the exception of one table. The one nearest the door. A group of wannabe cowboys looked Raine over with the slow, easy confidence of being on their home turf, then went back to the business of beer and bullshit.

Raine took his time, checking out the place as he crossed to the bar. He ordered a beer and asked about the room in the back. The solemn-faced bartender plopped a cold, long-neck bottle in front of Raine and angled his head toward a door at the far end of the room. Raine paid the man and took a long pull from the bottle as he settled onto a stool. The cold liquid slid down his throat and pooled in his stomach, doing nothing to quench the fire burning inside him. He forced himself to drink the rest despite the tension urging him to act. He had wanted to rush over here and wait for Dillon's arrival the minute he'd hung up the phone. But he had forced himself to wait. To fill the time, Raine had showered and shaved, then changed into the new clothes he had bought that day. He knew Dillon too well, he would have considered the possibility of an early arrival. Most likely, he had already been at this joint when he'd called.

Raine glanced at the Red Dog clock above the mirror behind the bar. Twelve-ten. Dillon had waited long enough, any longer and he might take his anger out on Kate. Raine slid off the stool and strode to the door, opened it and stepped inside. His gut clenched at the sight of Kate sitting at a table with Dillon standing behind her, caressing her hair. Raine's jaw tightened. Dillon looked mad as hell, his tall, thin features taut, his eyes as dark as smoke off burning rubber. Raine's gaze flicked from the pompous twisted bastard back to Kate. She was scared to death. His thoughts went immediately to the bottle of little blue pills in his pocket, but that would have to wait.

The door slammed shut behind Raine. Danny and Vinny stepped up to stand on either side of him.

"You're late," Dillon hissed.

Raine lifted one eyebrow in the beginnings of a shrug that didn't quite make it to his shoulders. "I know."

"I *hate* to be kept waiting," Dillon added, his knuckles going white as he grasped the back of Kate's chair.

"I know," Raine intoned.

Vinny jabbed him hard in the gut, but Raine absorbed the blow with nothing more than a soft grunt. He stood statue-still while Danny patted him down and removed the weapon at the small of his back, then held up the Beretta like a trophy.

Vinny sneered at Raine. "You shoulda killed me while

you had the chance, Ricky boy. Now I'm gonna watch you die.''

Raine smiled mockingly down at the shorter man. Vinny knew his real name wasn't Rick, but he kept up the pretense. ''I'm saving you for later, Vinny, when it's just you and me.'' Raine instinctively tightened his stomach muscles a split second before the next blow was delivered.

Muttering expletives, Vinny moved back to stand guard at the door. Danny followed suit.

''Kate leaves now.'' Raine leveled his gaze on Dillon's. ''That was the deal. I'm here, she goes.'' He shifted his gaze to Kate. ''The car's outside, the engine's running,'' he added so she'd know which car he meant. The surprise and momentary disapproval that flitted across her face told him that she understood that he'd stolen another vehicle.

Kate stood. Raine saw the violent tremble that rocked her body. Her brown eyes were huge and liquid. A single, crystalline tear slid down one cheek. Something inside Raine twisted and he felt weak with regret that any of this had happened to her. If he had learned nothing else, he now knew that Kate was in no way connected to Dillon.

''Let's not be in such a hurry, Raine.'' Dillon snaked an arm around Kate's waist and pulled her against him, knocking over the chair she'd vacated. She gasped, her fingers automatically working to pry loose his restraining arm. ''I was rather enjoying Kate's company.''

Raine tamped down the rage that jolted him. ''I'm not in the mood to debate the point. I'm here, so let her go.''

Dillon rubbed his cheek against her hair. Kate whimpered and closed her eyes. Before he could prevent it, Raine's fists clenched at his sides. Dillon smiled at the reaction and Raine cursed himself for allowing it.

''So this one means something to you?'' Dillon scrutinized Kate for a time, then righted the chair and pushed her into it. His gaze moved back to Raine. "Don't worry, I'll take good care of her for you."

Raine moved in Dillon's direction, ignoring the snap of weapons engaging behind him. "*I said,* let her go," he repeated, the sound coming from some foreign, guttural place deep inside him.

Dillon rounded Kate's chair, waved a hand at his two henchmen then took the final three steps to bring himself face-to-face with Raine. He drew his weapon and aimed it at Raine's heart, the tip of the silencer creasing his shirt. Kate's sharp intake of breath broke the quiet that followed.

Raine briefly considered announcing that Dillon was the one who had killed Ballatore's son, but why bother? Kate wouldn't know what he was talking about, and the other two in the room would never believe him. Besides, Raine still needed Dillon—at least until he could draw out the mole. He had no choice but to play the hand he'd been dealt. As bad as it sucked, this was it.

"The old man wanted me to bring you in alive." Dillon shook his head and sighed. "But I think I'll save him the trouble of dealing with you personally. I wouldn't want to further tax his failing health." Dillon smirked and pressed the barrel more firmly into Raine's chest. "Are you prepared to die, Raine?"

Raine flashed an answering smile. "I'm always prepared, *amigo.*"

Dillon flinched. He hated to be reminded of his heritage. Raine leaned into the weapon. "Why don't you cut the small talk and just do me? No need to complicate things. I'm here, the weapon's engaged with the target, why waste time yapping? *Just do it,*" Raine challenged.

Dillon's face contorted with rage. "I say when. I set the pace." His face relaxed into a feigned smile. "And I say, *now.*" Dillon's grip tightened on the weapon in anticipation of the recoil.

"There's just one thing," Raine began, his words stopping Dillon a heartbeat before his trigger finger applied the slight pressure required to fire the weapon.

"What the hell would that be?" Dillon snapped. Sweat beaded on his forehead, anger blazed in his eyes.

"The money," Raine offered with a nonchalant shrug. "If you kill me, you'll never know where I hid the money."

Irritation flared in Dillon's angry gaze. "To hell with the money! There will be more where that came from."

It was during that fleeting moment of transition between anger and irritation, just before the final decision was made, that Raine acted. His left arm darted under Dillon's right and shoved it upward. A shot hissed through the silencer and lodged in the ceiling. Before either of the other two could assimilate what had happened, Raine had the .22 automatic pressed to Dillon's temple.

"Hold it right there," Raine ordered when Vinny would have moved closer. "Everybody just take a breath." Two beads held steady on Raine. "Kate, move over here behind me." She quickly obeyed.

"Now." Raine tightened his choke hold on Dillon's scrawny neck. "Place your weapons on the table." Nobody moved. Raine nudged the .22 a little deeper into the thin skin protecting Dillon's temple. "*Now,* gentlemen." Dillon tossed his Ruger on the table. The two men on the other side of the room remained motionless.

"Do it!" Dillon screeched when Raine's finger snugged around the trigger.

First Vinny, then Danny relented, placing their weapons on the table and backing away.

"And mine," Raine reminded Vinny.

His insolent gaze fixed on Raine, Vinny slid the Beretta across the table. "Good." Raine smiled his appreciation, which only earned him a heated glare from both men.

"You two, back over here—" he angled his head toward the far side of the room "—on the floor, facedown."

When the two were prone on the floor, Raine shoved Dillon in their direction with one hand and snatched up his Beretta with the other. He watched Dillon reluctantly slide into place next to his cohorts. "Kate, grab those weapons."

He didn't have to tell her twice, Raine noticed when he shot a glance in her direction. To his surprise she snatched up the Ruger, deftly unscrewed the silencer and slid it into her back pocket, then put the weapon on safety and set it aside. Despite the rampant trembling he had observed in her only moments ago, her hands were steady and efficient now. She put each of the other two weapons on safety as well before stowing them in the waistband of her jeans beneath her sweatshirt.

Watching her warily, Raine took the Ruger from her and shoved it into his waistband. Now wasn't the time to ask how she knew her way around a handgun. Getting the hell out of here was top priority.

"It's only a matter of time before I catch up to you again," Dillon said from his position on the floor. "You're a dead man walking, my friend."

Raine ushered Kate across the room, keeping his gaze trained on the three men on the floor. "Well," Raine said as he reached behind him to snag the doorknob, "at least I'm walking." He turned and propelled Kate into the crowded barroom. He pulled the door closed behind him, leaned toward her and ordered, "Get in the black T-Bird. The engine's running. I'm right behind you."

She spared him a panicked glance, but took off without question. Raine knew Dillon would burst through the door any moment. He waded quickly through the crowd, but paused when he got to the door. He moved back to the last table he'd passed and leaned down to speak to the nearest wannabe cowboy.

He had to shout to be heard over the jukebox, which had just boomed back to life. "Hey, buddy, that fag with the ponytail—" Raine glanced up just in time to see Dillon's anger-twisted mug glaring at him from across the room "—called you and your friends here a bunch of redneck yahoos."

Raine straightened and backed up the four steps between him and the door. A quick glance over his shoulder before he slipped out revealed Bubba and his five buddies forming an intimidating line across Dillon's path. Raine smiled. Satisfied that he had a few minutes to put some distance between them, he headed for the T-Bird.

"Are they right behind you?" Kate's frightened voice met him when he opened the driver's-side door.

"They'll be busy for a few minutes." Raine shoved the car into gear and spun out of the parking lot.

"What are we going to do now?" she demanded, twisting around to peer out the rear window.

"Slide those weapons under my seat." Raine suppressed the other demand he wanted to make. Now wasn't the time.

"What?" She shifted her wide-eyed gaze to him.

"Put the Smith & Wesson and the Beretta under my seat," he said slowly, watching her reaction in his peripheral vision.

"You have the Beretta and the Ruger, the two I have are both Smith & Wessons," she clarified as she pulled the weapons one at a time from beneath her sweatshirt and slid them under his seat just as he had instructed. The silencer followed.

Raine clenched his jaw and drew in his first deep breath since walking into the hotel room and finding Kate missing. She was safe now and that gave him some sense of relief. But he had seen more than enough to resurrect his suspicions about her identity. And that made him madder than hell—mostly at himself. He took a right onto the unpaved side road that led to the doc's house. A couple miles down the rutted, muddy passage he took another right. Water and mud from the day's storm splashed from the deeper ruts. The driveway to the house-cum-clinic was more than a mile long and dark as pitch save for the unearthly glow of the moon bearing down on them through the barren treetops.

Raine parked a good distance from the house, cut the engine and got out. He skirted the hood, anger and questions pounding in his head, then jerked Kate's door open and demanded, "Get out."

"Where are we?" she asked hesitantly, glancing from side to side with mounting uncertainty. Despite the reluctance in her voice, she scrambled out of the car.

Raine slammed the door and glared at her. She shivered and rubbed her hands up and down her arms. Dillon had dragged her off without her coat. The coat was in the car, but Raine was too pissed off right now to offer it to her.

"What's wrong? Why are you staring at me that way?" Her eyes were wide with fear, her lips trembled, and Raine hated himself, which only pissed him off all the more. He reached behind him and drew his weapon. Kate gasped and edged back against the T-Bird.

Brutally squashing the guilt that immediately rose, Raine forced her chin up with the cold, steel barrel. The weapon wasn't aimed at her, but the effect was the same, she trembled and tears welled in those big dark eyes. "Tell me about the weapon I'm holding," he rasped.

"I don't know what you mean," she shuddered the words. A tear slid down her cheek, then another and another. She blinked furiously, but they came anyway. "Why are you doing this?"

Raine clenched his teeth until he had ruthlessly steadied his control. "How did you know that the two nine millimeters you carried out of there were Smith & Wessons?" His tone was fierce and Kate all but crumpled under his glare.

She shook her head. "I don't know. I just knew."

"You removed that silencer without thought, Kate." Raine leaned in closer, keeping the weapon between them, his fisted knuckles hard against the slim column of her throat. "As if you'd done it many times before."

"I...saw Dillon attach it." She pressed a shaky hand against his chest, a frail attempt at protecting herself. "It was simple. And maybe they mentioned the names of their guns. I just don't know!" A sob shook her body with such force that it pained him to watch.

With a disgusted exhale, Raine shoved his weapon back into his waistband. He braced his hands against the car on either side of Kate and held her fearful gaze a long moment before he spoke. "Here's what I know." He paused for effect. She trembled. "I know that I didn't make any mistakes, and still Dillon walked right up to my door. How do you suppose he knew where we were, Kate?"

She shook her head and pushed a handful of dark hair behind her ear. "I don't know," she insisted. "I didn't tell him. I'd never seen the man before in my life until he dragged me out of the closet." She shuddered in a harsh breath. The pulse at the base of her throat fluttered too fast, way too fast.

Raine wrenched himself away from her. He muttered a colorful phrase about his birthright. Here the woman might have a heart condition and he was doing his level best to send her into cardiac arrest. Damn him all to hell.

"All right." He reached out to brush the fresh tears from her cheek and she flinched at his touch. His gut twisted with regret when she trembled beneath that simple caress. Her skin was unbelievably soft. Raine willed away the desire that immediately rose inside him. How could he want her so much? He couldn't let his guard down around her, that was becoming all too clear, but he wanted her anyway. She drew in another shaky breath and he longed to press his lips to hers. To soothe away the fear. But something about Kate Roberts didn't add up.

"Let's go," he said tiredly, and took a step back, out of her personal space.

"Where are we going?" she murmured, her voice weak with relief.

Raine turned from her. "We need a doctor," he said, then started toward the house he couldn't yet see.

Kate grabbed his arm and pulled him back around to face her. Concern had replaced the fear. Her gaze moved frantically over him and then landed back on his. "Are you hurt?"

Guilt stabbed like a knife deep into the center of his chest. "Don't ask questions, Kate," he said tightly.

She glanced around, and frowned. "But where are we going to find a doctor at this time of night around here?"

"Trust me, I have a plan."

Chapter Eight

"Just stay calm, Doc, and there won't be a problem."

Kate glared, agog, first at Raine and then at the elderly man staring into the business end of Raine's Beretta.

This was his plan?

"What are you doing?" she demanded. "*This* is your idea of a plan?"

Raine looked at her for a long, charged moment, then smiled. It wasn't pleasant. Turning his attention back to the doctor, he shoved the unmarked prescription bottle Kate had completely forgotten about into the man's hand. "I'm told this is Inderal. I need you to tell me if my friend here has a bum ticker."

Kate drew in an audible breath. Was he talking about her? On cue, her chest ached and her heart fluttered. Oh, God! Was it possible that she could have some sort of heart problem and not remember? What other horrible things had she forgotten? Panic surged through her veins, urging her possibly faulty heart into an erratic rhythm.

His eyes huge behind the bifocal lenses, the doctor nodded his understanding of the question. "I'll…" He cleared his throat. "I'll need some background information on the patient."

Raine shook his head slowly from side to side. "No questions, Doc, just answers."

Still somewhat reluctant, the doctor opened the door wider and allowed them entrance into his home. "This way," he said as he started down the long, dimly lit hall.

Pressing his hand to the small of her back, Raine urged Kate forward. "This is insane," she hissed, and shot him an irritated glare. She was young. How could she have a heart condition? The poor old doctor, on the other hand, could very well drop dead of fright, considering his age and the weapon Raine was waving around.

Raine ignored her. "You live here alone, Doc?" he asked as if he'd just commented on the lovely country decorating of the man's home.

Kate gaped at Raine's audacity. "Why don't you just ask him where he keeps his life's savings buried while you're at it?" she huffed in a stage whisper.

"I stopped burying my money years ago, missy," the doctor called over one stooped shoulder.

Heat flooded Kate's face as humiliation dropped around her like a black cloud. Raine coughed in an obvious attempt to cover a chuckle, which earned him the nastiest look Kate could marshal. How did she get mixed up in all this? Though she still couldn't remember anything, she knew in the farthest reaches of her soul that she was not a criminal. Except, she grimaced, for the fact that she had participated in using two stolen vehicles and now, in holding a poor, innocent old man at gunpoint.

The doctor opened a door at the end of the hall and flipped on a light. "To answer your question, young fella—" he stood aside so Kate could pass "—yes, I live alone. Does that make a difference in the services you require of me?"

"No." Raine shrugged, a faint smile playing on his lips. "I just don't like surprises."

"You won't find any surprises here. I'm fresh out." The doctor eyed him speculatively. "You won't need that firearm either. The only one I own is upstairs behind the bedroom door. Hasn't been fired in more than twenty years, so I doubt that it would even work.''

"That's good to know." Raine angled his head toward the open door. "After you, Doc."

The doctor appraised Raine a moment longer before he relented. Kate released the breath she had been holding when the two men seemed to reach some sort of unspoken understanding. The doctor shuffled over to an examination table. Raine, perpetually wary, settled into a chair near the door. At least clean shaven he didn't look quite so dangerous. Her eyes had feasted on the sight of him when he'd walked through that door to rescue her. Freshly showered and wearing the new clothes he had bought earlier that day, he took her breath away.

"On the table, missy. But first you'll need to shed some of those clothes."

Kate shrugged out of her coat and purse, then pulled the sweatshirt over her head, leaving just the T-shirt. She tossed them aside, then braced her hands on the examination table and hoisted herself onto it. Thankfully, Raine had put his gun away, or at least it was no longer in sight. The doctor placed his stethoscope around his neck.

Kate took her first good look at the old man. He had on flannel pajamas and well-worn house slippers. She had to clamp down on her lower lip to prevent a smile at his bedtime attire.

"It *is* the middle of the night," he offered, one shaggy gray eyebrow arched as if he'd just read her mind and taken good-hearted offense. "Besides—" he scrutinized her face, then angled her head to get a better look at her bruised temple "—you look a fright yourself."

Kate smiled then, warming to the old man's fatherly nature. "I've been through a lot lately."

"This," he said quietly as he touched the fading bruise

on her temple, "doesn't have anything to do with your companion, does it?"

Kate shook her head. Her gaze flitted to Raine, who didn't seem to be paying any attention to their conversation. "I was in an automobile accident."

He nodded. "I see. Are you in trouble?" he asked quietly, his gaze searching hers.

"No." Kate hoped he couldn't read the truth in her eyes.

"Are you afraid of him?" He inclined his head in Raine's direction. This time Raine's jaw tightened and he shot the doctor's back an impatient look.

Kate moistened her wind-chapped lips. She summoned the small amount of strength she had left to keep her voice steady. "He saved my life."

"Who prescribed the heart medication for you?"

Before Kate could answer, Raine broke in. "No questions, Doc. That was our agreement." His tone left no room for bartering.

The doctor released a breath, then nodded. "Let's see what we can find then," he suggested. He settled the stethoscope into place, then warmed the contact piece in the palm of his hand before reaching beneath Kate's T-shirt to press it to her chest.

Kate tried to smile kindly for the old doctor, but Raine's words kept replaying in her ears. *I need you to tell me if my friend here has a bum ticker.*

"WHAT'S THE BOTTOM LINE, DOC?" Raine asked over his second cup of coffee.

Kate couldn't finish her first cup. She'd managed to swallow the little blue pill, but nothing else wanted to go down. She didn't want to hear any of this. This whole heart thing made her want to run away and hide her head in the sand. The feeling wasn't new. Kate recognized the familiarity of the old pain, but the recognition gave her no comfort. This was something she didn't want to know. Maybe that's why she had forgotten it.

"Mitral valve prolapse is a fairly common heart disorder and isn't usually much of a problem." The doctor glanced meaningfully at Kate. "Some patients have more severe symptoms, which require medication and can affect daily living. Of course, I can't be completely sure since there are other more precise tests required to give an accurate diagnosis. But I would hazard to guess that Kate falls into that category."

Kate swallowed tightly. Tears burned the backs of her eyes. She wanted out of here. Away from this—she didn't want to know. She knotted her hands in her lap and forced her body to stay put. She couldn't just up and run out the door. Raine would only drag her back to face this ugly reality anyway. She stole a glance in his direction. He listened quietly while the doctor spoke, his face wiped clean of emotion.

"She is physically fit. There's no reason to think she can't live a normal life as long as she takes her medication and doesn't overextend herself physically. It would be best, however, for a cardiologist to do a full evaluation."

Something indiscernible flickered across Raine's face, but he quickly banished it. "What's the medication dosage?"

"Without more in-depth testing, I would suggest one tablet per day. And rest," he added quickly. "She needs rest. From the look of her, I'd say that she is already seriously overextended physically, and possibly otherwise." The doctor eyed Raine for a long moment before he spoke again. "I won't ask why she doesn't remember all this or where you got the Inderal."

Raine met his gaze. "It would be better if you didn't."

"I'm going to assume that the bruise on her temple explains her lack of knowledge about her health history, and warn you again that she needs rest.'' He held Raine's gaze for a beat before continuing. ''You're welcome to stay here for the night,'' he offered hesitantly, as if he knew the answer before he spoke.

''Thanks, but we have some ground to cover before morning.'' Raine stood and reached for his wallet. ''What do I owe you, Doc?''

Kate took her cue from Raine. She shot to her feet, anxious to do anything but sit and listen to more gory details about her physical limitations. A sickening sense of dread welled inside her, making her heart flutter. Anxiety pressed down on her like a load of bricks.

The doctor pushed to his feet and extended his hand, which Raine hesitantly accepted. ''This one's on me.'' His cheeks flushed a bit. ''I haven't had this much excitement since Josh Miller shot his best friend in the foot for taking his girlfriend to the Fourth of July barn dance.''

A few minutes later, Kate exchanged goodbyes with the doctor and followed Raine into the darkness. She had a bad feeling that her heart condition played a strong role in her life. A negative role. A sob twisted deep in her throat. She didn't want to have to take these stupid blue pills. She didn't want some doctor to listen to her insides and hear unacceptable sounds. She wanted to be normal. To be a cop like her brother!

Kate jerked to a stop. She struggled to suck a breath into her seemingly too-tight chest. Her brother? She had a brother and he was a cop? The memory was there, on the tip of her consciousness but she couldn't quite grasp it.

Raine turned back to her. ''You okay?''

She felt as if she might explode at any moment. An overwhelming sense of doom settled over her, pushing away rational thought. She felt the urge to run, run as fast as she could. The need consumed all other thought.

"Kate?" This time he was right beside her. "We have to go."

All but catatonic, Kate allowed Raine to guide her the rest of the way to the car. He had insisted on leaving the damn thing parked what felt like a mile from the house. So the old doc couldn't see the make and model in case he decided to call the police later. Her savior, she mused. He didn't miss a detail when it came to covering his tracks.

Kate opened the passenger-side door and plopped onto the bucket seat. She shoved her fingers through her hair and willed herself to calm, to think rationally. But it did no good. Raine worked his magic under the dash to start the engine.

The interior of the car suddenly seemed too confining for Kate to breathe. She had to get out. *Now.* Kate opened the door and bolted out. She sucked in breath after breath, but she just couldn't get enough oxygen to her lungs. Her heart pounded harder and harder. Oh, God. She was going to die. In the dark, in the middle of nowhere. Realization slammed into her like a blow to her midsection.

Panic. She was having a panic attack. She used to have them all the time.

How did she know that? She didn't want to know it! She didn't want to feel any of this.

Kate paced back and forth, alternately hugging her arms around herself and threading her fingers through her hair. She wanted to run. Run fast. Run off all the extra adrenaline. Run until she collapsed in a pathetic heap.

Raine rounded the rear end of the car and moved toward her. "Kate."

He came too close. She felt crowded. Kate backed away, but he kept coming. A cold sweat broke out on her forehead. Her hands were clammy. God, she needed to run. But she couldn't. She had nowhere to go. She couldn't escape this reality. It was hers. She was defective, less than acceptable.

"Kate, it's okay," he said in a soothing voice.

"It's not okay!" she shouted, backing up another step. Kate closed her eyes and let the uncontrollable emotion have its way with her. "It's definitely not okay," she muttered. The open car door halted her backward movement. Frustrated and very near tears, she snapped her eyes open and banged her chest with her fist. "I don't want to have this." She surveyed her dark surroundings. "I don't want to be here." God, she needed more air. "And I don't want to know anything else about my past."

Raine braced one arm on top of the car and the other on the open door, then leaned in close, forcing her to look at him, to listen to him, crowding her with his nearness. "Kate, it's not the end of the world."

"How do you know what constitutes the beginning or the end of *my* world?" She glared at him, wishing with all her might that she could make him feel what she felt at this moment. He was perfect. What would he know about not measuring up? "Just go away and leave me alone!"

"Look," he said more sternly. "We don't have time for you to fall apart right now. We have to get the hell out of here. In case you've forgotten, we both almost met our maker tonight. Dillon and his men are out there right now trying to figure out which way we went. So if you're through feeling sorry for yourself, I'd like to get on the road."

Anger flared inside Kate, devouring her anxiety in one hot flash. "Don't you preach to me about feeling sorry for myself, you—you bastard. You're the one who got me into this mess. If anyone should be sorry it's you!" Kate punctuated her statement by shoving against his chest. She needed some space. He was too close. Why wouldn't he just leave her alone?

Even in the waning moonlight, Kate didn't miss the irritation that flickered in Raine's eyes. "Don't think I haven't been sorry since day one," he said hotly. "But now that I'm stuck with you, I am trying to make the best of it."

Kate crossed her arms over her chest and lifted her chin a notch. "Ha! You call dragging me around like a rag doll and almost getting me killed making the best of it?"

"I haven't gotten you killed yet," he pointed out. He leaned a tad closer, close enough that his breath fanned her face. Kate shivered. "I told you I wouldn't let anything happen to you, and I've kept my word."

Kate trembled then, as much with awareness of the man towering over her as with delayed fear from the night's events. "Why did you come for me?"

Raine frowned. "What do you mean?"

"Why didn't you just take off? Why risk your life to save mine?" She had to know. The answer was suddenly the most important bit of knowledge in the universe. If she never knew anything else, she needed to know this. Why didn't he just let her die? What good was she?

Confusion claimed his features briefly before he contained the outward display. "When I said I would keep you safe, I meant it. I'll do whatever it takes."

Kate hugged her arms more tightly around herself as a softer emotion crowded out all others. "You don't even know me, why would you die for me?"

"I've risked my life for a lot less in the past." The truth of his words burned in his eyes like an eternal flame of tribute to a past he'd just as soon not discuss.

She had to touch him. Kate lifted her hand to his face, to caress his tense jaw. The warmth of his skin felt devastatingly erotic beneath her palm. "You confuse me, Raine. I can't decide if you're a good guy or a bad guy."

He moistened his lips, placed his hand over hers, then kissed her palm. "I stopped wondering that myself a long time ago."

Kate pushed her arms around his neck and closed her eyes. She held him close. Somehow, this man, this stranger, cared about her. He might be a murderer, and he might be the worst of the bad guys, but he cared about her. Right now that's all that mattered. His lips felt firm and hot against her neck. She tilted her head and gave him full access to her throat. Heat and desire churned, warming her from the inside out. Kate tangled her fingers in his hair and pulled his mouth to hers. She wanted to taste him, to feel his lips against hers.

She gasped at the shock of his hard body pressing into hers. Instinct took control. Instead of pushing him away, she melted into the kiss, allowing him to mold her fully to him. His tongue pushed into her mouth, caressing hers. She tightened her hold, needing him closer when he was already practically a part of her. She demanded more and he gave it. His kiss deepened. He delved beneath the bulky layers of clothing with one long-fingered hand and found her breast. Kate groaned with need and arched into the thick arousal already straining against the front of his jeans.

Raine squeezed and caressed her breast. Kate's heart pounded frantically beneath his touch. Raine suddenly tensed, then broke the kiss, but kept her body trapped with his.

He slowly removed the hand that covered her breast and softly touched her cheek with his fingertips as he smiled, but the surface convention was strained. "We have to go."

Before she could protest, he stepped away and waited for her to get back into the car. Kate took a deep breath to steady herself and climbed inside without looking back. If she'd had any doubts about what was happening between them, none existed now. This relationship was no longer one of captor and hostage. And he didn't seem to mind at all that she wasn't perfect. Of course, he probably didn't have his mind on her heart, she admitted ruefully.

"Where are we going?" she asked when Raine had gotten behind the wheel and started down the long, rutted side road.

"Someplace safe."

Kate swallowed. She doubted that anyplace on earth would be safe from a man like Dillon. Her gaze moved over Raine's strong profile. Or him, for that matter.

RAINE DROVE SOUTH for more than two hours before he reached the city limits of Russellville. He glanced at Kate, asleep in the seat beside him. She had slept most of the way and that was good, she needed the rest. He, on the other hand, had been awake for twenty-four hours straight, and probably would be for most of the next twenty-four. Lack of sleep didn't bother him much though. During his stint in the special forces he had learned to function for days at a time with almost no sleep at all, catching a few minutes here and there.

The sun peeked over the mountaintops just in time to highlight the carefully restored historic buildings lining both sides of the main street that divided Russellville. Banks, coffee shops and other businesses occupied the federalist-style structures. Just before he reached the bridge that crossed the river, Raine turned left onto a narrow country road. He drove parallel to the river on his right. Farmhouses dotted the landscape on the left.

He slowed for a hairpin curve, then turned left at the top of the hill onto a gravel road. Over a mile later, a two-story farmhouse came into view and Raine smiled. Although the place had never really been his home, it felt like home.

Early-morning sunlight glinted from the damp-with-dew, green metal roof. A wide porch graced the front of the house like the apron on a proud southern lady. Fresh white paint coated the century-old clapboard siding, and green louvered shutters framed each window. The house didn't have much in the way of contemporary amenities, but it belonged to Raine. And so did the land, wooded and pastured, for as far as the eye could see. Raine definitely approved of the new fence that was almost complete, acres and acres of white split-rail fencing.

No one knew about this place, not even Lucas. Raine had bought it two years ago under an assumed name. A local contractor had made the essential renovations and repairs, like central heat and air and a new roof. Raine could live without a lot of things, but efficient heat and air-conditioning were not among them.

He had only been here three times, the time he'd found the place, again to close the deal, and once more six months ago to look over the renovations. But it was home, or, at least, the closest thing to a home Raine had known since he was a child. He had lain awake many, many nights and planned a life here. A new life as far away and as different from his old one as could be found. Of course, he had always known there was a strong possibility he would never have the chance to enjoy that life. He lived each day with death just one step behind him.

He might never have the opportunity to live in this house, Raine decided, but if the place served no other purpose than to keep Kate safe then that was fine with him. He drove past the house and parked the Thunderbird in one of the open side sections of the enormous barn.

Raine turned to Kate and watched her sleep. He clenched his jaw as regret washed over him. It was a miracle he hadn't killed her on that damn mountain. Without her medication and with him pushing her to the breaking point, her heart had surely been stressed to the limit. He shook his head at the emotion twisting his insides. What a fool he was. Selfish, too. Even after the doctor had emphasized that she needed rest, Raine had kissed her. Kissed her with much more than kissing on his mind. The feel of her heart fluttering in her chest had forced him to realize what he was doing and he had stopped.

Selfish, he repeated silently.

Well, it wouldn't happen again. He would protect Kate not only from Dillon, but from himself as well. He would stay with her for a little while to make sure she was okay, and then he would go. He still couldn't be sure that someone hadn't sent her for him—that she wasn't, in effect, his enemy. If Kate was his enemy, she didn't know it, and, as far as he was concerned, that made her innocent. But what happened when she got her memory back? Time was running out for him. This last unexpected run-in with Dillon had been entirely too close for comfort.

He couldn't take anymore unnecessary risks.

"Kate." Raine gently shook her.

She jerked to attention and surveyed her surroundings like a sentry caught sleeping on his watch. "Where are we?" she asked when her gaze met his.

Instinct nagged at Raine again, an instinct he knew better than to ignore, but he ignored it all the same. More mystery definitely lay behind that pretty face, but he didn't want to analyze that right now. "My place," he told her, then smiled when confusion stole into her eyes.

Raine got out, skirted the hood and opened Kate's door. He took her by the hand and led the way to the house. He reached beneath the third rock from the bottom step and retrieved his key. Inside what had once been a back porch and was now a mudroom, Raine flipped the necessary breaker for the hot-water heater. The real estate agent who had sold him the house checked on the place monthly and maintained the utilities. Raine would need to adjust the thermostat to a higher setting, since the heat was only set at a level necessary to prevent frozen plumbing.

"You live here?" Kate asked as they entered the kitchen.

"Well, I've stayed here a total of seven nights, does that qualify?"

"I suppose so," she said distractedly as she followed him into the hallway.

He moved the thermostat to a more comfortable setting and tried to remember what canned goods, if any, he had in the pantry. Kate wandered down the hall past him, obviously ready to explore. "Make yourself at home," he told her. "I'll get our things from the car."

Kate had already disappeared into the living room before he finished speaking. It pleased him immensely to share this place with her. Raine recognized the feeling for what it was. He had grown entirely too fond of Kate in the last few days, a dangerous allowance for a man like him. Those emotions had no place in his world, but he couldn't escape them where Kate was concerned.

When he returned from the car with their purchases from the day before, Kate was upstairs checking out the second floor. Since there were only three bedrooms and one bathroom up there, it didn't take Raine long to find her. He leaned against the doorway and watched her survey a bedroom.

Kate smiled when her gaze came to rest on him. "This place is wonderful. I love all the antiques." She gestured to the sparse furnishings.

"Most of them came with the house." He straightened and scanned the room. "My real estate agent picked up the rest." Tiny bouquets of pink and blue flowers dotted the faded wallpaper. Rich mahogany flooring and white painted trim made this bedroom just like the other two, only the finish on the walls differentiated the rooms. One had yellow-and-white-striped paper, while beige paint dressed the walls of the third. Raine had decided, on his first look at the house, that he favored the painted room. Flowers and stripes just weren't to his taste. Luckily all the rooms had beds. "How about you take this room?" he suggested, bringing his gaze back to his very first houseguest. This room was the farthest from the stairs and had only one window, therefore the most secure.

A look of mild surprise clouded her expression, but she recovered quickly. "This one will be fine."

Raine's heart thumped in his chest. Had she expected to share one with him? His groin tightened at the thought. "Okay." He crossed the room and placed the shopping bag containing her new clothes on the bed. "The water should be hot in a few minutes if you'd like to have a shower or bath. I'll go see what I can find to eat."

"Thanks," she said on a smile.

Instead of doing something completely crazy like pulling her into his arms for another kiss as he so wanted to, Raine pivoted and left the room. He strode down the hall and left his own bag on the bed in the room next to hers. He would have preferred something on the other side of the globe, but a single wall would have to suffice. He only hoped that a mere wall would prove an adequate barrier to the temptation she represented.

Raine had a bad feeling that the day and night to come were going to be the longest of his life.

Chapter Nine

Steam curled around Kate, feathering against her skin like an angel's caress. The deep, hot water eased her sore, aching muscles. She relaxed fully against the smooth porcelain surface of the old claw-footed tub. Moisture beaded on her face, and Kate brushed back a strand of freshly washed hair. How could anything else on earth feel quite this heavenly? she wondered.

Kate had to admit that Raine's kiss had been pretty heavenly as well. The memory of his kiss flooded her mind, resurrecting that intense desire. A thousand sensations bombarded her. The way he touched her, the way his hard, muscular body felt against hers. His scent, his taste. Those amazing blue eyes.

She knew that allowing herself to dwell on thoughts of Raine's mind-boggling kisses wasn't safe, but she just couldn't help herself. Had any other man ever made her feel that way? Kate searched her mind for any memory of a former boyfriend or lover, but nothing came.

She sighed and slipped farther into the water's comforting depths. Maybe if she never remembered her past it would be best. Considering what she had learned about herself so far, Kate had a feeling the rest could be devastating.

She pressed her hand next to her left breast and felt for

her heartbeat. She extended one leg at a time out of the water and scrutinized its muscle tone, then looked long and hard at her arms. How could she appear to be in such good physical condition, and have something so terribly wrong with her? Anxiety shuddered through her at the thought of just how wrong her problem was.

Fearing another panic attack, Kate forced the troublesome thoughts away and concentrated on relaxing. Raine probably thought she was mental already. Another bout of hysteria wouldn't help. She suddenly longed for the time before the doctor had revealed her heart problem. The time in the mountains when it had been just she and Raine. When she'd been a "normal" person who'd bumped her head and lost her memory. For a little while she had been free of the big, ugly problem that haunted the past she couldn't remember.

Kate focused on the warmth surrounding her. She inhaled deeply of the moist, clean air. Slowly, the heat plied her exhausted body into a state just shy of sleep. Her thoughts whirled, unhampered. Snatches of short-term memory flitted through her mind in no particular order. Raine kissing her in the darkness. Dillon's evil smile. The doctor's kind voice. Raine holding her naked against him in the shower. Danny telling her how many men Raine had killed. Raine facing Dillon to save her. She examined that last bit of memory more closely. Raine could have been killed trying to save her. But he had come for her all the same. Why had he done that? Was it merely a dogmatic sense of responsibility, as he claimed? Or could there be more to it?

Sleep tugged at Kate, enticing her toward oblivion. She was so tired and so warm. There was no reason not to give in, to escape the reality of what might lay in store for Raine, for her. Her thoughts slowed and focused inward. A kind of calmness enveloped her. She was safe for the

moment, and so was Raine. She could rest. A sigh of surrender eased past her lips as sleep captured her in its serene
embrace…

Kate wore black….

The man next to her wore a navy blue uniform. A
policeman's uniform. Her heartbeat accelerated. Kate
peered through the haze of billowing steam to more closely
see the man sitting next to her. She couldn't make out his
features through the thick steam. No, it wasn't steam. It
was more like fog. She was dreaming, she realized. The
haze cleared then. The man beside her looked at Kate with
sad, dark eyes.

Her father. The man was her father.

An ache, soul deep, rushed through her. Kate was sitting
on a church pew with her father. She forced her gaze forward, to the man speaking from the podium. A priest. His
long, white robes and gray hair looked stark against the
darkness of her dream. Where was she?

A funeral.

A polished oak coffin stood in front of the podium. The
priest continued to chant some sort of prayer. Kate looked
to her father, who wept at her side.

"He's gone, Katie." He shook his head in resignation.
"He's gone."

"But I'm here, Daddy," Kate insisted, confused.

Her father smiled sadly. "I know. But you don't understand the special bond he and I shared." Then he began
to weep again, louder than before.

Kate frowned. She looked at the priest for answers but
he wasn't paying attention to her. A mixture of fear and
sorrow tightening her throat, Kate stood and stepped toward the open coffin. Why couldn't she reach her father?
What was it she didn't understand? Whose funeral was
this?

She looked down, into the white satin interior of the

beautifully crafted oak box, and saw what it was she didn't understand.

Her brother, Joseph.

Tears slid down Kate's cheeks. Joseph was as handsome as ever. His dark hair short and styled a bit more stiffly than he would have liked. His dark eyes closed in eternal sleep. His usually smiling lips, permanently drawn into a line that wasn't quite frown nor smile. His uniform crisp and decorated, a deep blue against the white satin. His hands folded beneath his policeman's cap.

Kate could never be like him. Never live up to his super-cop reputation. Never have the place in her father's heart that Joseph held, even in death.

She would never measure up. She would always fall short of the mark. Her heart would never allow her to be all that her brother had been, all her father was....

Kate sat straight up. Water sloshed around her and over the edge of the tub. Her heart pounded while she fought to catch her breath. Her brother, her only sibling, was dead. And he had been a cop. A cop like her father, and his father and grandfather before him. She could never be a cop. She had failed the required physical.

She had failed her father.

The tradition stopped with her, because she didn't measure up. And Joseph was dead. He wouldn't be able to father a son or daughter to keep the tradition alive. Tears crowded her throat. She should have been the one to die. Joseph was perfect, handsome and healthy. He should have lived. But a twelve-year-old boy on crack cocaine had killed him with a stolen handgun. Kate's heart fluttered wildly as tears slid down her cheeks. Her stupid faulty heart. She should have died in that alley, not Joe.

A loud knock on the door penetrated the fog of grief shrouding her. "Kate, what's wrong? I heard you cry out all the way downstairs."

Kate shivered as the coolness of the water penetrated her consciousness. How long had she been dozing? Why did her dream feel so real, yet make no sense at all? She swiped at her cheeks and willed her heart to calm. She could examine those new snatches of memory later, when she was calmer. "I'm...I'm fine," she managed to say, knowing if she didn't say something Raine would grow suspicious.

"You're not fine," he argued. "Now open this damned door before I break it down."

Kate splashed the cool water on her heated face before she stood on shaky legs. She pulled the plug so the tub would drain, then stepped out onto the cold tile floor. She drew in a long, deep breath and let it out slowly. She had to pull herself together before facing him.

"Open the door, Kate," he demanded impatiently.

"Give me a minute!" she snapped right back. Kate squeezed her hair dry, then quickly blotted the water from her skin. She remembered belatedly that she had forgotten to bring clean clothes into the bathroom with her. "Damn," she muttered. She snatched up her dirty sweatshirt, but it was wet from the water that had sloshed over the side of the tub. She swore again and swiped the damp hair from her face. She had to put on something.

Kate glanced at the wet towel and considered it. At least it was clean. Before she could make a decision, something draped on the pedestal mirror in the corner caught her eye. She dropped the towel and crossed to the mirror. A white dress shirt hung on one of the decorative arms that supported the full-length oval-shaped mirror. Kate picked up the shirt and examined it more closely. From all indications it had been hanging there for a while, but it appeared fairly clean. She shook it, then held the short-sleeved garment to her face and inhaled deeply. The slightest hint of

Raine's unique scent lingered on the fabric. He must have left it the last time he stayed here, she decided.

"Your minute is up." The deep timbre of his voice rumbled through the closed door.

A surge of renewed warmth flowed through Kate as the sound shivered across her nerve endings, pushing aside the sadness she couldn't bear to think about. She donned the shirt, made fast work of the buttons and opened the door before he carried through with his threat to break it down.

"What the hell took you so long?" he demanded, his shoulders rigid, concern creasing his forehead.

Kate propped her hands on her hips and stared up into those fierce blue eyes. "I had to put something on, you know," she retorted, shooting for nonchalance but not quite achieving it.

His lips parted as if he might say something else, but he changed his mind when his gaze slid down her body. Kate's stomach flip-flopped when he lingered on her breasts. The shirt clung to her still-damp skin, the white material becoming transparent and revealing almost as much as if she wore nothing at all.

"I...ah...heated up some canned soup," he said distractedly.

He lifted his gaze back to hers and Kate panicked. Her heart stumbled at the longing in his eyes. "I'm not hungry," she said quickly. No way could she trust herself in the same room with the man right now. His hunger was too strong, and she was weak—and none of it had anything to do with soup. What they both needed right now was distance. At least until she could sort out all these crazy, mixed-up memories and emotions.

He blinked twice, vacating his gaze of lust. "You need to eat."

"I'll eat later." Kate manufactured a smile. "I think I'll rest for a while." She crossed her arms over her chest and

prayed he would leave. He made entirely too tempting a
picture in those tight-fitting jeans and faded gray T-shirt.
Early-morning stubble glistened on his jaw, inviting her
touch.

Raine shrugged. "Suit yourself."

Kate blew out a relieved breath when he sauntered
away. She closed her eyes and shook off the desire buzzing
inside her. Her situation was screwed up enough without
allowing herself to fall for a man like Jack Raine.

...he's the best in the business.

If she could only remember what business.

THE IMAGES weren't clear, the voices slightly muffled, but
the dream pulled Kate deeper into the abyss of nothing-
ness. *It's your job to find out if he's turned,* the voice told
her. *And to bring him in either way.* The words echoed
inside her head, making her restless. She tossed and turned
in the bed, lingering just the other side of consciousness.
She wanted to wake up, but the dreams wouldn't release
her. She relaxed when Raine's kiss replayed behind her
closed lids. Warmth shimmered through her body, heating
all the right spots. She wanted to hold him close, to show
him he could trust her, to believe she could trust him.

...you're our best shot at getting close to this guy.
Raine's image shattered in Kate's dream, replaced by the
words, by sensations she couldn't quite identify and faces
she didn't recognize. *Someplace safe.* Raine's voice rushed
into her head. He wanted her to be safe. *Ballatore wants
him dead. It's only a matter of time before I catch up to
you again. You're a dead man walking, my friend.*

Kate's eyes snapped open and the room slowly came
into focus. She pushed the hair from her face and took a
long, shaky breath. Dreaming. She'd only been dreaming.
She quickly scanned her quiet surroundings. Raine's

house. She was safe. Sunlight spilled through the window and reached across the room.

Safe. The solitary word tugged at something buried way behind all the strange images and voices in her head.

And bring him in either way. The voice was Aunt Vicky's, whoever she was.

Kate frowned and struggled to recall her mixed-up dreams. Bits and pieces of conversation, snatches of images. Her father was a cop. Her brother was a cop and had died in the line of duty. She had wanted to be a cop and couldn't because of her heart problem. She couldn't measure up.

Kate blinked back the sting of tears. Tears for a loss she couldn't quite comprehend. She had lost a brother, but didn't remember much about that brother. How could that be possible? She could remember something as life-altering as her brother's death and still the rest of her past was a black hole in her brain.

And bring him in either way. Who did she have to bring in? And why? If she wasn't a cop, why would she be bringing in anyone? None of it made sense.

She was safe.

Raine had called this someplace safe. Safe for whom? Her? Him? *Ballatore wants him dead.* Would Raine hide here for the rest of his life? She didn't think so. Raine didn't strike Kate as the type to hide from anything.

Then why come here? *Someplace safe.*

Kate sat up with a start. He had brought her here so *she* would be safe. Jack Raine wasn't afraid of death. He had risked his life for a lot less in the past. He had told her that. He had been on his way to New York—to Ballatore. Kate knew that fact with a certainty of which she could only guess the source. Raine's only reason for this out-of-the-way stop was to tuck her away someplace safe.

"Damn!" Kate threw back the cover and shot out of

bed. He planned to leave her here—someplace safe—while he finished his business with Dillon and Ballatore. Lucas Camp was probably right. Raine intended to prove his innocence before he came in. Somehow he believed the usual channels had been breached, and he intended to do things his own way.

Lucas Camp? Kate paused, her eyes rounded in bewilderment. Who the hell was Lucas Camp? Why did Raine need to prove his innocence? Innocence of what? Kate pushed her fingers through her hair. She had no idea what any of this meant. The only thing she knew with any measure of certainty was that Raine would not hide from his enemies. He would face them. He wasn't concerned about his own safety.

Kate stood absolutely still in the middle of the room and listened. Complete silence hung heavily around her. He was probably already gone. Kate dashed out of the room, checked the other bedrooms and the bathroom before taking the stairs two at a time. She searched the downstairs. Raine was nowhere in the house.

The car. If he had left, he would have taken the car. Kate flung the back door open and raced across the yard. Though the sun beat down unusually warm for a November day, the ground still felt cool beneath her bare feet, but there was no time to worry about that at the moment. She skidded to a stop next to the muddy, black Thunderbird inside its makeshift garage. The car was exactly as Raine had left it. Even if someone drove up to the house, they would never be able to see the stolen vehicle without walking into this attached side section of the barn with a flashlight. Despite the lack of a door, it was dark as a cave this far inside.

Kate frowned. If Raine hadn't left in the car, then where the hell was he? Though she had no idea why, Kate knew that she could not allow Jack Raine to slip through her fingers....

RAINE SHOVED the oil stick back into the engine and wiped his hands on a shop cloth. Everything checked out. He would have to give the real estate agent a bonus for going above and beyond the call of duty. The man had kept Raine's house and vehicle in tiptop shape. He glanced up at the lights hanging overhead in the barn, if you didn't count the one fluorescent bulb blinking overhead, that is. Of course, the lights out here probably didn't stay on long enough for the blinking bulb to be noticed.

For the time being, Raine used the barn for a garage to store his truck. But someday soon, he hoped to fill the numerous stalls with horses. He smiled to himself. He'd always wanted to be a cowboy. His smile faded into a frown. A pipe dream, nothing more. He knew better than to expect anything beyond this minute.

Forcing his attention to the present, Raine glanced at his watch. There was still time for a quick shower before taking off. If he left now he could be in New York well before midnight. He couldn't risk waiting any longer. Raine had already stored what he would need in the vehicle. An extra clip or two for the Beretta, and the Glock, his favorite weapon next to the Beretta. He didn't like being caught without backup protection.

A low creak sounded near the front entrance, jerking him from his unpleasant strategizing. Raine tossed aside the shop cloth and drew his Beretta. He eased around the fender and down the driver's side of his Range Rover, then scanned the front of the barn. One side of the double doors stood open. His senses moved to a higher state of alert as his gaze followed the almost imperceptible sound of fabric rustling.

He rounded the tailgate and stood column straight at the

edge of the bumper. Raine braced himself, then swung around the end of the vehicle, arms extended, weapon leveled on the first thing that moved.

Kate.

Raine swore.

Kate whirled around. Raine took a breath and lowered his weapon. "What the hell are you doing sneaking up on me like that? Announce yourself when you walk into a room with an armed man," he said crossly as he shoved the Beretta into his waistband at the small of his back.

"I...I thought you left," she stammered uncertainly. She shoved a handful of sleep-mussed hair behind her ear and met his gaze. "I was afraid...you had left..." Her voice trailed off.

She didn't say the word *me*, but Raine knew that's what she meant. Her words twisted his insides. She had been afraid that he'd left her, and that's exactly what he intended. Because he couldn't trust her, and he desperately wanted to keep her safe. "I came out to check on..." He gestured toward the vehicle, but words failed him as his gaze moved over her body.

Did she have no idea how tempting she looked standing there, all innocent and vulnerable? His shirt caressed her body in ways that made Raine's mouth go dry. Barely covering the tops of her thighs and with one too many buttons left undone, the shirt revealed a great deal more than it concealed. He remembered how it had looked against her skin after her bath. Her long, mahogany hair fell around her shoulders like a waterfall of silk. The bruise on her temple had almost completely faded now. Those dark eyes were wide with worry as she braced one hand against the front fender to steady herself. Obviously he'd scared the hell out of her as well.

He frowned. "Where's your coat?" Though the temperature was unseasonably warm and he'd shed his own coat hours ago, dressed like that, she had to be cold. He allowed his gaze to sweep over her once more.

She looked down at herself as if realizing for the first time her state of undress. "I was worried. I didn't know where you were," she murmured self-consciously. She slid one bare foot behind the other, as if trying to hide its nakedness. That innocent gesture pulled at him, made him want to protect her from any and all threats.

Raine averted his gaze and plowed his fingers through his hair. There was nothing in this world he wanted more than to take her in his arms right now. To promise her that he would never leave her, that he would always protect her, but he couldn't do that. If he touched her now, there would be no turning back. He couldn't do that to himself, and he wouldn't do it to her. Raine planted his hands on his hips and leveled an indifferent gaze in her direction. "I wouldn't leave without telling you."

She moistened her lips. "So you are planning to leave."

Raine restrained the urge to shift. He'd spent a lifetime holding his reactions in check, emotional as well as physical. Nothing had changed, he told himself. The lie proved hard to swallow. "I didn't say that."

"But you are, aren't you?" She crossed her arms over her chest and lifted her chin a notch. "You have to, don't you?"

Raine ignored the alarms going off in his head and took two steps in her direction. "My plans aren't concrete yet," he hedged. He'd actually planned to spend the night, but recognized the risk that he wouldn't be able to stay away from Kate.

She choked out a laugh and shook her head slowly from side to side. "You really expect me to believe that?" Kate pinned him with a gaze that shredded several more layers of his defenses. "My long-term memory may be off-line at the moment, but don't insult my intelligence. I know why we're here, Raine. This is where I get off, right? Did you plan to just dump me, or is this where you tie up *your* loose ends? Isn't that what a professional does? I mean, you are a professional, right?''

Disregarding his better judgment, Raine allowed the anger to erupt inside him as he closed the distance between them. He needed that particular emotion right now for protection—protection against the other much more precarious emotion he refused to acknowledge. He never second-guessed himself, he wasn't about to start.

He walked right up to Kate, directly into her personal space, and gave her his most intimidating glare. ''When I've made up my mind I'll let you know.'' He kept his tone low and purposely threatening. ''Until then, I would suggest that you don't antagonize me further. I do things my way.''

Kate met his glare with lead in her own. His anger seemed to strengthen her resolve. All signs of uncertainty had vanished. ''I tell you what, tough guy, why don't I save you the trouble. I'll just take the T-Bird and leave now. Then you and your nice friends can play all you want without having me around to worry about.''

Raine felt a muscle jerk in his jaw. ''You'll do whatever I damn well tell you to do,'' he said quietly, coldly.

Something changed in her eyes. A subtle, impossible-to-read shift. Instinct told Raine that he wasn't going to like it.

''Just try and make me,'' she challenged, then brushed past him as she strode away.

Hands still jammed at his waist, Raine watched in amazement as she stormed out of the barn. No, he didn't like this at all. He didn't tolerate insubordination. Grappling for control, he stalked after her. Halfway across the yard he snagged her by the arm and swung her around. She glowered at him, those dark eyes glittering with anger.

"Don't push me, Kate," he cautioned. "I won't let you get in the way of what I have to do."

"I'd say you're a little late." She struggled to free her arm, but he tightened his hold. "What will you do now, Raine?" She stilled and stared up at him. "Shoot me?"

Raine clenched his jaw and jerked her hard against him. "Don't tempt me."

Seconds ticked by as she stared fiercely at him, unwilling to relent. Through the thin layers of clothing separating their tense bodies, Raine could feel her heat. He wanted simultaneously to kiss her and shake some sense into her, the urge to do one or the other almost overwhelming. He had spent too many endless hours denying his desire for her, denying his needs, his feelings. Years of banished emotion threatened to crash in on him, showering Kate with its fallout.

She moved first, slamming her right fist into his gut. Raine grunted in surprise at the force behind her blow. He didn't have time to consider how the hell she could pack such a powerful wallop. He manacled her wrist while deftly deflecting her knee. Kate twisted, lost her balance and pulled him down with her. Raine shifted, holding her close and allowing his shoulder to take the brunt of impact when they hit the grass.

"Let me go, you bastard!"

"Stop squirming!" Raine pinned her beneath him, holding her hands above her head and trapping her legs with his own. She fought to throw him off, her body grinding into his. "Don't move," he growled. Desire warred with his common sense. Need bordered on physical pain, gnawing at his crumbling resolve.

She glared at him, the same battle between desire and anger taking place in her own dark eyes. The sound of her short, shallow breaths played havoc with Raine's weakening control. This was wrong, a mistake. He knew it. But he couldn't keep himself from wanting her, needing her. His gaze locked on her mouth. Her tongue darted out and moistened her lips. His control vaporized.

He took her mouth with his own, forcing her to accept him. Plying her soft lips with his firmer ones. A fierce longing shuddered through Raine, followed by a tormented groan that echoed inside her mouth.

Still fighting, Kate bit his lower lip. Raine swore, but refused to retreat. The tang of his blood mixed with her warm, sweet taste. She writhed beneath him and he kissed her harder, sucked at her tongue. Kate stopped struggling then, whether with desire or defeat, he couldn't be sure. Despite the risk that she might scratch his eyes out, Raine released his brutal hold on her hands to thread his fingers into her silky hair. Her hands went immediately to his chest, but she didn't push him away. Instead, her fingers fisted in the fabric of his T-shirt and pulled him nearer. Relief washed through him, followed by a rush of desire heightened by her acceptance.

Raine rested his weight on his forearms to keep from crushing her soft body into the ground. He cradled her head and deepened the kiss, invading her mouth with his tongue, stroking hers, teasing sensitive places. She responded wildly and his body contracted with want. The fact that they were lying outside in broad daylight no longer mattered. His need to have Kate consumed all else.

Kate tugged his shirt from his jeans and slipped her hands beneath it. He groaned when her delicate fingers traced the contours of his bare chest. He had wanted to be like this with her for so damn long. Heat sizzled wherever she touched. Raine ground his hips into hers, allowing her to feel just how much he wanted her. He drew his mouth from hers and kissed the tip of her nose, her closed lids, the shell of ear, and then lower. She lay panting, her passion-clouded eyes now following his every move, her chest heaving as harshly as his own.

Kate smoothed her palms over his heated flesh, down his chest to his abdomen, then around to his back. Her every touch left a trail of fire. She squeezed his buttocks and he almost lost it. He had to close his eyes and concentrate with all his might to slow his body's plunge toward release. He needed to be inside her, *now.* Her hands moved higher, kneading, massaging, urging him against her arching hips.

Raine knew instinctively the moment her fingers curled around the butt of the Beretta. He didn't move, didn't even breathe for one long moment. He lifted his mouth from the naked flesh he was plundering at the base of her throat, his gaze meeting hers. A beat of uncertainty passed. In that split second, something distinctly adversarial flashed in her dark eyes, then it was gone. Kate extended her arm above her head and placed the Beretta on the ground in plain sight.

A look of primal intent in her eyes, she raised her mouth to his. She sucked his injured lip, moaning softly at the taste of him. Renewed desire roared through his veins, bringing the need inside him to a boiling point and hardening already tight muscles. Again and again her lips teased his until Raine took her mouth hard, thrusting his tongue inside. Her fingers labored with the snap and fly of his jeans.

She reached inside, touched him, then circled his aching flesh with her soft fingers. Raine groaned harshly, suppressing the urge to explode in her gentle caress. Crazy with want now, he wrenched his mouth from hers, ripped open the shirt she wore and covered one straining breast. Her essence filled his mouth as he sucked first one breast, and then the other. Kate screamed her pleasure. He wanted to taste her, to touch her all over, to take her. Now, right now.

His heart pounded with impatience as she struggled to shove his jeans and briefs down his hips. She whimpered her own frustration. He kneed her thighs farther apart as he glided one hand over her feminine shape. He touched her, surprised when he didn't find panties. Kate gasped as he tangled his fingers in her nest of soft curls, slid one finger along her feminine channel, then dipped inside. She was so hot. Kate moaned with pleasure, momentarily distracted from her struggle with his jeans. Raine buried that one finger deep inside her, pressing the heel of his hand hard against her swollen nub. She arched her hips, her hands suddenly frantic to push away his restraining clothes.

Raine grunted a primal sound when his shaft leaped free. There was no time for civilized foreplay, no patience for decorum. He entered her in one savage thrust. Tight and hot, she gripped him. Kate cried out his name and he soothed her mouth with his own, murmuring unintelligible sounds between kisses.

Kate clung to him, her arms around his neck, her legs locked around his as he started to move. She lifted her hips to meet each thrust and Raine slid his arms beneath her to protect her from the cold ground. Harder and harder he pounded into Kate, driving closer and closer to release. He couldn't slow the pace, couldn't draw out the pleasure for her. Giving was out of the question, he could only take. He would make this up to her if it was the last thing he did.

Heat and sensation crashed down on him, propelling him over the edge. Raine pressed his forehead to hers and thrust one last time, shuddering with the force of it. He slowed, emptying himself into her heat.

Kate groaned her protest when he would have slumped

to a stop. She quivered against him and her feminine muscles clutched urgently around his shaft. Unable to form coherent thought, instinct took control. Raine clenched his jaw and drove fully into her again and again, bringing her to the completion he hadn't expected. She buried her nails in his back, a sweet pleasure-pain, as she convulsed around him.

Exhausted and sated, they lay together without speaking, their frantic breathing and the wind shifting in the trees the only sounds around them. Kate shivered. Raine realized then how cold she must be, lying in his arms against the frigid ground.

"We should go inside," he murmured, and brushed a strand of windblown hair from her cheek.

She silently searched his gaze. Raine hoped she couldn't see how deeply this desperate act had affected him. For the first time in his life, he couldn't push away how he felt. It threatened to burst out of him in ways and words he couldn't yet acknowledge.

He looked away, disengaged from Kate and shifted to a kneeling position. He shouldn't be feeling any of this. He was a fool. He righted his clothes, then offered her his hand. She accepted it, and they stood together. Raine swallowed tightly as he quickly analyzed what had just happened between them. He'd never let anything get this far out of bounds before. He always maintained control of a situation—any situation.

What the hell was wrong with him? People were trying to kill them, for Christ's sake. And what was he doing? Having sex like a horny teenager with no consideration to their safety or the consequences of the unprotected act.

His gaze swept over Kate as she tugged the now-buttonless shirt around herself. He had sworn that he wouldn't do this to her. It was bad enough that he had endangered her life, he didn't want to hurt her emotionally as well. She might not be totally innocent in all this, but her amnesia had left her vulnerable. And he had taken advantage of that vulnerability. She needed his protection, not his barbaric abuse.

Holding the sides of the shirt together with one hand, Kate flipped her long hair over one shoulder and leveled her gaze on his. "Just so you know," she said with more challenge than he would have expected. "This doesn't change anything. I'm still not going to let you tell me what to do."

Before Raine could respond, she gave him her back and walked away.

Chapter Ten

Kate watched Raine pace the length of the living room once more. She shifted in her chair and waited for the inquisition to begin again. Impatient with dread, she crossed her legs, clasped her hands around her knee and tried her level best not to appear nervous. She swallowed tightly when she considered that only an hour ago she and Raine had made love outside, *on the ground.* The only evidence of that temporary lapse in sanity were the grass stains on the knees of his jeans. Kate resisted the urge to grimace at the memory of the primitive act. One minute he had been on top of her, lost to the desires of their heated bodies, the next he had grabbed back control and tucked all emotion into an iron fist of restraint.

The transition hadn't been so easy for Kate. It had taken a shower, clean clothes and several minutes of self-chastisement to shake the intensity of the emotions she had experienced. Coming back downstairs to face him had surely been one of the hardest things she had ever done. No matter how much her heart wanted to, she could not allow herself to make more of their encounter than was warranted. Sex, that's all it had been. Desperate people in desperate situations did desperate things. As if to deny that reasoning, Kate shivered when the memory of his touch flooded her being once more.

And now he wanted some answers. Answers, for the most part, she couldn't give.

"You don't remember anything else?"

Kate avoided his penetrating gaze. She wasn't nearly so good as he at masking her emotions. "No," she lied.

Raine scrubbed his hand over his jaw as he slowly turned to retrace his steps. When he stopped he ran his fingers through his blond hair and seemed to consider long and hard Kate's response. She knew he didn't quite believe her, and certainly didn't trust her. She could only hope that what she had told him would be enough. The dreams she'd had didn't make a lot of sense, but there were parts that instinct told her were accurate.

Though Kate still couldn't recall having a father, she knew she did and that he was a cop. She'd had a brother too. A brother who had been a cop and had died in the line of duty. This information she shared with Raine, but nothing more. Kate felt the need to protect the rest of the mysterious snatches of memory. The really scary part was the bad feeling she had that her instinct to conceal this information had something to do with who Raine was and all this insanity going on around them.

"Look," Raine said, breaking into her unsettling thoughts. He sat down on the edge of the coffee table in front of Kate, his forearms braced on his thighs, his wide-spread knees on either side of hers. Those clear blue eyes settled onto Kate's, sending a spear of heat through her. "It's becoming more and more apparent that your turning up at my doorstep was no accident—"

"But you said that I had wrecked my car near your driveway," she interjected quickly. She knew exactly where this was headed and somehow she had to keep him from going there.

"That's the way it appeared."

"The way it appeared?" Indignation surged through her

veins. "Do you think I hit the ditch and risked killing myself on purpose? That I'm walking around here with no clue to my past because I enjoy the mystery of it?" Realization washed over Kate, leaving her weak with disbelief. Though she had her own doubts as to exactly why she showed up in Gatlinburg, the amnesia was all too real. "You think I'm faking the amnesia." Shé breathed that sudden awareness aloud.

It wasn't a question, she already knew the answer. Kate saw the quick flash of indecision in his eyes. The possibility had crossed his mind.

He exhaled and looked away. There was no uncertainty in his gaze when it focused again on hers. "I don't think you're faking," he said finally. His tone was reassuring but measured. "The accident and the head injury were real. The amnesia is real. I'm just not convinced that your being on that particular stretch of road was coincidental."

"What's that supposed to mean?" Kate felt her heart flutter. She frowned, trying to remember if she had taken her medication. Yes, she had. Raine had asked her that same question right after…after they'd come back into the house. Kate willed herself to relax, to pay attention to what he had to say next.

"I think maybe someone sent you there to find me," he said carefully. He watched her closely, poised to analyze any reaction, no matter how remote.

Kate shot to her feet and stepped away from him. She couldn't be sure that she could adequately shield her emotions if he probed too deeply. There were too many unanswered questions floating around in her head. Too many pieces of the puzzle that didn't quite fit together. And a whole slew of gut feelings that skirted too close to the conclusion he had verbalized. She crossed the room and stared out the window at the clear, warm day.

"My father is the cop, not me." Kate folded her arms

across her middle and looked over her shoulder at him. His expression gave away nothing of what he might be thinking. "I have a bum ticker, remember?" She injected a healthy dose of sarcasm into the repetition of his own words.

Raine stood, his height alone immensely intimidating. Those long fingers sifted through his thick blond hair once more. His body language revealed as much about his own uneasiness as her eyes likely revealed about hers, Kate decided. He seemed uncomfortable with accusing her, or, distressed by the reminder of her heart condition. Kate felt certain that, whichever was true, sentiment of that nature was way out of character for a man like Jack Raine.

"I remember." He took several steps in her direction. "But that might not keep someone from using you to get to me," he said softly, as if trying to lessen the ugly meaning behind his words. He stood right beside her now, crowding her with his nearness.

…you're our best shot at getting close to this guy. The now-familiar voice mocked, the words reverberating in Kate's skull. She shuddered and shoved that foreboding intrusion away. If Raine was right, then whoever sent her could be just one step behind them, or waiting for Kate to make a move. She was still convinced that the phone call she had made had given away their location, bringing Dillon to their door. But she couldn't be working for Ballatore…could she?

And to bring him in either way.

Kate's breath caught, she blinked, then examined the absolute finality of the mental prompting some dark recess of her mind had just given. There was no question. Raine had hit the nail square on the head. She had been sent to find him and to bring him in despite what he had or had not done. *He needs protection, Ballatore wants him dead,* the voice reminded. If she were trying to protect him from Ballatore, she couldn't be working for him.

"You're sure you didn't know me before—" Kate swallowed the constricting lump rising in her throat "—before I showed up at your door?"

Raine shook his head, then allowed one of those rare, breath-stealing smiles. "I would definitely remember if I had ever met you."

Kate braced herself against the assorted flutters and shivers his nearness evoked. She couldn't allow those feelings right now. Like him, she needed answers. "Why would anyone be after you? What did you do?" She had really wanted to ask why someone would want him dead, but hadn't been able to manage that much courage.

Raine shifted to stare out the window. "It's not what I did, it's what I didn't do."

"What didn't you do?" Anticipation pounded through her veins as she waited for his response. The answer to this one question was somehow pivotal, Kate felt it with every fiber of her being.

That disconcerting, analyzing gaze landed on hers once more. "I didn't see it coming. That's what I didn't do." He let go a heavy breath, then swallowed hard. The play of muscle beneath tanned skin momentarily distracted Kate from the question his words would have naturally prompted.

"I should have anticipated Dillon's move," he answered without her asking. Raine shook his head. "He killed Michael Ballatore right in front of me and I didn't have a clue what he was up to until it was too late."

"That's why Ballatore wants you dead," Kate realized out loud, talking more to herself than to Raine. "He thinks you killed his son." Somehow she had known that, too.

"That about sums it up," he agreed dispassionately.

"What are you going to do about it?" she prodded,

suddenly overwhelmed with the urge to develop a plan to
clear him. "You can't just keep running forever. He won't
stop sending men after you. Even if you kill Dillon, Ballatore will just send someone else." Fear snaked around
Kate's heart. She knew without a doubt that her summation
was accurate. Sal Ballatore was not the kind of man who
ever gave up. Raine needed a plan—she needed a plan.

"I have to set the record straight," he said in that cold,
emotionless voice that sent a different kind of shiver danc-
ing up Kate's spine. She didn't like that side of Raine.
*He's spent the last twelve years of his life living on the
edge...*

"How do you propose to do that?" she asked, shaking
her head to clear it of the now too-familiar voice. She
didn't want to remember anything else. Raine's plan
wasn't exactly the kind of plan she had in mind. "It's not
like you can call up his secretary and make an appointment."

One corner of his sensuous mouth kicked up into a
wicked tilt. "I don't plan to make an appointment."

Kate's mouth dropped open, and she quickly snapped it
shut, then made a sound of skepticism, half sigh, half
chuckle. "You said yourself that Ballatore has an army of
trained killers like Dillon on his side; just what do you
have?"

Raine cocked his head and allowed that one-sided tilt to
widen into a grin. "*I* have the element of surprise."

"I CAN'T BELIEVE you're doing this," Kate hissed. She
glared at Raine through the darkness of the car's interior.
A shaft of dim light from a nearby street lamp highlighted
the angles of his handsome profile. She shouldn't let him
do it. But how could she stop him?

"It's the only way, Kate," he told her again. The words
weren't any more convincing this time than they had been

the other two times he'd repeated them. A muscle twitched in his tense jaw. She knew he'd become impatient with her resistance to his strategy, but she just couldn't help protesting what could only be called suicidal. No more than she could help the way she felt...

She cared too much. And she knew deep in her heart that when this was all over—when she had her memory back—things would never be the same. He would hate her for lying to him. Trust was a matter Raine took deadly serious. Of course, none of that would matter if the damn fool got himself killed tonight.

"What I can't believe is that I let you talk me into allowing you to come along," he said incredulously.

"Like you could have stopped me," Kate retorted.

Raine tossed her a look that spoke louder than words. The real decision had been his and she knew it.

Kate exhaled a burst of helpless frustration that had been hampering her ability to take a deep breath for the last ten hours. Raine had driven nine of those hours with only one stop for refueling before they entered the city of New York. Now they sat in his black Range Rover less than a block from Sal Ballatore's East Side estate. And there was nothing, short of shooting Raine herself, that she could do to stop what was about to take place.

"Dillon was right." Kate breathed the words into the tense stillness. "You are a dead man walking. You believe you have nothing to lose, so you don't think twice about taking a risk like this." Ice-cold fingers of dread nudged at Kate. Raine had a death wish and he was about to make it a reality.

Raine shifted to face her, leather squeaked beneath faded denim. That glimmer of light spread across his full lips and intense blue eyes now. "The old man won't kill me until he hears what I have to say."

"And if he doesn't believe you?" Kate couldn't mask

the fear in her voice. She didn't want Raine to die. Damn him! He'd made her have…all these feelings, and she wasn't prepared to let him go just yet—even if they had no future together.

"Kate—"

"What if Dillon is here?" she demanded, cutting off whatever he would have said.

"Dillon won't be here," Raine assured her. His voice had taken on a placating tone she'd heard only once before—when they had made love on the cold ground beneath the sun's warm kiss.

"Dillon and I were the only two people in the room when Michael died. He's as guilty as I am in Ballatore's eyes. That's why he was ordered to find me. Failure would be a death sentence. He won't come back until he eliminates the possibility that Ballatore might hear my side of the story. This is the last place Dillon will expect me to show up."

Kate searched his eyes, hoping against hope that she might actually be able to read his true feelings. But Raine was too good at hiding things. "Is there any chance Ballatore will believe you?"

Raine lifted one shoulder in a halfhearted shrug. "Maybe."

"Maybe?" Kate shook her head. "How can you walk in there knowing that you'll probably never walk out again?"

"I don't have a choice." Raine fixed her with a gaze that chilled Kate to the bone. "If Ballatore backs off, then it'll be just Dillon and me. Dillon has information I need."

"Information? About the money?" As soon as the words were out of her mouth, Kate recognized the stupidity of them. None of this was about the money.

When he didn't respond immediately, she said, "Who are you, Raine?" That was the missing link. Raine was the key. The realization hit Kate with sudden, amazing clarity. She needed him alive for more than one reason. She needed him to complete her *assignment*. ''You can't go in there,'' she managed to say despite the sensations and voices whirling inside her head.

''If I'm not back in one hour, drive until you find a pay phone and call Lucas.'' Raine pressed a folded piece of paper into her trembling hand. ''He's your only shot at getting out of this mess alive.''

Lucas Camp. Kate stared first at the small white square, then back at the man who had placed it in her hand. ''Do you trust Lucas?'' *There's only one person I trust, Kate, and that's me.* Raine's words joined the medley of others inside her head.

He exhaled and cast a glance in the direction of Ballatore's dark house. ''If Lucas can't be trusted, there's no one else.''

Raine didn't give her a chance to ask anything else, he slid his hand around her nape and pulled her mouth to his. Kate didn't fight him, instead she melted into his kiss. His taste filled her, sent heat straight to her center where it bloomed and spread throughout her body. She couldn't deny her need for him any more than she could deny the truth that was unfolding inside her and around them. Though the facts were still vague, Kate knew he was right—they were enemies, or, at the very least, on opposing sides in all this insanity. But none of that mattered when he kissed her.

Raine pulled back all too soon. Before Kate could protest, he had opened the driver's-side door, gotten out and was disappearing into the darkness on the other side of the street. She strained to make out his form moving toward the iron gate that guarded the entrance to Ballatore's property. She watched for several minutes, but there was no further sign of Raine.

…he's an infiltrator. He can get in and out of places no one else can.

Right now, Kate hoped with all her heart that Raine really was the best in the business.

RAINE HAD ONLY to wait until the perimeter guard made his rounds. Twice an hour, one guard walked the grounds inside the security fence and another outside. The one outside could always be counted on to be the newest and probably the youngest member of the security staff. He would be considered the most expendable, and walking outside the fence certainly represented the greatest risk to surviving night shift.

While he waited he considered the chance he had taken bringing Kate along. But he couldn't leave her as he had planned. Though it pained him to believe that she might be working for the enemy, he had to trust his instincts. Instinct told him not to risk her alerting *anyone* to his plans. Outside locking her up or killing her—and he could not do either—he'd had no choice but to bring her. He never took that kind of risk—he wouldn't now. No matter that some small foolish part of him wanted to take Kate and run. Leave it all behind. Disappear where no one would ever find them. Raine silently laughed at himself. *Great plan.* The only problem was, what happened when she got her memory back?

Before Raine could consider the answer to that question, the guard stopped to check the side gate. Raine pressed the barrel of his Beretta against the man's temple and stepped out of the shadows. "Take me to the old man," he said quietly.

The guard tensed. Raine could imagine the man's short life was passing before his eyes at that precise moment. "I can't do that," he replied in a clipped tone. "You could blow my head off for all they care, man, and they still wouldn't let you in.''

Raine clenched his jaw, then forced himself to relax. ''Just tell them Jack Raine is here to see Mr. Ballatore.''

A few minutes later Raine stood in Sal Ballatore's private study. No one had roughed him up as he had fully expected. The head of security had thoroughly searched him, however, and taken his Beretta, but other than that, things had gone rather smoothly. Raine was alone now. Four men waited outside the closed doors to do Ballatore's bidding. There would be others somewhere inside and at least two still patrolling the grounds. There was always a minimum of eight men on duty. The old man had grown a bit paranoid in his twilight years.

Of course, in this business, operating a crime syndicate in a city the size of New York, it paid to be a little on the paranoid side.

A sense of déjà vu shrouded Raine with memories of another night much like this one. The night he'd had to pass Ballatore's personal inspection. As sharp as the old man was, he had accepted Raine almost without question. But that was what he did best, Raine reminded himself. He made people trust him. At one time that particular skill had meant a great deal to him. Now it only disgusted him.

Raine turned at the sound of the opening door. He felt the muscle in his jaw jump when his gaze met Ballatore's. The loss of his only son evidenced itself in every line on his face, but the eyes were the worst. Those gray eyes no longer held the spark of life, or the power that had once radiated from their world-wise depths. They were empty. Regret, unbidden, trickled through Raine. He had experienced remorse over few things in his life, but he truly regretted the senseless death of Michael Ballatore.

Sal Ballatore, clad in silk pajamas and matching robe,

crossed the room to stand directly in front of Raine. He held Raine's weapon in his right hand.

"Dillon and my men have been searching for you for quite some time now." He lifted one gray eyebrow a fraction higher than the other. "How is it that in all this time they could not find you, yet you waltz into my home in the middle of the night of your own free will?"

"I didn't come here to discuss the lack of skill possessed by the men you employ," Raine told him, careful to keep his tone as unrevealing as his gaze. "I was told that you wanted to ask me a question. I've driven all night for this little tête-à-tête, so let's get on with it."

"You never were one to waste time on idle chitchat," Ballatore noted aloud, then focused his attention on the weapon in his hand. "Before I end your worthless life, I would like you to tell me why you killed my son." The old man's voice wavered slightly when he continued. "Michael was a good boy, and he did not deserve to die by your hand, Jack Raine." He lifted his gaze back to Raine, something primal shifted in those lackluster eyes.

Vengeance. Raine recognized and understood the desire for vengeance that suddenly filled that empty gaze.

"I despise killing." Ballatore grimaced. "It's so messy, especially when you shoot a man in the head with a weapon like this at close range." He glanced around the elegant study then. "But Michael was born in this room." He smiled, remembering. "His mother waited too long before she told me it was time to go. So my son took his first breath right here in this study. And you—" his gaze lit on Raine once more "—will take your last here."

"I did not kill Michael," Raine offered quietly, firmly.

Contempt stole across Ballatore's grief-stricken features. "You are a liar," he spat. "I know who you are, Jack Raine, and you killed my son. You and that bastard government you work for!"

"Dillon killed Michael for the money," Raine countered.

"*You* took the money. Danny and Vinny have attested to that fact." Rage darkened his cheeks. "*My* money."

"I took the money only to keep Dillon from taking it." Raine opened his hand and held out a small brass key. "It's in a locker at the Port Authority bus terminal."

Ballatore slapped away the key with the back of his hand. "You think you can come here and buy redemption with my own money?"

Raine allowed his hand to drop to his side. "I don't need your absolution, old man, I didn't kill your son. I only came here to set the record straight."

"You came here all those months ago," Ballatore growled, "to destroy my family. You ingratiated yourself into this household and then you destroyed my only flesh and blood." His body trembled with the rage Raine could see building in his eyes. "*You* were like a second son to me. I trusted you with my life—with Michael's life." Ballatore shook his head slowly from side to side. "First you betrayed my trust, then you killed my son."

"I came here *for you,* old man, not your son," Raine said pointedly. "The organization that hired me had no interest in Michael. Dillon killed your son. Somehow Dillon found out who I was and used that knowledge as an opportunity to make himself a couple million and to get rid of me at the same time." Raine leaned closer to the shorter man. "Think about it. With Michael and me out of the way, that puts Dillon at the top of the food chain."

Ballatore considered Raine's words for several long, tense moments before he spoke. "Why should I believe what you say?" His eyes narrowed as he scrutinized Raine's face for the truth in the response he was about to give.

"I could have taken your money and disappeared."

Raine held his gaze. "And, trust me, you and your men would never have found me."

"You don't want my money and you didn't kill my son, so why are you here?" Though some of his conviction had dissolved, sarcasm still weighted Ballatore's tone.

"I want Dillon. He has information that I need."

Realization dawned in the aged gray eyes. "You want to know who sold you out?"

"That's right," Raine agreed.

Ballatore snorted his disbelief. "What does it matter? Your cover is blown for this operation. Why do you care?"

"I can't walk away knowing that someone might be selling out others like me."

The old man nodded then. "Ah, I see. You think I give one damn what happens to the others like you?"

"No, but I'm sure you want to punish the man who killed your son."

"And you want me to believe that it wasn't you?" He smirked. "Again I ask, why should I believe you?"

"Because I'm telling the truth."

Ballatore regarded Raine warily for another beat or two. His expression slowly relaxed, as did his posture, and finally he spoke again. "What do you want from me?"

"I want Dillon," Raine said simply.

The older man's chin went up a notch, unaccustomed to acquiescing to anyone's demands. "You ask a great deal for a man whose life means nothing to me, and who has less than nothing to offer in return."

Raine mentally acknowledged his new standing with Ballatore. He hadn't come here tonight to make amends. He'd come, Raine reiterated silently, to set things straight with the old man and to set up Dillon. "You asked what I wanted, that's what I want," he replied.

Ballatore lifted his silk-covered shoulders and then

dropped them in a careless shrug. "That could be arranged."

A new surge of adrenaline rushed through Raine, anticipation of the hunt. "You keep this meeting quiet for the next twenty-four hours. I'll call in a location for you to pass along to Dillon. Tell him I've asked for a meet to explain what really happened. When he comes for me, I'll be ready."

The old man's gaze locked with Raine's once more. "There are two conditions."

Raine's tension escalated to a new level.

"When you have extracted your information, Dillon is mine." He paused long enough for Raine to absorb the impact of the statement. "And, you tell your people that the next man they send for me will die a slow and painful death. Salvador Ballatore doesn't make the same mistake twice."

Raine nodded, then extended his open hand. "Done."

Ballatore placed the butt of the Beretta into Raine's palm. "Good. Maria will be glad." He gave a short, wry chuckle. "There will be no mess for her to clean up in here tomorrow."

His relief near-palpable, Raine tucked the Beretta into his waistband at the small of his back. "I'll contact you in the next twenty-four hours." He gave Ballatore one final glance, then strode toward the door.

"One more thing." The voice of the man who still held Raine's life in his hands echoed across the room.

Raine paused at the door and turned back to face him.

"Find a new line of work, Jack Raine. This one will get you killed."

Chapter Eleven

Kate sat in the near darkness of the hotel room and watched Raine sleep. It was the first time she had actually seen the man with his guard down completely. She remembered thinking that maybe he was a machine and didn't have such basic needs as sleep. She smiled and hugged the cool sheet more tightly around her naked body. She definitely knew better now. Raine was all too human. He had needs. Needs so strong they were almost frightening. Like her own. She shivered at the thought of how important he had become to her in the last few days. More important to her than remembering the truth about who she was and why she had been sent to find him.

When Raine had returned to the truck, alive and unharmed, from his meeting with Ballatore, Kate had been beside herself with relief. She had no idea if in her past life she'd been a spiritual person or even attended church, but she had thanked God over and over the moment Raine had appeared out of the darkness.

Raine hadn't given any details about the meeting, only that everything was set. Whatever that meant. Then he had driven straight to a hotel in Manhattan, checked into a room and dragged her into bed before she could so much as get a good look at the place. Like the first time, their lovemaking had been hot and frantic, neither of them taking the time to undress, only pulling down or pushing aside the absolute essentials.

Kate had sensed his desperation, the same desperation she felt even now, that this might be the last time they were together. The unrestrainable instinct to celebrate life and survival when mortality threatened. She could have resisted and he would have stopped, but she hadn't. Instead, she'd urged him on with her own frenzied response.

Afterward Raine seemed to regret that he had taken her so crudely, with no pretty words or proper foreplay. As if to make up for his actions, he'd gently removed her disheveled clothing, then carried her to the bathroom, where they had showered together. Slowly, chastely, he had washed every square inch of her body. Later, when he'd tenderly tucked her into the wide, inviting bed, Kate had given in to the exhaustion almost immediately.

Surprised at finding Raine asleep when she had awakened, Kate had pulled the sheet around her and moved to a chair so she could watch him. Dawn was still hours away, but the soft glow of light from the bathroom filtered through the room's darkness and caressed his bare chest. The ivory brocade coverlet concealed his lower body, leaving the rest for her admiration. His strong arms were flung over his head and draped across the pillow. Kate's gaze slid over his handsome profile and down his tanned throat, across his muscled chest, and then down the lean terrain of his stomach. His navel peeked above the edge of the rich cloth.

Kate's insides warmed from just looking at him. She had no memory of making love before Raine, but she could not imagine anyone else making her feel quite the way he did.

But they had no future together. Though she still didn't know all the details, Kate knew enough to be certain about where she would stand when Raine discovered the truth.

Would the man, who had made love to her only a few short hours ago, kill her when he found out she had been sent to find him? To bring him in?

As she scanned his beautifully sculpted body once more, she decided that in repose he looked almost vulnerable. But Jack Raine was anything but vulnerable.

Dangerous. A man who lived by a different set of rules.

"See anything you like?"

Kate's breath caught when her errant gaze collided with eyes so blue and piercing they seemed to reach past her defenses and touch a place no one else could. Longing welled inside her, shoving away all other thoughts.

She managed a smile despite the blood roaring in her ears and the tremble of her lips. "I see a good many things I like," she told him.

Raine threw back the cover and stood in one fluid motion. Kate's heart lurched when he moved toward her. His body was already, *or still,* semi-aroused. She shivered when she considered the mild discomfort associated with his size. He was a big man, his body strong and powerful. In the brief moments required for Raine to take the three steps separating them, her body moistened in anticipation of the desire evidencing itself in his.

Raine crouched in front of her and pressed his lips to hers. The kiss was lingering, undemanding. Kate's fingers found their way into his tousled blond hair and she urged him closer. With her movement, the sheet fell away from her shoulders, freeing her breasts so that her nipples grazed his bare chest. Desire stung her core and Kate moaned low in her throat, the sound echoed between them, intensifying her need.

He broke the kiss, pulling back despite her groan of protest. Kate frowned her frustration that their lips were no longer touching. He smiled, the expression wicked and insanely sexy. "This time's going to be different," he assured her. His deep, sensual tone raised goose bumps on Kate's skin.

Raine stood and offered his hand. When she placed her hand in his and rose, the sheet slid down her body to puddle around her ankles. His gaze followed that same route, leaving a fission of heat wherever it lingered. Kate stepped into his open arms and he pulled her against him, maintaining the contact of their bodies as he eased her down onto the bed.

"This time," he said, pausing to place a kiss along her throat between each word, "we're going to do this right." When he reached her collarbone, he lifted his head to smile down at her and repeated, "So right."

The utter sweetness of that smile touched a place deep inside her. Kate closed her eyes and absorbed the impact to her heart. She loved this man. There was no denying it now. Whether they were enemies or not, whether she lived or died come sunrise, she loved Jack Raine. No matter who she was or what he had done in the past, nothing could change how she felt.

Not even a husband.

Honey, it's Nick.

Kate tensed, her eyes flew open. That man's voice. The one who had answered when she'd called the number…he'd called her *honey*. What if she did have a husband, children?

"What's wrong?"

Only when he spoke did Kate become aware that the tantalizing movement of his lips on her skin had stopped. She blinked rapidly to mask the fear of uncertainty in her eyes as he moved back up to lie alongside her. He propped on one elbow and swept a wisp of hair back from her cheek with his fingertips.

"What's wrong?" he repeated.

Kate forced her lips into a tremulous smile, but quickly

averted her eyes from the ones examining her so closely. She focused on his broad chest. "I'm fine," she said, then struggled for something else to say when he remained silent, waiting. Her attention suddenly lit on one of the thin, jagged lines marring his tanned flesh. "I...was just wondering how you got these scars."

He chuckled, a short, breathy sound, then pressed a kiss to her temple. "Talking isn't exactly what I had on my mind, but if that's what you want to do..." His words trailed off as he captured her gaze, his own full of mischief but still hot with desire. "A few of those hundred men someone told you I'd killed didn't go down without a fight," he teased.

Kate felt suddenly helpless when faced with the reality that he had likely skated close to death numerous times. Her pulse quickened at the thought, panic tightened her chest. "What you do—" with the tip of her finger she traced one pale pattern that angled downward just beneath his right nipple "—is it always this dangerous?" Kate held her breath as she waited for the answer she already knew.

"Yes." There was no humor in his tone now.

She lifted her gaze to his. "Can you stop?" A knot of fear and uncertainty, as hard and cold as a rock, settled in Kate's stomach. "Can you just walk away?"

He searched her eyes for what felt like a lifetime, then moistened his lips and drew in a heavy breath. "No." The simple, one-syllable response tightened that knot of fear growing inside Kate.

Raine snuggled closer, offering the only thing he had to give, Kate realized. His warm, muscled body fit perfectly against hers. Hard angles and lean planes in all the right places to mesh with her fuller curves and softer valleys. There was no hiding just how much he wanted her, every hardened inch of him pressed against her hip. But he waited.

Kate shuddered at the rush of renewed need that surged through her at his patience. She wanted him so very much. Surely if she had a husband she would remember something about him. She didn't wear a ring and there had been nothing in her purse to indicate she was married, she rationalized. Everything inside her resisted the notion of children. She couldn't have children and not remember. Could a mother really forget her own child?

"Kate," he whispered, the deep timbre of his voice gliding over her like silk.

She studied his face, his chiseled jaw, those full sensuous lips before allowing her gaze to meet his. Kate braced herself for the intensity she would find there, and be unable to resist. "What if there's someone else?" She felt her frown deepen at the reaction she saw in his stormy blue eyes. Some unreadable emotion flickered fiercely but briefly before he banished it. "What if I have a husband?" she clarified softly.

A beat of silence passed, then those sinfully tempting lips slid into a wicked smile. "Then he's a fool for letting you out of his sight." He nipped at her lower lip, gently suckled it, then murmured, "Tonight you're mine, Kate."

She nodded, her breath catching as his lips moved along the line of her jaw toward the supersensitive curve of her neck. She didn't want to analyze the situation anymore, she only wanted to feel. Long fingers and a roughened palm skimmed over her heated flesh, touching, torturing, taking her body to a new level of desire. Urgent and exploratory, his hungry mouth moved lower. A wave of sensations splashed through Kate's body again and again, rising and then falling like the relentless pounding of the ocean against the shore. She arched her back, thrusting her breasts forward for his attention.

When his hot, moist mouth closed over one nipple, Kate cried out, the sound a primal plea of approval as well as a demand for more. His tongue flicked over her nipple, then slowly circled the straining, swollen peak before moving to her other breast. Her fingers threaded into his golden hair and held him in place as he drew on her more strongly. Kate writhed with pleasure at the intensified assault. His hand traced a path down her rib cage and across her abdomen, his tantalizing tongue followed, hesitating briefly at her belly button to dip repeatedly inside. The cool brush of his fingertips sent pleasant jolts through Kate. Her body arched instinctively when he parted her thighs and tangled his fingers in the triangle of hair there.

"Raine," she gasped. Anything else she would have said, as well as coherent thought, evaporated when one long finger slid along the part of her feminine folds, and then slipped inside. Colored lights pulsed behind Kate's lids as he tortured her intimately with those skilled fingers. His lips caressed the curve of her hip, her mound, his tongue darting out to scorch her shivering flesh. Kate moaned her surrender to the urgent desire. Her concentration focused inward as her tremors began. The gentle quakes vibrated from her center outward. She cried his name again when the burning sweetness erupted into full-body shudders and stole her breath.

Kate was vaguely aware of him moving over her, but the vortex of erotic sensations would not allow her to open her eyes. The scent of his clean, masculine body filled her with a sense of completeness and well-being. She reached for him, circling his lean waist with her arms and drawing him closer, until his strong body covered hers and she could feel his ragged breath on her face. "Raine," she murmured, her lips brushing whisper-soft against his. "There's no one else but you." And in that ethereal moment she knew the words were true.

His mouth claimed hers as his weight crushed down on her, pressing her into the softness of the mattress beneath them. His tongue swept into her mouth at the same instant that he entered her in one long, powerful thrust, filling her, possessing her. Her body stretched to accommodate him, her feminine muscles contracting as she exploded once more around him. She was his and he was hers in an elemental way that no power on earth could change. When he moved against her, within her, everything else ceased to exist.

Raine took her to the pinnacle yet a third time, and this time he followed her into oblivion, bursting inside her with his own hot, sweet release. Kate clung to him, stunned by the intensity of the moment, frightened by what she felt in her heart. She could feel his heart pounding against his chest, echoing hers. Had he felt it too? Tears welled in her eyes when she considered the foolishness of that thought. How could she possibly mean anything to a man like him?

Raine rested his forehead against hers. ''Are you all right?''

Since she didn't trust her voice, she nodded, though she was anything but all right. He rolled to his back, pulling Kate close against him as he did. She fought the almost overwhelming urge to cry—to sob—in his arms. Oh God, how could she have fallen in love with this man? A man who would surely walk away from her if he didn't get himself killed first. As if sensing her distress, Raine's arms tightened around her and he held her that way, until her breathing slowed and sleep claimed her.

RAINE TRANSFERRED the white bag containing the coffee he'd picked up in the restaurant downstairs to his left hand and checked the Glock beneath his jacket. When the elevator doors slid open he stepped out onto the sixth floor and headed toward the room where he'd left Kate sleeping.

He had dreaded this moment for most of the night. After Kate had fallen asleep in his arms, he had spent endless hours kicking himself for allowing her so close. What he and Kate had shared had gone way beyond lust and mere physical need. He was in hazardous, uncharted territory now. Territory he'd sworn he would never allow himself to stumble into. Jack Raine didn't need anyone. He never had. He'd always done his job, taken what he wanted and walked away. Nothing more. No strings, no complications.

He couldn't change now, no matter how his insides twisted at the thought of leaving Kate behind. It was for her own good, and he had no choice in the matter. She would realize that soon enough. Taking down Dillon and revealing the mole in Lucas's organization was a mission he could not walk away from—he'd never walked away from a mission, even one he'd taken upon himself. If he survived, he would count himself lucky. The odds were stacked heavily against him, and the risk was only increased by his strong personal involvement. Though it was a risk he would have to take, there was no way in hell he would risk Kate's life.

No way, he repeated silently as he slid the key card into the slot near the door's handle. She would forget him in no time at all. And maybe there was a Mr. Roberts waiting somewhere out there for her. Someone who had a nice safe life to offer her.

Raine swallowed tightly. The idea of Kate with another man—any man—turned him inside out. If his instincts were right about her, though, the sooner they parted ways the better. He couldn't be sure who she worked for, but there was little doubt left in his mind that her appearance at his door was not coincidental.

Ignoring the lock's blinking green light, Raine clenched his jaw at the reality of his "relationship" with Kate. No one had ever gotten this close to him before. The fact that she had, and under increasingly suspicious circumstances, attested to his total loss of perspective. But he couldn't leave her behind until he was sure she would be safe and unable to interfere with his plans. Now was the time. In just a few hours it would all be over—one way or another. Selfishly, Raine had taken one last night with her…one final taste of her lips. He closed his eyes and remembered the smell of her hair…the sound of her voice. He would always remember.

But now he had to go.

To leave her behind, the way he should have done in the first place.

Raine reinserted the key card, pushed the door open and entered the room. Bright morning sun poured in through the open drapes. Kate was up. He hadn't wanted to wake her when he'd gone down to the parking garage. He needed to retrieve the Glock from its hiding place behind the truck's back seat. He planned to leave his Beretta with Kate. He surveyed the room. His gaze settled on the closed bathroom door as it opened and Kate stepped out.

Though she was fully clothed in jeans and a T-shirt, her hair was still damp and Raine could smell her freshly showered scent clear across the room. The sight of her shifted something entirely too close to his heart.

"Morning," he said, and gave her his best attempt at a smile. He wasn't very good at this sort of thing. He didn't have a lot of practice at explaining himself, or dealing with the unfamiliar compulsion to do so. He extended the bag he held in her direction. "Coffee?"

She approached him cautiously, the expression in her dark brown eyes wary. "Where have you been? I thought…"

She didn't have to say the rest. She thought he'd left her. Just like back at the house when she'd come out to the barn looking for him. And, just like then, leaving her was exactly what he intended to do. Only this time, he would. Raine ignored the alien sensation in the pit of his stomach that accompanied that line of thinking.

When she didn't accept the coffee, he strode across the room to the table. "There was something I needed in the truck," he told her as he removed the two disposable cups from the bag. She moved to his side, his body reacted instantly to her nearness.

"I thought you'd left without saying goodbye," she explained softly.

He crushed the bag into a wad and tossed it aside, then held one of the cups out to her. "I told you I wouldn't do that," he replied without allowing his gaze to meet hers.

Kate accepted the cup this time. She padded across the lush carpet to the other side of the table and sat down. She pretended to be relaxed, but was far from it. The rigid set of her shoulders and the overprotective way she held her cup spoke volumes. She'd weaved her long brown hair into a braid. Her T-shirt hugged her firm, round breasts. The jeans she wore were a little loose now. She'd lost a few pounds on this trip, and that bothered Raine. He should have taken better care of her. A ghost of a smile touched his lips when he considered the delicious curves and contours that lay beneath those ill-fitting jeans. Vivid images of their lovemaking had haunted him all morning. The creamy, soft feel of her skin, the way her silky hair felt between his fingers, the way her body—snug and hot— welcomed him so completely.

Averting his gaze, Raine forced himself to sip his coffee. He had to think clearly this morning. He had already decided on a place right here in New York to meet Dillon, and he had informed Ballatore. This city was as much Raine's home turf as any other place. The memory of making love with Kate at his house in Virginia invaded his concentration, but he quickly shut it out. He'd had high hopes when he'd bought the place, but it didn't really seem to matter all that much anymore. He'd always been a loner, but now the thought of living in that house alone held no appeal. Assuming he stayed alive beyond the next twenty-four hours to need a place to live, he ruminated.

Raine took another long sip of the warm, dark liquid. Right now he had to focus on the mission. Tomorrow would take care of itself, it always had.

"You didn't say much about your meeting with Ballatore," Kate reminded him quietly.

You were like a second son to me. Raine could still hear the hint of pain in the old man's voice, see the deep sadness in his eyes. Maybe Raine had allowed Ballatore a little closer than he had planned as well. He shook his head. He was definitely getting too soft for this business. Maybe that's why he hadn't seen Dillon coming, and hadn't been able to keep Kate at arm's length. At least the old man had been right about one thing, this line of work could definitely get him killed.

"Raine?"

He jerked to attention, his gaze focusing back on Kate. She'd asked about the meeting. "I accomplished my goal," he hedged. She already knew too much, he wasn't about to give her anything else that could be used against him.

Kate set her cup on the table and stood. "You told me that part already," she said impatiently. "I want to know if he believed you when you told him that you didn't kill his son."

Raine set his own cup down and leveled his gaze on hers. "If he hadn't, I'd be dead right now."

Kate flinched. "I don't understand," she murmured as she brushed a loose tendril of hair from her cheek. "Why would he believe you over Dillon?"

"Just lucky I guess," Raine retorted, aiming for flippant.

Her eyes narrowed suspiciously as she shook her head slowly from side to side. "No, I don't think so. I think there was something more to your relationship with Ballatore."

Raine rounded the table and pinned her with his most intimidating stare. Her accusation struck a little too close to home. "I get close to people, Kate. I make them trust me." He leaned nearer and her eyes widened slightly. "I infiltrated Ballatore's organization first, then his family. If Dillon hadn't blown my cover, I would have taken the old man down no matter what our relationship." He felt a muscle contract in his jaw when he paused. "That's what I do. And I'm very good at what I do."

Kate blinked, her dark eyes misty. "Is that what we've been about?" She swallowed visibly. "Getting close and making me trust you?"

The hurt in her eyes had the effect of an unexpected kick in the stomach. How could he have allowed himself to get in this deep? He'd sworn he wouldn't. Denial of her charge burned in his chest, but he ruthlessly tamped it down. This was the turning point. He recognized the necessity of what he had to do, despite the fierce desire to do just the opposite. He had lived on the edge for far too long. He had worked to gain trust and then betrayed it too many times in the name of God and country. He couldn't change now. Spend too many years with the scum of the earth and you become like them, Raine reminded himself.

He had to remember that Kate was most likely his enemy in all this. Raine just had no way of knowing which of his enemies had sent her. But he knew for certain that she was not like him. Maybe she was new to the business or maybe she was simply being used by someone to get to Raine. Whatever the case, he recognized the innocence in Kate that he had long ago lost to the world of deceit in which he lived. She would have plenty of regrets when she regained her memory. She would hate him then for taking advantage of her vulnerability. It would be better for her to believe that, he decided. Let her believe that he was the ruthless bastard of which his reputation boasted.

"Was last night just part of what you do?"

Raine struggled with his conscience—the one he hadn't even realized existed until he met Kate. "You don't want to know the answer to that," he lied, drawing the necessary line in the sand.

She quickly masked the flicker of hurt in her eyes, then lifted her chin in defiance of his indifference. "I guess that makes me as big a fool as Ballatore," she suggested, her voice lacking any kind of inflection. "I suppose that since Ballatore obviously believed you—considering you're not dead—now you have his blessings to go after Dillon?"

Raine ignored her question. He stepped past her to the bed, reached beneath the pillow he had used and removed the Beretta he'd hidden there. "Take this." He offered the weapon to Kate, but she only glared at him. Raine captured her hand and forced her to take the weapon. "You'll be safe here. The room is guaranteed with a credit card that can't be traced back to me." He held her wrist tighter when she would have jerked away. "Don't go out for anything. Use room service for whatever you need."

"How long do you expect me to stay here?"

"As long as it takes," he said, impatient with her resistance, as well as with his own ridiculous emotions.

"Once you walk out that door, what's to keep me from doing the same?" she retorted hotly.

Raine yanked her closer, anger overriding all else. "If you want to stay alive, you'll stay put until this is over."

"Dillon will do whatever it takes to kill you, you know that, don't you?" The hurt was back in her eyes now. She was afraid for him—another unfamiliar and unexpected glitch.

"I know," Raine replied quietly. He released her, then blew out a disgusted breath. He was a fool. He had swallowed the bait, hook, line and sinker. Kate's inadvertent amnesia only made her more effective against him. No one had ever held this much power over him. Raine swallowed, hard. But that wouldn't stop him from doing what he had to do.

"And that doesn't matter? Why can't you let Ballatore settle the score with Dillon? The mission you were assigned is over!"

"You don't know all there is to know," he argued in spite of himself. Why didn't he just leave?

"Well, fill me in," she demanded. She braced one hand on her hip, the Beretta hanging loosely at her side from the other.

Raine closed his mind, his heart, to what she wanted from him. She was hurt and confused. She wanted him to tell her everything would be all right, but he couldn't. And he shouldn't care, but, damn him, he did. "I can't do that," he said simply, allowing the coldness of his tone to speak for itself.

"Can't or won't?" she countered.

"Take your pick." Raine plowed his fingers through his hair and looked away. He didn't have time for this, and he sure as hell couldn't bear to watch the hurt in her eyes a moment longer. "I have to go now. If you'll follow my instructions you'll be safe." He turned and started toward the door, a sick feeling eating at his gut despite the knowledge that he was doing the right thing—taking the steps necessary to ensure her safety as well as the success of his mission.

"You're not coming back, are you?"

The faint glimmer of desperate hope in her voice stopped him halfway to his destination. He closed his eyes and willed away the emotions twisting inside him. He shouldn't feel any of this. "No," he admitted, brutally squashing that tiny seed of hope to which he knew she still clung.

"And if I try to stop you?"

Raine turned around slowly to face her. Her grip tightened on the Beretta, but she made no move to take aim. *Don't do this, Kate.* No way could he bring himself to hurt her. Pushing aside the unfamiliar emotions that bound him to Kate, he reached deep inside until he found that desolate place where he felt nothing at all. "Attempting to stop me would be a mistake."

Silence screamed around them for several tense seconds before she spoke again. "I can't let you go."

Despite having fully anticipated this possibility, betrayal stung Raine. He almost laughed out loud. The great Jack Raine, who made a career out of betrayal, had just gotten his in spades. What a fool he was.

Kate lifted her right arm, holding the Beretta like a practiced professional. A cold emptiness stealing through him, Raine watched her determined stride as she moved toward him.

She stopped directly in front of him, a bead dead center of his chest, her gaze locked on his. "I won't let you go."

"Don't leave the room," he told her again, as if she'd said nothing at all, as if the weapon were not in her hand and aimed at his heart. "I'll call to let you know when it's safe to leave. Don't believe anything until you hear it from me."

"I said," she repeated, "I'm not letting you walk out that door."

"Then shoot me." Raine turned his back on her, took the final steps to the door and walked out without looking back.

Chapter Twelve

Kate stood in the middle of the hotel room with nothing but the echo of the closing door to break the absolute silence. He was gone. Her entire body shook from the receding fear and adrenaline. She glanced at the gun in her hand. Could she have stopped him? No, not without using the gun, and she knew she couldn't and wouldn't have done that. Would she? Fear and confusion twisted inside her. She blinked, feeling as if she was coming out of some sort of trance. Why did she draw the weapon on him in the first place? Is that what she was supposed to do? Stop him? She frowned, trying with all her might to remember.

What did it matter now anyway? He was gone.

Kate blinked again, then slowly surveyed the luxurious room. Without Raine's presence, previously insignificant details seemed to rush in on her all at once. The crystal chandelier hanging overhead. The lavish arrangement of fresh-cut flowers setting on the mantel above the marble fireplace. The lush burgundy carpet and drapes with gold intricately woven throughout. The perfectly coordinated French provincial furniture. And the wide inviting bed with its ivory brocade coverlet and tangled sheets still scented with their lovemaking.

...he needs protection.

Kate drew in a shuddering breath. She had to go after

him. *The assignment.* She had to salvage this assignment. *…to bring him in either way.* Kate raced across the room and fumbled with the lock on the door.

Don't go out for anything. Raine's words slammed into her head, stilling her trembling fingers on the ornate gold lever that would disengage the dead bolt. Kate squeezed her eyes shut against the confusion, against the words and voices churning in her head.

What should she do?

She pressed her forehead to the door's cool surface and willed herself to relax, willed the panic rising inside her to retreat. Her heart thumped frantically in her rib cage, ignoring the command to slow.

Her medicine, she needed her medicine. With all that had happened since their arrival at the hotel, Kate had forgotten to take the little blue pill that kept her heart condition under control. Her condition—the bane of her existence. Kate opened her eyes and exhaled shakily. She straightened and pushed away from the door.

Smooth move, Robertson, she chastised as she retraced her steps across the room and located her purse. Kate froze, the prescription bottle in her hand.

Robertson? Kate frowned as the name whirled around her like a tiny tornado. Katherine Robertson. Katherine. Katie. Her father called her Katie. But she preferred to go by Katherine, it sounded more professional.

Adrenaline rushing through her, Kate set the pills aside and dug through the purse until she came up with her driver's license. Anticipation pulling at her, she studied the picture, then the name listed. Why would she be using the name Kate Roberts if her real name was Katherine Robertson?

That wouldn't keep someone from using you to get to me. Raine was right. Her own suspicions were right on the mark. She had been sent to find him…to get close to him.

And to bring him in. That was her assignment. But she'd failed. Though she had no idea who had sent her, the fact that she had failed—failed miserably—resurrected a pain that was all too familiar. It squeezed at her already tight chest. Tears stung her eyes. She was a failure. *Again.*

Kate clenched her jaw against the self-pity that threatened. Her inability to get the job done didn't matter right now. What mattered was that Raine was about to get himself killed while she stood around feeling sorry for herself.

"Damn," she hissed, throwing the bottle against the wall. Kate closed her eyes and rubbed at her forehead with the heels of both hands. Losing it wasn't going to help. Reaching for calm, she crossed the room and snatched up the bottle and twisted off the cap. Pill in hand, she trudged to the sideboard and poured water from the crystal decanter into a matching goblet. After taking her medication, Kate stared into the large, gilt-framed mirror hanging on the wall.

"Who the hell are you?" she muttered to the familiar yet strangely alien woman staring back at her. Kate placed the ornate goblet on the silver tray and turned her back to the puzzling reflection that seemed to mock her.

To her way of thinking she had two options. She could stay put as Raine had instructed or she could call for help. *Call in,* the voice she recognized as Aunt Vicky's urged. Kate concentrated hard on the voice of the woman who identified herself as Kate's aunt, but no further recognition came. Aunt Vicky was probably an alias. Maybe this Vicky person had hired Kate to find Raine. She couldn't take the chance that whoever sent her might be out to hurt Raine. Dillon and Vicky could be partners. Kate hadn't forgotten that Dillon had shown up at their motel in Charlottesville only hours after her call to *Aunt* Vicky.

No, Kate had to call someone Raine trusted. *If Lucas can't be trusted, there's no one else,* he'd said. Kate

reached into her jeans pocket and withdrew the slip of
paper that contained Lucas's number. Fear welled inside
her again as she studied the bold handwriting that belonged
to the man she loved. No matter that he would never want
to see her again, and certainly would never trust her again.
Somehow she had to help Raine. Lucas Camp was her only
hope.

TWO GUT-WRENCHING, hand-twisting hours passed before
the expected knock came. The gun in hand and her purse
strap looped over her shoulder, Kate jumped from her seat
and rushed to the door. She peered through the peephole
at the man standing on the other side. He was tall, dark-
haired, and he wore a suit. Kate frowned at his spit-and-
polished appearance. She'd somehow expected Lucas
Camp to be a little older, and a lot less stiff-looking. His
phone voice in no way matched his image.

When the man knocked again, Kate swallowed back her
indecision and summoned a businesslike tone. "Yes?"

"Miss Roberts, I'm Agent Hanson. Lucas sent me here
to see that you're escorted to a safe house," he said with
a definite air of authority.

Kate moistened her lips as she mulled over his voice.
He sounded trustworthy enough. "I need to see some ID,"
she told him, adhering to the side of caution.

"Of course." He reached inside his jacket and removed
the leather case containing a picture ID, which he held in
front of the peephole for her perusal.

Hanson, Zachary P., Agent, Special Operations. The ID
looked authentic enough, Kate decided. She had no choice
but to take the chance. It was the only shot she had at
helping Raine. With a deep bolstering breath she opened
the door, the gun still gripped firmly in her right hand.
Agent Hanson surveyed the room before stepping inside.

He turned to Kate and smiled. "You'll need your coat, Miss Roberts."

Kate nodded and started to turn away.

"I'll have to take that for you," he offered kindly as he reached for the gun she held. "Regulations," he explained when she hesitated.

For a moment Kate considered refusing to release the weapon, but what choice did she have? In his eyes she was an unknown factor, a loose cannon, she supposed. He probably didn't relish the idea of riding in a confined automobile with an armed woman. She would do the same if the situation were reversed. Kate allowed Agent Hanson to take Raine's Beretta, then retrieved her coat and preceded him out the door.

The trip to the lobby was made in silence. They stepped off the elevator and onto the white mosaic tile that stretched across the elegant lobby. A towering vase of fresh-cut flowers sat atop a pedestal table beneath a huge crystal chandelier that sprinkled shards of light over the shiny floor. Kate managed a smile for the blue-jacketed clerk as she passed the mahogany-paneled registration desk. A lush red runner carpeted the foyer and led the way past a security guard and through the brass revolving doors.

"This way, Miss Roberts," Agent Hanson said as he paused beneath the canopied marquee.

With another friendly smile, he led Kate to a dark sedan parked at the curb. The windows were tinted, making it impossible to see anyone who might be inside. Reminding herself that she was doing the right thing, Kate thanked him when he opened the door. She had just taken her seat and reached for the seat belt when someone spoke.

"Nice to see you again, Kate."

The air in her lungs evaporated as her senses absorbed,

analyzed and recognized the voice of the man who had spoken.

Dillon.

DUSK HAD ALREADY SETTLED before Raine entered the deserted warehouse. The place hadn't been used in years, and time and the elements were wearing on the huge structure. At one time the warehouses on this dock had been in high demand. But not so much anymore. Like several others along this stretch of waterfront, the one Raine had selected for his meeting with Dillon now amounted to nothing more than a crumbling relic of a different time and way of life.

Raine took up a position inside that would give him an unobstructed view of the entrance. A streetlight provided just enough illumination for him to see any comings and goings near the open door leading into the building. He checked the Glock under his jacket, then the cellular phone in his right pocket. The old man had insisted that Raine contact him immediately after his business with Dillon was complete, and since there were no working phones in the vicinity, Ballatore had provided a means of communication as well.

Raine never allowed himself to develop any sort of attachment to his assignments. He shook his head when he considered the strange relationship that had evolved between him and Sal Ballatore. Maybe it was because Raine had never known his own parents, and had spent his juvenile years in one foster home after the other. He and the old man'd had that in common.

Distrustful of relationships, just like Raine, Ballatore hadn't married until well past middle age. He was pushing seventy now, and his twenty-year-old son had been the light of his life. Raine supposed that being thirty-four, he had served somewhat as a generational bridge between the old man and his son. Michael had taken to Raine from the start. Raine almost smiled as he recalled the serious case of hero worship the kid had had. The reputation the agency had set up for Raine, too realistic and ruthless, had intrigued Michael.

Raine shifted against the cold invading his body. He pushed away any further thoughts of Ballatore or his son. That mission was over, and once Dillon had been taken care of, Raine and Ballatore would never have contact again. That was the way it was supposed to be—the way it had always been.

Permanent ties weren't a part of Raine's life, professional or personal. The only long-lasting relationship he had allowed was the one with Lucas, and it only bordered on friendship, staying for the most part a professional relationship. That suited Raine just fine. He'd never had any desire for long-term on a personal level.

As if to refute the thought, Kate's image filled his mind. Raine blinked to dispel the vivid mental picture, but she refused to go away. Those dark eyes, going even darker with desire for him. Those tempting lips that made him ache for another taste of her. And all that long, silky hair begging for his touch. No one had ever made him feel the way Kate did. The range of emotions that tightened his chest were so foreign, he felt at a complete loss to try to sort the tangle. How one woman could hold this kind of power over him baffled Raine.

He had never been in love with anyone, and he assured himself that he wasn't in love now. But the denial sat like a stone in his gut, and that annoyed him beyond reason. He felt responsible for Kate, protective even. But he didn't love her—he couldn't love her. Surely some skill was involved in an emotion that strong, and Raine had never mastered any such talents. This thing between him and Kate was nothing more than physical attraction complicated by her vulnerability. It just couldn't be anything else.

Besides, what kind of life could he offer a woman like her? She had a family somewhere, one that loved her like he wouldn't begin to know how to. She might already have a husband or boyfriend. His jaw tightened at the notion. He didn't want to think about that part of Kate's life. He would never see her again anyway. Like Ballatore, she would be just another part of Raine's murky past.

Kate didn't need a man like him anyway. He didn't know the first thing about family or any of those other forever kind of things. He lived from one mission to the next. Hell, he didn't even know if he could survive retirement. He had lived on the edge so long with nothing but adrenaline for a companion, that he wasn't even sure he could pull off a "normal" life.

Raine folded his arms over his chest to ward off the increasing chill that seemed to come more from inside him than from around him. Kate would be much better off without him. He knew it, and deep down she knew it or, at least, would come to realize it later. He hadn't intended to let their relationship go so far. She would have enough regrets when her memory returned. She would regret letting him walk out of that hotel room alive. Whether she had a boyfriend or husband or not, she would regret sleeping with Raine. He closed his eyes to block out that image.

Kate was better off without him.

He was better off without her.

Especially considering their entire relationship was built on lies. Nothing had been what it seemed. Raine laughed at himself. Was it ever?

The almost imperceptible squeak of leather drew Raine's full attention back to the door. Tension and adrenaline did their job as he reached for his Glock. Two seconds later a dark silhouette moved in the shadows just outside the circle of light bathing the entrance. Raine clenched his jaw when Dillon stepped into the light and proceeded through the open door as confidently as one who had already decided that this battle belonged to him.

Dillon was alone and that didn't sit well with Raine. Danny and Vinny were probably right outside, but Dillon wasn't a man who took unnecessary risks. And Dillon had a lot riding on this little showdown. Something didn't add up.

As though he owned the place and had absolutely nothing to fear, Dillon walked just beyond the reach of the light and waited, facing the entrance, his back to anything that might be lurking in the dark warehouse. Sensing a setup, Raine silently made his way to the right until he stood directly behind Dillon's position. Less than a dozen soundless steps later, Raine had the barrel of his weapon nestled at the base of Dillon's skull.

Dillon turned around slowly, his hands held high in a gesture of surrender, a sadistic smile curving his thin lips. "I told you it'd only be a matter of time until we met again."

"Too bad I'm the one with the bead between your eyes," Raine returned, carefully diverting the rage building too quickly inside him to something more appropriate for the moment—revenge.

Dillon shrugged. "You know, it doesn't have to be this way. We could split the money. With your expertise, Ballatore would never find you, and, of course, I'll be long gone."

"I don't think so, Dillon." Raine felt one corner of his own mouth lift into a satisfied tilt. Was that desperation he heard in Dillon's voice? Good, Raine mused, he liked to see that in an adversary. For all his cockiness, maybe Dillon wasn't quite as sure of himself as he pretended to be. "I don't want to make a deal, *amigo.*"

Dillon shook his head, frowning dramatically. "Gee,

Raine, that's too bad. I guess that leaves us with nothing to talk about.''

"Not quite." Raine snugged his finger around the trigger. The line of sweat on Dillon's upper lip provided instant gratification. "We still have to discuss that little detail of who dropped the dime on me."

Dillon's smile returned. "You don't really expect me to reveal my sources, now, do you? Especially since you're so unwilling to share the spoils of victory. And surely you've been in the spook business long enough to know what happens to those who kiss and tell."

"In that case—" Raine leaned closer, dropping his voice to a deadly level "—I'm afraid you don't have an option. Fact is, if you don't start singing the tune I requested, I'm going to hand you over to the old man. And he knows you killed his son."

Dillon didn't flinch. Raine's gaze narrowed. *He knew.* Somehow Dillon already knew.

Wariness, much stronger than before, gnawed at his gut as Raine continued, "But if you give me what I want, I'll put you out of your misery right now."

"Oh, that's a tough one." Dillon pursed his lips in exaggerated indecision. "I can either die now, or later—after endless hours of less than imaginative torture."

Raine nodded succinctly. "That's pretty much the bottom line."

Dillon leveled his evil gaze on Raine's. "I think I'll take door number three, Monty."

Anger seared through Raine's control. "There is no door number three, you low-life scumbag. Now tell me the name of your source." Raine pressed the barrel of the Glock to Dillon's forehead. "I'm fresh out of patience."

Dillon smirked. "Oh, but you don't understand, my friend. This is my game and I set the rules."

"Say good night, Dillon," Raine warned.

"Rule number one," Dillon continued despite Raine's warning. "If you kill me, Kate dies."

Raine blinked, his heart skipped one beat, then another.

That satanic smile spread across Dillon's face once more. "Ah, I thought that would get your attention."

"Go to hell," Raine snarled.

"Been there, and it wasn't half as much fun as being here with you. Or being with sweet little Kate."

"You're a liar."

"When it suits my purpose," Dillon agreed.

"Kate's safe." Raine could feel the muscle in his jaw jerking rhythmically. "And you're dead." Raine tightened his grip on the butt of the Glock in anticipation of the recoil.

"For the moment, she's safe." Dillon knitted his eyebrows as if trying to remember some important detail. "What was it she said?" He hummed a note of irritation, ignoring Raine's mushrooming agitation. "Oh yes. She shouldn't have believed anything until she heard from you."

Dillon's words stabbed into Raine's chest and cut right through his heart. He'd warned Kate not to believe anything until she heard it from him. How could Dillon know that? He couldn't possibly know where Kate was. She was safe.

"You lying son of a bitch," Raine muttered as he refocused his attention on putting a bullet between Dillon's eyes.

"She should have trusted you, Raine." Dillon shook his head. "But she didn't. She shouldn't have believed anything until she heard it from you, but *she did.*"

"What do you want?" Raine demanded, barely able to restrain the rage trembling inside him.

"The same thing I've wanted all along. I want you." Dillon lifted one dark eyebrow. "And the money, of course."

Chapter Thirteen

Raine sat in a chair next to the telephone in the hotel room he had shared with Kate less than twenty-four hours ago. Housekeeping had changed the sheets and made the bed, and left clean towels sometime since he'd left. But nothing could erase the memory of her sweet scent from his mind. The taste of her skin and the feel of her welcoming body around him was imprinted forever in his soul. But she was gone.

He'd walked out on her.

It shouldn't have mattered how she'd wound up on his doorstep or who had sent her. He should not have allowed anything to come between them—not her true identity or this mission.

But he had.

Raine drew in a harsh breath and set his jaw against the pain that shuddered through him at the thought of Dillon touching Kate. Raine had suffered death a thousand times over during the seemingly endless hours since his meeting with Dillon. And now, as the lighted display on the clock blinked from 2:00 to 2:01 a.m., Raine still waited for Dillon's call.

Ballatore hadn't been too happy about Raine letting Dillon walk out of that warehouse alive, but the old man had been willing to back off and let Raine handle Dillon. "As

long as he dies,'' Ballatore had said when he'd given Raine
the case containing the bait.

Oh, he would die. Raine intended to watch Dillon die.
At the moment, that single goal was all that kept Raine
from losing his mind. He just didn't know if he'd be able
to live with himself afterward if the bastard had hurt Kate.

The telephone rang and Raine snatched it up before the
first ring ended. ''Yeah,'' he rasped, his voice rusty from
the long hours of disuse.

''Take a walk in the park. Head in the direction of the
zoo. We'll be waiting.''

A click ended the brief call. Raine placed the receiver
back in its cradle and stood. He bent to pick up the leather
case that held Ballatore's money. The bag actually contained only a quarter of a million. The rest of the bulk was
plain paper cut and banded into stacks. Dillon wouldn't
know the difference until it was too late.

Raine mentally reviewed the vague orders as he crossed
the room. The hotel overlooked Central Park, but there was
a hell of a lot of territory between it and the zoo. Raine
recognized the strategy. Dillon would be watching, and
when Raine was where he wanted him, Dillon would make
his move.

And Raine would be ready.

AT THIS TIME OF NIGHT, not much moved in the park, and
what did should be avoided if possible. The idea of Kate
somewhere in this asphalt and foliage jungle urged Raine
forward. He hunched his shoulders against the cold, his
leather jacket proving less than adequate against the
coldest night New York had seen this season.

The occasional antique-reproduction street lamp didn't
help much in the way of visibility. Trees, shrubbery and
benches provided ample cover for anyone who didn't want

to be seen, yet allowed for freedom of movement. Dillon definitely had the advantage.

Dillon had selected a location that would provide him with the best cover, as well as numerous routes of escape. If anything went wrong, disappearing into the shadows would be simple. Why not stack the deck in his favor? It was Dillon's favorite way to play the game—a win-win situation.

Raine moved quietly past an artfully designed wall of boulders, his gaze shifting quickly from left to right. Nothing moved. The zoo entrance loomed in the distance. It wouldn't be long now. Raine's tension escalated, sharpening his senses.

Ten minutes later and midway between street lamps, Dillon stepped out of the shadows, Kate at his side. Raine stopped several feet away. His gaze slid swiftly over Kate and found no indication that Dillon had harmed her, at least as best Raine could see in the faint light.

"Nothing like a stroll in the moonlight," Dillon taunted as he pulled Kate closer.

Kate struggled against his hold but Dillon only laughed at her attempts to free herself. Raine willed himself not to react. Any reaction would be just that much more ammunition for Dillon. Raine needed distance. He had to separate himself from his emotions. To think, not feel.

"Did you come here to talk, Dillon, or did you come to deal?" Raine asked curtly.

"Is that the money?" Dillon gestured toward the bag Raine held.

Raine nodded and tossed the bag on the ground in front of Dillon. "You have your money, now let Kate go."

"Lose the piece." Dillon gestured to his left. Raine drew the Glock from beneath his jacket, reached down and placed it on the ground, then kicked it away.

"Nothing up your sleeve?" Dillon asked sardonically.

Raine shouldered out of his jacket and dropped it to the ground. The night air's bite made his muscles contract as he held his arms high in the air and turned slowly around, allowing Dillon to see that he wasn't hiding anything. Saving Kate was too important. Raine wouldn't risk her life by pulling any fast ones this time. Dillon was hovering too close to the edge. Raine would just have to fly this one by the seat of his pants.

"Good." Dillon smiled his approval, then pulled the bag containing the money a little closer with one booted foot. "Just to prove what a good sport I am, I'm going to give you two things, my friend, *before* I kill you."

"I thought we agreed that I would take him down."

Raine snapped his gaze in the direction of the familiar sound of a male voice. Raymond Cuddahy, director of Special Operations for the past two years, stepped out of the shadows to stand next to Dillon. Shock vibrated through Raine as he mentally acknowledged the seriousness of the situation. No one—at any level—was safe with a man like this at the top of the heap. For about two seconds Raine felt some sense of relief at having been right about Lucas, then the graveness of the situation hit him all over again.

Cuddahy smiled, seeming to enjoy Raine's surprise. Raine had always despised the man's cocky attitude. Short and stubby, Cuddahy had a major Napoleon complex.

As if reading Raine's mind, Dillon laughed and cut Director Cuddahy a glance. "That's one." Dillon pushed Kate away from him. She hit the ground hard. "That's the other."

Kate scrambled to stand, but froze when Dillon trained his Ruger in her direction. "Stay," he commanded roughly.

Kate's frightened gaze jerked from Dillon to Raine. Raine nodded once, willing her to stay put with his eyes.

Raine suffered a twinge of panic when Cuddahy picked up the leather case, but relaxed when he didn't seem inclined to open it just yet.

"Why?" Raine heard himself ask.

It was Cuddahy's turn to laugh this time. "For the money, what else?" He shrugged. "I've taken advantage of my *position* on several occasions. The opportunity is always there. Especially with a sting this big. What's a couple mil to a man like Ballatore? You just have to find the right man for the job. One who's willing to take the ultimate risk and end up with nothing."

Before the meaning behind the words could penetrate Dillon's thick skull, Cuddahy had turned his weapon on him and pumped two silenced shots into the center of his chest. Dillon dropped like a rock, a look of disbelief permanently etched on his thin face. Kate screamed her horror, but to her credit, she quickly composed herself.

"Of course, killing Michael Ballatore wasn't part of the deal." Cuddahy shrugged. "It's hard to find good help these days." He glanced down at Dillon and shook his head. "Oh, well, there's plenty more where he came from." He smiled then. "One down, and two to go."

Raine heard the depth of the breath Kate took. Her heart condition flitted across his mind, and he wondered briefly if she had taken her medication. Of course, there was a good possibility that in a few minutes it wouldn't matter one way or the other.

Cuddahy shook his head, his dislike for Raine obvious. "You and your glorious reputation. Well, you sure as hell slithered into the wrong den of snakes this time, hotshot."

"I did what I was contracted to do," Raine replied evenly.

"But you still screwed up, didn't you? You had no idea Dillon was on to you until it was too late." He smirked.

"No going out in a blaze of glory for Jack Raine. Hell, you even let *her* pull the wool over your eyes."

Raine looked from Cuddahy to Kate and back, waiting for the other shoe to drop. Could Kate be working for Cuddahy? Raine couldn't bring himself to believe that.

"Your old friend Lucas hired some big-time private agency to find you when you disappeared," he explained, his hatred for Lucas as evident as his distaste for Raine.

"You mean, when your people couldn't?" Raine suggested, purposely antagonizing him.

Cuddahy glared at Raine. "Well, she found you." He stepped closer to Raine. "It was her call that alerted us to your whereabouts in Gatlinburg, and then in Charlottesville," he sneered, leaning nearer.

Cuddahy's words only confirmed what Raine had already figured out. His instincts were seldom wrong. But now wasn't the time to dwell on that. "Where's Lucas?" he asked. If Lucas had caught on to Cuddahy's extracurricular activities...

"He had himself a little accident," Cuddahy said glibly. "Your little friend here called to let him know what was going on with you, and, like any good deputy, Lucas passed the information on to me. Unfortunately, he had himself an accident on his way here. He'll be out of commission for quite some time I'd say."

"Lucas is no fool. He'll figure out what went down eventually." Raine saw the flash of insanity in Cuddahy's eyes. Power and greed had done their work. He also saw in his peripheral vision, to his extreme horror, Kate inching her way toward the weapon on the ground. Raine clenched his jaw and forced his attention to stay on Cuddahy.

"Maybe, maybe not," Cuddahy jeered. "I'm not opposed to recruiting myself another deputy. Maybe I'll just drop by Bethesda on my way home and make sure that Lucas stays permanently out of commission."

"The only place you're going, you sleazy bastard, is the county morgue if you make one wrong move," Kate countered in a tone so ruthless that Raine barely recognized the voice as hers.

Raine glanced over Cuddahy's shoulder and saw Kate with the Glock pressed against the back of his head. Raine smiled and shifted his gaze back to Cuddahy. The mild surprise that registered in the man's expression was swiftly replaced by insolence.

"Now, now, Miss Robertson. Lucas told me how this was your first field assignment. Are you sure you know how to handle a precision piece of weaponry like that." Cuddahy laughed, then added, "Are you sure you know how to take it off safety?"

Even in the dim light, Raine saw the killer instinct glaze Kate's eyes before she spoke. "I'll tell you what I know, Director Cuddahy," she said coldly, calculatingly. "I know this is a Glock 19 nine millimeter with a barrel length of a hundred and two millimeters, a magazine capacity of fifteen plus two, and if my impression of Raine so far is accurate, it probably has a modified hair trigger." She paused, Cuddahy's mouth sagged open in disbelief. "And just so *you* know," she continued. "I took it off safety when I picked it up. Now, if you don't drop your weapon, I will pull this trigger."

Several charged seconds passed before Cuddahy, his eyes wild and his chest heaving frantically with fear, reacted. He leveled his silenced weapon on Raine's chest. Less than three feet separated them. "I'll kill him," he barked, all signs of his previous cockiness gone now.

"I can't stop you from pulling that trigger, Cuddahy, but considering the trajectory and range of my weapon, you'll die first."

A split second before he fired, Raine saw the decision in Cuddahy's cold eyes. Raine moved, pitching himself to the right, but he wasn't quite fast enough. By the time the hissing puff of the silencer reached his ears, the burn of metal had seared into his flesh. Raine hit the ground and rolled, momentarily dazed.

Two more quick, thudding pops sounded in the cold night air. Cuddahy crumpled to the ground. Kate stared at the downed man, then at the weapon in her hand. The shots hadn't come from the Glock. Raine hadn't bothered with a silencer. If Kate had fired, everyone in Central Park would have known it.

Groaning at the pain shooting through his side, Raine pushed to a kneeling position and turned to see who had put Cuddahy down.

Ballatore.

Raine shook his head and muttered, "Stupid old bastard."

Kate dropped to her knees next to Raine and laid the weapon aside. "Where are you hit?" she demanded, hysteria rising in her voice.

"I'm fine." Raine struggled to his feet, his left hand not quite stemming the flow of blood leaking from his side. He didn't miss the hurt that marred her expression at his rebuff.

"I believe this belongs to me," Ballatore said as he nodded to one of his men who immediately snatched up the leather case containing the money.

"I thought I told you to stay the hell out of this," Raine growled.

Ballatore shrugged carelessly. "I've never taken orders well, and I'm too old to change now," he countered, then smiled. "That's why I'm the boss."

"How did you find us?" Raine had to ask, he knew he hadn't been followed.

Ballatore smiled, some of the old shine back in his eyes. "I knew you'd spot a tail in a heartbeat, so I put one on

Dillon when he left the warehouse last night,'' he said proudly. ''The stupid bastard couldn't spot a tail if he tripped over it.''

Raine frowned. ''You were at the warehouse last night?''

''Did you expect me to pretend it wasn't happening?'' He pinned Raine with a steely gaze. ''This is my city, Jack Raine, don't forget that.''

''Get the hell out of here, old man, you just killed a government agent.'' Raine fought the vertigo interfering with his ability to remain standing.

''I just did the feds a favor, and saved your pathetic excuse for a life in the process,'' Ballatore challenged.

''Go,'' Raine repeated harshly.

Ballatore hesitated as if he might say something else, but thought better of it. He and his four henchmen disappeared into the shadows.

''We have to get you to a hospital.'' Kate tried to visually assess his condition in the near darkness. Raine's shirtfront was soaked with blood and he could still feel the warm, sticky stuff seeping between his fingers.

''You should go, too, Kate,'' he suggested.

''I won't leave you,'' she argued, concern tightening her voice and evidencing itself on her sweet face.

Raine bit down on his lower lip, but couldn't stifle a groan of pain. He dropped to his knees. He wouldn't be able to hang on to consciousness much longer. ''Well, you're in for a hell of a cold night, because I can't walk out of here.'' Why hadn't he kept that damn cell phone?

Kate draped his jacket around his shoulders, then reached for the Glock. To put him out of his misery? Raine wondered through the fog filling his head. He jerked when the loud, repeated report of the weapon sounded into the quiet night. After firing several shots into the ground, Kate returned to his side.

"There," she said, obviously pleased with her ingenuity. "That ought to get us some attention.

Raine attempted a smile. "Creative, Kate," he mumbled. "Very creative." Pain ripped through his side. He squeezed his eyes shut and doubled over with the intensity of it.

"Don't you dare die on me, Jack Raine," she pleaded, but her voice sounded oddly distorted and far away.

Don't worry, I won't, he wanted to say, but his lips wouldn't form the words. *I won't ever leave you again. I love you, Kate.* A sense of relief and calm came with the realization.

And then her sweet face blurred out and the world faded into oblivion.

Chapter Fourteen

Katherine sat on the front pew in the deserted hospital chapel. The room was lit by what looked like, in her opinion, upside-down seashells posing as wall sconces. They didn't provide much in the way of illumination, but she supposed that they had been selected for the ambience they provided rather than the candlepower. An elaborate crucifix overwhelmed the front of the room, but its presence was somehow comforting.

She'd spent several hours in the waiting room, but felt restless, and she'd eventually found herself here. Katherine shifted on the hard bench and surveyed the chapel once more. Did being in a place like this put you any closer to God? she wondered. She frowned, trying to remember the last time she'd been in church. Too long ago to recall, she decided. Or lost forever thanks to the amnesia she'd suffered. Was this confusion and uncertainty residual effects of her slowly returning memory?

But not being able to remember her spirituality or lack thereof didn't stop her from reaching to that higher power now in her time of despair. Katherine had prayed, pleaded with God to spare Raine's life. She closed her eyes and fought the hot sting of tears. She should probably go back to the waiting room, but she felt too numb to move, and too dazed to deal with the police and the other assorted agents and investigators lurking there.

She clasped her hands in her lap. Her skin felt unnaturally cold and more than a little clammy. She needed to sleep, but couldn't. The very thought of food sickened her. Raine was still in surgery and no one would tell her anything. The only thing anybody wanted to do was ask questions. She shuddered when her last images of him replayed before her eyes. So much blood. Raine had been unconscious for several minutes before help had arrived. And the paramedics wouldn't have arrived then—even before the police—had it not been for an anonymous tip called in on a cellular phone.

Ballatore no doubt.

When they had arrived at the emergency-room entrance, Raine had looked so pale. Katherine swallowed tightly at the memory of the hospital staff wheeling him away from her. He had to make it, he just had to.

And then what?

He had told her that he wasn't coming back. Raine had intended to walk away and never look back. How could she possibly believe that he had changed his mind? If she hadn't made that call to Lucas, there would have been no reason for him to see her again. It was only his sense of responsibility to save her from Dillon that had brought him to that park, she felt sure. Even then, after he'd been shot, he had told her to go. Her heart squeezed painfully at the memory. He knew now that she had been sent to find him. That made her his enemy—a traitor. He would probably never forgive her, amnesia or not. But she just couldn't think about that right now. She had to concentrate on willing him to live.

She was so very tired. Her eyes closed in exhaustion. Maybe if she could marshal the strength to walk back to the waiting room, some of the vultures would have gone by now. She shook her head at the improbability of it. Would her life ever be normal again?

Normal? Ha! Had it ever been normal? On cue, her heart fluttered in her chest. Hardly, she admitted ruefully.

"Katie?"

Recognition washed over her, bringing with it a sense of having come home. She turned around slowly, her gaze lifting to meet the man who had spoken.

"Daddy." She breathed the word, her head whirling from sensory overload. Images, voices, sped across the landscape of her mind, too fast to analyze fully, and all belonging to the past she had forgotten. With warp speed, she was back. Her life, her family, the fact that she loved pepperoni pizza and chocolate ice cream, it was all there!

Before Katherine realized she'd moved, she had rushed into her father's arms. He held her tightly, his arms strong and reassuring. The tang of Old Spice as familiar as the man himself. How could she have forgotten this man? The man who'd been both mother and father since she was eight years old.

He drew back to look down at her, cradling her face in his big hands. "Little girl, you gave me a hell of a scare," he said gently.

Everything hit her at once, the good as well as the bad. The old doubts and fears, the overwhelming sense of not quite measuring up flooded her. Katherine wilted in her father's arms, giving in to the tears she had managed to hold at bay for the last few hours.

She had failed. She'd had such high hopes for her career at the Colby Agency. Now she would lose the man she loved as well as her job. A heart-wrenching sob tore past her lips.

"Shh now, Katie." Her father held her tighter. "Everything's going to be fine."

"It's not ever...going to be fine," she stammered. "I

really screwed up this time. And Raine...Raine's..." She couldn't say her worst fears out loud. She just couldn't.

"Don't say it, Katie." He patted her back as he gently rocked her from side to side. "From what I hear, you did a tremendous job and that fella you brought in is going to be just fine."

...and bring him in either way. Victoria's words rushed into Katherine's head, pushing aside all else.

She drew back and swiped at the tears streaming down her cheeks. "How do you know he's going to be fine? And I didn't do a good job. I blew it," she blurted, her words tumbling out over each other. "I failed. I'll never be like Joe." She shook her head. "Never."

A deep frown marred her father's features and sadness filled his coffee-colored eyes. "Katie, I don't want you to be like Joe. I want you to be yourself." He smiled, and some of the sadness disappeared. "I love you just like you are. I always have. Don't you know that?"

Kate realized then that he did love her. Her father hadn't held Joe as a measuring stick of success, she had. She threw her arms around his neck and hugged him close. "I love you, Daddy." Just as abruptly, Katherine pulled away. "How did you know I was here? So much has happened, I didn't even think to call you."

"That's what I was about to tell you." He glanced back over his shoulder. "Nick brought me here."

Katherine followed her father's gaze to the tall black-haired man who stood waiting at the back of the chapel. "Nick?"

A wide smile broke across Nick's handsome face as he slowly closed the distance between them, his limp a bit more pronounced than usual. "Hey, gorgeous," he said as he pulled her into his strong embrace.

Katherine hugged him back. Nick Foster was a good friend, as well as her co-worker at the Colby Agency.

"Thank you for coming," she managed to say past the lump rising in her throat. He wasn't her husband or her boyfriend. He was simply Nick, her friend. And he had given her the book of matches. *You never know when you'll need 'em, he'd said.* The man always carried matches, despite having quit smoking more than two years ago.

Katherine frowned as she remembered that Nick hadn't been the same since a job he'd taken around that time, in Mississippi. She didn't know the details, but she sensed something bad had happened, and it was still eating away at him.

Nick held Katherine at arm's length and gave her a slow once-over with those assessing green eyes of his. "Technically I'm here on business." He smiled when he had completed his visual survey and seemed satisfied with Katherine's well-being. "But you know I would have come anyway."

Katherine moistened her dry lips. "Victoria knows, doesn't she? I'm surprised she didn't come herself." Katherine knew her voice sounded stilted, but it was the best she could do under the circumstances. She had worked so hard to make a place for herself at the Colby Agency. How had she managed to screw up so badly?

"She's at Bethesda checking up on Lucas," Nick explained. "And, yes," he added quietly. "She does know. I had to tell her. When I arrived at the rendezvous point to find you and the target gone, and your car in a ditch, we knew the assignment had gone sour. I couldn't risk not telling her."

Katherine nodded numbly. "Do I still have a job?"

Nick chuckled. "Are you kidding? The whole agency is talking about how you tracked down some big-time secret-agent guy. You'll have to tell me the whole story one of these days." He playfully chucked her under the chin.

"Hell, Katherine, you're a regular celebrity back in Chicago. I plan to throw you a victory party when you get home."

Home. Katherine frowned at the emptiness that word suddenly conjured. What good was home or a career without the man she loved? How could she go back to her old life and just forget about Raine? "I should get back to the waiting room. There may be news about Raine by now."

"He's doing great. They moved him to recovery," Nick told her. "When I stopped in the waiting room looking for you, I heard the doctor giving the detective in charge an update."

Katherine closed her eyes and breathed a heartfelt sigh of relief. *Thank you, God.* Raine was going to be all right and that was all that mattered. She would learn to accept and live with her heart condition—but she wasn't sure she could live without Raine.

RAINE FOUGHT the thick blackness that surrounded him. He could hear someone calling his name, but he couldn't quite rise to the surface of the overwhelming darkness. He couldn't wake up. He tried, God knows he tried. But he just couldn't. Sleep, like a millstone around his neck, kept dragging him back into the abyss of nothing.

Later, a lifetime later it seemed, he struggled again to find his way to the surface, to break through that inky veil that hung between him and consciousness.

Finally, by slow degrees, his eyes opened. At first he squeezed them shut again, the light was too bright. But he couldn't find Kate if he didn't wake up. And he had to find Kate. He had to tell her that he'd been wrong to walk out on her. That she meant the world to him. That the past didn't matter. *That he loved her.* That realization still shook him, but there was no denying it any longer. He would tell her. He doubted it would change anything, but he had to say the words just the same.

But what if she'd already left?

He opened his eyes again. He blinked until his vision adjusted to the sterile, white brightness of the room. He moved his right arm and grimaced. Tubes from a nearby IV were attached to that arm. So he moved his left instead. He touched his parched lips with his fingers. Man, he could use a drink of anything wet.

Raine turned to his right to look at the array of beeping machines next to his bed. Pain speared through him, almost sending him back into the blackness. Frowning and confused, the fingers of his left hand found the bandage wrapped tightly around his midsection. Oh, yeah. He remembered now. Cuddahy, the son of a bitch, had shot him.

Gingerly, he looked to his left, making sure that nothing below his neck moved. His heart bumped into overdrive when he found Kate sleeping in a chair beside his bed. Her long hair fell around her shoulders. Those wide, expressive eyes were closed in what he felt sure was much-needed sleep. Had she been with him all this time?

Raine's frown deepened. Hell, he didn't even know how long he'd been here. Had it been days, or only hours? Lucas? He needed to find out about Lucas.

Raine licked his dry lips again. A water pitcher was on the table next to his bed. Maybe he could reach it. He cautiously stretched his left arm in that direction and the room spun wildly. A groan escaped when pain seared through him again. Raine swore under his breath, gritted his teeth and tried a second time.

"Raine." Kate moved to his side. "Don't try to move," She filled the cup sitting next to the pitcher with water, and peeled the wrapper off a bendable straw. "Here." She placed the straw against his lips and Raine took a small sip.

"Thanks," he said, feeling tremendously better just knowing she was nearby.

"If you want me to leave now I will," she said hesitantly. "I just wanted to make sure you were all right."

He frowned. "I don't want you to leave."

"Good." Kate smiled down at him then. She looked nervous and tired and more beautiful than any woman he had ever seen in his entire life. "You're going to be fine," she assured him.

"Lucas?" He had to know about Lucas.

"Lucas is fine. Victoria, my boss, called this afternoon. He has a concussion and a few cracked ribs, but he'll be out of the hospital in a couple of days."

Raine nodded. "Good." His gaze focused on hers. Had she only stayed to make sure he was all right? Would she go now? Now that she'd done what Lucas had hired her to do?

Kate averted her gaze for a long moment before she met his once more. Her eyes were suspiciously bright then. Raine saw the tremendous effort it took for her to gather her courage. He waited. This was the part when she would tell him that her job was done and she had to go back to wherever she'd come from. She was safe now, and he should be pleased that Kate could get back to her life. But he wasn't.

"I've done a lot of thinking during the last twenty-four hours," she finally said. She smiled crookedly and Raine's heart ached with the thought of never seeing that smile again. "I made a little list." She retrieved a small, wrinkled piece of paper from her jeans' pocket. She studied it a moment. "First I wanted to thank you for saving my life—more than once. And I want to apologize for not telling you the whole truth. I mean, as it came to me. I didn't tell you everything and I should have. I was afraid—"

"Kate, you don't have to do this." He couldn't bear the hurt on her face or the pain in her voice.

"Just let me finish, okay?"

"Okay," he relented.

"Second, I want to properly introduce myself." She essayed another tremulous smile. "I'm Katherine Robertson. My dad calls me Katie, but you can still call me Kate. I lived my whole life in Arlington, Virginia, until I moved out to Chicago to join the Colby Agency. I wanted to be a police officer, like my dad, but my 'bum ticker' got in the way." She released a shaky breath. "I'm a private investigator, and I'm pretty good, despite my physical shortcomings, if I do say so myself."

Raine felt his lips spread into a grin. "Pretty damn good," he agreed.

"Lucas hired the Colby Agency to find you because he wanted to help you. He didn't fully trust anyone in his own organization. He wanted to know the truth about what really happened." She smiled. "Finding you wasn't so difficult since you called and left that telephone number on Lucas's voice mail." Kate looked away a moment then. "I know I betrayed you, but I was only—"

"Kate," he interrupted.

"I'm almost finished," she insisted, then glanced nervously at her paper. "Third." Kate wet her lips and swallowed visibly. "Could I just do one thing before I tell you number three?"

A mixture of worry and uncertainty tugged at Raine. "Sure."

Kate leaned forward slightly, hesitated, her gaze locked with his. Her own uncertainty flickered in those deep brown eyes. She inhaled sharply, parted her lips as if she might say something, but closed her eyes and pressed her lips to his instead.

She kissed him softly, sweetly, the essence of hot chocolate lingering on her lips. Raine threaded the fingers of his left hand into her silky hair and pulled her mouth more firmly against his. He traced the seam of her lips with his tongue and she opened, inviting him inside. He stroked her tongue and all those other sensitive spots inside her soft, warm mouth until they both struggled for breath.

"Raine," she breathed. "Can I…is it okay if I touch you?"

Nipping her lower lip to draw her mouth back to his, Raine responded by taking her hand and placing it on his jaw. He groaned with pleasure when her soft palm stroked his beard-roughened skin. Her answering moan sent heat straight to his groin.

When she broke the contact of their lips again, Raine swore, caught her chin and pulled her mouth back to his.

"Wait," she protested, flicking a concerned glance at the quickening staccato of the monitor that tracked his heart rate. "We shouldn't be doing this, you're hurt." She licked her lips, no doubt tasting their kiss. "Besides, if I don't finish this now, I might just lose my nerve."

Raine exhaled in frustration, but relented. "For the record," he rasped. "I'd have to be dead not to want you to kiss me." Despite having just had major surgery, his loins were tight with desire. No one had ever shattered his control the way Kate did.

"Just be quiet and listen," she scolded gently.

He gave her his full attention and kept his mouth shut.

"Okay," she said, more to assure herself than him, he decided. "I hadn't anticipated this happening anytime soon in my life, but that's beside the point. It did and…and I'm glad." She leveled her gaze on his. "I love you, Jack Raine."

He felt stunned. He couldn't have uttered one word had his life depended on it. Could this woman—the kind of woman he'd never dreamed of having—really love him? Even knowing what she must know about his past?

"I...I know our lives are worlds apart and that it might never work even if you forgive me for not being completely honest with you." She fiddled with the edge of the white sheet covering him, her attention concentrated there for a time. Raine waited, he had to know what else she had to say, what *she* wanted.

"And I know that my heart condition is considerably less than appealing, but I..." She looked up then. "I just wanted you to know that I'll never, ever forget you and—" she swallowed "—that I'll always love you."

Raine searched her face, unsure what to say. No one had ever told him that before. No one. He had known that Kate had feelings for him, but he'd never expected her to love him.

She forced a smile. "That's all I wanted to say." She looked anywhere but at him. "I should go. You need your rest." She shoved a handful of hair behind her ear. "Goodbye, Raine." Kate wheeled away from him. Her movements jerky, she grabbed her purse and coat and headed to the door.

She was almost there before Raine found his voice. "Don't go, Kate."

She hesitated but didn't turn around.

Unsure of himself in this emotional territory, he plodded ahead, "I didn't get my chance."

She turned around slowly, her expression as uncertain as his own must surely be.

Raine attempted a shrug, but wound up grimacing. "I mean, I don't have a list or anything, but I do have some things to say."

Kate took two hesitant steps in his direction. "I'm listening."

He took a deep breath for courage and went for broke.

"First, I want to apologize for being so rough on you." Fear of what could have happened plagued him again. Without her medication and with a concussion, anything could have happened in those damn mountains. His gut knotted at the thought.

She smiled hesitantly. "It's okay. I'm tougher than I look."

That was true, he knew, but he'd been a real ass. Admitting that to himself hadn't been so bad, but saying it out loud to Kate was another story. Raine cringed inwardly. This touchy-feely stuff would take some getting used to. But Kate was worth every moment of discomfort. "Second, I thought you'd want to be the first to know that I plan to officially inform Lucas that I'm out of the business as soon as he's back on the job."

"I'm glad for you," she said quietly.

Her reaction was entirely too reserved. He'd hoped for something more, like maybe her throwing her arms around his neck and then begging him to take her with him. I'm glad *for you*, she'd said. He wanted her ecstatic for both of them.

"The downside is, I don't know what I'm going to do with myself." He frowned in speculation, then chuckled wryly. "I'm not sure my particular skills are in high demand in the private sector."

A full-fledged smile spread across her sweet face with that remark. "I'm sure you'll find something to do."

Now for the serious stuff. Raine swallowed tightly at the lump swelling in his throat. This was where he had to climb out on that flimsy emotional limb. And damned if he didn't suddenly feel afraid of heights. "Well, I have that place in Virginia and I was kind of thinking of horses," he ventured cautiously.

"Horses?" Her eyes lit up. "Oh, that'd be great." She took the final steps that separated her from his side. "I love horses." A hint of hopeful expectation joined that twinkle in her eyes.

"It would only be great if you shared it with me."

Her eyes rounded in what looked like surprise. "We really don't know each other that well, Raine. Most of what we do know is half truths and speculation. You might change your mind when you get to know me better."

Raine resisted the urge to cut his losses before taking the next step. "I love you, Kate." He took her hand in his and laced their fingers. "That's all that matters."

"But you said you weren't coming back," she argued, obviously still not ready to believe him. "You intended to walk away."

"I was afraid to trust you with my heart." He heard the slight tremor in his own voice, but he didn't care. Stretching the IV tubes and earning himself another stab of pain, he reached up and touched her soft cheek with the fingertips of his right hand. "But it's too late. You already own my heart. You have almost since the moment we met. And now I have to trust you. I do trust you," he added firmly. "I hope you can find it in your heart to trust me."

"So, it all comes down to a matter of trust," she suggested carefully.

"Can you trust me, Kate? Trust me with the rest of your life?" His breath stalled as he waited for her reaction.

Her lips quivered into a smile. "Oh, yes. I've trusted you this far, why change now?" Kate leaned forward and kissed him thoroughly, with all the love Raine knew was in her heart.

Epilogue

"The Colby Agency cost me the best contract agent I had."

Victoria lifted a speculative eyebrow at the man sitting on the other side of her immense oak desk. "The way I see it, *you* cost my agency one of our best trackers."

Lucas Camp sighed, then twisted his lips into that one-sided smile that Victoria found entirely too charming. "Touché, Victoria," he admitted.

"It is nice to see two people so much in love," she said wistfully. She and Lucas had attended the private ceremony for Katherine and Raine, which had been held in a tiny wedding chapel in the Smoky Mountains. Victoria felt a pang of regret at the reminder that she would never again share that special bond with a man.

Lucas nodded his agreement, his silvery gaze too knowing.

"Well," Victoria began, pushing the matters of the heart aside. "Nick tells me that you were rather impressed with his final report."

"Very impressed. And not just with the report." Lucas sat a little straighter and pulled a businesslike face. "I could use a man like Nick on my team."

"Don't even think about it, Lucas. Nick is too valuable

to this agency. Don't you dare try to recruit him. I won't stand for it.''

"Okay, okay," Lucas placated. "Nick's a hell of a guy, but I would never recruit him behind your back. It was just a thought. It never happened,'' he offered by way of apology.

"I'll hold you to that," Victoria stated pointedly, giving him notice.

Lucas got to his feet. "I should be going."

Victoria stood, feeling oddly reluctant to let him go. "When is your flight back to D.C.?"

"Tomorrow morning." Lucas reached for his cane propped against the nearby table. "If you don't have any plans," he said slowly, "perhaps you'd like to join me for dinner tonight."

Victoria swallowed at the tight little lump that had lodged in her throat the moment Lucas entered her office. "I thought you never mixed business with pleasure."

That crooked smile tilted his lips once more. "There's a first time for everything," he suggested. "Of course, we could talk shop if you prefer."

Victoria surveyed the tall, distinguished man before her for a long moment. The gray peppering his coal-black hair hadn't detracted from his good looks. Nor had the passing of nearly half a century since his birth softened his rugged frame. He still commanded a presence that made a woman breathless. When Victoria's gaze settled back on his, she noted the uncertainty her scrutiny had generated.

"Dinner would be lovely, Lucas." Victoria smiled and the doubt in his eyes vanished. "And I would prefer to discuss anything but shop."

"I'll call for you at seven then," he said before he turned toward the door.

Victoria nodded and then watched his slow, labored progress as he crossed the room. Her attention riveted to his right leg. She knew that beneath the classic wool slacks he wore a prosthesis. Tears stung her eyes as memories flooded her mind. In that cage, all those years ago, during a war that no one wanted to remember, the price of one young lieutenant's life had been the right leg of another.

And Victoria would always owe Lucas for that.

* * * * *

The Bodyguard's Baby

by
Debra Webb

This book is dedicated to some of the people
I love most—my family. Erica, Melissa,
Tanya, Johnny, Chad, Chris and Robby,
you mean the world to me.
A special thanks to Robby for being the
adorable inspiration for Laura's child.

Prologue

Victoria Colby studied Nick Foster's handsome profile for a long moment as he stared out the wall of glass that made up one side of her office. Nick kept his dark hair trimmed at precisely the perfect style and length, fashionably short, to accentuate his classic features. His attire received the same attention to detail. He dressed well and in a manner that drew one's eye to the breadth of his shoulders and the leanness of his waist. He looked more model than investigator.

The man was a perfectionist, personally and professionally. In this line of work those traits could be a definite plus. Victoria had worked hard to make the Colby Agency the best in the business. And carrying on the dream that had driven James, her beloved late husband, was all that mattered to Victoria now.

The Colby Agency was much more than just another private investigations firm; it had a staff second to none. All personnel recruited and employed were on the cutting edge of their field. And Victoria made it a point to see that they stayed at their best, physically and mentally.

Victoria cleared her throat, unnecessarily announcing her presence, and crossed the thick, beige Berber that carpeted her spacious office. Nick was probably aware of her the moment she stepped off the elevator. He missed nothing. "Good afternoon, Nick," she said, smiling pleasantly as she settled into the chair behind her desk.

"Victoria," he returned warily before taking the two steps necessary to reach the overstuffed wing chair in front of her desk. "You wanted to see me?" He grimaced slightly as he lowered his tall frame into the chair, but quickly masked the pain of the old injury and relaxed fully into the supple leather upholstery.

"Yes," she confirmed. Victoria had dreaded this meeting all day, but there was no putting it off any longer. She had noted the deepening lines around his mouth, the darkening circles beneath his eyes. The man was on a full-speed-ahead trip toward crash and burn. Firming her resolve, Victoria began, "Nick, we've worked together for five years, and I know you too well to pretend any longer that nothing is wrong. I've watched the change in you over the past two years. You haven't been the same since—"

"I do my job," he interrupted sharply, his assessing green eyes growing more wary.

"Yes," Victoria agreed. "You're a valuable asset to this agency. You do your job *and more*." She understood all too well what Nick was attempting to do. She had been there. After losing James she'd buried herself in work, too. "And I'm sure you'll understand that what I'm doing now is *my* job." She paused a beat, allowing Nick to prepare himself for her next words. "As of today, you're on mandatory R-and-R. You will not set foot back in this building, nor will you conduct any business even remotely related to this agency for a period of fourteen days."

Instantly his gaze hardened, as did the usually pleasant lines of his angular face. "That's not necessary, Victoria. I'm ready for—"

"No," she cut him off, her tone final. "I've always

trusted your judgment, Nick.'' She shook her head. ''But not this time. I'd hoped that your need to assuage your conscience would fade with time, but it hasn't. You're still struggling with demons you can't possibly hope to conquer by driving yourself into the ground.'' Victoria raised a hand to stay his protests. He snapped his mouth shut, but his tension escalated, manifesting itself in his posture and the grim set of his jaw.

Regret weighed heavily on Victoria's shoulders at having to call her top investigator, her second in charge actually, on the carpet like this. ''You can't run forever, Nick. You'll either burn out or get yourself killed trying to prove whatever it is you feel the need to prove. When Sloan left I wasn't sure I would ever be able to work so closely with anyone else, but I was wrong. I don't want to lose you, Nick, but I won't allow you to self-destruct on my time either. Go home, spend some time with your brother, or find yourself a hobby.'' Victoria raised a speculative brow. ''Or maybe a woman. Lord knows you could use one...or both.''

Nick's gaze narrowed. ''I don't recall seeing a category marked 'personal life' on my performance evaluation.''

Necessity and irritation overrode Victoria's regret. ''You see this desk?'' With one manicured nail she tapped the polished oak surface of the desk that had once belonged to her husband. ''The buck stops here, mister. When you go home at night you can thank God in heaven for whatever blessings you may have received that day. But here, in this building, I am the highest power. And, despite your long standing at this agency, whatever I say is the final word. You, Mr. Foster, are on vacation. Is that understood?''

He didn't flinch. ''Absolutely.''

''Good.''

Nick got to his feet. The only indication that the move

cost him was the muscle that ticced in his jaw and the thin line into which his lips compressed.

"Two weeks, Nick," Victoria reiterated as he strode slowly toward the door, his trademark limp a bit more pronounced than usual. "Get a life, and when you return to work I want to see a new attitude."

He paused at the door and shifted to face her. The other trademark gesture for which Nick Foster was known spread across his handsome face. Victoria imagined that the intensity and appeal of that smile had made many a heart flutter wildly.

"Yes ma'am," he drawled, then walked out the door.

TWO WEEKS.

What the hell was he supposed to do for two weeks? Nick slammed his final report into the outbox on his desk. Victoria just didn't get it. He had a life—*here*. Nick surveyed his upscale, corner office. Work was his life. He didn't care what the shrinks said—Nick Foster didn't need anything else.

Especially not a woman.

Ire twisted inside him when he considered Victoria's words again. Yeah, he always did a hell of a job on his assignments. Especially this last one. Victoria could always count on him. No one else at the agency would have gone so far out on a limb for a client, but unlike the rest, it didn't bother Nick.

He had nothing to lose.

If he had gotten himself killed, who the hell would have missed him?

Nick shrugged off the answer to that question. He stood, gritting his teeth at the pain that radiated through his right knee and up his thigh. Nothing like a needling reminder from the past, he mused, to keep a guy in touch with reality.

Reality had royally screwed him three years ago when he'd gotten this bum knee while protecting a client. Bad knee or no, he still did the best job possible. In fact, in all his years of service to the Colby Agency he had never failed—except once. He brutally squashed the memories that accompanied that line of thinking. That would never happen again. You couldn't lose if you weren't looking for anything to gain.

Nick jerked on his suit coat and grabbed his briefcase. What the hell? He hadn't been camping or fishing in a while. Maybe he would hone his survival skills with a couple of weeks in the wilderness. And maybe he would call Chad and make it a family venture—considering the two of them were all that was left of the Foster clan. Nick's right knee protested painfully when he skirted his desk too quickly.

He muttered a colorful expletive and then forced his attention away from the burning throb. He had ignored a hell of a lot worse.

The ergonomically modulated buzz from the telephone halted his thoughts as well as his indignant exit. Nick stared at the flickering red light with a mixture of annoyance and curiosity. Everyone else at the agency, including Victoria, had no doubt already left for the day. No one ever stayed this late but him. Why should he bother answering the phone? Hadn't Victoria ordered him to take a vacation starting immediately?

Just when he thought he could walk out the door without answering the damned thing, he snatched up the receiver and barked his usual greeting, "Foster."

"Nick, it's Ray Ingle."

Nick froze, his tension rocketed to a new level. "Ray," he echoed, certain that he must have heard wrong. Maybe his mind was playing tricks on him. Maybe he should have listened to the shrinks after all.

"It's been too long, buddy." Ray's chastisement was subtle.

"Yeah, it has," Nick said slowly as he leaned one hip against the edge of his desk, taking the weight off his bum leg. He dropped his briefcase to the floor and raked his fingers through his hair as he waited for Ray to make the next move.

"I haven't called in a while." *Since we gave up on finding her,* he didn't have to add. "You haven't returned any of my calls in so long, I guess I didn't see the point anymore."

"I've been really busy, man," Nick offered by way of explanation, but the truth of the matter was he just hadn't wanted to make time. He and Ray, a Natchez police detective, had worked closely for months on that one case. And to no avail. Guilt congealed in Nick's gut.

"Sure, I know," Ray acknowledged quietly.

Nick straightened. "Look, I was just on my way out the door, is everything okay?" He hated himself for trying to cut the call short, but just hearing Ray's voice evoked more memories than Nick was prepared to deal with right now. He didn't know if he'd ever be able to deal with those memories.

"I saw *her.*"

The hair on the back of Nick's neck stood on end as adrenaline flowed swiftly through his rigid body. "Laura?" he murmured in disbelief, the sound of her name sending an old ache through his soul. If Ray had seen her…she couldn't be dead. Nick had known it all along.

"If it wasn't her, it was her frigging twin."

Nick moistened his suddenly dry lips. "Where?"

"I was following up on a possible homicide witness down in Bay Break and—"

"You're sure it was her?" Nick prodded, suddenly impatient with the need to know.

"I'm pretty sure, Nick. Hell, we turned a good portion of the good old South upside down looking for that girl. And there she was, plain as day." Ray sighed. "I don't know how and I don't know why, but it had to be her. I haven't told anyone else yet. I hate to upset our Governor on the eve of an election." He paused. "And, I figured you'd want to know first. I can give you a few hours head start, but then I'll have to inform him."

Emotion squeezed Nick's chest, he swallowed tightly. "I'm on my way."

Chapter One

She was being followed.

Oh God, *no*.

Panic shot through Laura Proctor, the surge of adrenaline urging her forward. The November wind whipped her hair across her face as she turned toward the town's square and scanned the sidewalk for the closest shop entrance. The last of autumn's leaves ripped from the trees at the wind's insistence, swirling and tumbling across the empty street. Someone bumped Laura's shoulder as they walked by, making her aware that she had suddenly stopped when she should be running.

Running for her life.

Instinctively her feet carried her along with the handful of passing pedestrians. She hadn't taken the time to disguise herself as she should have. The desire to avoid the possibility of being recognized was no longer a priority. The only thing that mattered now was finding a place to hide.

Any place.

She had to get away.

To get back to her baby. She couldn't be caught now. *Not now.*

The knot of people crowding into the eastern entrance of the courthouse drew Laura's frenzied attention.

Election day. Thank God.

Laura rushed deep into the chattering throng. Once up the exterior steps, she allowed herself to be carried by the crowd into the huge marbled lobby. Weaving between the exuberant voters, she made her way to the stairwell. Almost stumbling in her haste, Laura flew down the stairs leading to the basement level.

If she could just make it to the west end, up the stairs, and onto the street on the opposite side of the square, she would be home free. She had to make it, she determined as she licked her dry lips. The alternative was unthinkable.

Don't dwell on the negative. *Think, Laura, think!*

Okay, okay, she told herself as she glanced over her shoulder one last time before starting down the dimly lit, deserted corridor. If she cut through the alley next to Patterson's Mercantile, then circled around behind the assortment of shops until she reached Vine Street, she would have a straight shot to the house.

Mrs. Leeton's house.

And her son. God, she had to get to Robby.

Laura skidded to a halt at the foot of the west stairs. "No," she muttered, shaking her head. The door to the stairwell was draped with yellow tape. A handwritten sign read, Closed—Wet Paint. Laura grasped the knob and twisted, denial jetting through her.

She was trapped.

Laura blinked and forced herself to think harder.

Slow, deliberate footsteps echoed in the otherwise complete silence. She swung around toward the sound. He was coming down the stairs. In mere seconds he would cross the landing and descend the final steps leading to the basement…

To her.

Oh God. She had to hide. Now! Laura ran to a door, but it was locked. As was the next, and the next. Why were all the offices locked?

Election day.

Only the office serving as the voting polls remained open today. Fear tightened its mighty grip, shattering all rational thought. Laura bolted for the next possibility. Blessedly, the ladies' room door gave way, pushing inward with her weight. Moving silently past each unoccupied stall, Laura slipped inside the last one and closed the rickety old door behind her. She traced the flimsy lock with icy, trembling fingers only to find it broken. Climbing onto the toilet, she placed one foot on either side of the seat and hunkered into a crouch. Knowing her pursuer to be only seconds behind her, Laura uttered one more silent prayer.

Trembling with the effort to remain perfectly still, she swallowed the metallic taste of fear and concentrated on slowing and quieting her breathing. The heart that had stilled in her chest, now slammed mercilessly against her rib cage. Laura refused to consider how he could have found her. She had been so careful since returning to Bay Break. She fought back a wave of tears as she briefly wondered just how much her brother was willing to pay the men he sent after his only sister.

How could this keep happening?

Why didn't he just leave her alone?

How did they keep finding her?

And, God, what would happen to Robby if she were killed in the next three minutes as she fully expected to be if discovered? Anguish tore at her throat as she thought of her sweet, sweet baby. She wanted to scream…to cry…to run!

Stupid! Stupid! How could she have been so careless?

She should never have left the house without taking precautions to conceal her identity. But Mrs. Leeton had insisted that Doc needed her at the clinic—that it was urgent. After all Doc had done for her son, how could Laura have refused to go? She closed her eyes and banished the tears that would not help the situation.

The slow groan of the bathroom door opening temporarily halted Laura's galloping heart. Everything inside her stilled as her too-short life flashed before her eyes.

She had failed.

Failed herself.

Failed to protect the only man she had ever loved.

And, most important, failed to make the proper arrangements for her son's safety in the event of this very moment.

Now she would die.

What would become of Robby? Who would care for him? Love him, as she loved him?

No one.

The answer twisted inside her like a mass of tangled barbed wire, shredding all hope. She had no one to turn to…no one to count on. A single tear rolled past her lashes and slid slowly down her cheek only to halt in a salty puddle at the corner of her mouth.

Something deep and primal inside Laura snapped.

By God, she wouldn't go down without a fight.

Laura's heart pounded back to warp speed. She swallowed the bitter bile that had risen in her throat as she heard the whoosh of the door closing and the solid thunk of boot heels against the tile floor. Each harsh, seemingly deafening sound brought death one step closer.

The first stall door banged against its enclosure as the hunter shoved the door inward looking for his prey. Then the second door, and the next and the next. Hinges whined and metal whacked against metal as he came ever closer to Laura's hiding place.

To her.

Her heart climbed higher in her throat. Her breath vaporized in her lungs. Tears burned in her eyes. She focused inward to her last image of Robby, all big toothy smiles, toddling across the floor, arms outstretched.

Blood roared in Laura's ears as her killer took the final step then paused before the gray, graffiti-covered metal door that stood between them. Did he know that she was there? Could he smell her fear? Could he hear her heart pounding?

Bracing her hands against the cold metal walls, Laura gritted her teeth and kicked the door outward as hard as she could. The answering grunt told her she had connected with her target—his face hopefully. Laura quickly scrambled to the floor, beneath the enclosure and into the next stall. Hot oaths and the scraping of boot heels echoed around her. Her body shaking, her breath coming in ragged spurts, Laura crawled from one stall to the next to retain cover. She had to get out of here. Had to run!

To get to Robby!

The door of the stall she had just wriggled into suddenly swung open. "Don't move," an angry male voice ordered.

Laura frowned. There was something vaguely familiar about that low, masculine drawl. As if in slow motion, her gaze traveled from the polished black boots, up the long jean-clad legs to the business end of the handgun trained on her. She blinked, feeling strangely disconnected from her body. Then her gaze shifted upward to look into the face of death.

Nick.

It was Nick.

DON'T MAKE ME SORRY I put my weapon away,'' Nick
growled close to her ear. Awareness punched him square
in the gut when he inhaled the gentle fragrance that was
Laura's alone. No store-bought perfume could ever match
that natural sweetness. He clenched his jaw and simultaneously tightened his grip on her arm as they moved toward
his rental car.

Hell, the Beretta had been overkill, he knew. Laura
hadn't even been carrying a purse, much less a weapon of
any sort. But Nick wasn't taking any chances this time. She
hadn't had a weapon the last time either.

His right leg throbbed insistently, but he gritted his teeth
and ignored the pulsing burn. He had found Laura, alive
and well, and that's all he cared about right now.

Lucky for him Bay Break streets were deserted as far as
he could see. He supposed that most of the residents out
and about this morning were huddled in and around voting
booths inside the courthouse, or sitting around a table in
the local diner discussing how the election would turn out.
Nick didn't keep up with Mississippi politics, but James Ed
Proctor III's sensational reputation was hard to miss in the
media. And, from what Nick had heard, whomever the man
supported for Congress or the Senate was a sure winner.

The cold wind slapped at Nick's unshaven face. After a
late night flight, a long drive, and an even longer surveillance of the little town's streets before Laura made her
midmorning appearance, Nick welcomed the unseasonably
cold temperature to help keep him alert.

He had fully expected Bay Break to be a good deal
warmer than Chicago, but he'd gotten fooled. According to
the old-timers hanging around the general store, all the
signs warned of an early snow. Nick didn't plan to hang
around long enough to see if their predictions panned out.
Between twelve hours of mainlining caffeine and the un-

anticipated cold, Nick felt more alert than one would expe
after virtually no sleep in the last thirty hours. But by tl
time he drove to Jackson and did what he had to do, l
would be in desperate need of some serious shut-eye. An
of course, there was that R-and-R Victoria had ordere
Yeah, right, Nick thought sarcastically.

Laura struggled in his grasp, yanking his attention ba
to the here and now. Nick frowned when he considered tl
woman he was all but dragging down the sidewalk. The
was something different about her, but he couldn't qui
put his finger on it. She seemed softer somehow. I
scowled at the path his thoughts wanted to take. He kne
just how soft and delicate Laura Proctor was in all t
places that made a man want a woman—except one. It to
a woman with a cold, hard heart to walk away from a m
who lay bleeding to death.

"You can't do this," Laura muttered heatedly. S
scanned the sidewalks and streets. Looking for someone
call out to for help, Nick surmised.

"Who the hell do you think you are? You're not a cop
she added vehemently. "And I have rights!"

Anger kicked aside his foolish awareness of her as
woman and resurrected more bitter memories. Nick paus
then jerked her closer, his brutal hold eliciting a muffl
yelp of pain, or maybe fear, at the moment he didn't rea
care which. "When somebody put a bullet into my ch
and *you* left me to die, you lost your rights as far as I
concerned."

Seconds ticked by as Laura tried her best to stare h
down, her sky blue gaze watery behind thick lashes. S
could cry a river of tears and he would still feel no sy
pathy for her. Nick mercilessly ignored the vulnerabil
peeking past that drop-dead stare, and turned the intir

lation up a couple of notches. Laura's defiant expression
wilted.

His point made, Nick escorted her the last few steps to
the car. After unlocking the driver's side door, he pulled it
open and ushered Laura inside. Her long blond hair trailed
over his hand, momentarily distracting him and making his
groin tighten. He squeezed his hand into a fist and forced
way the unwanted desire. He had come here to take her
back, not take up where they had left off. Laura Proctor
would never make a fool of him again. And this time, he
would be the one walking away.

As he had anticipated, once in the car she bolted for the
passenger side. With a smug smile, Nick slid behind the
wheel and started the engine, almost drowning out her surprised gasp when she couldn't open the door.

"You bastard," she snarled, her eyes unnaturally dark
with anger. Her breasts rose and fell with her every frustrated breath. "This is kidnapping!"

Nick's smile widened into a grin of pure satisfaction.
"Consider it a citizen's arrest," he offered. Before he could
back out of the parking slot Laura flew at him, a clawing,
kicking tangle of arms and legs.

Nick shoved the gearshift back into park. After several
seconds of heated battle he subdued her, but not without a
gash across his throat from her nails. He shook her, none
too gently. "Look," he ground out. "I'm trying *not* to hurt
you."

"Sure," she hissed. "You don't want to hurt me, you
just want to get me killed."

For one fleeting instant Nick allowed himself to feel her
fear. There had supposedly been a couple of attempts on
her life two years ago. Could she still be in danger? Even
now, after all she had put him through, Nick's gut clenched
at the thought. Hell, he couldn't say for sure that there had

ever been any real danger in the first place. According to the reports he had been privy to, Laura had possessed wild streak, not to mention an overactive imagination. He older brother, Mississippi's esteemed Governor, was alway getting her out of one scrape or another. Who was to sa that the whole thing was anything more than her vivi imagination? And the guy she had been romantically linke to back then was over the edge in Nick's opinion. H doubted her poor taste in associates had changed since.

Nick swallowed hard at the thought of Laura with an other man.

Did he care?

No, he told himself. The lie, unspoken, soured in hi throat.

"You don't have to worry, Laura. I'm taking you bac home, to your brother. I'm—"

"My brother?" She quickly retreated to the passenge side of the car, as far away from Nick as possible. "I can go back home! Don't you understand? It's not safe."

Nick leveled a ruthless gaze on her panicked one. He lower lip quivered beneath his visual assault, he suppresse the emotion that instantly clutched at his chest. How coul she look so innocent? So truly frightened for her life? An damn him, how could he still care? "You don't have a option. In fact, if you'll remember correctly, the last tim *you* were supposedly in danger *I'm* the one who almo bought the farm."

Something in her eyes changed, softened with wh looked like regret. But it was too late for that now. Wa too late.

Their gazes still locked, Nick shifted to reverse. "Buck up, baby, we're out of here," he ground out, then glance over his shoulder before backing into the street.

Laura Proctor was going back to face her brother an

e law. Nick had every intention of uncovering the real
ory about what happened their last day together at her
rother's cabin as well. Protecting Laura and seeing her
afely returned to the new Governor after the election two
ears ago had been Nick's assignment. But things had gone
rong fast, and Laura was hiding at least part of the an-
wers.

Including the part where she recognized the man who
most killed Nick. The one she had obviously disappeared
ith that same day. Ironic, Nick thought wryly, that he had
und her and would be delivering her to her brother right
ter an election—just two years later than planned.

AURA HAD TO DO something. Nick, the arrogant bastard,
as going to get her killed. She glared at his perfect profile
d winced inwardly. God, the man was breathtaking. It
urt to look at him and know what she knew. He had
unted her dreams every night for the past two years. He'd
ined her for anyone else. A dozen snippets of memory
ashed before her eyes. The way it felt to be held by Nick.
he way he made love to her. Her heart squeezed with
membered pain. He had been fully prepared to give his
e to protect hers. Yet she could never trust him with her
cret, and she sure couldn't go back to Jackson with him.

The small sense of relief Laura had felt when she had
alized the man holding the gun on her was Nick instead
some hired killer died a sure and swift death when he
nounced why he had tracked her down.

He still wanted to finish the job he had been assigned
o years ago, to return her safely to her brother. And that
as exactly the reason Laura had not been able to go to
ick for help. He was too honorable a man to ignore his
sponsibility to James Ed. No way would Nick have done
ings Laura's way. He took his job way too seriously.

She had always known that Nick could have found he
eventually if he had really wanted to—but he hadn't. H
had apparently stopped trying. Unlike James Ed's me
whom she gave the slip without much difficulty, Nic
wouldn't be so easy. He was too damned good, the best.
anyone could have caught Laura during the past two year
he could have. Why now, she wondered, after all this time
But the answer to that question didn't really matter at th
moment. Right now Laura desperately needed to think
something fast. Something that would give her an oppo
tunity to escape. She glared at the space where the unloc
button used to be, and then at the useless door handle
had somehow disabled. Nick Foster was just a little to
smart for his own good.

And hers.

Well, Laura decided, she hadn't eluded her brother th
long without being pretty smart herself. She would find
way. Going back to James Ed was suicide. And she cou
never allow anyone—especially Nick—to discover her s
cret. She had to protect Robby at all costs. Even if aft
getting Robby settled some place safe it meant going bac
to her brother, Laura would do it to lead any threat aw
from her child.

She would never let anyone harm her son.

Never.

But how would Doc know what had happened to he
Would Mrs. Leeton be able to take care of Robby if Lau
never returned? Unsettled by the thought, Laura snapp
from her disturbing contemplation, and realized that th
were already headed out of town.

To Jackson.

Desperation crowded her throat.

She needed to go back to Mrs. Leeton's house first.

To her son. She couldn't leave without making some sort of arrangements.

There was no other option at the moment.

"We have to go back," she said quickly.

"Forget it." Nick's focus remained steady on the road. A muscle flexed in his square jaw, the only visible indication of his own tension.

Laura frantically groped for some reasonable explanation he would find acceptable for turning around. Nothing came. A new kind of fear mushroomed inside her. She had to think of something.

Now!

"My baby!" she blurted when the Please Come Again sign loomed closer. "I have to get my baby."

Nick threw a suspicious glance in her direction. "What baby?" he asked, sarcasm dripping from his tone.

"My...I have...a son," she admitted, defeat sucking the heart from her chest. How would she ever protect her baby?

Nick's expression shifted from suspicious to incredulous. "I'm not falling for any of your tricks, Laura."

Trembling with the crazy mixture of emotions flooding her body, Laura swiped at the tears she had only just noticed were slipping down her cheeks. Dammit, why did she have to cry? She was supposed to be tough—had to be tough. "Please take me back, Nick. I have to get my son," she pleaded, any hope of appearing even remotely tough dashed.

Something, some emotion, flitted across his handsome face so fast Laura couldn't quite read it. She fought to ignore what looked entirely too much like hurt that remained. She knew just how much Nick had suffered because of her. He had almost died. She winced inwardly at the memory. But she couldn't permit herself to feel any sympathy for him. He certainly harbored none for her. She had to stay focused on keeping her son safe. Robby was all that really mattered. And she could never allow Nick to suspect the truth about her child.

Laura didn't even want to imagine what Nick would do if he found out he had a son.

A child she had kept from him for almost two years.

NICK PARKED the rented sedan on the street in front of the small white frame house Laura identified as belonging to a Mrs. Leeton. Emotions churned in his gut. What was it to him if Laura Proctor had gotten herself pregnant since he had last seen her? Or, hell, maybe even shortly before he had met her.

Nothing.

Less than nothing, he reiterated for good measure.

She had simply been an assignment back then, and Nick's sole motivation for taking her back to her brother now was to clear up his record. Laura Proctor represented a black mark on his otherwise perfect record, and he was about to wipe it clean. If he had kept his head on straight back then he wouldn't have screwed up the assignment in the first place. And he sure as hell wouldn't have allowed himself to believe the woman almost virginal. What a joke.

On him.

Nick reached for the door handle, but Laura grabbed his arm. He stared for a long moment at the small, pale hand clutching at him before he met her fearful gaze. "What?" he growled.

"Please don't do this, Nick," she begged. "Please just walk away. Pretend you never saw me." She moistened her full, lush lips and blinked back the tears shining in her eyes. "Please, just let us go."

"Save your breath, Laura." A muscle jumped in his jaw, keeping time with the pounding in his skull. Don't even think about feeling sorry for her, man, he reminded himself. You let your guard down once and it almost cost you your life. "Nothing you can say will change my mind," he added, the recall of Laura's betrayal making his tone harsh.

Her desperate grip tightened on the sleeve of his jacket. "You don't understand. He'll kill me, and maybe even my son." She squeezed her eyes shut, her breath hitched as it slipped past her pink lips. "Oh, God, what am I going to do?"

Nick tamped down the surge of protectiveness that surfaced where Laura was concerned. His chest tightened with an emotion he refused to label. He focused his attention on the street and dredged up the memory of waking up alone and barely alive in the hospital. "Who will kill you, Laura? The guy you watched put a bullet in me before you ran away?" He turned back to her then, the look of pain in her eyes giving him perverse pleasure. "Just how far were you willing to go to cause your brother trouble? Was it all just some kind of game to you?"

Her eyes closed again, fresh tears trickled down those soft cheeks. She was good. She looked the picture of innocence and sweetness. He almost laughed at that. Obviously the hotshot she had been involved with two years ago, or someone since had left her with an unexpected gift. Maybe it had been the guy who had put the bullet in Nick. Laura Proctor would have a hell of a time promoting that innocent act with an illegitimate baby on her hip. Well, that wasn't his problem, even if the thought did make some prehistoric territorial male gene rage inside him.

"Are we going in, or do we head straight for Jackson?" he demanded impatiently, drumming his fingers on the steering wheel for effect.

Laura brushed her cheek with the back of her hand. "I

want to get my son first," she murmured, defeat sagging her slim shoulders.

"Well, let's do it then," he shot back, trying his level best not to think about Laura having sex with another man, much less having the man's child. Damn, he shouldn't care.

But, somehow, he still did.

Nick called himself every kind of fool as he emerged from the car, years of training overriding his distraction as he surveyed their surroundings. Vine was a short, dead-end street dotted with half a dozen small frame houses. A dog barked at one of the houses on the far end of the quiet street. Two driveways had vehicles parked in them, indicating someone could be home. Either Mrs. Leeton didn't own a car or she wasn't home, he noted after another scan of the house before them. Nick reached beneath his jacket and adjusted the weapon at the small of his back. There was no way of knowing what to expect next out of Laura or the people with whom she associated.

Laura scrambled out of the car and into the vee created by his body and the open car door. It took Nick a full five seconds to check his body's reaction at her nearness. Laura's gaze collided with his, the startled expression in her eyes giving away her own physical reaction. Nick breathed a crude, four-letter word. Laura shrank from him as if he had slapped her. He didn't want to feel any of this, he only wanted to do what had to be done. But his male equipment obviously had other ideas.

"I know you'll never believe me, but it didn't happen the way you think," Laura said softly, defeatedly. She looked so vulnerable in that worn denim jacket that was at least two sizes too big, the overlong sleeves rolled up so that her small hands just barely peeked out. But the faded denim encasing her tiny waist and slender hips was breathstealingly snug, as was the dirt-streaked T-shirt that snuggled against her breasts.

Nick swallowed hard and lifted his gaze to the face he had never wanted to see again, yet prayed with all his heart he would find just around the next corner. For months after her disappearance his heart rate had accelerated at the sight of any woman on the street with hair the color of spun gold and whose walk or build reminded him of Laura. Each time, hoping he had found her, his disappointment had proven devastating. And now she stood right before him, alive and every bit as beautiful as the day he had first laid eyes on her. Could he have found her long ago had he truly wanted to? Or was believing the possibility that she was dead or, at the very least, lost to him forever simply easier?

Victoria had ordered him to stop looking for Laura. Her own brother had believed her dead. But Nick had never fully believed it. Yet he had stopped looking all the same. If she was alive and she didn't want to contact him, he wasn't going after her. Then Ray had called and the need for revenge had blotted out all else.

A wisp of hair fluttered against her soft, creamy cheek and Nick resisted the urge to touch her there. To wrap those golden strands around his fingers and then allow his thumb to slide over her full, lush lips.

"Please don't make me go back, Nick," she said, shattering the trance he had slipped into.

Briefly he wondered if she still felt it too, then chastised himself for even allowing the thought to materialize. Laura Proctor had no warm, fuzzy feelings for him. Actions speak louder than words, Nick reminded the part of him that stupidly clung to hope, and her actions had been crystal clear two years ago. She had left him to die.

"If you want to pick up your kid, I would suggest that you do it before I lose patience," he snapped, using his anger to fight the other crazy, mixed-up emotions roiling inside him.

"Yes," she murmured. "I want to pick up my son." She looked away, then reached up to sweep the tendrils of hair from her face.

The ugly slash on the inside of her wrist caught Nick's eye. He captured that hand in his and forced her to allow him to inspect it. He clenched his jaw at the memory that she had allegedly tried to commit suicide only a few weeks before they had met. But the woman he had known for such a short time in that quiet cabin by the river would never have done anything like that. She had been too full of life and anticipation of what came next. She wouldn't have walked away leaving him to die, either—but Laura had.

And that was the bottom line: she couldn't be trusted.

His hold on her hand bordering brutal, Nick led Laura up the walk and across the porch of the silent house. The whole damned street looked and felt deserted. He glanced down at the woman at his side. If this turned out to be a ploy of some sort, she would definitely regret it. He nodded at her questioning look, and she rapped against the door.

Laura held her breath as she waited for Mrs. Leeton, a retired nurse, to answer the door. The woman was old and riddled with arthritis, so Laura waited as patiently as she could for the key to turn in the lock. Until three years ago, Mrs. Leeton had worked with Doc for what seemed like forever. When Laura showed up a week ago needing Doc's help, he had asked Mrs. Leeton to take Laura and Robby in. The elderly woman had readily agreed. Laura hadn't really liked the idea of leaving Robby alone with Mrs. Leeton this morning, but what else could she do? Mrs. Leeton had insisted that Doc needed Laura right away.

When the door's lock finally turned, anxiety tightened

Laura's chest and that breath she had been holding seeped out of its own accord. Would Nick recognize his own child? Would he demand that she turn his son over to him? Nick wasn't the same man she had known two years ago. He was harder now, *colder*.

Would he take Robby to get back at her? Or would he simply take him out of fear for his son's well-being? Just another reason she could never have turned to Nick for help no matter how bad things got. James Ed had convinced Nick and everyone else that she was mentally unstable. Nick would never in a million years have allowed a woman considered mentally unstable to raise his son. He would have taken Robby, Laura knew it with all her heart.

Oh, God, was she doing the wrong thing by even coming back here? Why didn't she just let Nick take her back to Jackson without mentioning Robby? Doc would have taken care of her baby until Laura could figure out a way to escape…*if* she figured out a way.

The door creaked open a bit and old Mrs. Leeton peered through the narrow gap. Laura frowned at the look of distrust and caution in the woman's eyes. Did she not recognize Laura? That was impossible. Laura and Robby had been living here for a week. The idea was ludicrous. Hysteria was obviously affecting Laura's judgment.

"Mrs. Leeton, I've had a change in plans. I have to leave right away," Laura told her as calmly as she could. "Please let Doc know for me. I just—" she glanced at the brooding man at her side "—need to get Robby and we'll be on our way."

"Who are you and what do you want?"

Alarm rushed through Laura's veins at the unexpected question. "Mrs. Leeton, it's me, Laura. I've come back to get Robby. Please let me in." Nick shifted beside her, but

Laura didn't take her eyes off the old woman. Something was wrong. Very wrong.

"I don't know who you are or what you want, but if you don't leave I'm going to call the police," Mrs. Leeton said crossly.

Outright panic slammed into Laura then. "I need to get my son." Ignoring her protests, Laura pushed past the woman and into her living room. Nick apparently followed. Laura was vaguely aware of his soothing tone as he tried to placate the shrieking old woman.

"Robby!" Laura rushed from room to room, her heart pounding harder and harder. Oh God, oh God, oh God. *He's not here.* The cold, hard reality raced through her veins. Laura shook her head as if to deny the words that formed in her head. No, that can't be! She had left him here less than an hour ago. It can't be!

Laura turned around in the middle of the living room, slowly surveying the floor and furniture for any evidence of her son.

Nothing.

Not one single toy or diaper. Not the first item that would indicate that her son had ever even been there.

He was gone.

She could feel the emptiness.

Frantic, Laura pressed her fist to her lips, then looked from Nick, who was staring at her with a peculiar expression, to the old woman who glared at her accusingly. Laura clasped her hands in front of her as she drew in a long, shaky breath. "Mrs. Leeton, please, where is my baby?"

The old woman's gaze narrowed, something distinctly evil flashed in her eyes. "Like I said before, I don't know you, and there is no baby here. There has never been a baby here."

Chapter Two

"There's no need to call the police, Mrs. Leeton," Nick assured the agitated old woman. He shot a pointed look at Laura. "We've obviously made a mistake."

Laura jerked out of his grasp. "I'm not leaving without my son!" She grabbed the old woman's shoulders, forcing Mrs. Leeton to look directly at her. "Mrs. Leeton, why are you doing this? Where's Robby? Who took him?"

"Get out! Get out!" the old woman screeched. "Or I'll call the police!"

"We're leaving right now." Nick carefully, but firmly, pulled Laura away from the protesting old woman. "Now," he repeated when she resisted.

"I can't go without my baby." The haunted look on Laura's face tore at Nick's already scarred heart. "She's lying. She knows where he is!" Laura insisted. Her eyes, huge and round with panic, overflowed with the emotion ripping at her own heart. How could he not believe her?

But he had trusted her once before....

Nick forced his gaze from Laura to the old woman. "I apologize for the confusion, Mrs. Leeton." He tightened his grip on Laura when she fought his hold. "We won't bother you again." This time Nick snaked his left arm around Laura's waist and pulled her against him. His gaze connected with hers and he warned her with his eyes that she had better listen up. "We're leaving—*now*," he ground out for emphasis. Laura sagged against him, emotion shaking her petite frame.

"If that crazy girl sets foot back on my property I'm calling the police!" Mrs. Leeton shouted behind them.

Nick didn't respond to her threat. He had no intention of returning to the woman's house. If Laura had a son, he wasn't here, that much was clear.

Laura clung helplessly to Nick as he strode back to the rental car, her violent sobs rattling him like nothing else in the past two years had. He automatically tuned out the intensifying pain radiating from his knee upward. He didn't have time for that now. He glanced down at the woman at his side. Whether she had a child and where that child might be was not his concern. He ignored the instant protest that tightened his chest. Taking her back to James Ed was all he came to do, Nick reminded himself. Laura had a brother, an influential brother, who could help her with whatever personal problems—real or imagined—she might have.

Nick opened the car door, intent on ushering Laura inside. Hell, it was too damned cold to stand outside and debate anything. He could calm Laura down once they were in the car. As if suddenly realizing that they were actually leaving, she twisted around to face him.

"I have to find Robby," she said, her voice breaking on a harsh sob. "You have to believe me, Nick. I left him with Mrs. Leeton not more than an hour ago." Another shudder wracked her body.

Nick pulled her close again, his own body automatically seeking to comfort hers. He forced himself to think rationally, ruthlessly suppressing the urge to take her sweet face in his hands and promise her anything. "Show me some proof that you have a son, Laura. Convince me."

For the space of two foolish heartbeats Laura stared into his eyes, the blue of hers growing almost translucent with some emotion Nick couldn't quite identify. Her upturned face too close for comfort.

"He's real," she whispered, her breath feathering across his lips, making him yearn to taste her, to hold her tighter.

"Prove it," he demanded instead. "Show me pictures, a birth certificate, a favorite toy, clothing, any evidence that you have a child."

She shifted, her body brushing against his and sending a jolt of desire through him. "My purse..." Laura frowned, then looked toward Mrs. Leeton's house. "I left my purse and what few clothes we brought with us in there."

Nick followed her gaze and studied the small white frame house for a moment. "We definitely aren't going back," he said flatly, then returned his attention to the woman putting his defenses through an emotional wringer. "I don't want the local police involved."

Instantly, Laura recoiled from him. Anger and bitterness etched themselves across the tender landscape of her face. Her eyes were still red-rimmed from her tears, but sparks of rage flew from their watery blue depths. "Of course not," she spat the words with heated contempt. "We wouldn't want to do anything that would bring the wrong kind of attention to the almighty Governor of Mississippi, now would we?"

"Get in the car, Laura." Irritation stiffened Nick's spine. He had no intention of making the Proctors' domestic difficulties personal this go-around. "Now," he added when she didn't immediately move.

Her eyes still shooting daggers at him, Laura turned to

obey, but suddenly whipped back around. "Doc," she said. "Doc will back me up. He'll tell you about Robby."

Tired of beating a dead horse, Nick blew out a loud, impatient breath. "Who's Doc?"

"My doctor," Laura explained. "Robby was really sick. Doc's the reason I came back here, I knew I could trust him," she added quickly as she slid behind the wheel, then scooted to the passenger side of the car. "Let's go!"

Nick braced his forearm on the roof of the car and leaned down to look her in the eye. He held her gaze for a long moment, some warped inner compulsion urging him to believe her. He straightened, taking a moment to scan the quiet neighborhood, then Mrs. Leeton's house once more. Something about this whole situation just didn't feel right. Maybe there was some truth to Laura's story. Nick had always trusted his instincts. And they had never let him down...except once.

"Hurry, Nick, we're wasting time!"

Still warring with himself, Nick dropped behind the wheel and started the engine. He turned to his passenger and leveled his most intimidating gaze on hers. "If you're yanking me around, Laura, you're going to regret it."

LAURA STARED at the scrawled writing on the crudely crafted sign hanging in the window of Doc's clinic. The breath rushed past her lips, leaving a cloud of white in the cold air as she read the words that obliterated the last of her hope. "Gone out of town, be back as soon as possible." This couldn't be. She shook her head as denial surged through her.

It just could not be.

Her pulse pounded in her ears. Her heart threatened to burst from her chest. Laura squeezed her burning eyes shut.

Robby, where are you? Please, God, she prayed, *don't let them hurt my baby. Please, don't let them hurt my baby.*

"That's rather convenient," Nick remarked dryly from somewhere behind her.

Laura clamped one hand over her mouth to hold back the agonizing scream that burgeoned in her throat. How could she make Nick believe her now? Mrs. Leeton was lying or crazy, or maybe both. Doc had disappeared. Doc's new nurse would be where? Laura wondered. The woman worked part-time with another doctor in some nearby small town. Where? Laura wracked her brain, mentally ticking off the closest ones. She couldn't remember what Doc had told her. His longtime secretary had retired and moved to Florida months ago. He hadn't hired anyone else, preferring to do the paperwork himself now. Who could Laura call? She couldn't think. She closed her eyes again and stifled a sob that threatened to break loose. She had to keep her head on straight. She had to think clearly.

Who could have taken Robby?

Why?

Realization struck like lightning on a sultry summer night, acknowledging pain hot on its heels like answering thunder.

James Ed.

It had to be him, or one of his henchmen. They had found out about Robby and taken him to get to Laura. That would be the one surefire way to bring her home. She had realized that day two years ago at the cabin that her dear brother intended to kill her. She just hadn't known why. But that epiphany had come to her eventually. *The money.* He wanted Laura's trust fund. He was willing to kill her to get it. And now Robby was caught in the middle.

What about Doc? Could he be in on it? Was his sudden disappearance planned? Laura shook her head emphatically. No way. Doc loved her. And she trusted him. He wouldn't do that. Laura read the sign in the window again. But where could he be? He had asked her to come to the clinic. He'd told Mrs. Leeton it was urgent. Had he somehow heard that someone was in town looking for her? Maybe he wanted to warn her. Could he have taken Robby somewhere to safety?

Laura prayed that was the case. But how could she be sure? Could she leave town without knowing that her son was safe? She swallowed tightly.

No. She had to find him.

"I know Doc's here," she said aloud, as if that would make it so. "He has to be."

"Let's go, Laura. I'm tired of playing games with you."

Laura turned around slowly and faced the man who seemed to have set all this in motion. The man she still loved deep in her heart. The man who had given her the child that she could not bear to lose. But she could never tell him the truth.

Never.

Nick's green eyes were accusing, and full of bitterness. Defeat weighed heavily on Laura's shoulders as she met that unsympathetic gaze. Pain riddled her insides. She had lost her son and no one on earth cared or wanted to help her. She was alone, just as she had been alone since the day her parents had died when she was ten years old. Nothing but a burden to her much older brother, Laura had known from day one that he couldn't wait to be rid of her. As soon as she had come home from college, James Ed had tried to push her into marrying the son of one of his business associates, but Laura had refused. Then the attempts on her life had begun.

She supposed that it was poetic justice of sorts. James Ed had considered her a nuisance her entire life, but being the responsible, upstanding man he wanted everyone to believe he was, he had offered Laura an out—marry Rafe Manning. Rafe was young, reasonably handsome, and rich. What more should she want? Why couldn't she be the good, obedient sister James Ed wanted her to be?

If only James Ed had known. Rafe's wild stunts had made Laura's little exploits look like adolescent mishaps. Between the alcohol and the cocaine, Rafe was anything but marriage material. Not to mention the apparently insignificant fact that Laura had no desire to marry Rafe or anyone else at the time. She had been too mixed up herself, too young.

So Laura had thumbed her nose at her big brother's offer, and he had chosen an alternative method of ridding himself of his apparently troublesome sister. Maybe Rafe had been in on it, as well. How much would James Ed have paid him to see that his new bride had a fatal accident? James Ed always preferred the easy way out. Hiring someone to do his dirty work for him was a way of life.

Perversely, Laura wondered if her showing up now would be an inconvenience considering James Ed had no doubt already taken control of her trust fund. Only weeks from her twenty-fifth birthday, Laura would be entitled to the money herself. Then again, that might be the whole point to this little reunion. James Ed would make sure that she didn't show up to claim her trust fund. What would a man, brother or not, do to maintain control of that much money?

Nick stepped closer and Laura jerked back to the here and now. Robby was gone. Doc was gone. What did anything else matter? Panic skittering up her spine once more, she backed away when Nick reached for her. She had to find Robby and Doc. Laura rushed to the door of the house that served as both clinic and home to Doc Holland. She banged on the old oak-and-glass door and called out his name. He had to be here. He simply would not just disappear. She twisted the knob and shook the door. It was locked up tight.

Doc never locked the door to his clinic.

"This isn't right," she muttered. Laura moved to the parlor window. She cupped her hands around her eyes and peered through the ancient, slightly wavy, translucent glass. Everything looked to be in order. But it couldn't be.

"He wouldn't just leave like this," she reminded herself aloud. Bounding off the porch, Laura rushed to the next window at the side of the house. The kitchen appeared neat and tidy, the way Doc always kept it.

But something was wrong. Laura could feel it all the way to her bones. Something very bad had happened to Doc. Her heart thudded painfully. She knew Doc too well. He would never just disappear with Robby without leaving her some sort of word. "They've gotten to him, too," she whispered, the words lost to the biting wind. Forcing herself to act rather than react, Laura ran to the next window, then the next one after that.

That same sense of emptiness she had felt at Mrs. Leeton's echoed inside her.

"No one's here, Laura."

She struggled against the fresh onslaught of tears, then turned on Nick. "He has to be here," she snapped. Her heart couldn't bear the possibility that her child was in the hands of strangers who might want to harm him. Or that something bad had happened to Doc. "Don't you understand? Without him…" Anguish constricted her throat, she couldn't say the rest out loud.

Nick lifted one brow and glared at her unsympathetically. "We're leaving *now*. No more chasing our tails." He snagged her right arm before she could retreat. "Don't make this any more difficult than it already is," he warned.

Difficult? Laura could only stare at him, vaguely aware that he was now leading her back to the car. Did he truly think her situation was merely difficult? Could he not see that someone had cut her heart right out of her chest? Her child was missing! And she had to find him. Somehow...no matter what it cost her.

Another thought suddenly occurred to Laura—Doc's fishing cabin. Maybe he had gone to the cabin to hide Robby. Hope bloomed in Laura's chest. It wasn't totally outside the realm of possibility, she assured herself. She paused before getting into the car and closed her eyes for a moment to allow that hope to warm her. Please, God, she prayed once more, let me find my baby.

Now, all she had to do was convince Nick to take her there. She opened her eyes and her gaze immediately collided with his intense green one. Despite everything, desire sparked inside her. How she wanted to tell Nick the truth—to make him believe in her again. But she couldn't. And when they arrived at the cabin, if her son was not there, Laura would do whatever she had to in order to escape. She would go to James Ed all right. But she would go alone and on her own terms. Somehow Laura would devise a fail-safe plan to get her son back.

Whatever it took, she would do it.

NICK KEPT a firm hold on Laura as they emerged from the car outside Dr. Holland's rustic fishing cabin. The place was in the middle of nowhere, surrounded by woods on three sides and the unpredictable Mississippi River on the fourth. The cabin sat so close to the water's edge, Nick felt sure it flooded regularly. But from the looks of things, there appeared to be no amenities like electricity. It served only as modest shelter for the hard-core fisherman or hunter. So what did a little water hurt now and then? he mused. Most likely nothing.

Now that he had gotten a good look at the place, Nick was surprised there had been a road accessible by car at all. Once again, quiet surrounded them. Only the occasional lapping of the water against a primitive old dock broke the utter silence. The sun had peaked and was now making its trek westward. Nick would give Laura five minutes to look around and then they were heading to Jackson. They had already wasted entirely too much time.

She hadn't spoken other than to give him directions since they left the clinic. Nick glanced at her solemn face now and wondered what was going on in that head of hers. His gut told him he didn't want to know. And his gut was seldom wrong.

At the steps to the dilapidated porch, Laura pulled free of his loosening grip and raced to the door. Nick followed more slowly, allowing her some space to discover what he already knew: there was no one here. Considering nothing about the cabin's environment appeared disturbed in any way, and the lack of tracks, human or otherwise, there hadn't been anyone here in quite a while. Nick swore softly at the pain that knifed through his knee when he took the final step up onto the porch.

Damn his knee injury, and damn this place. He plowed his fingers through his hair and shifted his weight to his left side.

The wind rustled through the treetops, momentarily interrupting the rhythmic sound of the lapping water. Nick scanned the dense woods and then the murky river, a definite sense of unease pricked at him. Maybe it was because the remote location reminded him of the place he and Laura had shared two years ago, or maybe it was just restlessness—the need to get on with this. Whatever the case, Nick's tension escalated to a higher state of alert. If he still smoked, he'd sure as hell light up now. But he'd quit long ago. He had even stopped carrying matches.

"Doc's not here. No one's here."

Nick met Laura's fearful gaze. Drawing in a halting breath, she rubbed at the renewed tears with the back of her hand. She looked so vulnerable, so fragile. He wanted to hold her and assure her that everything would be all right as soon as she was back home. But what if he was wrong? What if someone still intended to harm her?

And what if he were the biggest fool that ever put one foot in front of the other? Don't swallow the bait, Foster. You've seen this song and dance before. "Let's get on the road then," he suggested, self-disgust making his tone more curt than he had intended.

She blinked those long, thick lashes and backed away a step. "I can't go with you, Nick." Laura shook her head slowly from side to side. "I have to find Robby. I…I can't leave without him. If you won't help me, I'll just have to do it alone."

Keeping his gaze leveled on hers, Nick cautiously closed the distance between them. "Don't do anything stupid, Laura," he warned. "If you say you have a kid, I'm sure it's true. And if you do, I can't imagine why anyone would want to take him, can you? What about the boy's father?"

The cornered-animal look that stole across her face gave her away about two seconds before she darted back inside the cabin. She had almost made it across the solitary room and to the back door when Nick caught, then trapped her between his body and a makeshift kitchen cabinet. Anger and pain battled for immediate attention, but at the moment jealousy of a man he had never even met had him by the throat. He leaned in close, pressing her against the rough wood counter, forcing her to acknowledge his superior physical strength.

"Does Rafe know about his son? Or is there some other unlucky fellow still wondering whatever happened to his sweet little Laura?" Nick snarled like the wounded animal he was.

In a self-protective gesture, Laura braced her hands against his chest, unknowingly wreaking havoc with his senses. How could she still affect him this way? Her scent tantalized him, made him want to touch her, taste her, in all the ways he had that one night. Every muscle in his body hardened at the imagined sensation of touching Laura again. When she turned that sweet face up to his, her eyes wide with worry and pleading for his understanding, his resolve cracked....

"He doesn't know about Robby." She licked those full pink lips and a single tear slid slowly down one porcelain cheek. "I'm afraid I won't find him, Nick. Please help me."

...his resolve crumbled. Nick allowed himself to touch her. His fingertips glided over smooth, perfect skin, tracing the path of that lone tear. The sensation of touching Laura like he had dreamed of doing for so very long short-circuited all rational thought.

Slowly, regret nipping at his heels already, Nick lowered his head. He saw her lips tremble just before he took them with his own. Her soft, yielding sigh sent a ripple of sensual pleasure through him. She tasted just like he remembered, sweet and innocent and so very delicate. Like a cherished rose trustingly opening to the sun's warmth, Laura opened for him. And when he thrust his tongue inside her sweet, inviting mouth the past slipped away. Only the moment remained...touching Laura, tasting her and holding her close, then closer still.

Nick threaded his fingers into her long blond hair, reveling in the silky texture as he cradled the back of her head. "Laura," he murmured against her mouth, and she responded, knotting her fists in his shirt and pulling him closer. His body melded with hers, her softness molding to his every hard contour as he deepened the already mind-blowing kiss.

Lust pounded through him with every beat of his heart. Nick traced the outline of Laura's soft body, his palms lingering over the rise of her breasts, then moved lower to cup her bottom and pull her more firmly into him. She slid one tentative hand down his chest, then between their grinding bodies. Laura caressed him intimately. Nick groaned loudly into her mouth as she rubbed his erection again and again through his jeans.

Her tongue dueled with his, taking control of the kiss, just as her body now controlled his. Her firm breasts pressed into his chest, her nipples pebbled peaks beneath the thin cotton of her T-shirt. The urge to make love to Laura—here, now—overwhelmed all else as she propelled him ever closer toward climax with nothing more than her hand, and in spite of the layers of clothing still separating them.

The unexpected blow to the side of his head sent Nick's equilibrium reeling. He staggered back a couple of steps and Laura took off like a shot. He stared at the thick ceramic mug shattered on the primitive wooden floor. He hadn't even noticed it on the counter. Nick shook his head to clear it and took several halting steps in the general direction of the door. When he got his hands on Laura he intended to wring her neck. At the moment he had to focus on reversing the flow of blood from below his belt to above his neck.

She was already at the car when he stumbled across the

porch, his body still reeling from her touch. He rubbed the throbbing place just behind his temple then checked his fingertips for any sign of blood. No blood, just a hell of a lump rising. A half dozen or so four-letter words tumbled from his mouth as he lurched toward the car, his knee throbbing with each unsteady step. Pure, unadulterated rage flashed through him like a wild fire. She would regret this, he promised himself.

Nick knew by Laura's horrified expression that she had just discovered that the keys weren't in the ignition. Did she think he was stupid as well as gullible? In a last-ditch effort to save herself, she locked the doors.

Grinning like the idiot he now recognized himself to be, Nick reached into his pocket and retrieved the keys, then proceeded to dangle them at her. "Going somewhere?" He inserted the key into the door's lock and glared at her. "I don't think so." He jerked the door open and leaned inside.

Laura tried to climb over the seat and into the back but Nick caught her by the waist.

"Let me go!" she screamed, slapping, scratching and kicking with all her might. "I have to find my son!"

Once Nick had restrained her against the passenger-side door, he glowered at Laura for three long beats before he spoke. "You have two choices," he growled. "You can sit here quietly while I drive to Jackson, or I can tie you up and put you in the trunk. It's your call, Laura, what's it going to be?"

Chapter Three

Laura sat absolutely still as Nick parked the car at the rear of James Ed's private estate per security's instructions. She forced away the thoughts and emotions that tugged at her senses. Nick's touch, his kiss, the feel of his arms around her once more. She still wanted him, no matter that her whole world was spinning out of control. Commanding her attention back to the newest level of her nightmare, Laura lifted her gaze to the stately residence before her. The place was every bit as ostentatious as she had expected. Nothing but the best for James Ed, she thought with disgust.

In a few hours every available space out front would be filled with Mercedes, Cadillacs and limousines as the official victory party got under way. According to Nick's telephone conversation with James Ed, of which Laura had only overheard Nick's end, a celebration was planned for the Governor's cohorts who had won big in today's election. Laura was to be taken in through the back. That way there would be no chance that a guest arriving early or some of the hired help might see her. James Ed was still protecting his good name.

But Laura didn't care. A kind of numbness had settled over her at this point. The knowledge that she might never see Robby again, and that she was going to die had drained her of all energy. She felt spent, useless.

She surveyed again the well-lit mansion and considered what appeared to make her brother happy. Money and power. Those were the things that mattered to him. He could keep Laura's trust fund. She didn't care. She only wanted her son back. But James Ed wouldn't care what Laura wanted. He had never cared about her. Otherwise he would have left her alone after she disappeared rather than hunting her down like an animal. She had barely escaped his hired gunmen on two other occasions. And now Laura would answer doubly to James Ed for all the trouble she had caused him.

But he couldn't hurt her anymore, that was a fact. He had already taken away the only thing in this world that mattered to Laura.

Laura looked up to find Nick reaching back inside the car to unbuckle her seat belt. His lips were moving, so she knew he was speaking to her, but his words didn't register. On autopilot, Laura scooted across the seat and pushed out into the cold night air to stand next to Nick. She looked up at him, the light from a nearby lamppost casting his handsome face in shadows and angles. She knew Nick was a good man, but he had been blinded by her brother's charisma just like everyone else. None of this was Nick's fault, not really. He was only doing what he thought was right. His job.

Would Robby look like him when he grew up? she suddenly wondered. Even at fifteen months, he already had those devilish green eyes and that thick black hair.

Yes, Laura decided, her son would grow up to be every bit as handsome as his father. She frowned and her mouth went unbearably dry. The father he would never know…and the mother he wouldn't remember. She blinked—too late. Hot tears leaked past her lashes.

"They're waiting for us inside," Nick said, drawing her back to the present.

Laura swallowed but it didn't help. She brushed the moisture from her cheeks with the back of her hands and took a deep, fortifying breath. She might as well get this over with. No point in dragging it out.

"I'm ready," she managed.

"Good."

Nick smiled then and Laura's heart fluttered beneath her breast. It was the first time today she had seen him smile, and just like she remembered, it was breathtaking. Robby would have a heart-stopping smile like that, too.

"This way, Mr. Foster."

Startled, Laura turned toward the unfamiliar male voice. The order came from a man in a black suit. A member of her brother's security staff, Laura realized upon closer inspection. She noted the wire that extended from his starched white collar to the small earpiece he wore. The lack of inflection in his tone as well as his deadpan gaze confirmed Laura's assumption.

Nick took Laura by the arm and ushered her forward as he followed the security guy. No one spoke as they moved across the verandah and toward the French doors at the back of the house. Laura instinctively absorbed every detail of the house's exterior. Her brother had spared no expense on exterior lighting. Of course that could be a hindrance if she somehow managed to escape. The darkness proved an ally at times. Not that her chance of escaping was likely. Laura eyed the man in black's tall frame with diminishing hope. Still, she needed to pay attention to the details. As long as she was still breathing, there was hope. *Focus, Laura,* she commanded her foggy brain.

A wide balcony spanned the rear of the house, supported by massive, ornate white columns. Three sets of French doors lined the first as well as the second floor. At least there were several avenues of escape, Laura noted, allowing that small measure of hope to seed inside her hollow heart. Maybe, just maybe, she would live long enough to at least attempt a getaway.

They crossed a very deserted, very elegant dining room and entered an enormous kitchen. Gleaming cabinetry and stainless steel monopolized the decorating scheme. The delicious scents of exquisite entrées and baked goods hung in the warm, moist air. Laura remembered then that she hadn't eaten today, but her stomach felt queasy rather than empty. Besides, she had no desire to share her last meal with her brother, or to eat it in his house. She would starve first.

Several pots with lids steamed on the stovetop. Security had apparently temporarily vacated the staff upon hearing of her arrival. As soon as the all clear signal was given the kitchen would quickly refill with the staff required to pull off this late night gala.

James Ed always rode the side of caution. And he never passed up an occasion to celebrate, to show off his many assets.

Laura's stomach knotted with the knowledge that her own brother hated her this much—or maybe it had nothing to do with her. Maybe it was simply the money.

Maybe…

Maybe Robby was here. A new kind of expectation shot through Laura. James Ed could have brought Robby here to use him as leverage to get what he wanted.

Nick firmed his grip on her right arm as if somehow sensing that her emotions had shifted. She had to get away from him. He read her entirely too well. Escape scenarios flashed through her mind as they mounted the service stairs.

Laura's heart pounded harder with each step she took. She felt hot and cold at the same time. She rubbed the clammy palm of her free hand against her hip, then squeezed her eyes shut for just a second against the dizziness that threatened. She could do this. Laura would do whatever it took to find her son and escape. James Ed would not win.

"Governor Proctor asked that you wait in here."

Nick thanked the man, then led Laura into what appeared to be James Ed's private study. Flames crackled in the fireplace, the warmth suffusing with the rich, dark paneling of the room. A wide mahogany desk with accompanying leather-tufted chair occupied one side of the room. Behind the desk, shelves filled with law books lined the wall from floor to ceiling. Leather wing chairs were stationed strategically before the massive desk. An ornate sideboard displayed fine crystal and exquisite decanters of expensive liquors. No one could accuse James Ed of lacking good taste, it was loyalty that escaped him.

Anxiety tightened Laura's chest, making it difficult to breathe. She had to concentrate. If she somehow freed herself from Nick's grasp and found Robby, could she make it off the grounds without being caught? Nick narrowed his gaze at her as if he had again read her thoughts. The man was entirely too perceptive.

"Take it easy, Laura, your brother will take good care of you," he said almost gently.

Laura shook her head, a pitiful outward display of her inner turmoil. "You just don't get it." She moistened her painfully dry lips and manufactured Nick a weak smile, hoping her words would penetrate that thick skull of his. "It would have been simpler if you'd just killed me yourself."

Laura knew she would not soon forget the expression that stole across Nick's features at that moment. The combination of emotions that danced across his face were as clear as writing on the wall. He cared for her, but he was confused. He trusted James Ed, just like everyone else, and he didn't quite trust Laura. Because she had hurt him badly. Left him to die—he thought. But she hadn't. And now he would never know what really happened, and, what was worse, he would never know his son.

"Laura, I'm sure—"

"Laura?"

A bone-deep chill settled over Laura at the sound of James Ed's distinctive voice. Nick turned immediately to greet the Governor. James Ed, tall, still thin and handsome, hadn't changed much, except for the sprinkling of gray at his sandy temples, and that was likely store-bought to give him a more distinguished appearance. Laura couldn't read the strange mixture of emotions on his face as he approached her. Fear sent her stumbling back several steps when he came too close, but his huge desk halted her.

"Laura, sweet Jesus, I didn't think I would ever see you again. I thought…I thought—dear God, you really are *alive*."

Feeling as trapped as a deer in the headlights of oncoming traffic, Laura froze when her brother threw his arms around her and hugged her tight. He murmured over and over how glad he was to see her. Resisting the urge to retch, Laura closed her eyes and prayed for a miracle. At this point, deep in her heart, she knew it would take nothing short of a miracle to escape and find her child.

James Ed's uncharacteristic actions dumbfounded Laura, adding confusion to the anxiety already tearing at her heart. He had never been the touchy-feely type. Then realization hit her. It was a show for Nick's benefit. James Ed wanted Nick to believe that he truly was thankful to have his baby sister home. When her brother drew back, tears clung to his salon-tanned face, further evidence of his feigned sincerity. The man was a master at misrepresentation and deceit. A true politician, heart and soul.

Laura slumped against the desk when he finally released her. She felt boneless with an exhaustion that went too deep. Nick had no way of knowing that he had just delivered her like the sacrificial lamb for slaughter. It was his job, she reminded herself. Nick worked for James Ed. She had known he would do this if he ever found her, just as she had known he would take her son away if he discovered his existence. And suddenly Laura understood what she had wanted to deny all day. It was over, and she had lost.

Robby was lost.

Laura's eyes closed against the pain that accompanied that thought, and the memory of her baby's smile haunted her soul.

"Nick, thank you so much for bringing her back to us. I don't know how to repay you."

Nick accepted the hand James Ed offered. "I was only doing what I was assigned to do two years ago." Nick wondered why it suddenly felt all wrong.

"You're a man of your word." James Ed gave Nick's hand another hearty shake. "I like that. If there's ever anything I can do for you, don't hesitate to ask."

Nick studied the Governor's sincere expression. He considered himself a good judge of character, and Laura's fears just didn't ring true when Nick looked her brother square in the eye. He read no deceit or hatred in the man's gaze. But his gut reaction told him that Laura truly believed in the threat.

"There is one thing," Nick began, hesitant to offend the man, but certain he couldn't leave without clearing the air.

"*Laura!*" Sandra, James Ed's wife, flew across the room and pulled Laura into her arms. "Honey, I am so glad to have you back home. You don't know how your brother and I have prayed that somehow you really were alive and would come back to us.''

Nick couldn't reconcile what Laura had described with the reunion happening right in front of him, and still something didn't feel right about the whole situation. Something elemental that he couldn't quite put his finger on.

''You were saying, Nick,'' James Ed prompted, the relieved smile on his face further evidence that Laura had to be wrong.

Nick studied the Governor for another long moment before he began once more. He knew that what he was about to say would definitely put a damper on this seemingly happy event. A few feet away he could hear Sandra fussing over a near catatonic Laura. What the hell, Nick had always been a straightforward kind of guy. Why stop now?

''Laura is convinced that you're the one behind the threat to her life, two years ago and now,'' Nick stated flatly.

You could have heard the proverbial pin drop for the next ten seconds. The look of profound disbelief on James Ed's face morphed into horror right before Nick's eyes. Nick would have staked his life on the man's innocence right then and there. James Ed couldn't possibly be guilty of what Laura had accused him. Slowly, James Ed turned to face his sister, whose defeated, lifeless expression had not changed.

''Laura, you can't really believe that. My God, I'm your brother.''

''Honey, James Ed has been beside himself since the day you disappeared. How could you think that he had anything to do with trying to harm you?'' Sandra stroked Laura's long, blond hair as a mother would a beloved daughter. But Laura made no response. In spite of everything she had done, Nick ached to give Laura that kind of comfort himself—to see if she would respond to him as she had that one night.

Suddenly, Laura straightened, dodging Sandra's touch and pushing away from the desk that had likely kept her vertical. She took several shaky steps until she was face-to-face with her brother. She stared up at him. Nick tensed, remembering the hefty mug she had used to bash him upside the head. Luckily for James Ed there was nothing in her reach at the moment.

"If you really mean what you say, big brother, then do me one favor," Laura challenged, her voice strangely emotionless, but much stronger than Nick would have believed her capable at the moment.

Nick readied himself to tackle her if she started swinging at James Ed. The lump on the side of his head undeniable proof that Laura could be a wildcat when the urge struck her.

"Laura." She flinched when James Ed took her by the shoulders, but she didn't back off. "I will do anything within my power for you. Anything," he repeated passionately. "Just name it, honey."

"Give me back my son," she demanded, her voice cracking with the emotion she could no longer conceal. Laura's whole body trembled then, her upright position in serious jeopardy.

Nick moved to her side, pulled her from a stunned James Ed's grasp and into his own arms. "Shh, Laura, it's okay," he murmured against her soft hair as he held her tight. Her sobs would be contained no longer, she shook with the force of them.

"Nick, I don't know what she's talking about." James Ed threw up his hands, his exasperation clear.

"What on earth can she mean?" Sandra reiterated as she

hurried to her husband's side. She looked every bit as confused and genuinely concerned as James Ed.

"Please make him tell you, Nick, please," Laura begged, her fists clenched in the lapels of his jacket. "I don't care what he does to me, but don't let him hurt my baby." The look of pure fear and absolute pain on her sweet face wrenched his gut.

Confusion reigned. For the first time in his entire life, Nick didn't know what to do. As much as he knew he shouldn't, he wanted desperately to believe Laura. To take her away from here and keep her safe from any and all harm.

"Tell me, *please,*" James Ed urged. "What is this about a child?"

In abbreviated form, Nick recited the events that had taken place in Bay Break, all the while holding Laura close, giving her the only comfort he could. "Laura insists that she has a son," he concluded. "I didn't find any evidence to corroborate her story, but—" he shrugged "—she stands by it."

Laura pounded her fists against his chest, demanding Nick's full attention. "I do have a son! His name is Robby and he's—"

"Laura," James Ed broke in, his tone calm and soothing despite the unnerving story Nick had just related to him.

Laura whirled in Nick's arms, but he held her back when she would have flung herself at James Ed. "You stole my son! Don't try to tell me you didn't!"

"Laura, please!" Sandra scolded gently. "You aren't making sense. What child?"

Laura turned to her. "Sandra, make him tell me!"

Nick tightened his hold on Laura, his protective instincts kicking into high gear. He still felt connected to her; he couldn't pretend that he didn't. "So you don't have her son?" he asked the Governor pointedly.

James Ed closed his eyes and pinched the bridge of his nose. Several long seconds passed before he released a heavy breath, opened his eyes, and then spoke, "It's worse than I thought."

"What's that supposed to mean?" Laura challenged, her voice strained.

James Ed settled a sympathetic gaze on his sister. "Laura, there can't possibly be any baby." He held up his hands to stay her protests, a look of pained defeat revealing itself on his face. "Just hear me out."

Laura sagged against Nick then, the fight going out of her. Nick wasn't sure how much more she would be able to stand before collapsing completely.

"Laura," James Ed began hesitantly. "Until the day before yesterday, when you escaped, you had spent the last eighteen months in a mental institution in New Orleans."

Nick felt Laura's gasp of disbelief. "That's a lie," she cried.

James Ed massaged his right temple as if an ache had begun there. "Apparently when you ran away two years ago, you wound up in New Orleans. You were found in an alley a few months later and hospitalized." He paused to stare at the floor. "The diagnosis was trauma-induced amnesia, and schizophrenia. The doctor says you haven't responded well to the drug therapy, but there's still hope."

Laura shook her head. "That's a lie. I've never been to New Orleans."

"Laura, honey, please listen to your brother," Sandra coaxed.

"You had no ID, no money. They assumed you were homeless and really didn't attempt to find out where you'd come from. And that's where you've been ever since. If you hadn't escaped, we might never have known you were even alive." His gaze softened with sadness. "You were considered a threat to yourself...as well as others." A beat of sickening silence passed. "Detective Ingle spotted you yesterday." James Ed looked to Nick then. "Ray told me you would be bringing Laura home. He received a copy of the New Orleans APB on the Jane Doe escapee just a few hours ago. It didn't take long to put two and two together. We've already contacted the hospital. The treating physician there faxed me a copy of his report."

Laura turned back to face Nick. "He's lying, Nick. You have to believe me!"

Nick searched her eyes, trying to look past the panic and fear for the truth. "Laura, why would he lie?" All the cards were stacked against her, James Ed had no motivation that Nick could see for wanting to harm her. And Laura had no proof of any of her accusations, or that she had a child.

"Honey, I would never lie to you." James Ed moved closer. "I am so sorry that this has happened. If we had known how sick you were two years ago, maybe we could have prevented this total breakdown—"

"Why are you doing this?" Laura cried. "I'm not crazy. I just want my son back!"

"I think it's time to call Dr. Beckman in," Sandra suggested quietly.

"Who?" Laura demanded. Her body shook so badly now that Nick's arms were all that kept her upright. Nick's own concern mounted swiftly.

"Wait," James Ed told Sandra, then turned to Laura. He studied her for a time before continuing. "All right, Laura, tell us where you've been if not in New Orleans."

"Darling, don't put yourself and Laura through this now," Sandra pleaded softly.

James Ed shook his head. "I want to hear Laura's side.

I won't be guilty of failing to listen again." He gave Sandra a pointed look. "I want to know where *she* believes she has been."

"You know where I've been," Laura snapped. "You've had someone tracking me like an animal."

"Please, Laura, you can't believe that." James Ed reached for her, but she shunned his touch.

"Stay away from me!"

"Surely we can sort all this out in the morning after Laura's had a good night's rest," Sandra offered quickly. "We're all upset. Let's not make things worse by pushing Laura when she's obviously exhausted." Sandra placed a comforting hand on James Ed's arm. "And we do have guests arriving shortly, unless you'd like me to cancel...."

"You're right, of course, dear," James Ed relented with a heavy sigh. "Laura needs to rest. Canceling dinner is probably wise, too. I should have realized that earlier. We've all had a shock."

"I'll get the doctor." Sandra hurried toward the door.

Laura stiffened. "I don't need a doctor."

"Honey, this is for your own good," James Ed assured her. "We've had Dr. Beckman, a close friend, standing by since we found out...what happened. He has spoken with the doctor in New Orleans and understands the specifics of your case. He'll give you something to calm you down, and we can work all this out in the morning."

"No!" Laura struggled in Nick's arms. "Don't do this, James Ed, please!"

Nick didn't like the way this was going. Before he could protest, Sandra rushed back into the room followed by a short, older man carrying a small black case.

"Nick, please don't let them do this to me."

Nick looked from Laura to the doctor who had just taken a hypodermic needle from his bag. Nick's uncertain gaze shifted to the Governor. "I don't know about this, James Ed," Nick said slowly.

"It's okay, Nick, he's only going to give her a sedative," James Ed explained tiredly. "It's for her own good. Considering the state she's in she might hurt herself."

The image of the scars on Laura's wrists flashed through Nick's mind. Maybe James Ed knew what he was doing. She was his sister. If there was no child, then Laura was seriously delusional. But—

"Don't!" Laura shouted when the doctor came closer. "Help me, Nick! You have to help me!"

"Nick, you're going to have to help *us*," James Ed pressed as he reached for Laura. "You must see that she desperately needs a sedative."

Nick pulled Laura closer, the look he shot James Ed stopped him cold. "This doesn't feel right."

"It's perfectly safe, Mr. Foster," the doctor assured Nick. "She needs rest right now. Her present condition isn't conducive to her own welfare."

Nick felt confused. His head ached from the blow Laura had dealt him. The image of her scarred wrists kept flitting through his mind. He wasn't sure how to proceed. His heart said one thing, but his brain another. He stared down at the trembling woman in his arms. What was the best thing for her? The dark circles beneath her wide blue eyes and the even paler cast to her complexion gave him his answer. She needed to rest. She needed the kind of help Nick couldn't give her. But *this* just didn't feel right.

Sandra reached for Laura this time. "No," Nick said harshly. "I don't think—"

"Your job is over now, Nick," Sandra interrupted calmly, patiently. "You should let us do ours."

"It's for the best, Nick," James Ed said with defeat.

"Mr. Foster, I'll have to ask you to leave now."

Nick's gaze shot over his shoulder toward the man who had just spoken. A suit from James Ed's private security staff stood directly behind Nick. His jaw hardened at the realization that he had been so caught up in Laura's plight that he hadn't heard him approach.

"Get lost," Nick warned.

"Let's not make this anymore unpleasant than necessary, sir," the man in black suggested pointedly.

Nick held his challenging stare for several tense seconds, then reluctantly released Laura. He wouldn't do anything to make bad matters worse...at least not right now.

When Sandra and Dr. Beckman closed in on Laura, the look of betrayal in her eyes ripped the heart right out of Nick's chest. "Please don't let them hurt my baby," she murmured, then winced when the needle penetrated the soft skin of her delicate shoulder.

Nick turned to James Ed, a white-hot rage suddenly detonating inside him. "If you're holding anything back—"

The Governor shook his head in solemn defeat. "Trust me, Nick."

Chapter Four

"She isn't well," Sandra said softly.

"I know."

"What are you going to do?"

"I don't know," James Ed answered hesitantly. His pause before continuing seemed an eternity. "But I have to do something. I can't allow her to continue this way."

"What do you mean?" Caution and the barest hint of uncertainty tinged Sandra's words. "Laura is your sister," she reminded softly. "Now that she's back, there are changes..."

James Ed breathed a heavy sigh. "Do you think I could forget that significant detail?"

"I'm sorry. Of course not."

Laura struggled to maintain her focus on the quiet conversation going on above her. Blackness hovered very near, threatening to drag her back into the abyss of unconsciousness. Her entire body felt leaden, lifeless. She wasn't sure she could move if she tried. She could open her eyes. Laura had managed to lift her heavy lids once or twice before Sandra and James Ed entered the room.

How long had she been here? she wondered. Long enough that the sedative the doctor had administered had begun to wear off. Though still groggy, Laura's mind was slowly clearing. But she couldn't have been here too long. Twenty-four hours, maybe? Though Laura had no way of knowing the precise drug she had been given, she recognized the aftereffects. Whatever it was, it was strong and long lasting. She'd had it before....

Before she had escaped her brother's clutches. Before she fell in love with Nick and had Robby.

A soul-deep ache wrenched through her. Laura moaned in spite of herself. Where was Robby? Was he safe? Oh God, she had to find her baby. But if she opened her eyes now they would know she was listening. Why hadn't Nick helped her? Because he was one of them, Laura reminded herself. He had always been on their side. No one believed her. No one would help her.

"She's waking up," James Ed warned, something that sounded vaguely like fear in his tone. "Where is the medication Dr. Beckman left?"

"You go ahead and get ready for bed," Sandra suggested. "You didn't get much sleep last night with Laura's arrival. I'll see to her, and then I'll join you."

James Ed released a long breath. "All right."

Laura heard the door close as James Ed left the room. Her heart thudded against her ribcage. She had to do something. Maybe Sandra would believe her. She opened her eyes and struggled to focus on her sister-in-law's image. A golden glow from the lamp on the bedside table defined Sandra's dark, slender features. Smiling, she sat down on the edge of the mattress at Laura's side. Laura's lethargic fingers fisted in the cool sheet and dragged it up around her neck, as if the thin linen would somehow protect her. She had to get away from here. Somehow.

"Help me," Laura whispered.

"Oh, now, don't you worry, everything is going to be fine." Sandra smoothed a soothing hand over Laura's hair.

"You shouldn't be frightened. James Ed and I only want the best for you, dear. Don't you see that?"

Her lids drooping with the overwhelming need to surrender, Laura mentally fought the sedative. She would not go back to sleep. She concentrated on staying awake. Don't go to sleep, she told herself. You have to do this for Robby. Robby…oh God, would she ever see her baby again? And Nick? Nick was lost to her, too.

Sandra retrieved something from the night table. Laura's drowsy gaze followed her movements. A prescription bottle. Sandra slipped off the top and tapped two small pills into her palm. Laura frowned, trying to focus…to see more clearly. More medicine! She didn't want more.

"Here." Sandra placed the medication against Laura's lips. "Take these and rest, Laura. We want you to get well as soon as possible. Dr. Beckman said these would help."

Laura pressed her lips together and turned her head. She would not take anything else. She had to wake up. Tears burned her eyes and her body trembled with the effort required to resist.

Sandra shook her head sympathetically. "Honey, if you don't take the medication, James Ed will only make me call Dr. Beckman again. You don't want that, do you?"

A sob constricted Laura's throat. Slowly, her lips trembling with the effort, she opened her mouth. Tears blurred her vision as Sandra pushed the pills past Laura's lips. Laura took a small sip of the water Sandra offered next.

"That's a good girl," Sandra said softly. She fussed with the covers around Laura and then stood. "You rest, honey. I'll be right down the hall."

Laura watched as Sandra closed the door behind her. Laura quickly spat the two pills into her hand. She shuddered at the bitter aftertaste they left in her mouth. Her fingers curled into a fist around the dissolving medication.

She cursed her brother, cursed God for allowing this to happen, then cursed herself for being a fool. Gritting her teeth with the effort, Laura forced her sluggish body to a sitting position. With the back of her hand she wiped at the bitter taste on her tongue. She shuddered again, barely restraining the urge to gag.

Laura took a deep breath and surveyed the dimly lit room. She had to get out of here. But how would she get out? She would most likely be caught the moment she stepped into the hallway. Security was probably lurking out there somewhere. French doors and several windows lined one wall. The balcony, she remembered. The balcony at the back of the house. Maybe she could get out that way. A single door, probably to a bathroom or a closet, Laura surmised, stood partially open on the other side of the room. Still wearing the clothes she had arrived in, Laura pushed to her feet, then staggered across the room to what she hoped was a bathroom. Her legs were rubbery, and her head felt as if it might just roll off her shoulders like a runaway bowling ball.

Cool tile suddenly took the place of the plush carpeting beneath her feet. Laura breathed a sigh of relief that the door did, in fact, lead to a bathroom. She lurched to the vanity and lowered her head to the faucet. Water. She moaned her relief at the feel of the refreshing liquid against her lips, on her tongue, and then as it slid down her parched throat. Laura rinsed the bitter taste from her mouth, then washed the gritty pill residue from her hand. She shivered as her foggy brain reacted to the sound of the running water, making her keenly aware of the need to relieve herself in another way.

After taking care of that necessity, Laura caught sight of her reflection as she paused to wash her hands. The dim glow from the other room offered little illumination, but

Laura could see that her eyes were swollen and red, and her face looked pale and puffy. She splashed cold water onto her face several times to help her wake up, then finger-combed her tousled hair. All she had to do was pull herself together enough to find a way to climb down from the balcony. Laura frowned when the coldness of the tile floor again invaded her senses. She needed her shoes. Where were her shoes?

Laura lurched back into the bedroom. She searched the room, the closet, under the bed, everywhere she knew to look and to no avail. Her shoes were not to be found. Exhausted, Laura plopped onto the edge of the bed. She had to have shoes. It was too damned cold to make a run for it barefoot. She would have to head for some sort of cover—the woods, maybe. How could she run without her shoes?

Think, Laura, she ordered her fuzzy brain. They must have removed her shoes when they took her jacket. She stared down at the stained T-shirt she wore. She had to remember. What room was she in when they took her jacket? The study or in this bedroom? Robby was depending on her. She had to get out of here. But somehow she needed to search the house first. Robby could be here. Her heart bumped into overdrive at the thought of how long it had been since she had seen her son. She let go a halting breath. He had been missing over twenty-four hours now, if her calculations were correct. She scanned the room for a clock, but didn't see one. Laura squeezed her eyes shut then.

Please God, keep my baby safe. I don't care if I die tonight, she beseeched, *just don't let anything happen to my baby.*

Her body weak and trembling, Laura dropped to her hands and knees on the floor. For one long moment she wanted to curl into the fetal position and cry. Laura shook off the urge to close her eyes and allow the drug to drag her back into oblivion. She had to find those damned shoes. Slowly, carefully, she crawled around the large room and searched every square foot again. Still nothing. Too weary now to even crawl back to the bed. Laura leaned her head against the wall and allowed her eyes to close. She was so tired. She could rest for just one minute. She scrubbed a hand over her face…she could not go back to sleep…she had to find her shoes.

To find Robby.

All she needed was one more moment of rest….

The blackness embraced Laura as she surrendered to the inevitable.

LAURA WASN'T SURE how much time had passed when she awoke. Hours probably, her muscles cramped from the position in which she had fallen asleep. It was still night she knew since only the dimmest glow of light filtered through her closed, immensely heavy lids. Groaning, she sat up straighter and stretched her shoulders, first one side, then the other. She frowned, trying to remember what she was supposed to do. Her shoes. That's right. She needed to find her shoes and get out of here. Laura shoved the hair back from her face and licked her dry lips.

"Okay," she mumbled. Shoes, she needed her shoes. She had to get up first. Laura forced her reluctant lids open and blinked to focus in the near darkness. Eerie pink eyes behind a black ski mask met her bleary gaze. Laura opened her mouth to scream, but a gloved hand clamped over her lips.

"So, Sleeping Beauty is awake," a male voice rasped.

Laura drew back from the threat, the wall halted her retreat, his hand pressed down more brutally over her mouth. She shook her head and tried to beg for her life, but her words were stifled by black leather.

"You," he said disgustedly. "Have caused me a great deal of extra trouble." Something sharp pricked her neck. Laura's heart slammed mercilessly against her rib cage. He had a knife. A cry twisted in her throat.

He jerked Laura to her feet. The remaining fog in her brain cleared instantly. This man had come to kill her. She was going to die.

No! her mind screamed. She had to find Robby.

Laura stiffened against him. He was strong, but not very large. If she struggled hard enough—

"Don't move," he growled next to her ear. The tip of the knife pierced the skin at the base of her throat again.

Laura suppressed the violent tremble that threatened to wrack her body. Blood trickled down and over her collarbone. Hysteria threatened her flimsy hold on calm. She had to think! Her frantic gaze latched on to the open French doors. He had probably entered her room from the balcony. If he could come in that way, she could escape by the same route. All she had to do was get away from him…from the knife.

His arm tightened around her as if she had uttered her thoughts aloud. "Time to die, princess," he murmured, then licked her cheek. The foul stench of his breath sent nausea rising into her throat.

Laura swallowed convulsively. She squeezed her eyes shut and focused on a mental picture of her son to escape the reality of what was happening. Her sweet, sweet child. The tip of the knife trailed over one breast.

"Too bad you didn't stay gone." He twisted her face up to his. Those icy eyes flashed with rage.

The air vaporized in Laura's lungs. He was going to kill her and there was no one to help her. No one. Nick didn't believe her. And her own brother had probably hired this man.

"Now you have to die." He eased his hand from her lips only to press his mouth over hers. The feel of wool from his ski mask chafed her cheeks. Laura struggled. The knife blade quickly came up to her throat again.

Laura wilted when he forced his tongue into her mouth. Tears seeped past her tightly closed lids. Her entire body convulsed at the sickening invasion. Rage like she had never experienced before surged through her next. Laura's eyes opened wide and she clamped down hard with her teeth on the bastard's tongue. The sting of the knife blade slid down her chest when he snapped his head back. Laura jerked out of his momentarily slack hold. She flung herself toward the balcony. She had to escape.

"Come back here, you bitch," he growled, his words slightly slurred.

Laura slammed the French doors shut behind her. He pushed hard against them. Laura fought with all her body weight to prevent the doors from opening. Her feet slipped on the slick painted surface of the balcony. One door opened slightly before she could regain her footing. He reached a hand between the doors and grabbed her by the hair. Laura screamed. The sound echoed in the darkness around her. She slammed against the door with every ounce of force she had. The man swore, released her and jerked his arm back inside.

Too weak to stand any longer, Laura dropped to her knees. She held on to the door handles with all her might. The handles shook in her hold. She leaned harder against the doors. Surely someone would come into her room at any moment. James Ed had around-the-clock security, Laura was certain. If they would come, then she would have proof that she had been telling the truth all along.

Seconds clicked by. Someone had to come, didn't they? A sob twisted inside her chest. She was so tired. And no one was coming. No one cared.

Laura screamed when the door shoved hard against her, hard enough to dislodge her weight. She scrambled away from the threat. Panic had obliterated all reason. She had to get away. To find her child.

"Laura!"

Laura stilled. Was that Nick's voice? Hope welled in her chest. He was coming back for her.

"Laura." James Ed crouched next to her. "What happened?"

Laura lifted her gaze to his, disappointment shuddered through her. It wasn't Nick. She must have imagined his voice. "Please help me," she pleaded with her brother.

"Sweet Jesus!" James Ed stared at her chest. "Laura, are you hurt?"

She stared down at herself. Blood. Her T-shirt was red with blood. Her blood. The blackness threatened again. Laura struggled to remain conscious. She was bleeding. The knife. Her gaze flew to her brother's. "He tried to kill me," she murmured.

James Ed shook his head, his face lined with worry. "Who tried to kill you, Laura? There's no one here."

Laura looked past James Ed to the bedroom she had barely escaped with her life. The overhead lights were on now. A man in a black suit stood in the middle of the room. Security. Laura remembered him from when she had first arrived. She frowned. Security had to have seen the intruder. Surely he couldn't have gotten past a professional security team. Could he be hiding somewhere in the house? Why weren't they looking for him?

Sandra was next to her now. "Let's get you back inside and see exactly what you've done to yourself."

"No," Laura denied. "There was a man. He tried to kill me. He had a knife."

"Come on, Laura." James Ed helped Laura to her feet. "Don't make this any worse than it already is."

"I found this, sir."

The man held a large kitchen knife gingerly between his thumb and forefinger. Light glistened from the wide blade. Blood—her blood, Laura realized—stained the otherwise shiny edge.

Sandra scrutinized the knife. "It's from *our* kitchen," she said slowly, her gaze shifting quickly to James Ed.

"Dear God," he breathed.

Despite the lingering effects of the sedative, Laura realized the implications. "No," she protested. "There was someone here. He—"

"That's enough, Laura," James Ed commanded harshly. She glared up at him. "We've had more than enough excitement for one night," he added a bit more calmly. "Now, let's get you back in bed and attend to your injuries."

Shaking her head, Laura jerked from his grasp. "You can't keep me here." Laura backed away from him. "I have to find my son."

James Ed only stared at her, something akin to sympathy glimmered in his blue eyes. For one fleeting instant Laura wondered if she could be wrong about her brother. Probably not.

"Miss Proctor, I have to insist that you cooperate with the Governor."

Laura turned slowly to face the man who had spoken. The security guy from the night before. She didn't know his name. Laura met his cold, dark gaze. He extended his hand, and Laura dragged her gaze down to stare at the offered assistance. She looked back to her brother, then to

Sandra. Laura swallowed the rush of fear that crowded into her throat. How could she fight all of them?

She shifted her gaze back to the man offering his hand. "They're going to kill me, you know," she said wearily. Laura blinked as tears burned her eyes.

"Laura, please don't say things like that," Sandra insisted gently. "Please lie down and let me take care of you. You've hurt yourself."

Laura shook her head. "It doesn't matter." She brushed past the guy in the black suit and walked to the bed. Laura climbed amid the tangled covers and squeezed her eyes shut. "Just go away," she murmured. "Just…go away."

A long moment of silence passed before anyone responded to her request.

"Lock it this time," James Ed ordered, his voice coming from near the door. "And I want someone stationed outside her room. I don't want her hurting herself again."

"Should we call Dr. Beckman?" Sandra suggested quietly.

"I think it's too late for that," James Ed returned just as quietly. "This has gone way beyond Beckman."

"Excuse me, sir," a new male voice interrupted. "There is a gentleman downstairs to see you."

"At this hour?" James Ed demanded. "Who is it?"

Silence.

"I think you had better come and see for yourself, Governor."

NICK STOOD in the middle of Governor Proctor's private study. He was mad as hell. He had no idea what the hell had gone on here tonight, but he had clearly seen Laura on that balcony. Fear and fury in equal measures twisted inside him. If tonight was any indication of James Ed's ability to take care of his sister, it stunk. And Nick had no intention of leaving her welfare to chance.

Maybe Victoria was right, maybe he had lost his perspective. Victoria had wanted to assign Ian Michaels to Laura's case when Nick called and informed her of his plan to hang around. She had stood by her assertion that Nick needed a vacation. But Nick had managed to convince her otherwise—against her better judgment. Nick blew out a disgusted breath. What the hell was wrong with him? He should have flown back to Chicago last night instead of skulking outside James Ed's house watching for trouble. If security had caught him, how would he have explained his uninvited presence? Nick had just about convinced himself to leave after more than twenty-four hours of surveillance, when Laura had flown out onto that balcony screaming bloody murder. Now, Nick didn't care what James Ed thought.

Nick closed his eyes and shook his head. Here he was allowing history to repeat itself—at his expense. Laura Proctor had almost gotten him killed once. And now he was back in her life as though nothing had ever happened between them. Nick swore softly, cursing his own stupidity.

But he just couldn't leave her like this.

"Nick, sorry you had to wait." Governor Proctor breezed in, a suit flanking him. "I thought you had to get back to Chicago? What's going on?"

"I was about to ask you the same question." Nick met him halfway across the room and accepted the hand he extended. "I saw Laura on the balcony." Nick had called out to her, but she hadn't heard him.

James Ed shook his hand firmly, then sighed mightily. Worry marred his face. "I'm not sure I know what happened."

"Where's Laura?" Nick felt a muscle tic in his tense jaw.

James Ed dropped his gaze and slowly shook his head. "She's in her room, heavily sedated." He lifted his gaze back to Nick's and shrugged listlessly. "Tonight's episode was intensely frightening. I was afraid she would—" he swallowed "—fall off the balcony."

Renewed fear slammed into Nick like a sucker punch to the gut. "Is she all right?"

"Physically she'll be okay," he explained. "But she's convinced that someone is trying to kill her."

"And you don't believe that?" Nick noted the lines of fatigue around the Governor's eyes and mouth before he looked away. "You're certain she's all right. I heard her scream and the next thing I knew she was struggling against the French doors as if someone were trying to get to her."

"That was me," James Ed explained. "I'll take you up in a moment and you can see for yourself." He shook his head wearily. "But honestly, Nick, I don't know what I believe." He gestured to the chair in front of his desk. "Please, have a seat. I have to do something. But first I have to think this through." He skirted the desk and settled heavily into the high-back leather chair behind it.

Nick didn't have to look to know that the Governor's bodyguard remained by the door. Slowly, Nick moved to stand behind one of the wing chairs near the desk. He wasn't ready to sit just yet. He watched James Ed's reaction closely as Nick asked his next question. "I don't know what's happening here, James Ed. Your actions indicate to me that you don't believe Laura, yet you believed her two years ago. That's why you hired me in the first place."

"Did I?" He met Nick's analyzing gaze. "Or was I simply desperate for someone else to take responsibility for my out-of-control sister?"

"And the man who shot me?" Nick lifted one brow in skepticism. "Was he another figment of her imagination as well?"

James Ed closed his eyes and let go a weary breath. "I don't know," he said quietly. "I only know that Laura is alive and she needs help." He opened his eyes, the same translucent blue as Laura's, and met Nick's gaze. "The kind of help I can't give her. I'm afraid for her life."

The image of Laura's scarred wrists loomed large in Nick's mind. He tensed. Maybe James Ed had a right to be scared of what Laura might do to herself. Nick couldn't be sure. Too much of what was going on still baffled him. Something had been nagging at him since he left her here last night. And he hadn't been able to leave because of it. Nick couldn't put his finger on it just yet, but something wasn't as it should be. Maybe he just needed to get Laura out of his system. Whatever it was, he had to do this. He needed closure with Laura and both their demons.

"Tomorrow I'm calling a private hospital that Dr. Beckman has recommended to me." James Ed lifted his gaze to Nick. "I don't know what else to do. Every waking moment she rants on about her child, then tonight she claims someone tried to kill her. I'm at a complete loss."

"And what if she's telling the truth," Nick offered.

James Ed searched his desk for a moment, then picked up a piece of paper and handed it to Nick. "There's the report from the hospital in Louisiana. See for yourself."

Nick scanned the report that had been faxed to Beckman. The conclusions it indicated were very incriminating. If half of this turned out to be true, Laura was a very sick lady. He leaned forward and passed the report back to James Ed. "I'm still not convinced."

James Ed stroked his forehead as if a headache had begun there. "What is it that you would suggest then, Nick?

I only want to keep her from hurting herself and to find a way to help her.'' He straightened abruptly and banged his fist against the polished desk. "Damn it! I love my sister. I want her to be well. If these doctors can help her, what choice do I have?''

Silence screamed between them for one long beat. "Give me a chance to see if I can get through to her.'' Nick shrugged. "Let me look into the allegations she has made.''

James Ed's weary expression grew guarded. "I'm listening.''

"Two weeks. I choose the place,'' Nick went on. "And there will be absolutely no interference from you or anyone else.''

James Ed frowned. "What do you mean interference?''

"You won't see Laura until I bring her back to you.''

"What kind of request is that?'' James Ed demanded crossly. "She's my sister!''

"What do you have to lose?'' Nick said flatly. He couldn't get to the bottom of what was going on with Laura unless he had her all to himself. There could be no distractions or interference.

The Governor pushed to his feet, irritation lining his distinguished features. "Fine.'' He glowered at Nick. "I'm only doing this because I'm desperate and I trust you. I hope you know that, Foster. Now, where are you planning to take her?''

"I'd like to take her to your country house near Bay Break. It's quiet and out of the way,'' Nick explained. "And Laura mentioned that her childhood there was happy.''

James Ed blinked, then looked away. "Laura did love it there as a child.'' He closed his eyes for a moment before he continued. "And that would protect Laura from the paparazzi that follows me.''

Nick considered the Governor's last words for a bit. Was his concern for his sister or for his image? Maybe Laura's accusations were making Nick paranoid. One thing was certain, before he left Laura this time, Nick would know exactly what and who was behind Laura's problems—even if it turned out to be Laura herself. That possibility went against Nick's instincts, but time would tell.

"When would you like to begin?" James Ed asked.

Nick couldn't be sure, but he thought he saw something resembling hope in James Ed's gaze. "We'll leave right away," Nick suggested.

"I'll call Rutherford and have him prepare the house." James Ed surveyed his desk as if looking for something he had just remembered. "Sandra will put some things together in a bag for Laura."

"Good." Nick turned to leave.

"Nick."

He shifted to face James Ed once more. "Yes."

"Take good care of her, would you?"

Nick dipped his head in silent acknowledgment.

NICK STOOD at the foot of Laura's bed and watched her sleep for several minutes. He closed his eyes and willed away the need to hold her. She looked so small and vulnerable. And Nick wanted more than anything to protect her. He opened his eyes and stared at the soft blond hair spread across her pillow. He wanted to hold her to him and protect her forever. That's what he really wanted. But could he do that? He had seen the report with his own eyes. He swallowed. Laura could be very ill.

That reality didn't stop him from wanting her. Laura's problems had almost cost him his life once before. Apparently that didn't carry much weight with Nick either, because it sure as hell hadn't kept him from hanging around when his assignment was technically over. Giving himself credit, there was more to his being here than simply bone-deep need and desire.

Something wasn't right with this whole picture. James Ed appeared every bit the loving, concerned brother. By the same token Laura seemed as sane as anyone else Nick knew. He lifted one brow sardonically. That didn't say much for Nick's selected associates.

Nick's thoughts turned somber once more. Laura was convinced that she had a child. He frowned. According to James Ed and the hospital report, that was impossible. Nick massaged his forehead. Well, he had two weeks to decide what the real truth was. And the only way he would ever be able to do that is if he kept his head screwed on straight. He couldn't allow her to get to him again. One way or another he would get to the truth. He owed it to himself…and he owed it to Laura. The image of her stricken face when he had left her haunted his every waking moment. Nick swallowed hard. He simply couldn't walk away without looking back. No matter what had happened in the past. He just couldn't do it.

Nick stepped quietly to the side of the bed. He sat down next to Laura and watched her breathe for a time. She was so beautiful. Nick cursed himself. He wasn't supposed to dwell on that undeniable fact. He lifted his hand to sweep the hair from her face, but hesitated before touching her. He swallowed hard as he allowed his fingertips to graze her soft cheek. That simple touch sent desire hurdling through his veins.

"Laura," he whispered tautly. "Wake up, Laura."

Her lids fluttered open to reveal those big, beautiful blue eyes. It took her a moment to focus on his face. Drugs, he realized grimly. James Ed had said she was heavily sedated.

"Nick?" She frowned, clearly confused.

"It's okay, Laura," he assured her.

She struggled to a sitting position. Nick's gaze riveted to her bloodstained T-shirt. The same T-shirt she had been wearing when he brought her here.

"What the hell happened?" he demanded softly. Before Nick could determine where the blood had come from, Laura flung her arms around him and buried her face in his neck.

"I prayed you'd come back for me," she murmured, her words catching on a tiny sob.

Hesitantly, Nick put his arms around her and pulled her close. "It's okay. I'm here now, and this time I'm not leaving without you." The feel of her fragile, trembling body in his arms made him want to scream at the injustice of it all. How could life be so unfair to her...and to him?

Laura drew back from him, her eyes were glassy, her movements sluggish. "Nick, I just need you to do one thing for me."

"What's that?" he asked, visually searching her upper body for signs of injury. The idea that someone had hurt Laura seared in his brain.

"Please, Nick," she murmured, "find my baby."

Chapter Five

"This child doesn't look neglected to me." Elsa touched the small dark head of the sleeping child. "Where was he found?"

"It's not our job to ask questions."

"I'm only saying that he looks perfectly healthy and well cared for in my opinion," Elsa argued irritably. The child slept like the dead. He rarely cried and ate like a horse. And when he was awake, he played with hardly any fuss. This was no neglected and abandoned child.

"Who's asking for your opinion?"

"I'm entitled to my opinion."

"That you are. You'd do well to remember your place and to keep your opinions to yourself."

"Don't you wonder where he came from?" Elsa wondered how her longtime friend could simply pretend not to notice the obvious inconsistencies.

"No. And if you know what's good for you, you'll put those silly notions out of your head and be about your work. There are some things we're better off not knowing."

Elsa's gaze again wandered to the sleeping child. He really was none of her concern—not in that way anyhow. And asking questions and jumping to conclusions weren't included in her duties.

Perhaps her friend was right.

NICK STARED at a framed photograph of Laura as a child while he waited for his call to be transferred to Ian's office. Perched in the saddle atop a sandy-colored pony, Laura beamed at the camera, her smile wide and bright. Nick decided the moment had been captured when she was about five. All that angel blond hair hung around her slim shoulders like a cape of silk. Her big brother, James Ed, who would have been about twenty-one, sported an Ole Miss letter sweater and gripped the lead line to the pony's bridal. His own smile appeared every bit as bright as his sister's.

A frown furrowed Nick's brow. What happened, he wondered, between then and now to change their lives so drastically? With a heavy sigh, he placed the picture in its original position on the oak mantel. Nick stared at the frozen frame in time for a second or two more. Had James Ed been a doting brother then? Did he really care about Laura the way he claimed to now? Laura certainly didn't think so.

Ian Michaels' accented voice sounded in Nick's ear, drawing his attention back to the cellular telephone and the call he had made. "Hey, Ian, it's Nick. I need you to check on a few things for me." Nick paused for Ian to grab a pen. "Review the file on Laura Proctor again and see if you can dig up anything new." Nick scrubbed a hand over his unshaven face, then frowned at the realization that he hadn't taken time to shave. After getting Laura settled in the Proctor country home, he had stayed up what was left of the night—early morning actually—watching over her.

"I didn't find anything when I ran that background check on her brother a couple of years ago." Another frown creased Nick's forehead. He'd been pretty distraught at the time; maybe he missed something. "I want you to look again. See if I overlooked anything at all. Something just isn't kosher down here. I can feel it,'' Nick added thoughtfully. He listened as Ian mentioned several areas that might turn up something new if he dug deeply enough.

"Sounds good," Nick agreed. "And, listen, check out that hospital in Louisiana that claims to have provided care for Laura for the past eighteen months. I want to know the kind of treatment she received, the medication she took—hell, I want to know what she ate for the last year and a half." Nick smiled at Ian's suggested means of collecting the requested and highly sensitive information. "Just don't get caught," Nick said. "Call me as soon as you have anything."

Nick flipped the mouthpiece closed and deposited the phone into his jacket pocket. He massaged his chin and considered his next move. There really wasn't much he could do until he heard from Ian. He let go a heavy breath. Except for keeping Laura out of trouble and, of course, getting the truth out of her. He should probably check on her now, he realized.

The Proctor country home was a ranch-style house of about three thousand square feet that was more mansion than home. Polished oak floors and rich, dark wainscoting and stark white walls represented the mainstay of the decor. The furnishings were an eclectic blend of antiques and contemporary, complemented by oriental wool rugs. The place was well maintained. The caretaker, Mr. Rutherford, appeared to stay on top of things. Upon James Ed's instructions, Rutherford had dropped by and adjusted the thermostat to a more comfortable setting, even stocked the refrigerator before Nick and Laura arrived. The old man had gone to a lot of trouble in the middle of the night. He also left a note with his telephone number in case they needed anything. Nick wasn't sure the guy could be of any real assistance to him unless the central heating unit died or the water heater went out, but he appreciated the gesture.

From the foyer Nick took the west hall and headed in the direction of Laura's bedroom. There were two bedrooms and two bathrooms at each end of the house. Laura's was the farthest from the main part of the house. Nick's was directly across the hall from hers. Nick opened the door and walked quietly across the plush carpeting to her bedside. She hadn't moved since the last time he checked on her. That bothered him. Laura hadn't shown any true violent tendencies in his opinion. A faint smile tilted his lips. Well, except for the way she crowned him with that coffee mug. Nick touched the still tender place at his temple. But that had been in self-defense, at least from Laura's standpoint. Yet they had kept her drugged as if she were a serious threat.

Nick considered the shallow knife wound on her chest and the tiny prick at the base of her throat. The injuries weren't consistent with anything self-inflicted in his opinion. Anger kindled inside him when he considered that no one had tended the injuries. He had done that himself, and then replaced the bloodstained T-shirt with a clean one Sandra had provided. Oh, Sandra had been apologetic enough. She had tried, she insisted, to take care of the wounds, but Laura had fought her touch. Nick wasn't sure he fully believed the woman, but that really didn't matter now.

Laura was safe for the moment. And one damned way or another he intended to see that she stayed that way. When she was up to it, he would get the answers he wanted. But first he had to unravel the mystery of where Laura had been and what she had been doing for the past two years. His gut told him that the answers he wanted about the man who shot him were somehow tangled in those missing months.

The pills Sandra had given him for Laura right before they left Jackson caught his eye. Nick sat down on the edge of the bed and picked up the prescription bottle to review the label. Take one or two every twelve hours. The pharmacist he had called this morning for information regarding the drug had said that the dosage was the strongest available. He had seemed surprised at the instructions to administer the medication more than once in a twenty-four hour period. Nick sighed and set the bottle back on the night table. The medication was strong enough that Laura hadn't moved a muscle.

Nick watched her breathe for a long while, just as he had done for hours last night. He closed his eyes and resisted the urge to touch her. Touching her would be a serious mistake. He had to stay in control of the situation this time. Nick pushed to his feet. Whenever she roused from the drug-induced slumber, she would likely be hungry. Nick left the room without looking back. A quick inventory of what the kitchen had to offer would keep him occupied for a while. If any supplies were needed he would just call Mr. Rutherford and put in an order.

When Nick reached the spacious kitchen a light knock sounded from the back door. A quick look through a nearby window revealed an older man, in his sixties maybe, waiting on the back stoop. Mr. Rutherford, Nick presumed from the overalls and the work boots.

"Howdie, young fella," the old man announced as soon as Nick opened the door. "I'm Carl Rutherford. Came by to see if you had everything you needed."

"Good morning, Mr. Rutherford. I'm Nick Foster." Nick pushed a smile into place and extended his hand.

"A pleasure to meet you, Mr. Foster." Rutherford clasped Nick's hand and shook it firmly

"Please, call me Nick. And thank you, you've taken care of everything here quite nicely."

Mr. Rutherford beamed with pride. "I've been seeing after this place for nearly thirty years." His expression grew suddenly somber. "How's Miss Laura this morning?"

Nick hesitated only a moment before stepping back. "Come in, Mr. Rutherford. I was about to have another cup of coffee."

"You can call me Carl," he insisted as he stepped inside.

Nick gestured for him to have a seat, then closed and locked the door. "How do you take it, Carl? Black?"

Carl settled himself into a chair at the breakfast table. "No sir, I like a little cream in mine if that's not too much trouble."

Nick shot him an amused look. "No trouble at all. You asked about Laura." Nick withdrew two cups from the cabinet near the sink and placed them on the counter. He had already gone through one pot. "She's sleeping right now." Nick frowned as he poured the dark liquid into the cups. "I'm not sure I can answer your question about her well-being with any real accuracy."

Carl huffed an indignant breath. "Was never a thing wrong with that little girl as long as she lived here."

Nick eyed the old man curiously as he stirred the cream into his coffee. "Tell me about Laura…before," he suggested cautiously. "Maybe that will give me some insight to what's going on now," he added at the older man's suspicious look.

Carl folded his arms over his chest and leaned back in his chair, lifting the two front legs off the floor. "She was a mighty sweet little thing growing up. Everybody loved her. Like an angel she was."

Nick had made that same connection several times himself. There was just something angelic and seemingly vulnerable about Laura's features. "She never got into trouble in school?" Nick placed both cups on the table and sat down across from his talkative visitor.

Carl shook his head adamantly. "No sir." He waved off the obvious conclusions. "Oh, the tale was that she got a little wild right before she went off to college." He made a scoffing sound in his throat. "That's why James Ed rushed her off to that fancy college up north."

"And you don't think that was the case?" Nick watched the older man's swiftly changing expressions.

"Land sakes no!" The chair legs plopped back to the floor. "Wasn't a thing wrong with that little girl except she had a mind of her own. She didn't fall into step like James Ed demanded." He harrumphed. "Why she was just like her daddy, that's all."

"Like her father how?" Nick's interest was piqued now. He sipped his coffee and listened patiently.

"You see, I worked for James Ed's granddaddy, James Senior, when I first moved to this county," Carl explained. "Right before James Ed's daddy, James Junior, went off to college he got a little wild."

Nick eyed him skeptically. "What do you mean wild?"

The old man shrugged. "Oh, you know, running with the wrong crowd. Even got himself involved with a girl from the wrong side of the tracks."

"Rebellious, like Laura?"

Carl nodded. "So the tale goes."

"What happened?"

"Well, James Junior got himself hustled off to one of them Ivy League law schools." The old man frowned in concentration. "Harvard, I believe it was. There was a bit of a stir about it. All the big shots hereabouts have always gone to Ole Miss. James Senior went to Ole Miss."

"But not James Ed's father?"

"Nope." Carl took a hefty swallow of his coffee. "When James Junior got back, he joined his daddy's law practice and married a girl of the right standing, if you know what I mean."

Nick considered his words for a time before he spoke. "What happened to the other girl?"

"Can't rightly say."

"So you think James Ed ushered Laura off to school in Boston in order to keep her out of trouble here."

"Yep." He leveled a pointed look at Nick. "But I think it amounted to nothing more than James Ed being too busy taking care of business and building his political career to deal with a hard-to-handle teenager." Red staining his cheeks as if realizing too late he had said too much, Carl scooted his chair back and got to his feet. "Thank you for the coffee, Nick. I'd better get going. Lots to do, you know." He turned before going out the door and met Nick's gaze one last time. "Give Laura my best, will you?"

Nick assured him that he would do just that. After the old man left Nick paced restlessly. He slid off his jacket and hung it on the back of a chair. For the next half hour he played the conversation over and over in his head, looking for any kind of connection. Each time he came up blank. Not taking any chances, he put in another quick call to Ian and added James Ed's daddy to the list of pasts to be looked into.

Maybe if he looked long and hard enough he would find at least some answers.

LAURA LICKED her dry lips and tried to swallow. Her throat felt like a dusty road. With a great deal of effort she opened her eyes. Focus came slowly. Where was she? Pink walls. Shelves lined with stuffed animals and a collection of dolls brought a smile to her parched lips.

Home.

She was home.

And Nick was here.

The events of the past few days came crashing into her consciousness. Laura wilted with reaction. *Her baby.* Oh, God, where was her baby? Clenching her jaw, she forced the overwhelming grief away. She had to get up. She couldn't find her baby like this.

Her arms trembling, Laura pushed to a sitting position. Her muscles were sore and one leg was asleep. Grimacing at the foul taste in her mouth and the bitter knots in her stomach, Laura stumbled out of bed. She made her way to the bathroom and took care of necessary business, including brushing her teeth. Using her hand, she thirstily drank from the faucet, then splashed some of the cool water on her face. Laura felt like she had been on a three-day drinking binge. She supposed she should be thankful for the dulling effects of the drugs, for if she were to have to face this nightmare with full command of her senses—

Laura couldn't complete the thought. Focus on something else, she ordered herself. Clumsily she fumbled through drawers until she found a hairbrush. Straightening out the mess her hair was in took some time and focused effort. Though still groggy, she felt at least a little human then.

Dressed in nothing but an oversized T-shirt and panties from the bag Sandra had sent along, Laura went in search of Nick. She needed to know if he had made any headway in the search for her son.

Laura's heart squeezed at the thought of her baby. A wave of dizziness washed over her. She sagged against the wall for a few seconds to allow the weakness to pass. *Please, God,* she prayed, *don't let anyone hurt my baby.*

She closed her eyes tightly to hold back the burn of tears. Crying would accomplish nothing.

Robby, where are you? she wanted to scream.

Laura forced her eyes open and pushed away from the wall. She had to be strong. Her son was depending on her. If no one would believe her, she would have to find a way to escape. Somehow she would find Robby herself.

Somehow...somehow.

A touch of warmth welled inside her when she considered that Nick had rescued her. Maybe he believed her just a little. That shred of hope meant more to her than he would ever know.

Laura passed through the foyer and checked both the den and the living room. No Nick. She frowned and for the first time noticed it was dark outside. Had she slept through another day? God, how long had her baby been missing now? She repressed the thought. One thing at a time. She had to find Nick first.

The scent of food suddenly hit her nostrils. Laura staggered with reaction. How long had it been since she had eaten? She shook her head. She had no idea. Following the mouthwatering aroma, Laura found Nick in the kitchen hovering over the stove. She opened her mouth to call his name, but caught herself. She propped against the doorjamb instead and took some time to admire the father of her child.

Nick wore his thick black hair shorter than she remembered, Laura realized for the first time. But it looked good on him, she admitted. Nick was one of those guys who had a perpetual tan, the kind you couldn't buy and you couldn't get on the beach. His skin was flawless. And those lips. Full and sensual, almost feminine. Laura took a long, deep breath to slow the rush of desire flowing through her. From the beginning she had been fiercely attracted to the man.

Laura had only made love with one other man, and that one time had proven more experimental than passionate.

There was just something about Nick. Laura closed her eyes and relived the night they had spent making love. A storm had raged outside, roaring like a wild beast with its thunder. Flash after flash of lightning had lit the room, silhouetting their entwined bodies in shadows on the wall. His kiss, his touch, the feel of his bare skin against hers....

"Laura?"

Laura's lids fluttered open, her attention drifted back from the sweet memory of making love with Nick, of making their baby. Those assessing green eyes, the color of polished jade met hers.

"Feeling better?"

A trembling smile curled her lips. Her heart wanted so to trust this man. Every fiber of her being cried out with need in his presence. "A little," she replied. Laura shoved a handful of hair behind her ear and trudged slowly across the room. Damn, she hated this zombie-status feeling. She leaned against the counter and peered into the steaming pot. Soup. She closed her eyes and inhaled deeply of the heavenly scent.

"Hungry? You slept through lunch."

The sound of his deep voice rasped through her soul. That knowing gaze remained on hers, analyzing. "Yes," she murmured. With Nick wearing jeans and a tight-fitting polo shirt, Laura had an amazing view of all that muscled terrain she remembered with unerring accuracy.

Nick reached for a bowl. "Have a seat," he suggested.

Laura frowned when she noted the gun tucked into his waistband, but the image of those strange pink eyes made her glad Nick was armed.

"Sit down, Laura."

She snapped her gaze to his. Food. Oh yeah. He wanted

her to eat. Though food would never fill the emptiness inside her, she knew she had to eat. But only the feel of her baby in her arms would ever make her whole again.

"Have you learned anything about my son?" she asked abruptly.

Nick shifted his intense gaze to the steaming soup. "I have a man working on it." After thoroughly stirring it, he met her gaze once more. "But to answer your question, no. We don't have any more details other than those you gave me."

Which were sketchy at best, he didn't add. Laura could hear the subtle censoring in his tone. Anxiety twisted in her chest. "I've got to find him, Nick." She sucked in a harsh breath. "Please, don't keep me here like a prisoner when my son is out there somewhere." She shook her head slowly. "I have to find him."

Nick clicked the stove off and turned his full attention to her. "You're not a prisoner, Laura. I didn't wake you this afternoon and give you the scheduled dose of medicine for that very reason. I want your head clear. I want to help you."

Hope bloomed in Laura's chest. "You believe me?" she whispered, weak with relief. Laura blinked back the moisture pooling in her eyes.

He studied her for a long moment before he answered. "Let's just say, I'm willing to go with that theory until I have reason *not* to." He cocked his head speculatively. "Can you live with that?"

Laura gave a jerky nod. "As long as we find my baby I can live with anything."

Warning flashed in those green depths. "If you make a run for it, or give me one second of grief—"

"I won't," Laura put in quickly. "I swear, Nick. I'll do whatever you say."

Tension throbbed in the silence that followed. "All right," he finally said, then gestured to the table. "Have a seat and I'll be your server for the evening." A smile slid across those full lips.

Laura nodded and made herself comfortable at the table. Nick might still have reservations, but at least he planned to give her the benefit of the doubt. That's all she could ask at this point. And he had effectively stalled James Ed's plans to send her away.

Her eyes drinking in his masculine beauty, and comparing each physical trait to that of her small son, Laura watched Nick prepare her dinner and set it before her. Robby looked so much like his father. Laura longed to share that secret with Nick.

But she couldn't.

Not until she proved her case—her sanity. She frowned. She had to find her son, and then prove herself a fit mother to the man who possessed the power to legally take her child from her. Laura's heart ached at the possibility that Nick would likely never forgive her for keeping his son from him. He would probably hate her. She shook off that particular dread. She had enough to worry about right now. Some things would have to wait their turn to add another scar to her heart.

"Water or milk?" he asked.

"Water is fine," she replied with a small smile. "I'm still feeling a little queasy." His answering smile as he sat down across the table from her took her breath away.

Laura squeezed her eyes shut and tried to clear the lingering haze that continued to make coherent thought a difficult task. Not to mention she couldn't keep drooling over Nick. Maybe once she got some food into her empty stomach she could think more rationally. Uncertain as to how her queasy stomach would react, Laura took a small taste of the soup. Swallowing proved the hardest step in the process. Finally, she managed.

"I hope that look on your face has nothing to do with the palatability of the cuisine."

With a wavering smile, Laura swallowed again, then shook her head. "It's wonderful. I'm just not as hungry as I first thought." Her stomach roiled in protest of that tiny taste.

Nick's concerned expression tugged at her raw emotions. "You need to eat, Laura."

She sipped her water, trying her level best not to rush from the table and purge her body of that single sip. "I know." How could she eat when she didn't know if her child had been fed? Laura froze, the glass of water halfway to her mouth. The glass plunked back to the table, her hand no longer able to support its weight. She couldn't.

Nick was suddenly at her side asking her if she was all right. Laura turned to him and stared into those green eyes that looked so much like Robby's. Don't lose it, Laura. She drew in an agitated breath. If you lose it he'll believe James Ed and the hospital report, and then you'll never find Robby. Laura blinked at the flash of fear she saw in Nick's eyes. He still cared, but would that be enough?

"I'm okay," Laura said stiffly. She clenched her hands into tight fists beneath the table. "I'm just not hungry that's all." She manufactured a dim smile for his benefit. "I'm sure it's just the medicine affecting my appetite."

Nick moved back to his own chair then. "You'll probably wake up in the middle of the night starved," he suggested warmly.

Laura nodded, struggling to keep her smile in place. He had gone to all this trouble for her, the least she could do was try to force down a few bites.

Nick folded his napkin carefully and laid it aside before

meeting her gaze again. Laura moistened her lips in anxious anticipation of what was coming next. Did he know something that he hadn't wanted to tell her? Her heart butted against her rib cage. Something about Robby?

"We need to talk, Laura," he said quietly.

Laura's heart stilled in her chest. Adrenaline surged then, urging her heart back into a panicked rhythm.

That penetrating gaze bored into hers. "I need you to start at the beginning and tell me everything." He pressed her with that intense gaze. "And I mean everything. I can't help you if you hold anything back."

This wasn't about Robby. Relief, so profound, shook her that Laura trembled in its aftermath. "You're right, Nick," she said wearily. "There's a lot we need to talk about." She shrugged halfheartedly. "But I'm still not thinking clearly. Is it all right if we wait until morning when my head is a bit clearer?" Please let him say yes! Her emotions were far too raw right now, and she still felt groggy. She had to be in better control of herself before answering any questions. She might make a mistake. Laura couldn't risk saying the wrong thing while under the lingering influence of the medication.

"Tomorrow then," Nick relented.

Laura stood, intent on getting back to her room before he changed his mind. "I think I'll have a bath and crawl back into bed." She turned and headed for the door, concentrating on putting one foot in front of the other without swaying.

"Laura."

She paused. Laura closed her eyes and took a fortifying breath before she turned back to him. "Yes."

Nick sipped his water, then licked his lips. She shivered. "Don't lock the door in case I need to check on you," he told her.

Irritation roared through Laura's veins at his blatant reminder that he didn't completely trust her. "Sure," she said tightly.

Her movements still spasmodic and somewhat sluggish, Laura stormed back to her room. She jerked off her clothes and threw them on the unmade bed. Once in the bathroom, she not only slammed the door, but locked it for spite. She was an adult. She could certainly bathe herself without incident, she fumed, as she adjusted the faucet to a temperature as hot as her body would tolerate. The warm water would relax her aching muscles. Laura grabbed a towel and tossed it onto the chair next to the tub. Her reflection in the mirror suddenly caught her attention. The shallow half-moon slash on her upper chest zoomed into vivid focus.

The memory of the intruder who tried to kill her shattered all other thought. Image after image flooded her mind. Glittering pinkish eyes. The oddest color she had ever seen. The black ski mask. The glint of light on the wide blade of the knife. Her blood. *Time to die, princess.* Laura grasped the cool porcelain of the sink basin. She clenched her teeth to prevent the scream that twisted in her throat.

You're okay, you're okay, she told herself over and over. *You're safe. Nick is here now. He'll keep you safe.* Laura drew in a long, harsh breath. She had to stay calm. *You can't find Robby if you're hysterical all the time.*

The sound of the water filling the expansive garden tub behind her finally invaded Laura's consciousness. She relaxed her white-knuckled grip on the basin and turned slowly toward the brimming bath. Cool night air caressed her heated skin. Laura closed her eyes and savored the coolness. Nick must have opened a window. She inhaled deeply of the fresh air. She would feel better tomorrow, be more clearheaded. And maybe tomorrow would bring news of Robby. Hope shimmered through Laura as she stepped into the tub. The sooner she took her bath and got into bed, the sooner she would go to sleep and tomorrow would come.

Please, God, please let me find my baby.

Laura turned off the water and settled into its warm depths. She closed her eyes and allowed the heat to do its work. Absolute quiet surrounded her, except for the occasional drip of the faucet. Each tiny droplet echoed as it splashed into the steaming water, the sound magnified by the utter silence. Laura softly moaned her surrender as complete calm overtook her. Tension and pain slipped away. Fear and anxiety evaporated as the warmth lulled her toward a tranquil state just this side of sleep. She was so very tired. So sleepy…

She was under the water.

Laura struggled upward, but powerful hands held her down. Strong fingers gouged into her shoulders. She opened her eyes to see but inky blackness greeted her. Who turned out the lights? Her lungs burned with the need for oxygen. She wanted to scream. Laura flailed her arms, reaching, searching, grasping at thin air. Mental darkness threatened. *Don't pass out! Fight!* Her nails made contact with bare skin. She dug in deep. The grip on her loosened. She plunged upward. Blessed air filled her lungs.

Laura screamed long and loud before her head was forced beneath the water once more.

Chapter Six

Nick loaded the soiled dinnerware and utensils into the dishwasher and closed the door. He braced his hands on the counter and stared into the darkness beyond the kitchen window. Tomorrow he would have to make sure Laura ate something. She wouldn't regain her strength without food, and she would need all her energy to get through the next few days.

She was going to have to make a believer out of Nick. Laura would have to prove to him that someone had tried to kill her and that a child did exist...somewhere.

Laura's child.

Nick frowned at that thought. The idea had niggled at him for a while now. He and Laura had only made love once. If she did have a child, and if...he were the father—an unfamiliar emotion stirred inside him—that would make the baby...about fifteen months old. He would simply ask her the child's age. He shook his head in denial. That wasn't possible. If Laura had been pregnant with his child, surely she would have come to him for help rather than...

Nick cut off that line of thinking. There was no point in running scenarios when he still didn't know exactly what had happened two years ago. Nor did he know the real story about the events that led up to Laura's disappearance. As soon as Laura was up to it, he intended to find out every detail. He would give her the benefit of the doubt on the kid. If she said she had a son, maybe she did. He couldn't imagine what purpose that particular lie served.

Unless, he considered reluctantly, she was suffering from the mental condition listed in the report from the hospital. Nick rubbed at the ache starting right between his eyes. And if she were in the hospital all that time, did that negate the possibility that there was a child? No point in working that angle until he had some word from Ian. In the meantime, Nick would just have to concentrate on getting some answers from Laura. He wasn't going to bring up the medication either—unless she asked for it. He had an uneasy feeling about those damned pills. Besides, he needed her head clear if he planned to ascertain any reliable answers.

Just another job, he told himself for the hundredth time. Nothing else. Laura Proctor was his assignment, and he damned sure intended to get the job done right this time. Getting to the bottom of this tangled mystery once and for all was the only thing that kept Nick here. That and his damned sense of justice. If there was any chance Laura was right and James Ed had set all this up…

Who was he kidding? Nick had spent more than twenty-four hours monitoring James Ed's house because he couldn't bear to leave Laura under those circumstances. Fool that he was, he still wanted to protect her. Poised to push the dishwasher's cycle button, a muffled sound made Nick hesitate. He quickly analyzed the auditory sensation. A scream? Dread pooled in his gut.

Laura.

Nick bolted from the kitchen, shouting her name. Dodging family heirlooms as he flew down the hall, Nick ticked off a mental checklist of items in a bathroom with which one could hurt oneself. Razor topped the accounting. Nick cursed himself for not checking the room first. Why the hell had he allowed her even this much free rein? His heart pounded with the fear mushrooming inside him.

He skidded to a stop outside the closed door and twisted the knob. Locked. "Laura!" he banged hard on the door. "Laura, answer me, dammit!"

Water sloshed and something clattered to the floor. He could hear Laura's frantic gasps for air between coughing jags. "Laura!" Nick clenched his jaw and slammed his shoulder into the door, once, twice. The lock gave way and he shoved into the dark, humid room. He flipped on the overhead light.

Naked and dripping wet, Laura was on her hands and knees next to the tub. She struggled to catch her breath, water pooled on the tiled floor around her. An assortment of scented candles and a silver tray were scattered about near the end of the tub. No blood anywhere that he could see. Relief rushed through Nick. He grabbed the towel draped across a chair and, ignoring the pain roaring in his knee, knelt next to Laura. Gently, he wrapped the towel around her trembling body and drew her into his arms.

Nick sat down on the edge of the tub and pulled Laura onto his lap. "It's okay," he murmured against her damp hair. "I've got you." Nick swiped back the wet strands clinging to her face. "What happened, honey, did you fall asleep in the water?" Nick called himself every kind of fool for not considering that the drugs still in her system might make her drowsy again. His gut clenched at the idea of what could have happened.

Still gulping in uneven breaths, Laura lifted her face to his. "He…he tried to drown me. I…" She sucked in another shaky breath. "I screamed…" Her eyes were huge with fear. "The window." Laura lifted one trembling hand and pointed to the window. "He went out the window."

Frowning, Nick followed her gesture. He stared at the half-open window and the curtain shifting in the cold night air. "Why did you open the window? It's freezing outside."

Laura drew back and searched his gaze, confusion cluttering her sweet face. "I didn't," she said slowly. "I thought you did." She frowned. "He must have come—"

"Now why the hell would I do something as stupid as leaving the window open?" he demanded, disbelief coloring his tone.

One blond brow arched, accenting the irritation that captured her features. "But you thought I did *something that stupid?*"

Nick shook his head. "I didn't mean it like that," he defended.

"Sure you did." Laura struggled out of his grasp, jerked to her feet, and promptly slipped on the wet tile.

He steadied her, his grasp firm on her damp arms. Nick stood then, and glared down at her. He refused to acknowledge all the naked flesh available for admiration. He couldn't think about that right now. "I only meant," he ground out impatiently, "that *someone* opened the window and it wasn't me."

She smiled saccharinely. "So, of course, it was me."

"Well, there doesn't seem to be anyone else around," he said hotly. A muscle jumped in his tightly clenched jaw, adding another degree of tension to the annoyance already building inside him.

Laura shrugged out of his grasp. "No joke, Sherlock." She adjusted the towel so that it covered more of her upper chest, including the healing injuries from her last encounter with...who or whatever.

Nick forced away the unreasonable fear that accompanied that memory. There was no evidence that anyone else was in the damned room but Laura that time either. The image of her naked body slammed into his brain, reminding him of what he had seen with his own eyes. Nick had memorized every perfect inch of her two years ago, tonight's refresher had only made bad matters worse. She was still as beautiful, as vulnerable as she had been then.

Focusing on the task to counter his other emotions, Nick stepped to the window, closed and locked it before turning back to a fuming Laura. "I'll have to check the security system to find out why the alarm didn't go off when the window was opened. In the meantime, why don't you tell me exactly what happened," he suggested as calmly as possible.

"We're wasting time," she snapped. "Whoever tried to hold my head under the water—" she shuddered visibly, then stiffened "—is getting away." Laura fanned back a drying tendril of blond silk. "You're the one with the gun. Are you going to help me or what?"

Nick released a disgusted breath. "Laura, there is no one else here."

"Fine." She pivoted and stamped determinedly toward the door, slipping again in her haste.

Nick reached for her but she quickly regained her balance and stormed out the door. His arm dropped back to his side. Now this, he mused, was the Laura he remembered. Sassy and determined. Grimacing with each step, Nick stalked into the bedroom after her. He snapped to attention at the sight of Laura shimmying into her jeans, the tight denim catching on the damp skin of her shapely backside. Apparently deciding time was of the essence, she had foregone panties.

"What—" Nick cleared his throat. "What the hell do you think you're doing?"

Laura yanked an oversized T-shirt over her head and

turned to face him just as the soft cotton fell over her breasts. "I'm going after him."

Nick choked out a sound of disbelief. He braced his hands at his waist and shook his head. "No you're not."

Laura stepped into her sneakers, plopped down onto the end of the bed and tied first one and then the other, her fiercely determined gaze never leaving his. If this was a war of wills, she need not waste her time. Nick could out-wait Job himself when he set his mind to it.

"Just try and stop me," she challenged as she shot back to her feet. Laura flipped her still damp hair over her shoulders. "I'm tired of being treated like I'm a few bricks shy of a load. And I'm sick of no one believing anything I say." She walked right up to him. "Someone took my son. The same someone that's trying to kill me." She glowered at Nick, her eyes glittering with the rage mounting inside her. "You can either help me or get out of my way."

One second turned to five as Nick met her glower with lead in his own. When it was clear she had no intention of backing down, Nick's mouth slid into a slow smile. What the hell? He could use a walk in the cold air after this little encounter. The image of her naked, shapely rear flashed through his mind and sent a jolt of desire straight to his groin. "All right. We do it your way." Hope flashed in her eyes. "This time," he added firmly. Nick stepped aside and Laura darted past him.

"We need a flashlight," he called out as she disappeared around a corner.

"It's in the kitchen. I'll get it!" she shouted determinedly.

Nick moved his head slowly from side to side. He had to be crazier than she was supposed to be to do this. It was late. Laura should be in bed. His knee hurt like hell, and he could damned sure use a little shut-eye. He had hardly slept at all the last three nights. But he couldn't bring himself to deny her this. She was so sure…a part of him wanted to believe her. That same part that had fallen for a sassy, innocently seductive Laura two years ago.

"Got it." Laura almost hit him head-on when she barreled through the kitchen doorway.

"Good," he muttered. Nick followed Laura to the den but stopped her when she would have thrown the patio door open and burst out into the November darkness. "Hold on there, hotshot." She cast him a withering look. "I'm the one with the gun, remember?"

Laura blinked. "Right." She stepped back, yielding to Nick's lead.

More for her benefit than anything else, Nick drew his weapon from its position at the small of his back. "Stay behind me," he instructed. She bobbed her head up and down in adamant agreement. "And don't turn the flashlight on unless I tell you."

Nick flipped the latch and slid the door open. Instantly, the cold air slapped him in the face, escalating his senses to a higher state of alert. He surveyed the backyard for a full thirty seconds before stepping onto the patio. Slowly, with as much stealth as possible with Laura right behind him, he made his way down the back of the house until he reached the window outside the bathroom that connected to Laura's bedroom.

"Give me the light." Nick took the yellow plastic instrument and slid the switch to the on position. As thoroughly as possible with nothing but a small circle of illumination, Nick examined the area around the window. The window itself, the ledge, the portion of brick wall from the ledge to the ground, then the ground. Nothing. The window showed no signs of forced entry. With the ground frozen, there wouldn't be any tracks, and the nearby shrubbery appeared undisturbed. Nick crouched down and examined the dormant-for-the-winter grass a little closer just to be sure. He saw absolutely no indication that anyone had been there, but with the current weather conditions that determination would not be conclusive.

"Did you find anything?" Laura chafed her bare arms with her hands for warmth.

"Let's go back inside," Nick urged. "It's freezing out here."

Laura dug in her heels when he would have ushered her toward the patio. She lifted her chin defiantly. "You still don't believe me."

"Look." Nick tucked his weapon back into his waistband. "It's not a matter of whether or not I believe you." His grip tightened on the smooth plastic of the flashlight, its beam lighting the ground around their feet. "The fact of the matter is there's nothing to go on—either way."

Nick caught her by one arm when she would have walked away. "*If* anyone was here, there's no one here now and—"

"Go to hell, Foster," she said from between clenched teeth.

His fingers tightened around her smooth flesh. "And," he repeated, "there is no indication that anyone climbed in or out this window."

"He was here," she insisted, her voice low and fierce with anger. "He tried to drown me. And you know what?" She jerked with emotion. "I think he's going to keep trying to kill me until he succeeds. Will you believe me then, Nick?"

This time Nick released her. He watched until she disappeared through the patio door. He closed his eyes and fought the need to run after her. To assure her that he would never let that happen. What was he supposed to believe?

All the facts pointed to Laura as being mentally unstable, suicidal even. Nick flinched at the idea. Not one single shred of evidence existed to support her claims, except the knife wounds James Ed wanted him to believe were self-inflicted. James Ed didn't appear to have any reason to lie. Nick opened his eyes and shook his head. Then why the hell did he want—need—to believe her so badly?

Disgusted with himself as well as the situation, Nick strode slowly toward the still-open door. Maybe he was the wrong man for this job. Apparently he couldn't maintain a proper perspective in Laura's presence. "Big surprise," he muttered.

Nick's gut suddenly clenched. The hair on the back of his neck stood on end. He stopped stock-still. Someone was watching. He felt it as strongly as he felt his own heart beating in his chest. Nick turned around ever so slowly and surveyed the yard once more. Taking his time, he studied each dark corner, watching, waiting for any movement whatsoever.

Nothing.

Nick scrubbed a hand over his beard-roughened face and considered the possibility that maybe he couldn't trust his own instincts anymore. Maybe paranoia was like hysteria, contagious.

One thing was certain, time would tell the tale. In Nick's experience, given time all things became clear.

Nick just hoped that time would be on their side.

"HARDHEADED JERK," Laura muttered as she flung another dresser drawer open. She rifled through the contents, then slammed it shut. She needed a change of clothes. Her own clothes. Surely there would be something here she could wear.

Laura paused in her search and tried to remember the

last time she had been here and what she had brought with her. Two years ago. The final barbecue bash of the summer. She remembered. James Ed had insisted she come along. He had invited Rafe. It was Labor Day weekend. Only two months before...

Closing her eyes, Laura fought the memories that tugged at her ability to stay focused. Two months before she met Nick, fell in love with his self-assurance and intensity. Ten years older than her, he seemed to know everything, to be able to do anything. He was so strong, yet so tender. The way he had made love to her changed something deep inside her forever. And he had given her Robby. Tears threatened her flimsy composure. Laura clutched the edge of the dresser when emotion kicked her hard in the stomach. How was she supposed to go on when she didn't know if her baby was safe or not. Had he eaten? Was someone bathing him and keeping his diapers changed? Pain slashed through her, making her knees weak.

No! Laura straightened with a jerk. No. Robby was fine and she was going to find him. She refused to believe anything else. Somehow she would get away and find him. Somehow...

Laura jerked the next drawer open and forced herself to continue her search. The next drawer contained some underclothes and socks, the one after that an old pink sweater. Laura exhaled a puff of relief. At least it was a start. All she had to do was get away from Nick, then she would go back to Doc's clinic and look for clues—

"Laura."

Startled from her plans, she met his gaze in the mirror above the dresser. He stood in the doorway, looking too concerned and too damned good. Laura willed away her heart's reaction to the father of her child. She didn't want to feel this way about Nick. She didn't want to love him.

He would never believe her. Never help her the way she needed him to. Laura clenched her teeth and blinked away the emotion shining in her eyes. She didn't need Nick. She could take care of herself and her son...

...if she could just find him.

"What are you doing?" His gaze strayed to the items she had stacked on top of the dresser.

To lie was her first thought, but Nick was too smart for that. He would see through her in about two seconds. "I'm packing myself a bag." Laura turned to face him. She gripped the edge of the dresser's polished wood surface for extra support. "Because the first chance I get I'm out of here."

Nick took two steps in her direction. He paused then and slowly looked the room over as if seeing her childhood summer sanctuary for the first time, and wanting to commit what he saw to memory. Finally, his gaze moved back to hers, dark, intense. Laura shivered with awareness. Heat stirred inside her. She wanted to touch him, to have him touch her. She swallowed.

"And you think I'm going to allow you to do that."

It wasn't a question, she knew. She leveled her gaze on his, and poured every ounce of determination she possessed into that unsettling eye contact. "You have to sleep sometime."

Two more steps disappeared behind him. "Is that a threat?"

"Yes." Laura's heart rate accelerated. "It is."

"Just for the moment, let's say you were successful in your plan." He paused, cocked his handsome head and assessed her thoroughly. Laura stiffened to prevent her body's need to tremble beneath his blatant act of intimidation. Did he have any idea how he still affected her? "What will you do?"

She held her spine rigid when her body wanted to sag with despair as her harsh reality momentarily pushed aside all else. "I'll find my baby," she told him.

He moved closer. The smooth movement of denim-encased muscle dragged her attention to those long legs and the limp that had first endeared him to her. Nick had gotten that limp by taking a bullet intended for a client he had been assigned to protect the year before Laura met him. He had taken a bullet for her, too. Because that's the kind of man he was. And despite his distrust of her, he had still come back to get her. To protect her. Laura's breathing grew shallow and irregular as renewed need twisted inside her. Giving herself a mental shake, Laura jerked her gaze back to his intense, analyzing one. She had to focus. But she was exhausted, mentally and physically. She needed so much for Nick to hold her right now. But at the same time, Laura needed to escape his watch.

"And the man who's trying to kill you?"

Laura's lips trembled then tightened with the blast of outrage that raced through her at his words. He didn't fully believe her. Why the hell was he asking? "I've been out-maneuvering him for two years. I can do it again."

"Until recently you mean," he suggested quietly. Another half yard of carpet disappeared between them.

"He would never have caught up with me and my son if it hadn't been for you," she told him tautly. Bottom line, Nick was one of the bad guys now. Why didn't he just leave her alone? Why had he come back for her? A tiny seed of hope sprouted in her heart despite her efforts to resist that very emotion.

"So you consider this to be my fault?"

"That's right." Laura pressed back against the dresser as he came closer still. "I hope you can live with it," she added bitterly.

He stopped two steps away. "Oh, I can live with it," he said with complete certainty. "If you can live with this."

Before Laura could fathom what he intended, Nick jerked his shirt from his waistband and pulled it over his head in one fluid motion. Laura's heart slammed mercilessly against her sternum. Her gaze riveted to his bare chest. Broad, tanned, muscled and sprinkled with dark hair. The memory of touching him, making love with him, swirled inside her. Then she saw it. The single jagged scar that marred that amazing terrain just beneath his heart. Laura's own heart dropped to her stomach then. A little higher and Nick would certainly have died.

"But I almost didn't live with it," he said, his voice dangerously low. A muscle flexed in that square jaw of his. "So while we're on the subject of blame, why don't you tell me about the guy you watched put this bullet hole in me. The one you disappeared with while I was bleeding to death." His fingers moved gently over the scar, but there was nothing gentle about his voice or his expression.

Fear, regret, pain churned inside her, but Laura fought to maintain her composure. She had to do this, had to say what needed to be said—for the good it would do. How could he think she had willingly left him to die? "It was my fault that you got shot," she said in a rush. Surprise flickered in Nick's gaze. "Not one day has gone by since that I haven't wished I could go back and somehow prevent what happened. But I swear to you, Nick, I didn't go anywhere with him. He tried to kill me, too."

Wariness slipped into his expression. "But you recognized him, Laura. I saw it in your eyes."

Laura raked her fingers through her wet hair. Her hands trembled so she clenched them into tight fists. God, how could she ever explain everything? "Look," she began wearily. "I admit that I got into some trouble in college."

She met Nick's guarded gaze. "Just like James Ed said. But I know now that I was just desperate for his attention." Laura closed her eyes and forced away the bitter memories twisting inside her brain. "I needed him and he was never there for me. He just wanted me away from him." She stared at the floor for a while before she continued. "When I came home after graduation, he tried to marry me off to Rafe Manning." Laura didn't miss Nick's reaction to Rafe's name. She tamped down the renewed burst of hope that maybe he did feel something for her.

"But you refused," he prompted.

Laura nodded. "James Ed wasn't very happy. And I pretty much made a fool of myself about it," she admitted. "But the car accident and all that other stuff was not my fault." She leveled her gaze on Nick's, hoping to convey the depth of her sincerity. "I tried to tell James Ed that the brakes failed, but he wouldn't listen to anything I had to say."

Nick snagged her hand. His thumb glided across the scar marking her wrist. "And this?"

Laura lifted her free hand and stared at the white slash of a scar. "All I know is that I came home from a party one night." She licked her dry lips. "James Ed and I had argued before I left. So I had a little too much to drink I guess. I came home and crashed on the bed. I woke up the next day in a hospital under suicide watch."

"You don't know for sure what happened then," Nick clarified.

She sucked in a weary breath. "I know I didn't do it. I was passed out. Besides, I had no reason to want to die."

Nick considered her words for a moment, then said, "Now, tell me about the man who shot me."

Laura tried without success to read Nick's closed expression. Did he believe anything she said? Would he believe what she was about to tell him now? Well, it was the truth. That's all she could do was give him the truth. "I saw him in James Ed's private office at the house a couple of times."

Nick's hands fisted at his sides, something fierce flashed in his eyes. "So you do know him?"

"I don't know him. I only saw him—"

"Be careful what you say next, Laura." There was no mistaking the emotion in his voice or his gaze then. Rage. Vengeance. "I know more than you think."

Laura shook her head in confused denial. "Why would you believe that? I did not know him. I still don't."

"I heard everything," Nick ground out.

"Everything?" She shook her head. "I don't understand what you mean." Laura had no idea what Nick was talking about.

Nick smiled, it was far from pleasant. "Oh you're good, Laura. Too good."

"What the hell are you talking about?"

"Before I blacked out completely, he told you that you didn't need me anymore, that it was just you and him now," Nick said coldly. "I heard him say it. You didn't deny it then, don't even think about denying it now."

Laura frowned, trying to remember. She allowed the painful memory to play out in her mind. She had screamed something like "why did you hurt him?" at the man after he shot Nick. Then he had said—oh God, she remembered. Laura met Nick's accusing glare. "He didn't mean it the way you think," she explained. "He meant that he had me where he wanted me—without protection."

"You expect me to believe that?"

Laura nodded. "I swear, Nick, it's the truth. I had never seen the man before in my life except the times I saw him in James Ed's office. That's what this is all about," she argued vehemently. "My brother wants me dead!"

"So you didn't leave willingly with the shooter?"

Astonishment struck her hard. Why wouldn't he believe her? "How could you think I left with him? That I left you hurt? He dragged me out to the riverbank and tried to kill me. He wanted it to look like a murder-suicide." Laura shook her head at Nick's still wary expression. How could she make him believe her? "The storm was still going strong. He lost his balance, and we both went over the edge. He hit his head on a rock on the way down. He never resurfaced, then I got swept away. I woke up the next day several miles down river. I was lost. It took me two days to find my way out of the woods."

"But you never came back, never let anyone know you were alive," Nick reminded her bitterly.

Laura slumped in defeat. "I thought you were dead. I knew my brother was trying to kill me. I didn't think coming back would be too bright."

"What about after you found out I was alive. Why not then? You could have come to me for help."

Uncertainty seized her. She had to tread carefully here. Laura couldn't risk allowing him to discover the truth about Robby. "You worked for James Ed. I knew you would take me back to him. And that's just exactly what you did," she reminded him curtly.

Nick hesitated, his green eyes bored relentlessly into hers. Something she couldn't read flickered in that fierce gaze. "Even after what we had shared, you didn't trust me?"

"Did you trust me? Our whole relationship stemmed from proximity and your desire to protect me. I…" Laura swallowed tightly. "I needed you so desperately. But how could I know that it was safe to trust you completely?"

The seconds turned to minutes before Nick responded. "You couldn't have," he offered flatly. "It's late. You should get some rest," he said, effectively changing the subject. "I'll check all the doors and windows, then I'll reset the alarm. Somehow it failed," he added. He picked up his shirt and started for the door.

Laura wasn't sure whether to be relieved or disappointed that he had left their discussion at a standoff of sorts. He had admitted what she knew as well. Two years ago everything had happened so fast there was no time to learn each other. What happened then hadn't been their fault. Just like now. Circumstances had brought them together, then torn them apart. She closed her eyes and took a slow, deep breath. She was tired. Sleep would come easily. Laura shivered. What if someone came into the house again? Maybe sleep wouldn't come so easily, she decided. The alarm system was obviously no deterrent. And Nick couldn't be everywhere at once.

At the door Nick turned back to her. "One more question," he said offhandedly.

Laura's gaze connected with his. "What's that?"

"How old is your baby?"

Laura's breath fled from her lungs. "Why do you ask?" she managed, her voice devoid of all inflection, her body paralyzed by uncertainty.

"Is there anything I should know about your child?"

She knew exactly what he meant. *Is the child mine?* Laura swallowed the words that wanted to spill out of her. "No," she said instead. Something in his expression changed. "There's nothing you need to know." She blinked back the tears that burned behind her eyes. "Except that I have to find him." She clamped down on her lower lip for a moment to hold her emotions at bay. "I'll die if anything happens to him."

He looked away. "Sleep. We'll talk more in the morning."

Laura watched him leave. Oh God. Why didn't she just tell him the truth?

Because she couldn't live without her son. And if Nick knew the truth, he would take Robby away. After all, Laura was considered unstable. And she couldn't prove any differently. Hadn't tonight's little episode added fuel to the fire? Laura shuddered at the memory of how those strong hands had held her beneath the water.

How would she ever be able to close her eyes now? Knowing her killer was near?

Panic slithering up her spine, Laura ran to first one window, then the next to make sure they were locked. She crawled into the bed and hugged her pillow to her chest.

No way would she be able to let her guard down tonight, even though Nick would be right next door.

All she had to do was stay awake....

Chapter Seven

Elsa smiled as she spooned another taste of strained carrots into the little boy's mouth. He was such a good child. How could anyone believe that this child had been neglected in any way? Elsa frowned. And the only way a mother would abandon a baby this healthy and sweet would be if she were dead.

She stalled, the spoon halfway to the baby's open mouth. If the mother and father were dead, why the abandonment story? The baby gurgled and swung his little fists about in protest. Elsa scolded herself for allowing her mind to drift.

"Okay, little one, be patient." She popped the next bite into his waiting mouth. "I'm just an old woman, and too slow for the lively likes of you," she cooed. The little boy loudly chanted his agreement in baby talk.

Elsa frowned again. This wasn't right. She had worked here for a very long time and nothing like this had ever happened before. Maybe she should slip and take a look at the child's file. There would be a perfect opportunity day after tomorrow with the director away.

Elsa nodded resolutely. Yes, she would see what she could find out. Not that it would really do any good, but it would put her mind at ease.

LAURA JERKED AWAKE. Sunlight streamed in through the partially opened blinds. She rubbed her eyes and tried to gather her thoughts. She had finally given in and fallen asleep a few hours ago. Laura stilled. She had been dreaming. The image of Robby smiling and playing with his food filled her mind's eye. Laura closed her eyes and allowed the dream to warm her. She prayed that it was a good sign. Robby had to be all right.

Two loud raps echoed from the door. "Laura, are you up in there? In about three seconds I'm coming in," he warned.

So that's what woke her. Laura bounded off the bed and hurried to the door. Today she would find a way to prove to Nick that Robby was real. Then maybe he would put some serious effort into helping her. If not, she would set out on her own. She reached the door just as Nick opened it.

The grim expression on his face loudly proclaimed his thoughts without his having to open his mouth. For at least a moment he must have thought she had made good on her threat to make a run for it. The realization that he had even considered her capable of giving him the slip lightened Laura's mood considerably.

"Good morning," she said with exaggerated cheer. God, why did he have to look so good? Her pulse reacted the moment her eyes lit on him.

He took stock of the room and then settled his searching gaze on hers. "Really, what's good about it?"

Laura studied his chiseled features as she shoved her unbrushed hair back from her face. She cringed inwardly when she considered how she must look. Her hair a mess, her clothes slept in, no makeup. But not Nick. He always looked picture-perfect. Never a hair out of place. He looked as if he had taken great pains with every aspect of his appearance. But Laura knew that wasn't the case. Perfection came naturally to Nick. It was the same with his lovemaking. Slow, thorough. Laura's mouth went unbearably dry.

"We're alive," she offered in answer to his question, and directing her mind away from his expertise between the sheets. "That's definitely good. And maybe today I'll find my son."

"There's coffee in the kitchen," he said impassively. He ignored her comment about Robby. "We should finish last night's discussion."

"Okay," Laura replied just as impassively. "Give me five minutes to change." Today was his last chance, she reminded that part of her that wanted so to believe in him. If he didn't help her today...

Nick's gaze traveled down the length of her and back. She didn't miss the glint of male appreciation, but his gaze was hard when he met hers once more. "Five minutes. I've got a lot of questions that need answers." Without another word, he turned and walked away.

Laura shoved the door closed behind him. She blew out a breath of annoyance. *Men.* She would never understand them. She was the victim here! Laura railed silently. Why did he make her feel like the villain? Someone tried to kill her last night. *Again.* Why wouldn't Nick believe her?

James Ed. Laura crossed her arms over her chest and considered her loving brother. He had done this to her. Taken her life away, taken her child and the man she loved. And for what? Laura shook her head in aversion. Money. It was all about the money.

To hell with the money.

Maybe it was time Laura got down on his level. James Ed wasn't the only one who could play dirty. Laura clenched her teeth until her jaws hurt. Whatever it takes, she promised herself. One way or another she would get her son back.

SEVEN MINUTES LATER, Nick noted impatiently, Laura breezed into the kitchen looking for all the world like a little girl. Jeans hugged her shapely legs while an oversized pink sweater engulfed the rest of her. Her hair was pulled back high on her head in a ponytail. Her sweet face was freshly scrubbed and bright with hope. Nick's chest constricted. He swallowed that damned burning need to take her in his arms and just hold her. He couldn't do that. It would jeopardize his perspective even further. He had a job to do. He shifted in his chair. Damn. Three seconds in her presence and his body was already reacting.

Things between them had always been like this—fast and furious. But neither was to blame. Their circumstances were equally fast and furious. Despite that fact, something drew Nick to her, made him want to believe her. To trust her. Whether Laura was telling the complete truth or not, something was wrong here. His instincts warned him that Laura was in real danger. Evidence or no, things just didn't add up.

Laura popped a slice of bread into the toaster. Nick sipped his coffee and watched her graceful, confident movements. The drug had worn off completely now, he decided. Good. That would make things a lot easier, unless, of course, she became overwrought. Nick set his cup on the table and started to speak but speech eluded him when Laura bent over and poked around in the fridge.

He averted his gaze from her heart-shaped rear and passed a hand over his face. "I'm glad to see your appetite is back."

"I just realized I was starving." Milk in one hand, jam in the other, Laura shoved the fridge door closed with one slender hip. "I have no idea when I ate last." She smiled as if knowing some secret he wasn't privy to. Nick almost groaned at the angelic gesture. "But I'm about to make up for at least part of it."

"The man," Nick began, drawing her attention from spreading strawberry jam on her toast to him. "Did he actually tell you that James Ed hired him to kill you?" Nick had replayed their conversation a dozen times during the night. He kept coming up with the same questions. Questions he needed answered. And only Laura could answer them. Half the night had been spent running scenarios, the other half fighting the need to go to her bed. Nick tensed. That couldn't happen—even if she were to invite him, which was highly unlikely. This go-around Nick had to remain as personally detached as possible. It was the only way to really protect Laura, and to get to the bottom of whatever was going on.

Laura placed the butter knife on the counter. She frowned thoughtfully. "No, not in so many words. But when I asked him why he was doing this, he said 'for the money, of course'." Laura shrugged. "Who would stand to gain from my death?" She met Nick's gaze then, hers certain in her conclusion. "James Ed."

"I checked his financial standing forward and backward. His assets were a bit shaky prior to the election two years ago, but he recovered. Most politicians barely skate through the election process without financial crisis. James Ed didn't seem to need your trust badly enough to kill for it, in my opinion." Nick pushed his now cold coffee aside. "He appeared to have enough money already."

Laura deposited her skimpy breakfast on the table and dropped into a chair. "Then why would that man have wanted to kill me if he weren't working for my brother?"

Nick lifted one shoulder in a semblance of a shrug. "It

could have been a kidnap-ransom plot gone awry,'' he suggested. That had been the police's theory two years ago.

Laura shook her head. ''No. He intended to kill me, then and there. What good's a ransom if the sacrificial lamb is already dead?''

She definitely had a point there. If only Nick had remembered more details about the man's physical features, maybe they could have nailed down his intent and his associates two years ago. But Nick had barely survived the gunshot and ensuing surgery. The entire event was forever a blur in his mind—except for the snatch of conversation he had heard. Nick would never forget that. The guy was dead according to Laura. Whatever had motivated him, he had gotten his in the end.

Nick took a deep breath and forced the old rage to retreat. ''Maybe he was just a nutcase who wanted to get back at James Ed,'' he suggested.

Laura laughed humorlessly. ''You just don't want to believe that James Ed is behind this little soap opera.'' She leveled her determined gaze on Nick's. ''He tried to marry me off, then he tried to prove me mentally unstable. And when all that failed, he got desperate and hired someone to kill me. Think about it,'' she urged fiercely. ''Ten million dollars is a lot of motivation. If I married, was pronounced mentally incompetent or dead before my twenty-fifth birthday, big brother gained control of the money. No matter what your investigation turned up, he wanted that money.'' Laura leaned back in her chair. ''He still does.'' Laura blinked. ''If he hasn't gotten it already.''

Nick shook his head, still denying her assertion. ''But why? He had enough of his own.''

''Is there ever enough?''

Nick just couldn't reconcile the picture Laura painted with the man he knew. James Ed had truly grieved after

Laura's disappearance. His happiness at having her back home was so clear a blind man could have seen it. "It just doesn't feel right," he countered.

Laura sighed. "I don't know anything to say that will convince you, but I know I'm right. And somehow he found out about my son and took him to get at me. He knows I won't go far as long as there's any chance my child is here somewhere." Her gaze grew distant. "How can I run from James Ed when he holds my heart in his hands?"

Laura's words touched Nick so deeply that he couldn't speak for a time. If Laura had a child, he would definitely help her find him. And if he discovered that James Ed was behind the threat to Laura, the man would not live to regret it. Finally, Nick looked from her untouched toast to her. "You should eat," he said quietly. No one was going to hurt Laura again. *But what about the hospital report?* his more logical side argued.

She shook her head. "No. You have something else to say." She pressed him with her gaze, reading him like an open book. "Say it."

"All right. How do you explain the hospital report? I read it myself." *Give me an answer I can live with,* Nick urged silently.

Laura pressed her lips together and blinked rapidly to fight the fresh tears shining in her eyes. "You know I've even considered that maybe I am crazy. Maybe I imagined the last two years." She shrugged one thin shoulder. "Maybe Robby isn't real." Laura flattened her palms on the table and slowly shook her head from side to side. "But I can't even imagine that. He is real, Nick. As real as you and me. And I have to find him, no matter what it takes." She drew in a bolstering breath. "There's no way I can live

without him. He's all I have in this world. Can you understand that?''

Long minutes passed with nothing but silence and a kind
of tension that only old lovers could feel between them.
Emotions he knew he shouldn't feel battled with his need
to stick with the facts. ''Prove it,'' he demanded softly. ''I
need hard evidence, Laura.''

''Okay.'' Laura licked her trembling lips. ''Take me to
the clinic where he was born. They have records. Would
that be proof enough?'' she asked sarcastically.

''Absolutely,'' he said gently.

''Fine.'' Laura stood. ''We should get started then. The
clinic is a good half-day drive from here.''

''First,'' Nick ordered, ''you'll eat. Then we'll go.'' Nick
held her gaze with his until she relented and settled back
into her chair. A single tear trekked down one soft cheek.
Every cell that made him who he was reacted to her pain,
ached to reach out to her. The strength and determination
radiating beneath all that vulnerability played havoc with
his defenses. ''You show me one slip of evidence and I
swear I'll move heaven and earth to find your child,'' he
vowed.

WELCOME TO PLEASANT RIDGE the sign read.

Laura's heart rate accelerated. She suppressed the excitement bubbling inside her at finally reaching the small
Alabama town where Robby was born. In just a few short
minutes she would have the proof she needed. Then Nick
would help her find her baby. Laura brushed back the tears
of relief. *Hold on, girl,* she told herself. *You'll find him.
Nick won't let you down. He promised.*

Laura glanced at the strong profile of the man behind the
wheel. He was so good-looking. She had fallen hard and
fast for him two years ago, and had loved him ever since.

A tiny smile tugged at Laura's lips. Confusion had reigned supreme in her life back then with the insanity revolving around the election and James Ed's strange behavior. Laura's smile dipped into a frown. And the attempts on her life. Nick had charged in and taken control of everything, including her heart. She had rebelled at first. Just another man trying to tell her what to do, and who would believe nothing she said, Laura had assumed. But Nick proved her wrong on that score. He reached out to her, made her want to trust him.

But nothing had prepared her for the way he made love to her. Only her second sexual experience, Laura's un-skilled enthusiasm couldn't hold a candle to Nick's com-plete mastery of the art. She trembled inside at the memory of how easily he had coaxed the woman in her to bloom with just his touch, his kiss. Then when he had been inside her, all else had ceased to exist. There was only Nick and the way he loved her.

Hours had melted away as they had loved each other that one night. Then that murderous thief had barged in unim-peded and stolen the life she could have had with Nick. Laura clutched the car door's armrest and closed her eyes as the painful pictures flashed through her mind. Her heart pounded harder and harder with each passing frame of memory. Nick had pushed her behind him to protect her. Unarmed, he had looked death square in the eye without hesitation.

The sound of the gun firing echoed in Laura's ears. Nick had fallen at her feet, but the other man had grabbed her before she could help Nick. He had forced the small hand-gun into her hand, closed her fingers around it, then pitched it to the floor a few feet away from where Nick lay bleeding to death. Laura hadn't understood then that he was setting her up as Nick's killer.

Laura shivered and forced the memories away. Nick was alive. Somehow he had managed to find his cell phone in the tangled sheet on the floor. The call to 9-1-1 before he had lost consciousness was all that had saved him. Laura had read the story in the newspaper. She had been listed as missing, possibly dead. She swallowed, but not dead enough to suit her brother. If the world thought she was dead, why hadn't James Ed left it at that? She was out of his hair. He could have the money. Why had he hunted her down and dragged her back home?

Maybe, Laura thought with a frown, he hadn't been able to access the trust fund without producing a body. Or maybe he was afraid she would show up when she turned twenty-five and demand *her* money. She considered her brother's obvious determination. He wanted her dead, whatever the reason. Laura turned her attention back to the driver. Unless she could convince Nick that she was right very soon, she was as good as dead. Eventually he would have to turn her over to James Ed.

And where would that leave Robby?

"Is this the place?"

Laura jerked from her disturbing reverie. Nick had parked and was watching her closely, too closely. Laura quickly surveyed the one-story building in front of them. She nodded. "Yeah, this is it." Pleasant Ridge Medical Clinic was lettered on the plate glass window. Not much had changed as far as Laura could see. Thankfully the clinic still opened on Saturdays. There were several other cars in the parking lot, but that was the norm. People came from all over the county for low-cost and, in some cases, free medical care. The cost was based on income, but the service was as good as anyplace else. Laura had been extremely pleased with her care, as well as Robby's, here.

"What name did you use?"

Laura turned to Nick, but hesitated. Would he find her choice of aliases suspicious? There was no other way. She needed those records. "Forester," she said quickly before she lost her nerve. "Rhonda Forester for me, Robert—" Laura's heart skidded to a halt in her chest. Her son's full name was Robert Nicholas Forester. Oh God. "I named my son Robert."

"Just follow my lead," Nick told her as he opened the car door. "Don't say anything unless I ask you a question."

Laura nodded and scooted out after him. She followed Nick toward the entrance. She clenched and unclenched her hands, then smoothed the damp palms over the fuzzy material of her bulky sweater. There was no other alternative. She had to do this. Laura would deal with Nick's suspicions later. Right now she had to do what she had to do. Proving Robby existed was her primary goal. Without proof Nick wouldn't help her. Laura shivered and hugged herself. She had forgotten her jacket in her rush this morning.

Nick pulled the door open and waited for Laura to enter first. She met his gaze one last time before going inside. Okay, Laura, you can do this. Laura forced a smile for the numerous patients who glanced her way as she crossed the waiting room. Nick followed close behind her. She stopped in front of the receptionist's window and waited for the young blond woman to look up from her work.

"May I help you?"

She was new, Laura noted. The receptionist before was blond as well, but a little older.

"I certainly hope so," Nick said with a charming smile. The receptionist warmed to him immediately.

"What can I do for you, sir?"

Laura looked away. She didn't need to see this interaction, and she sure didn't need to feel what she was feeling as a result. Women probably responded to Nick this way all the time.

Nick displayed his Colby Agency ID. "My name is Foster. I'm a private investigator from Chicago."

The woman was impressed, Laura noticed when she allowed herself a peek in her direction.

"I'm working on a child abduction case."

"Oh my," the receptionist named Jill, according to her name tag, said on a little gasp. "How can I help you?"

"The child, a boy, was born here last..." Nick looked to Laura.

"August sixth," she finished, praying that Nick wouldn't do the math. Jill looked doubtfully from Laura to Nick.

"Records you might have to corroborate that birth would be of tremendous assistance," he added.

"Well, our records are private," Jill said slowly, caution finally outweighing Nick's charm.

Nick smiled reassuringly at her. "I don't need to see your records. I just need you to verify the birth, and that the child was a boy and left this clinic alive and well. His name was Robert Forester, the mother was Rhonda."

Jill looked uncertain. "I don't see any harm in that."

"It's perfectly legal for you to answer that question," Nick offered placatingly. "I'm sure you would much rather answer that simple question than to be subpoenaed to court."

Jill's eyes widened. "It'll take just a minute to locate the file."

"Take your time."

Nick openly studied Laura then. What was he thinking? she wondered anxiously. Was he doing the mental calculations to determine Robby's date of conception? Laura swallowed hard and forced her attention to Jill's search at the file cabinets. Now Nick would know that Robby was real. That Laura had a child. That James Ed was lying. That the hospital report from Louisiana was a fake.

Frowning, Jill glanced back in their direction. "You're sure of the name?"

Nick looked to Laura for confirmation. She nodded stiffly. Ice filled her veins. No. The records had to be here.

Jill shook her head and stepped back to the window. "I'm sorry, but we have no record of a Forester, Robert or Rhonda. Are you certain that's the right name?"

"That can't be," Laura argued, a mixture of anger and fear gripping her heart. "Dr. Nader was the doctor on call. The records have to be here."

"I'm sorry. I looked twice. There is no Forester."

Laura leveled her gaze on the other woman's. "Where can I find Dr. Nader then?" she demanded.

Jill looked to Nick then back to Laura. "I've only worked here for six months. Dr. Nader left before I came. I think he moved somewhere out west."

Laura shook her head in denial. "That can't be. The records have to be here," she repeated.

"Ma'am, I'm sorry. I can't give you something I don't have," the receptionist offered apologetically. "All births are registered at the state office. You could check there."

"But—"

"Let's go, Laura." Nick was next to her now, ushering her away from the window. "Thank you," he said glancing back at the receptionist.

"No, Nick." Laura pulled out of his grasp. "She has to be wrong." Confusion added to the emotions already knotting inside her.

Nick leveled his steady gaze on hers. "Let's go."

Trembling with reaction to the multitude of emotions clutching at her, Laura surrendered to Nick's orders. What choice did she have? She sagged with defeat. How would she ever prove her case now?

"Wait!"

Nick turned back to the receptionist, pulling Laura around with him. "Yes."

How could he be so damned calm? Laura wanted to scream. She wanted to run hard and fast—somewhere, anywhere.

"I almost forgot," Jill explained. "Right after I came to work here there was a break-in. Some files were stolen."

"Some?" Nick pressed.

"I can't say for sure what files." Jill frowned. "It was the strangest thing. The files were stolen and our computer's database was wiped clean. But nothing else."

"No drugs were taken?"

Jill shook her head. "Not a one."

NICK SWORE silently as he watched Laura storm across the parking lot. He followed more slowly, taking the time to study her. He wasn't at all sure how much more she could take. The cool wind shifted all that long blond hair around her shoulders as she slumped against the locked car door. His instincts told him that whatever happened at this clinic it definitely wasn't a coincidence. The robbery was a blatant cover-up. If Laura had a child why would anyone want to conceal that fact? If James Ed was somehow involved in all this as Laura thought, what difference would the kid make? But something was all wrong.

He hoped like hell that Ian would call soon. Nick needed a break in this case. He needed something—anything—to go on. There was no way he could cover Laura and do the kind of research required to solve this enigma. But Ian Michaels was as good as they came at ferreting out the truth.

And right now, Nick needed the truth desperately. H

couldn't help Laura until he knew what was fact and what was fiction. One thing was certain, someone was trying to push Laura over the edge. Nick had no intention of allowing that to happen. He paused in front of her. "We should be getting back," he suggested quietly.

"He did this. I don't know how, but he did." Laura lifted her chin defiantly, but her eyes gave her away.

Nick couldn't bear to see that much hurt in her eyes. He tried to take a breath, but his chest was too heavy. How could he watch this happen and do nothing? But what could he do? He had no proof.

"Laura, we'll get to the bottom of this," he told her with as much assurance as he could impart.

She shook her head and blinked back her tears. "He's won," she admitted on a sob. "Look." She swallowed convulsively and swiped at her damp cheeks. "I've made a decision, I want you to take me back to Jackson…to my brother. Maybe if he gets what he wants he won't hurt Robby." She searched Nick's eyes for a time before she continued. "I just need you to promise me one thing." She trembled with the effort of maintaining her flimsy hold on composure.

Nick waited silently for her to finish, but his entire being screamed in agony. The need to touch her, to hold her was overwhelming.

"No matter how the chips fall, no matter what anyone tells you, find my son and take care of him for me, would you?"

His resolve crumbled. Nick took her in his arms and pulled her close. There were no words he could say because he didn't have any answers, the only thing he could do was hold her. Laura's arms went around his neck. Nick closed his eyes and savored the feel of her, the scent of her. He would gladly give his life right now to make her happy again.

"Nick."

Nick opened his eyes and drew back to find her looking up at him. That sweet face so filled with sadness.

"Promise me," she whispered. "Promise me you'll find him."

His gaze riveted to those full, pink lips. So soft, so sad, and so very close. Nick shook his head slowly, in answer to her question or in denial of what he wanted more than anything to do, he couldn't be sure. "I'm not taking you back until I know it's safe." His voice was rough with emotion. Emotions he could no longer hold at bay.

Challenge rose in her eyes. "You're going to let them put me in that hospital, aren't you?"

He had to touch her. He lifted one hand to her cheek and allowed his fingers to trace the hot, salty path of her tears. He swallowed hard. "No one is going to touch you until I have some answers."

She searched his gaze, something besides the sorrow flickered in her own. "You're touching me," she murmured.

His fingers stilled at the base of her throat. "Do you want me to stop?" It was his turn to do the searching this time. He wanted to see the same desire that was wreaking havoc with his senses mirrored in her eyes.

She moistened her lips and gifted him with a shaky smile. "No, I don't want you to stop."

Nick lowered his head when he saw that answering spark of desire in her blue eyes. Slowly, as if an eternity yawned between them, his lips descended to hers. How could he have survived the past two years without her? She tasted of that same sweet heat that had burned in his memory every waking moment of every day for those two long years. His body hardened at the rush of bittersweet need that saturated his being. Nick threaded his fingers into her silky hair, loosening it from its constraints, and deepened the kiss. Her lips opened slightly and Nick delved inside. The traffic on the nearby street, the cold November wind all ceased to exist.

Laura tiptoed to press her soft body more firmly against him. Nick groaned his approval. His left arm tightened around her waist, pulling her into his arousal. Laura whimpered her own response. The need to make love to her was staggering in its intensity.

He had to stop. To get back in control. Nick pulled back. His breath ragged, his loins screaming for release. Laura's lids fluttered open. Her swollen lips beckoned his.

He clenched his jaw and stepped away from her. "We should get back."

Laura nodded, the sadness rushing back into those big blue eyes.

Nick reached to insert the key into the lock but she stayed his hand. "Wait," she said breathlessly.

His gaze collided with hers. "What?"

"There's one more possibility," she said quickly, hope filling her gaze once more. "I can't believe I didn't think of her already."

"Laura, you're not making sense." Reality had just crashed in on Nick. He had allowed himself to fall into that same old trap. Dammit. How had he let that happen again? Yes, he had reason to believe her now. But he wasn't supposed to allow himself to cross the line this time. Hadn't he learned his lesson two years ago? Obviously not or he wouldn't have kissed her.

Laura snagged the keys and hurriedly unlocked her door. She pitched them back to him then. "Come on!"

He was a Class-A fool. Nick cursed himself repeatedly

as he rounded the hood and unlocked his own door. He slid behind the wheel and shot his passenger, the bane of his pathetic existence, a heated glower. ''Where are we going?''

She smiled, a wide, genuine smile and pointed to his left. ''That direction. I'll explain on the way.''

Chapter Eight

Laura stared in disbelief at the vacant house. The For Sale sign creaked as the wind shifted it, the sound heralding yet another failure. Jane Mallory had been Laura's last hope. Defeat weighed heavy on her shoulders. Laura closed her eyes and fought the sting of tears. It was as if destiny had determined her fate already. Now there was no one she could turn to. She and Robby had moved so often and stayed so much to themselves that few people would be able to verify Laura's story. And Jane Mallory had been the last one on the list.

"Do you mind telling me why we're standing on the front walk of an empty house?" Nick inquired in that nonchalant tone Laura hated.

She turned on him, a bolt of anger sending a burst of adrenaline through her. Even the memory of his kiss couldn't assuage her anger. Laura admitted to herself then and there that she was falling in love with the man all over again, but did he have to be so damned logical? *Because he's an honorable man, you idiot,* she scolded herself. Nick was only trying to be objective. To do what's right. Laura took a deep breath and summoned her patience.

"This is where Jane Mallory lived. She was the attending nurse at my son's delivery." Laura shot him an irritated look. "Robby and I stayed with her for a couple of weeks while I recovered."

Nick looked from Laura to the empty house. He tucked his hands into his pockets. "Looks like another dead end."

"You know, Foster, your perceptiveness amazes me."

Irritation flickered in his green eyes. "What do you want from me, Laura?" He raked the fingers of one hand through his hair. "I'm following up on every lead you toss my way. I've got one of the Agency's finest investigating your brother, your sister-in-law, and anybody else that has anything to gain by offing you. What else do you expect me to do?"

Laura leveled her gaze on his. "I want you to tell me that you believe me." Laura stepped closer to him. "Tell me that all these dead ends don't mean that all is lost." Laura stabbed his chest with her index finger as anger banished all else. "Tell me that my son is safe and that I'm going to find him—if not today, for sure tomorrow." A sob twisted in her throat, challenging her newfound bravado. "That's what I want from you, Nick."

The cold wind whipped around them, adding another layer of agony to her suffocating misery. How would she live without her son? She couldn't.

"Answer me, dammit," she demanded. Laura wilted when she saw the truth in his eyes. He couldn't make those kind of promises.

"I can't give you what you want, Laura. Not today, maybe not even tomorrow. But I will keep trying to find the answers you need until I've exhausted every possibility."

Laura looked up at the darkening sky. Why was this happening to her? What had she done to deserve this? She hugged herself to fight the chill coming more from the inside than the outside. What could she do now? *She needed a gun.* Nick's gun, she decided grimly. She would make James Ed tell her where her son was. Laura blinked at the irrational thought. With sudden clarity, she realized that she was now beyond simply desperate, and extreme measures might be the only way.

Next door an elderly woman shuffled onto her porch and retrieved the evening paper. She pulled her sweater more tightly around her as she surveyed the deserted street. She smiled when her gaze lit on Laura. Her movements slow with age, she turned and started back across the porch.

Nick was saying something but Laura ignored him. This was a small town. Neighbors kept up with neighbors in a place like this. Hope rushed through Laura, urging her to act. She put one foot in front of the other even before her brain made the decision to move. This woman would know where Mrs. Mallory had moved.

"Ma'am," Laura shouted before the old woman could disappear inside her house. "Ma'am!" She took the porch steps two at a time.

A welcoming smile greeted Laura. "Hello. Is there something I can help you with?" The woman shook her gray head. "I don't know a thing about what the real estate agent is asking for the house, but I can tell you it's a fine old place."

Laura returned her smile. "Hi, my name is Laura Proctor. Mrs. Mallory is a friend of mine. I was wondering where she had moved to."

The woman frowned. "Oh my." She clutched her newspaper to her chest. "I thought everyone knew."

A chunk of ice formed in Laura's stomach. "Knew what?" she asked faintly. Laura felt Nick's gaze heavy on her from his position on the steps.

"I'm sorry, dear, Jane passed away a few months back."

Laura's knees buckled but Nick was at her side now,

supporting her. "But I was here, with her, in August of last year. She was fine," Laura insisted.

The old woman nodded. "It was very sudden. A heart attack." She pointed to the neighboring yard. "She was always in that yard since she retired this spring, weeding and planting. Just got herself too hot, I reckon. It was a real shame. We had been neighbors for more than forty years."

Laura clamped her hand over her mouth for a moment to hold back the sob that wanted to break loose. When she had composed herself, she struggled with her next words, "Thank you for telling me." Laura closed her eyes and shook her head, exhaustion and anxiety sucking her toward panic. "I didn't know."

The old woman smiled kindly. "If you're not from around here, how could you have known? Jane never did marry and she didn't have any folks except one estranged brother." The woman shook her head. "A real shame that was. He didn't even come to her funeral. Course I'm not sure he even knew." She frowned. "Come to think of it, he probably didn't. At least his son hadn't known. Did you know Jane had a brother?"

Laura moistened her painfully dry lips. "No, I'm sorry I didn't know any of her family."

"Far as I knew that's all there was, but about four months ago, not long after Jane died, a fella showed up asking about her. A long-lost nephew it seems. Odd sort if you ask me."

A chill raced up Laura's spine. "Odd? What do you mean?"

The old woman rocked back on her heels. "Well I hate to speak poorly of Jane's folks, but he didn't look a thing like her or her brother. I'd never seen the brother, mind you, but I had seen his picture. Jane was a big woman, brawny even. So was that brother of hers. But this nephew, he was kinda short and stubby like. I suppose he took after his mama's side of the family. Strange fella,'' she added thoughtfully. ''Wore long sleeves even in the July heat.''

''What color were his eyes?'' The question came out of nowhere, but the image of those eerie pink-colored eyes flickered in Laura's mind.

''Can't rightly say. He wore them dark glasses. And gloves.'' She chuckled a rusty sound. ''I thought that was mighty strange myself.'' She tapped her chin with one finger. ''Maybe it was because he had such pale skin. Like a corpse.'' She frowned as if working hard to conjure the stranger's image. ''And the whitest hair I've ever seen on a young man.''

Nick's grip tightened on Laura's waist. Only then did she realize that she was leaning fully against him. Her legs had gone boneless. White hair, pink eyes, pale skin. *Albino.*

Laura turned in Nick's arms. ''It's him,'' she murmured. ''He's the one who broke into my room at James Ed's.'' Oh God. Laura closed her eyes and tried to slow the spinning inside her head. *The files were stolen and our computer's database was wiped clean. Jane passed away a few months back.*

The next thing Laura knew she was on the porch swing. She could hear Nick's deep voice as he questioned the woman about the strange nephew, but the words didn't quite register. *Time to die, princess.* Laura jerked at the memory. Why was this man trying to kill her? Why was he erasing all traces of Robby's existence? She swallowed. Laura didn't want to consider the reasons.

A wave of nausea washed over her. What did her sweet, innocent child have to do with any of this? *Nothing.* Laura trembled with the rage rising swiftly inside her.

Her child had nothing to do with any of this. And if

James Ed harmed one hair on her son's head, he was a dead man. Laura's breath raged in and out of her lungs. For the first time in her life the thought of someone's death brought a sense of comfort to her. Death would not be a harsh enough punishment for him if her child was hurt. Not nearly bad enough.

Laura's gaze moved to Nick. She had to get away from him. He would only hold her back. He would never allow her to do what she wanted to do. Nick was too honorable and straightforward to resort to what Laura had in mind. James Ed held all the answers.

And Laura intended to get them out of him one way or another.

"HE USED THE NAME Dirk Mallory." Nick paused while Ian made a note of the alias the albino guy had used. "He may or may not be connected to James Ed or the man who shot me, but it's worth checking into." Nick knew Laura was convinced that this was the man. He had no more to go on now in the way of hard evidence than he'd had three days ago, but his instincts told him to trust Laura on this one. Too many strange little coincidences and events added up to just one thing—a cover-up. "What do you have for me?"

"Governor Proctor has performed some pretty amazing financial acrobatics the past two years," Ian told him. "And he has definitely accessed Laura's trust fund. That would hardly be considered illegal since he had every right to do so with her sudden disappearance, and the assumption that she was dead. "

Nick swore under his breath. Maybe Laura was right. But, like Ian said, James Ed's use of the trust fund the last couple of years was strictly on the up-and-up. It still didn't prove that he tried to kill his own sister to get it.

"I also uncovered some rather strange details in Sandra's background."

Nick's attention jerked back to the conversation. "Good, anything is better than nothing."

"You already knew that she was adopted at the age of thirteen after spending one year in a state-run orphanage in Louisiana," Ian suggested.

Nick frowned in concentration. "Yeah, I remember that. The little wife was as clean as a whistle though. I remember that, too."

"Maybe, maybe not," Ian countered. "Her biological mother was one Sharon Spencer from a rural community just outside Bay Break."

"And?"

"And," Ian continued, "Sharon was involved with James Ed's father before he went off to college. There was a pretty big scandal before the Proctors enforced a gag order of sorts, and then sent their straying heir off to Harvard."

Rutherford's words echoed in Nick's head. "Damn," he breathed. The old man knew something, that's why he had innocently dropped that ancient gossip.

"Anything on what became of her?" Nick inquired hopefully.

"According to my source, she married the town drunk who died two years after Sandra's birth. Ten years after that, Sharon went off the deep end and the county took the child."

Nick passed a hand over his face. "So Sandra grew up, until the age of twelve at least, in a household where the Proctor name was mud. And her mother was a fruitcake."

"That would be my analysis," Ian agreed.

"I want to know everything you can find on Sandra Proctor, her first steps, her first kiss—everything."

"No problem," Ian assured him. "I should be able to get back to you later tomorrow on that. I have an excellent source."

Nick blew out a breath and plowed his fingers through his hair. "What about the report from the psychiatric hospital, Serenity Sanitarium?"

"That one's a bit more tricky."

"I need to know if that report's legit," Nick insisted. "That's the biggest fly in the ointment. I have to know if there's any chance Laura was really a patient there."

"Would you care to hazard a guess as to who one of the long-term residents of that facility is?" Ian inquired in a cocky tone.

Nick considered the question, then smiled with satisfaction. "One Sharon Spencer."

"Bingo."

"Excellent work, Ian," Nick praised. That gave Sandra a connection to the hospital. Maybe she or James Ed knew someone employed there who was willing to forge reports.

"Actually, it wasn't that difficult. I found a great source right up front."

Nick raised a speculative brow. "Who is your source?"

"Carl Rutherford."

"Son of a bitch," Nick hissed. "Why didn't that old geezer tell me all this?"

"He was afraid you were one of James Ed's bought-and-paid-for strong arms. He said more than he intended on the day the two of you met."

Nick didn't miss the amusement in Ian's tone. "Well, I guess you can't blame a guy for being cautious."

"That's it for now," Ian said. "I'll check in with you again within twenty-four hours."

"One more thing," Nick added before Ian could hang up. "Find out if the birth of a baby named Robert Forester was registered in the state of Alabama sometime in August last year.''

"No problem," Ian assured him.

"Thanks, Ian." Nick ended the call. He stood for a long moment and allowed the information to absorb more fully into his consciousness. He had no proof that Laura had a child or where she had actually been for the past two years. Despite Laura's claims, James Ed still surfaced from all this smelling pretty much like a rose in Nick's opinion. But then, there was this new light on Sandra. Nick massaged his chin as he considered the kind and demure first lady of Mississippi.

Sandra appeared as elated as anyone to have Laura back home. Sandra's school and college records indicated a disciplined, well-adjusted student. As first lady she was involved with numerous charities and a devoted churchgoer. The perfect wife to James Ed and surrogate mother to her young sister-in-law. No children of her own though. She and James Ed couldn't have children, Nick remembered. He wasn't sure of the reason, but he had found no indication that the problem was an issue. Sandra seemed to accept Laura as a substitute for a child of her own.

But how was that possible considering this new information? Sandra had grown up dirt-poor in a home with a drunk for a father and a mother who was mentally unstable. And where the Proctors represented everything she didn't have.

Uneasiness stole over Nick. That combination spelled trouble with a capital *T*. Nick exhaled heavily and passed a hand over his face. But why would Sandra go to such lengths to get Laura's money when James Ed would be in control of the trust fund, not her. Or did she have that much power over her husband? Nick wondered briefly. It just didn't ring true. James Ed was doing well on his own merit.

Is there ever enough? Laura's words filtered through his mind. Why would Sandra kidnap Laura's child if James Ed already had access to the trust fund? Maybe it was simply a matter of not wanting to have to pay it back. Even with Laura considered unstable, her child would be heir to her trust fund unless the will specified otherwise. That could be a distinct possibility, Nick decided.

The missing files, the knife wounds on Laura's throat and chest. The events in the cabin when he was shot. Laura's explanation of how the man had tried to kill her on that riverbank two years ago. Nick suppressed a shudder. He had lost his heart that night, and very nearly his life. That one incident might not have anything to do with the rest. The police labeled the case as a kidnapping gone sour. According to Laura, the man who shot Nick and tried to kill her died in the river that night. And she had seen him in James Ed's office more than once.

Anyone or thing that could provide hard evidence that Laura had a child had conveniently disappeared. Nick wondered again about the strange nephew who had shown up at Jane Mallory's neighbor's house. Nick supposed he could have been the real thing. And what about the hospital report? How convenient that Sandra's mother was a long-term resident of the very facility which provided the only hard evidence that existed as to Laura's whereabouts during the past months.

None of it actually added up to anything conclusive. And he doubted it would until he knew more facts. The only thing Nick knew for certain was that he had to protect Laura. He thought again about the way kissing her had made him feel, and the realization that he still cared deeply for her hit him hard. A weary breath slipped past Nick's lips. It was late. He couldn't deal with any of this right now. He glanced at the clock on the mantel above the fireplace. Midnight. He should check on Laura and get some sleep. Maybe Ian would come up with something more on Sandra tomorrow.

Rain pattered quietly on the roof. A storm had been threatening the entire drive home. Nick was glad the wet stuff had held off until they got back to Bay Break. The door to Laura's room was open. Nick slipped in soundlessly. The light from the bedside table cast a golden glow on her sweet face and silky hair. Laura had been so exhausted and overwhelmed, she had hardly spoken a word during the return trip. She had gone straight to bed as soon as they got home.

She was tired. Nick moved to her bedside and crouched down next to her. Tired or not, Laura was beautiful. Her bare shoulders made Nick wonder if she were naked beneath that sheet and thin cotton blanket. His mouth parched instantly at the thought. His eyes feasted on the perfection of the satiny skin revealed before him. Rage stirred inside him when his gaze traced the small slash mark, then flitted back to the tiny puncture wounds on her throat. Forcing the anger away, Nick shifted his slow perusal to her sweet face. All emotion melted, leaving him weak with want. Her lashes, a few shades darker than her blond hair, shadowed her soft cheeks. Those full, pink lips were parted slightly as if she were waiting for his kiss.

Cursing himself as a glutton for punishment, Nick allowed his gaze to trace her tempting jawline, then down the curve of her delicate throat to the pulse beating rhythmically there. He licked his lips hungrily and resisted the urge to touch her slender shoulder, to feel the warm smoothness of her skin. His body turned rock hard with desire.

Something snagged his attention. He frowned. Nick jerked his gaze back to her shoulder, near her neck. He moved closer to get a better look. The bottom fell out of Nick's stomach when his brain assimilated what his eyes found there.

Bruises. Small, oblong, barely visible marks that discolored her otherwise perfect, creamy skin.

He…he tried to drown me.

No way could Laura have made those bruises on herself. The position and size of which could only be labeled as finger marks. A churning mixture of rage and fear rising inside him, Nick eased down onto the side of the bed next to her. This, Nick seethed, was hard evidence.

"Laura." He shook her gently. "Laura, honey, wake up. We need to talk."

She moaned a protest and hugged her pillow. Nick's body ached with the need to hold her that way. "Laura." He shook her again. "We have to talk."

Laura sat up with a start. The sheet fell, exposing one high, firm breast briefly before she covered herself. "What?" she demanded irritably.

Nick leveled his determined gaze on her bleary one. "I want you to start at the beginning and tell me everything. Again."

LAURA WATCHED Nick pace back and forth across the room. She stood in the middle of the room, the sheet hugged close around her. She wished he had given her time to put some clothes on before he started this inquisition. After her long cry in the shower where Nick wouldn't hear or see her, she hadn't had the energy or the desire to dig up anything to sleep in. She had wanted to escape into sleep. She didn't want to think about the missing files or Mrs. Mallory's death.

Or the nephew.

Laura shivered. She blocked the memory of the man with

the strange eyes who had tried to kill her twice already. The bathroom had been dark and she hadn't actually seen his eyes that time. But she knew. Deep in her heart, Laura knew it was him. And with that instinct came the realization that he had probably been the one to take her son. James Ed would never have bothered himself with that part. Her heart shuddered at that thought.

"Does that about sum it up?"

Nick's question jerked Laura to attention. "What?" she asked as she forced herself to focus on him once more.

"Dammit, Laura," he growled. He jammed his hands at his waist and moved in her direction. "I need your full attention here."

"I'm sorry." She pushed the hair back from her face. "You're going to have to start over."

Nick swore under his breath. Those green eyes flashed with barely checked fury. What had him all worked up? Laura wondered, her own irritation kindling. Certainly nothing they had learned today. Though she knew with a measure of certainty that the nephew was the man after her, she couldn't prove that to Nick. She had proven *nothing* today.

The emptiness of that one word echoed around her. The only glimmer of hope in all this was that Nick was beginning to believe her.

"You came home that summer from college, and things were tense you said."

Laura nodded. "At first I thought it was because I hadn't put as much into school as James Ed had. He wanted me to be the perfect student, the perfect sister." She frowned, remembering her brother's disappointment. "But it didn't take long for me to figure out that it had nothing to do with me. It was the campaign for the Governor's office."

"And then Rafe Manning came on the scene."

Again Laura noted that change in Nick's eyes, in his posture, when he spoke of Rafe. "Right," she replied. "I dated him a few times because I was bored, but we didn't hit it off. James Ed tried to push the issue. Apparently he and Rafe's father were tight." Laura shrugged. "You know the rest."

Nick folded his arms over his chest and massaged his chin with his thumb and forefinger. The movement drew Laura's eyes to that sexy cleft in his chin. Emotion stirred inside her. Robby had a cleft just like that.

"Not once during all of this did you ever suspect Sandra of being involved?"

Taken aback by his question, Laura stared at him in amazement. "Sandra?" Laura shook her head slowly from side to side. "That's ridiculous. Sandra has never been anything but kind to me."

"What would you say if I told you that Sandra might not be who you think she is," Nick offered, his gaze intent on hers, watching, analyzing.

Laura frowned. "What does that mean?"

"Sandra's mother was involved with your father."

"That's not possible. Sandra's mother is dead."

"Did Sandra tell you that?"

Laura nodded, feeling as if another rug was about to be snatched from under her feet.

"Sandra's mother is a permanent ward at Serenity Sanitarium."

Laura stilled as her brain absorbed the impact of his words. That was the hospital James Ed claimed she had been committed to for the past eighteen months. Sandra's mother was alive? And a patient there? "Why would Sandra lie?" The question echoed in the room, only then did Laura realize she had said it aloud.

Nick placed a reassuring hand on her arm, his fingers

caressed her bare skin. That simple touch sent heat spearing through her. "I don't know, but we're damned sure going to find out."

Laura's gaze connected with his. "Why the sudden change of heart, Nick?" Laura examined his now impassive gaze closely. "Are you trying to tell me that you really do believe me now?"

He lifted those long fingers to her throat and touched her gingerly. He swallowed hard, the play of muscle beneath tanned skin made Laura ache to touch him there, the same way he was touching her.

"Believing you wasn't the problem, Laura. Let's just say I finally got that hard evidence." His gaze followed the movements of his fingers.

Laura stumbled away from him. She pivoted and hurried to the dresser, then stared at her reflection in the mirror. Several long, thin bruises marked her skin where strong fingers had held her beneath the water's surface.

Nick came up behind her, watching her in the mirror. "Laura, I'm sorry I let this happen. I should have believed you sooner." He touched her elbow. Laura flinched. "I won't let anyone hurt you again. I swear," he added softly.

Laura shunned his touch. "It took this," she gestured to the bruises, "to make you believe that someone was trying to kill me." Fury rose in Laura then. "What about my child? Do you believe in him yet?"

Nick's gaze wavered. "Of course I believe you, but we have to have proof."

"You bastard. You still don't really believe me."

Nick let go a heavy breath. "That's not true," he argued.

"Then look me in the eye and tell me that you believe I have a son. That his name is Robby and he's the most important thing in my life," she ground out, a sob knotting her chest.

Nick's concerned gaze collided with hers.

"Say it, damn you!" Laura trembled with the intensity of her fury. "Say it," she demanded when his response didn't come quickly enough.

Nick blinked. "It's not a matter of making me believe you—we have to be able to prove it to James Ed." He added quickly, "And the police."

She shoved at his chest with one hand and held the sheet to her breast with the other. "Get away from me! I don't give a damn about your proof!"

"Laura." Nick dodged her next attempt at doing him bodily harm. He grabbed her by both arms and held her still. "Laura, listen to me."

"I don't want to hear anything you have to say." Laura trembled, his long fingers splayed on her flesh and urged her closer.

"Laura." He breathed her name, the feel of his warm breath soft on her face. "I have to operate on facts, not assumptions. I can't go back to Jackson and demand to know where your son is when I have no physical proof that he exists."

Laura knew he was right. Deep in her heart, she knew. But that didn't stop the ache tearing at her insides. She needed to find her son more than she needed to take her next breath.

"I have to find him," she murmured. How many days had it been now? Laura squeezed her eyes shut. God, she didn't want to think about that.

"Please trust me, Laura," Nick pleaded. He angled his head down to look into her eyes when she opened them. "I won't let you down if you'll just trust me."

Laura met that intense green gaze and found herself drowning in the emotions reflected there. Desire, need... The same emotions she felt detonating inside her. She did trust Nick. He would never do anything to hurt her. She knew that. And she needed him so much. To hold her, to make her forget for just a little while. She needed him to love her the way he had before. She needed to reaffirm this thing between them, to feel his strong arms around her. Nick would help her, she knew he would. His strength was all that kept her sane right now.

"Hold me, Nick." Laura went into his arms. She slid her own arms around his lean waist and held him tightly. His scent, something spicy and male, enveloped her. And then his strong arms were around her, holding her, protecting her.

Nick pressed a tender kiss to her hair. "I just need you to trust me, honey, that's all." His lips found her temple and brushed another of those gentle kisses there. "Please trust me."

Laura closed her eyes and allowed instinct to take over. She needed Nick to take her away from this painful reality. To hold her and promise her that everything would be all right. Her hands moved over his strong back, feeling, caressing. She could feel the muscled landscape of his broad chest pressing against her breasts. Her nipples pebbled at the thought of how his warm skin would feel against hers.

His fingers threaded into her hair and pulled her face up to his. "You should get some rest," he said thickly, his gaze never left her mouth. "I won't be far away."

Laura shook her head, drawing his gaze to hers. "Don't leave me," she said in the barest of whispers. Laura tiptoed and quickly kissed his full lips. Nick sucked in a sharp breath. "I want you, Nick. I want you now."

He drew back slightly. "You're not thinking clearly, Laura." He searched her gaze, her face, then licked his lips, yearning clear in his eyes. "I don't want you to regret anything."

Determined to show him just how badly she wanted him, Laura stepped back and allowed the sheet to fall to the floor. "I do want," she told him. "I want you."

Nick's gaze moved slowly over her body. Laura felt its caress as surely as if he were touching her with those skilled hands.

"I want you, too," he admitted quietly. "But you're vulnerable right now and I don't want to take advantage of that." His eyes contradicted his words. He did want to do just that. He wanted it as badly as she did.

"The decision isn't yours," Laura concluded. "It's mine." She recovered the step she had retreated. Her eyes steady on his, Laura reached up and slowly began to unbutton his shirt. His gaze dropped to her hands and he watched as she bared his chest. The knowledge that he was watching her and responding sent a surge of power pulsing through her veins, heating her already too warm body.

Laura held out her hand. "Your weapon, sir."

Nick looked from her hand to her. Laura saw the flicker of hesitation in his eyes. She stepped back and opened the drawer to the night table. "I'm only going to put it away," she explained.

He nodded, then reached behind his back and retrieved the weapon. Nick's gaze held hers as he placed the ominous looking weapon in Laura's open palm.

She smiled, her lips trembling with the effort. "Thank you." Nick would never know how much that gesture meant to her. He could have put the gun away himself, but he hadn't. He trusted her at least a little.

Laura closed the drawer and turned to find him right behind her, she looked up into those sea green eyes and melted at what she saw. Savage need, overwhelming desire. Nick took her hand in his and pressed a kiss against her palm, then placed it over his heart. Laura felt weak with emotion. Knotting her hands in his shirt, she pulled it from his jeans, then pushed it off his broad shoulders until it dropped to the floor.

For a time Laura simply admired the exquisite terrain of his muscled chest. She touched the scar and electricity charged through her. Leaning forward, she kissed that place and thanked God once more that Nick was alive. Laura flattened her hands against his hair-roughened chest and allowed her palms to mold to the contours of that awesome torso. She closed her eyes and committed each ripple and ridge to memory. Desire sizzled inside her, making her bold, making her need. Her fingers slipped into the waistband of his jeans and circled his lean waist.

Nick groaned low in his throat. "Laura," he rasped. "How long do you plan to torture me this way?"

She released the button to his fly, then slowly lowered the zipper, the sound echoing around them. "As long as it takes," she assured him, her voice low and husky.

Laura knelt in front of him. The immense pleasure in his eyes added to her own. She pulled one boot off, then the other. The socks were rolled off next. Slowly, she tugged his jeans down those long, muscled legs. Each inch of flesh she revealed made breathing that much more difficult. When his jeans had been disposed of, Laura sat back on her heels and admired his amazing body. Wide, wide shoulders that narrowed into a lean waist and hips, then long, muscled legs. She studied the scarred right knee momentarily, remembering the life he had saved by taking a bullet. Laura closed her eyes and forced away the possibility that he might get caught in the crossfire of all this madness again. She couldn't bear the thought of Nick being hurt again. The realization that his getting hurt or worse was a very distinct possibility hit her hard. She had to make sure that didn't happen. Everyone around her that she cared about was being hurt or worse.

Suppressing the thought, Laura's gaze moved back up those long, powerful legs. Black briefs concealed the part of him that made her wet and achy. Nick had taught her what it was to be a woman in the purest, most primitive sense of the word. Not one day had gone by in the past two years that her body had not yearned for his. Now, at last, she would know that pleasure once more.

One last time.

With painstaking slowness, Laura slid his briefs down and off. Nick groaned loudly when she pressed a kiss to one lean hip. His arousal nudged her shoulder sending a shard of desire slicing through her. She wanted him inside her. Now.

Laura stood, braced her hands against his chest and tip-toed to kiss his firm lips. His eyes opened and the savage fire burning there seared her from the inside out.

"No more," he growled. Nick lifted her into his arms as if she weighed nothing at all. Three steps later and they were on the bed.

"My turn now," he warned.

Laura bit down on her lower lip to hold back her cry of need as he kissed his way down her body. He paused to love her breasts. Taking his time, he laved and suckled each until Laura thought she would die of it. He gave the same attention to her belly button, licking, sucking, arousing.

Nick suddenly stilled. His fingers traced her side. "What's this?" he murmured.

Trying to make sense of his question through her haze of lust, Laura stared down at where his fingers touched her. *Stretch marks.* Few and faint, but there just the same. Why hadn't she thought of that before?

"Stretch marks," she answered. "From my pregnancy. Everyone gets them."

Nick traced the pale marks hesitantly.

"Your evidence," Laura added when he remained silent.

Nick smiled at her then. "Absolutely," he concurred. A predatory gleam brightened his beautiful green eyes. "And my pleasure as well." His tongue followed the same path his fingers had taken.

Laura moaned her approval.

His fingers trailed down her skin until they found that part of her which throbbed for his touch. Laura arched upward when one long finger slipped inside her. His thumb made tiny circles around her most intimate place of desire.

"Nick," she murmured. Instinctively her hips moved against his hand. A second finger slipped inside and Laura cried out.

His mouth captured hers. Slowly, thoroughly he kissed her, his tongue mimicking the rhythm of his fingers. The feel of his lips, soft, yet firm and commanding, commanding her with devastating precision. His tongue touched all the sensitive places in her mouth, a sweet torture to which she gladly surrendered. Laura writhed with the tension coiling tighter and tighter inside her. She gasped for air when his mouth finally lifted from hers. His ragged breath fanned her lips, igniting another fire in her soul. Nick moved between her thighs. Those magic fingers, hot and moist from her body, slid over her hip and beneath her to lift her toward him. Release crashed down on Laura the moment he entered her, stretching, filling, completing.

Nick covered her mouth with his and took her scream just as she took him inside her. His fingers entwined with hers, pulling her hands above her head. Slowly, drawing out the exquisite pleasure, Nick thrust fully inside her again and again. Her tension building even faster than the first time, Laura met his thrusts, urging him to hurry. Her heart pounding, her breath trapped in her lungs, Laura spiraled toward release once more. One last thrust and Nick followed her to that special place of pure sensation.

His breathing as jagged and labored as hers, Nick pressed his forehead to Laura's. "Are you all right?"

Laura nodded once, unable to speak.

"Rest now. We'll talk later," he told her as he rolled over and pulled her into his protective embrace.

Laura closed her eyes against the tears. How she loved this man. But they would never be able to be a family. No matter how he felt about her at this moment, when he discovered the truth, he would despise her for keeping his son from him for so long.

Laura had to find a way to get away from Nick. He had been hurt by her too much already. Nick had taken a bullet and almost died for her. She had kept his son from him all this time. He deserved better. She could not risk him being hurt by James Ed's men again. If something happened to her Robby would need his father. Nick only had to take one look at Robby to know that the child belonged to him. And she knew in her heart that Nick would not stop looking for him now no matter what happened. He had urged James Ed to give him this time with Laura. Nick had stuck his neck out for her too many times already. Decision behind her, Laura considered her best course of action. Too much time had been wasted already. Doc's office might hold some clue to where he had gone. And maybe even some proof of her child's existence. Something she could take to the police.

Laura had to find her baby. But she had to make sure Nick stayed out of the line of fire this time.

This was between her and James Ed.

Chapter Nine

The scent of an angel tantalized him. Nick snuggled more deeply into his pillow. *Laura.* He smiled and opened his eyes to the bright morning light spilling into the room. He reached for the woman who had turned his world upside down once more.

"Good morning," she murmured.

Nick kissed the tip of her nose. "Morning," he rasped. "Did you know that you look like an angel when you wake up?"

Laura giggled. God, how good it felt to hear that. But Nick wanted more than a glimpse of the woman he had fallen in love with. He wanted her to laugh out loud. To drive him crazy like she did two years ago. While he watched, sadness filled her gaze once more, and Nick knew she had remembered that her son was still missing.

"Hungry?" he inquired, trying to keep the mood light. "I could eat a horse."

She smiled. "You're always hungry." Laura searched his gaze for what seemed like forever, as if she were afraid it might be the last time she could look at him this way. "You go take care of breakfast. I want a long, hot bath," she said suggestively. "Maybe you can even come join me."

"Maybe I'm not as hungry as I thought." Nick nuzzled her neck, then nipped the lobe of her ear.

Laura gasped and pulled away from his exploring mouth. "For once I am," she murmured.

Nick bowed his head. "Your wish is my command, madam."

Laura giggled again as she scurried from the room. Nick watched her departure in rapt appreciation. He loved every square inch of her petite little body.

"Don't lock the door," he called out after her. "I'll be there in fifteen minutes."

"I'll be waiting," she called from the bathroom. The sound of water rushing into the tub obliterated any possibility of further conversation.

Nick threw back the sheet and got out of bed. He stretched, feeling better than he had in a very long time. He pulled on his jeans, tucked his weapon into his waistband and started toward the kitchen. This was the way it should be, the two of them together making love, sharing moments like this morning.

But there was Laura's child. Nick slowed in his progress toward the kitchen. He scrubbed a hand over his stomach. The notion of a child would take some getting used to. Nick certainly wanted children of his own. He paused at the kitchen doorway. Did it matter to him that this child belonged to another man? A slow smile claimed Nick's mouth. Hell no. Nick would love Laura's child just like his own.

Feeling like a tremendous weight had been lifted from his shoulders, Nick set to the task of making breakfast. He whistled as he worked. Nothing like great sex with the woman you love to make a man happy, he decided. All he had to do now was sort all this insanity out.

Twenty minutes later and Nick was ready to join Laura.

At this point he might only get to dry her back. He grinned. But that was fine with him. Nick sauntered down the hall, anticipation pounding through his veins. He could make love to Laura for the rest of his life and never stop wanting more of her. He tapped on the closed bathroom door.

"Ready or not here I come," he teased. Nick turned the knob and pushed the door open. Steam billowed out to engulf him. Nick frowned. What the hell? He stepped into the bathroom and water pooled around his feet. His heart rate blasted into overdrive, pumping fear and adrenaline through his tense body. He fanned his arms to part the steam. Water was pouring over the side of the tub. Where was Laura? Fear hurdled through Nick's veins. He peered down at the tub. No Laura. Thank God. He swallowed hard as he leaned down and turned the swiftly flowing water off, then opened the drain.

Nick straightened and took a breath. His next thought sent anger rushing through him, neutralizing the fear he had felt. He crossed the wet floor to the window, parted the curtain and cleared a spot of fog from the glass. Peering out, his suspicion was confirmed. His rental car was gone.

Nick swore hotly.

Laura was gone.

His fury burning off the last of the fear lingering in his chest, Nick stamped into Laura's bedroom. Pain roared up his leg, and his knee almost buckled in protest. He closed his eyes and gritted his teeth until the pain subsided to a more tolerable level. Taking a bit more care, he tugged on his shirt and socks and stepped into his boots.

How the hell had he let last night happen? Nick cursed himself again. It was two years ago all over again, only this time he wasn't bleeding. At least not on the outside, he amended. With all that had happened, how could he still feel this way about Laura?

He was a fool, that's why.

He had sworn that he wouldn't get sucked into the Proctor family saga this time. He headed to the door, pulling his jacket on and automatically checking the weapon at the small of his back as he went. Damn it, damn it. Here he was, heart deep in tangled emotions and deadly deceptions.

He had really screwed up this time. He should have known Laura was up to something. She had given in to his plan of action last night all too easily. She was desperate to find her son. And desperate people did desperate things. Nick knew that all too well. He should have reassured her rather than pushing for answers about her pregnancy. She had ended up unwilling to discuss the issue. Nick cursed himself again. Making love to Laura again had only served to reinforce the feeling that she was his and his alone. The thought that she had been with another man, even once, still tore at his heart. He shouldn't have pressured her about the child's father. He should have insisted they do things his way and his way only. He should have realized that something was up this morning.

Damn it, he was a complete idiot.

Nick followed the driveway until it intersected the highway. He glanced left. That direction would take her to Jackson. He didn't think Laura would head that way, not alone and unarmed. His gaze shifted right. It was only five miles to town. That was the direction he needed to take. His knee complained sharply at the thought. Nick shifted his weight to the other leg. Why would Laura go into town?

Nick swore when he considered that she may have gone back to the old woman's house. That's all he needed was for the old hag to call the police and get Laura thrown into jail. James Ed would...

He didn't want to consider that his instincts had gone that far south where James Ed was concerned. Protecting

James Ed's interests, including Laura, was the job Nick had signed on to do. But solving the puzzle that was Laura Proctor's predicament was Nick's ultimate goal. Nick's gut instinct just wouldn't permit him to believe that James Ed was the villain here.

And neither was Laura. She had definitely been attacked. There was no question in his mind about that. And she had obviously been pregnant. The stretch marks were there and Nick had noticed other subtle changes to her body. Her breasts were fuller. However, making love to her had proven the same—mind-blowing. The scent of her still clung to his skin, the memory of her tight, hot body was tattooed across his brain, easily arousing him even now.

Nick shook himself from the memory. He didn't have time for that right now. He had to find Laura. His attention jerked to the road when an old truck slowed as it approached him. He squinted to identify the driver.

Rutherford.

Headed in the direction of Jackson, the old man passed slowly, did a precarious U-turn, then stopped on the edge of the road right in front of Nick.

"Need a ride young fella?"

Nick braced his hands on the door and leaned into the open window. "I suppose that depends upon where you're headed, old man," Nick said tersely. He was still annoyed that Rutherford had spilled his guts to Ian and not him. Maybe Nick had gotten too close to all this. Whatever the case, he didn't like being jerked around or bypassed.

The old man eyed him suspiciously for one long minute, then one side of his mouth hitched up in a smile. He pushed his John Deere cap up and scratched his forehead. "I'm headed to the same place you're headed, I reckon," he replied cryptically.

Nick eyed him with mounting skepticism. "Is that a fact?"

Rutherford settled his cap back into place and adopted a knowing look. "It is if it's an angel you're looking for."

"You know where Laura is?"

The old man grinned widely. "I sure do. I was out to the barn for a ladder." He nodded toward the large barn right off the pages of a New England calendar that sat behind and to one side of the Proctor house. "Planned on cleaning out the gutters today. That rain last night pretty much cleared the rest of the leaves from the trees."

"You saw her leave," Nick prodded impatiently.

"She come running outta that house like the devil himself was on her heels." Rutherford cocked a bushy gray brow. "But you never did come out."

Nick tamped down the response that immediately came to mind. "Which way did she go?" he said instead.

"She jumped into that car of yours and took off toward town." He frowned. "I figured something was up so I followed her. She drove straight to Doc Holland's office. Didn't appear to be nobody there though, but she went on around back like she knowed what she was about. Then I got to thinking that maybe I should come back and get you. Seeing as you're supposed to be keeping an eye on her and all."

Nick jerked the door open and climbed in. "Thanks," he snapped. The fact that the man was right didn't help Nick's disposition.

Rutherford pulled back out onto the highway. He cast Nick a conspiratorial wink. "You have to watch those angels, young fella, they got themselves wings. They can fly away before you know they're gone."

Nick manufactured a caustic smile. "Thanks, I'll remember that." When he caught up with Laura, he fully intended to clip those wings.

In no time at all Mr. Rutherford chugged into the driveway leading to Doc Holland's place. Nick's black rental car was parked at an odd angle next to the porch. He opened his door before Rutherford braked to a full stop. Nick slid out and closed the door behind him.

"Thanks for the ride," he said, taking another look at the old man behind the wheel. "And thanks for your help with Laura's situation," he added contritely. Hell, the man had done him a favor. Nick should be considerably more grateful.

Carl Rutherford's expression turned serious. "You just make sure that little girl don't do no permanent disappearing act."

Nick nodded and backed up a step as the old truck lurched forward. When Mr. Rutherford had exited the other end of the horseshoe-shaped drive, Nick turned his attention to the house-cum-clinic before him. What the hell was she doing here? Nick shook his head. Looking for more evidence to support her case, he felt sure. Or for the Doc, whichever she could find. Nick frowned. The place was awfully quiet for there to be anyone home—he glanced around the property—and no other vehicles besides his rental car were in the vicinity. Nick trudged slowly toward the house, the wet leaves made little sound beneath his feet as he crossed the tree-lined yard.

Not taking any chances on the possibility of anyone else having followed her, Nick withdrew his weapon. If "Pinkie" showed his ghostly mug, Nick would give him something to remember him by. The thought that the bastard had hurt Laura again and maybe taken her son burned in Nick's gut.

Nick moved cautiously across the porch to the front door.

It was locked. The sign officially proclaiming the doctor's absence still hung in a nearby window. He obviously hadn't returned. Surveying the quiet street, Nick moved down the side of the house. A couple of blocks off the small town square and lined by trees and shrubbery, the place was fairly secluded. The back of the house looked much like the front with a wide porch spanning the length of it. The back door stood open. Good. Nick preferred an avenue of access that didn't require breaking a window. An open door was invitation enough to skirt the boundaries of breaking and entering.

Not that a minor technicality would have kept him from going in, Nick mused. Upon reaching the door, he saw that Laura had beat him to it anyway. One glass pane in the door had been shattered. A handy rock lay on the painted porch floor. Nick swore under his breath. What the hell was she thinking? The police surely patrolled the area. Nick eased inside, scanning left to right as his eyes adjusted to the natural early morning interior light. The large old-fashioned kitchen looked homey and quite empty. Silently, Nick weaved between the massive oak furnishings and made his way to the dimly lit hall.

A sound reached him. He frowned in concentration. *Crying.* Laura! Hard as it proved, Nick remained absolutely still until he got a fix on the direction of the heartrending weeping. Farther down the hall and to the right. Nick moved soundlessly toward the door he had estimated would lead him to Laura. The soft sound of her tears echoed in the silent house. If anyone had hurt her...

Rage twisting inside him, Nick paused next to the open doorway and listened for any other sound coming from the room. Nothing. Taking a deep breath and firming his grip on his weapon, Nick swung into position in front of the door. He scanned what appeared to be an office for any threat. The place had been tossed. It looked as if a tornado had ripped through it. Maintaining his fire-ready stance, Nick dropped his gaze to the floor where Laura huddled...

...over what was obviously a very dead man.

BLOOD.

Laura stared at her hands. The warm, sticky red stuff oozed between her fingers. She had tried to help Doc but it was too late.

Too late.

Dizziness washed over her, making her want to give in to the darkness that threatened her consciousness. Who would do this to Doc? Laura's gaze riveted once more to the large kitchen knife protruding from his chest. She swallowed back the bitter bile rising in her throat.

She had done this. Laura moaned a sob. She had come back to Bay Break and brought nothing but pain, loss and death to those she loved most.

Robby...

Doc...

And Nick.

Laura closed her eyes and surrendered to the flood of emotion pressing against the back of her throat. She was responsible for this senseless violence.

''Oh, God,'' she murmured as she rocked back and forth. ''I killed him. I killed him,'' she chanted.

''Laura.''

Slowly, Laura looked up into the stony features of Nick's grim face. ''Doc's dead,'' she told him weakly.

Nick knelt next to her then and checked Doc's pulse.

''It's too late,'' she whispered. ''He's gone. Robby's gone, too.'' A heart-wrenching sob tore from her lips. Laura slumped in defeat. *Too late. Too late. Too late,* her mind screamed.

"Come on, Laura, we have to get you out of here."

Nick was moving her. She could feel his strong arms around her as he lifted her. Laura's head dropped onto his shoulder.

Doc was dead.

Robby was lost.

And it was all her fault.

Laura's stomach churned violently. The room spun wildly when Nick settled her back onto her feet near the kitchen sink. Laura moaned a protest when he began washing the blood from her hands. *No, no, no,* her mind chanted.

"Oh, God." Laura dropped her head into the sink and vomited violently. The image of Doc's blood pooling around his dead body was forever imprinted in her memory. The sound of Robby's cries for mommy rang in her ears.

"It's okay, baby, it's okay," Nick murmured softly as he held her hair back from her face. He turned on the tap to wash away the pungent bile.

When the urge to heave passed, Laura cupped her hand and cooled her mouth and throat with as much water as she dared drink with her stomach still quivering inside her. She splashed the liquid relief on her face, then swiped the excess moisture away with her hand. *Doc was dead.*

Nick lifted her onto the counter and inspected her closely, a mixture of fear and concern etched on his face. "You're not hurt?" He brushed the damp hair back from her face.

Laura shook her head. Nausea threatened at even that simple movement. *Doc was dead.*

She squeezed her eyes shut to block the horrifying images. "This is my fault. I shouldn't have come here."

"You have to tell me what happened," Nick urged gently. "Why did you run away from me?"

She swallowed, then shuddered, more from grief than the

bitter taste still clinging to the back of her throat. "I didn't run away," she told him. "I thought if I could find my file, that maybe Doc had made some sort of notations regarding Robby. Then James Ed couldn't pretend my son doesn't exist." Laura closed her eyes and suppressed the mental replay of the scene she had found. She opened her eyes to him then. "I want to do this alone, Nick. I don't want you to help me anymore. It's not safe. I won't risk you getting hurt again."

"There was no one else here when you arrived?" Nick seemed to ignore all that she had just said.

Laura shook her head. "Just...just..." She gestured vaguely toward the hall. "Doc," she finished weakly.

"Laura, I need you to think very carefully. Was the door open when you arrived?"

"I...I broke the glass and unlocked the door," she told him. Laura allowed her frantic gaze to meet his now unreadable one. Those piercing green eyes bored into hers, searching, analyzing.

"Did you touch anything besides the door?"

"What?"

"Did you touch anything at all, Laura, anything besides the door?" he demanded impatiently.

She thought hard. What did she touch? Nothing... everything, maybe. "I can't remember." What was he thinking?

His fingers, like steel bands, curled around her arms, he gave her a little shake. "Listen to me," he ground out. "The blood hasn't congealed yet. Do you know what that means?"

Laura's stomach roiled at the mental picture Nick's words evoked. "I don't want to hear this...." She tried to escape his firm hold. "Just let me go, Nick."

"Dammit, Laura," he growled. "Whoever killed Doc

hasn't been gone long. Doc was out of town, remember? He probably arrived back in town and surprised someone in his office. Think! Think about what you saw first when you came inside. What did you hear?''

Laura concentrated hard. She heard...silence. Her gaze connected to Nick's. "Nothing. There was silence." She swallowed. "But I could smell the blood." A sob snatched at Laura's flimsy hold on composure. "The moment I walked in I could smell it."

Nick swore under his breath. "You're sure," he repeated slowly, "that you didn't touch anything."

"I don't think so." Laura let go a shaky breath. "But I can't be sure. I was...I was hysterical." A kind of numbness had set in now, Laura realized. She didn't really feel anything at all, just tired. So very tired.

"Don't move," Nick instructed harshly.

Laura nodded. She clamped her hand over her mouth and fought the urge to scream. She felt her eyes go round with remembered horror. Doc was dead. Robby was lost. Oh, God. Oh, God. She had to do something.

But what?

Minutes or hours passed before Nick came back. Laura couldn't be sure which. He swiped the faucet and the area around the sink with a hand towel. Laura frowned. What was he doing?

"Can you stand?" he asked, his expression closed.

"Yes," she murmured.

Nick lifted her off the counter and settled Laura on her feet. "Don't move, don't touch anything," he ordered.

Laura blinked, confused. Nick swiped the counter, then ushered her toward the back door. Once they were on the porch, he gave the doorknob, the door, and its surrounding casing the same treatment. Still too dazed to marshal the strength to question his actions, Laura watched as he threw the rock she had used to break the glass deep into the woods at the back of the yard. She tried to think what all this meant, but her mind kept going back to the image of Doc lying dead on the floor. Laura shuddered and forced the images away.

Nick took her hand and led her back to the car. He pitched the towel he had used into the back seat. As if she were as fragile as glass, he settled Laura into the passenger seat and buckled her seat belt. Laura watched him move to the other side of the car and slide behind the wheel. Memories of their lovemaking suddenly filled her, warmed her. Laura closed her eyes and savored the remembered heat of Nick's skin against hers. His lips on her body, his kiss. The last time they had made love Robby had been conceived.

And now he was lost. Laura's heart shuddered in her chest. Her baby. She had to find her baby.

"Nick, we have to find my baby," she urged. Laura shifted in the seat. "Don't you see. They're erasing every trace of my baby's existence." She shook her head. "It's as if he has disappeared into thin air. Never existed."

Nick cast her an understanding look as he pulled the car out onto the street. "I'm calling Ian when we get back to the house." He glanced back at her then. "I'm making arrangements to take you some place safe. Too much I don't understand is going on around here. I'm not taking any chances."

Fear rolled over Laura in suffocating waves. "No! I can't leave without Robby."

"The point is not negotiable."

Laura caught a glimpse of Vine Street as Nick crossed town. Desperation like she had never known before slammed into Laura. She had left Robby with Mrs. Leeton. She had to know where he was. She wasn't the fragile old woman she pretended to be. She knew. She had to know.

"Take me to Mrs. Leeton's house." The quiet force in those few words surprised even Laura. She had to go back.

Nick cast a glance in her direction. "All right," he agreed without hesitation and to her complete surprise.

Laura closed her eyes and prayed that Mrs. Leeton would tell the truth...and that it wouldn't be too late.

NICK BANGED on the door again, louder this time. The old woman would have to be deaf not to hear him. Laura stood next to him, impatiently shifting her weight from one foot to the other.

"She's not going to answer because she knows you're on to her now," Laura insisted.

He glanced at his watch. "Give her a minute. It's early and she's old. Maybe she's still in bed."

Laura huffed a breath and crossed her arms over her chest.

Nick released a long, slow breath of his own. *I killed him. I killed him,* kept echoing in his brain. He passed a weary hand over his face. She couldn't have, of course. But someone had intended to make it look as though she had. Her file had been lying right next to the Doc's body, the contents missing.

Nick shook his head at his own stupidity. In his irrational desire to protect Laura, he had tampered with evidence by wiping down the place, including any prints the real killer might have left behind. He was a bigger fool than even he had imagined.

"She isn't coming to the door," Laura prodded.

Nick cut her a look. He reached into his pocket and retrieved his all-purpose key. Laura watched in silent amazement as he quickly and efficiently "unlocked" the door.

Laura rushed past him before he could step aside. Nick

surveyed the quiet parlor while Laura rushed from one room to the next calling the old woman's name.

Mrs. Leeton was history.

Nick scanned the parlor.

She had either gotten out of Dodge or she was pushing up daisies somewhere like the Doc. Laura rushed back into the room.

"She's not here," she said wearily.

Nick picked up a picture frame and studied the smiling couple inside. "She's gone."

"But her things are still here," Laura argued. "Her clothes, her pictures." She gestured to the frame in his hand.

Nick turned the silver frame so that Laura could see it. "Lovely couple," he noted. "But they came with the frame."

Laura frowned, then quickly scanned the two frames hanging on the far wall. "Why would she take the pictures and leave the frames hanging?"

Nick placed the frame back on the table. "She doesn't want anyone to know she's gone." He crossed the room, stared out the window at nothing in particular, then looked back to Laura. "Can you tell if any of her clothes are gone?"

Laura shrugged. "It's hard to tell. There are clothes in the closets and in the dresser drawers, but I can't be sure if they're all there."

"I'll bet they're not," he assured her. "Where's the kitchen?"

Laura led him to the small immaculate kitchen. The woman was definitely obsessive-compulsive about house-cleaning, he noted. He glanced at the shiny tile floors and sparkling white countertops. Nick walked to the refrigerator and opened the door. He leaned down and peered inside for a moment or two.

"She's been gone at least three days," he said when he had straightened and closed the door.

"How do you know that?"

"The milk expired day before yesterday," he explained. Nick nodded toward the calendar hanging from a magnet on the appliance door.

Laura stepped closer to see what had caught Nick's eyes. Mrs. Leeton had meticulously marked off each day until day before yesterday. "Oh, God," she murmured.

Laura swayed. Nick caught her. "Come on, Laura, there's nothing else we can do here."

Nick locked the door and led Laura to the car. He watched her for signs of shock or panic. She had seen too much today. He didn't see how she could tolerate much more defeat. It was a miracle she hadn't fallen completely apart.

Once they were back at the house, Nick would insist that Laura lie down. Then he would call Ian and set up a new location to take Laura. Things were definitely getting too hot around here. One way or another, he intended to get to the bottom of this mess. But first he had to make sure Laura was safe. It wouldn't be long before Dr. Holland's body was discovered. Time was running out for Laura's freedom. If James Ed suspected Laura was in any way involved with Doc's murder, he would insist that she be sent away now.

Maybe, Nick decided, he would tilt the odds in their favor. A quick call to his old friend Ray would set things in motion.

NICK PULLED the afghan over Laura. He hoped she would sleep for a while. She had been so despondent over the Doc's death that Nick had been worried out of his mind.

Shortly after finally lying down, she had fallen asleep on the couch and Nick was immensely thankful. He didn't think he could bear one more moment of her self-deprecation. She blamed herself for Doc's death. If she hadn't come back here, she kept saying. But her baby had been sick. With no insurance and no money, she hadn't known who else to turn to. Now Doc was dead.

Nick blew out a breath. He wished he could find one single shred of real proof that Laura did, in fact, have a child. The stretch marks indicated a pregnancy, but proved nothing as to her having had a live birth. He had to have solid evidence.

Shaking his head in disgust, Nick walked to the kitchen and numbly went through the motions of brewing coffee. Hell, he hadn't even had a cup of coffee today. He glanced at the clock on the wall, two o'clock. He had a feeling that this was going to be one hell of a long day. He had busied himself earlier with cleaning up the water in the bathroom, but now he felt that old restless feeling. They were getting closer to the truth now. He could feel it.

With a cup of strong coffee in his hand, Nick sat down at the table and pulled out his cellular phone. He hadn't wanted to make this call until he was certain Laura wouldn't hear. He punched in the number for information, then requested Ray's home number. Less than two minutes later he was holding for his old friend, Detective Ray Ingle.

"Hey buddyro, what's up?" Ray quipped, sounding a great deal more relaxed than the last time Nick had spoken to him.

"The easier question would be what's not," Nick told him with humor in his tone though he felt none at all.

"I hear you're hanging out in Mississippi for a week or two."

"Yeah, I just can't seem to learn my lesson right the first

time." Nick compressed his lips into a thin line. Beating around the bush wasn't going to make telling Ray what he had to tell him any easier.

"Hell." Ray laughed. "If you hang around down here long enough, maybe we'll make a real Southern gentleman out of you yet."

Nick smiled in spite of himself. "Thanks, but I think I'll stick with what I know best."

Silence waited between them for several long seconds.

"What's really up, man?" Ray ventured solemnly.

Nick stretched his neck in an effort to chase away the tension building there. "There's been a murder here in Bay Break."

"I see," Ray answered much more calmly than Nick had anticipated.

"Dr. Holland. Sometime this morning I think. His office has been trashed."

"Do the locals know yet?"

"Not yet."

"Is there anything else I should know?" Ray asked pointedly. "I won't even ask how you know all this."

"You may find Laura's prints in there," Nick admitted. "Hell, you'll probably find mine, too."

"Anything else?"

Nick hesitated only a second. "No."

Another long beat of silence passed.

"What is it you want me to do?" Ray asked finally.

"I know the locals will request a detective from your office to conduct the investigation." Nick moistened his lips. "I need you to make sure we're clean on this one."

"Are you?"

"I wouldn't ask if we weren't."

"Does the Governor know about this?"

"No," Nick said quickly. "And I'd appreciate it if you didn't tell him."

"What's going on, Nick?"

Nick heard the tension in Ray's voice. "I just need some more time to figure this out. I don't want Laura connected to anything that might muddy the waters."

"All right," Ray agreed. "I'll take care of it."

"Thanks, man," Nick said. "You know if you ever need anything at all, I'll be there for you."

"Don't think I'll forget it, slick," Ray said frankly.

"Let me know if you come up with any suspects," Nick added before he could hang up.

"Hey," Ray blurted before the connection was cut.

Nick pressed the phone back to his ear. "Yeah, Ray, I'm still here."

"What's the deal with the kid?"

Nick froze. Had James Ed told Ray about Laura's claims of having a child. Maybe James Ed had Ray looking into the possibility. Nick shook his head. No way. Ray would have told him right up front.

"What kid?" Nick asked slowly, reserving reaction.

Ray made a sound of disbelief. "Hell man, the kid Laura had with her when I spotted her down there. What kid did you think I meant?"

Nick's chest constricted. "Laura had a child with her when you saw her?"

"Yeah," Ray said, confusion coloring his tone. "A baby, maybe a year or so old. You couldn't miss him, he—"

"Her child is missing," Nick interrupted.

"Missing? What do—"

"Thanks, Ray," Nick said quickly, cutting him off. "Gotta go. I'll explain later." Nick closed the phone and tossed it onto the table.

He stood, the chair scraping across the floor in protest of his abrupt move. James Ed had definitely lied about Laura being in the hospital for the past eighteen months. She had been telling the truth all along. There really was a child.

Laura's child.

And now Nick had the evidence he needed to prove it.

Chapter Ten

Laura woke with a start. It was dark outside. She had slept the afternoon away again. She licked her dry lips and swallowed, the effort required to do so seeming monumental. How could she have slept so long? The medication was no longer in her system. Exhaustion, she supposed. Sleep had brought blessed relief. She had been able to leave reality behind. To escape...

Doc was dead.

The memory hit like a tidal wave. Laura squeezed her eyes shut and resisted the urge to cry. She refused to cry. Crying would accomplish nothing. She had to do something.

Doc was dead.

The files were missing.

Mrs. Mallory was gone.

Mrs. Leeton had disappeared.

Anyone who knew anything about Robby's birth was no longer available to help Laura. There was no one. Desperation crashed in on her all over again.

She would just have to help herself.

She could do it.

Nick would help her, but she wasn't going to allow him to take that risk. Doc had tried to help her and he was dead.

Laura clenched her teeth and forced her weary, grief-stricken mind to concentrate on forming a plan. If she could get her hands on a gun...

Nick would need his gun to protect himself.

Doc had a gun. She remembered seeing it on her first visit with Doc when she returned to Bay Break with Robby. Doc had shown her that he kept it loaded and in the drawer by his bed. If anyone showed up to cause trouble for Laura, he knew how to use it, too, he had said. Doc loved her. When this nightmare started she had hoped that maybe he had Robby with him, hiding out somewhere.

Another wave of fierce grief tore at Laura's heart. But he was dead. Gone forever. The albino had killed him. James Ed's henchman. Laura knew it as surely as she knew her own name. He would kill Nick, too, if he got in James Ed's way. Laura would not permit that to happen.

A sense of calm settled over Laura with the decision. It would be simple. All she had to do was take the car like she did this morning, drop by the clinic to get the gun, and head to Jackson. She would get the truth out of James Ed one way or another. Nick would never suspect that she would go back to her brother's house. At least not until it was too late. But first, she had to escape Nick's watchful eye. He would be monitoring her even more closely now.

Throwing back the afghan, Laura sat up and pushed the hair from her face. She looked around the den. No Nick. Maybe he had decided to take a shower. She listened. Nothing. She didn't smell food cooking either, so he probably wasn't in the kitchen. But he wouldn't be far away that was for sure.

Laura pushed to her feet. She closed her eyes and waited for the dizziness to pass. She needed to eat, but couldn't bring herself to even think of food. Her body was so weak. Laura took slow, deep breaths. When the walls had stopped spinning around her, she moved toward the kitchen. Though she rarely drank it, coffee would be good now. Laura shuffled into the hall and bumped straight into Nick. It was as if he had some sort of sixth sense about her. She smiled a secret smile. Except for this morning. She had definitely thrown him off balance then. Or maybe it was the lovemaking the night before. Warmth flowed instantly through Laura at the thought of making love with Nick.

"Laura." He smiled and brushed her cheek with gentle fingers. "I've been waiting for you to wake up. We need to talk, sweetheart."

The desire to tell Nick the truth about his son almost overwhelmed all else. She looked into those caring green eyes and remembered every detail of the way he had made love to her. The tenderness, the heat. The same as two years ago when she had fallen in love with this special man in the first place. Nick was the most caring, giving person she had ever met. He was the only person since her parents had died who believed in her at all. He was nothing like her brother. He was unlike any man she had ever met. And she had to protect Nick. He would willingly die for her if it came down to it. Laura had to make sure that didn't happen.

Laura shook off the lingering doubts regarding what she was about to do. She had to do it for Nick. "What did you want to talk about," she asked casually. Talking would give her time to devise a plan. She stilled. As long as he didn't start pressuring her again about her baby's father. God, if he suspected the truth for one minute...

"Let's go back into the den and get comfortable," he suggested.

For two long beats Laura could only stare into those caring jade depths. She loved this man so. The truth was going to forever change how he felt about her. Could she bear that? Finally, she nodded. "Okay." She allowed Nick to usher her back into the den and to the sofa. She sat down obediently and sent up a silent prayer that he hadn't figured things out yet. Laura knew she had to tell him eventually. Just not now. She couldn't deal with anything else right now.

Nick paced in a kind of circle for a moment as if he couldn't decide how to begin. Laura swallowed hard. Surely he didn't have bad news that he feared passing on to her. Laura closed her eyes for a second to calm herself. No, she couldn't take more bad news at the moment. The image of Doc lying lifeless on the floor of his office flashed before her eyes.

"I spoke with Detective Ingle this afternoon," Nick began, jerking her splintered attention back to him.

"Robby?" Terror snaked around Laura's heart and she instantly slammed a mental door shut on her fears. She had to be strong. Otherwise she wouldn't be able to find Robby or to lead the albino away from Nick.

Nick paused a few feet away, his back turned to her he bowed his head. "I'm sorry, Laura, I should—"

Shattering glass interrupted Nick's words. Laura's startled gaze darted to the window across the room. A gust of wind blew the curtains outward, they fluttered briefly then fell back into place. Fragments of glass littered the carpet. Laura frowned. She stood—

Nick's arms went around her and they hurtled to the floor, overturning the sofa table in the process. The telephone and lamp crashed to the floor. The dial tone buzzed from the dislodged receiver.

Stunned, Laura lay against the carpet for a several seconds before she could think. Nick's body covered her own protecting her. "Nick, what's going on?" she whispered hoarsely. The answer to her question struck her like a jolt of electricity. Her breath thinned in her lungs. Someone had shot through the window. Ice formed in Laura's stomach. *He* was out there. He was shooting at them.

"Nick!" Laura twisted her neck to an awkward angle to try and see his face. His eyes were closed, blood dripped down his forehead. She realized then that his full body weight was bearing down on her. Terror ignited within Laura. She pushed with all her might to roll herself and Nick over. She scrambled onto all fours and lowered her cheek to his face. He was breathing. Thank God. She quickly studied the injury that started an inch or so above his right eyebrow and disappeared into his hairline.

Please don't let him be hurt badly, she prayed.

Laura's hands shook as she traced the path the bullet had made with her fingers. Her lips trembled and she clamped down on her lower one to hold back the sobs twisting in her throat. Nick's warm blood stained her fingers. The vision of Doc lying in a pool of blood reeled past her eyes. Laura forced away the vivid memory. She had to help Nick. She frowned at the large bump rising on the left side of his forehead, near that temple. Laura glanced at the overturned table and broken lamp. He must have hit his head on the way down. The bullet appeared to have only grazed his head. She prayed she was right about that. He was still breathing but out cold. Could there be internal damage? Renewed terror zipped through her.

Laura shook him gently. "Nick. Nick, please wake up."

Laura's chest tightened with a rush of panic. She had to get help. She crawled to the other side of the table and snatched up the receiver and uprighted the telephone's base. Something cold and hard pressed to the back of her head.

"Hang it up," a coarse voice ordered.

It was him. She knew that voice. In her panic to help Nick, Laura had completely forgotten that he was somewhere outside. Now, he was here.

"Now," he commanded harshly. "Or I'll put another bullet in your boyfriend and finish him off."

Laura dropped the receiver onto its base and quickly stood. "He needs help," Laura pleaded. "Just let me call for help and then I'll do anything you want."

His weapon trained on her heart, the albino circled around her then glanced down at Nick. Laura gasped when he kicked Nick in the side.

"Stop!" she shrieked.

The albino grinned. "He'll live." He cocked one pale brow. "But he might not if you don't do exactly as I say."

Laura grabbed control of herself. She nodded adamantly. "What do you want me to do?"

He gestured toward the hall. "Outside, princess."

Laura led the way to the front door. She said one more silent prayer that Nick would be all right. Once outside, she turned to the man and asked, "What now?" Whatever it took to appease him and keep him away from Nick.

He glanced around the dark yard as if trying to decide. "The barn," he suggested. "Lots of imaginative possibilities in a barn."

Laura shuddered, but quickly composed herself. She needed calm. She needed to think. She had to think of a way to defend herself. If he killed her now, he might go back inside the house and kill Nick as well.

"Let's make this easy on the both of us," the man murmured next to her ear as he ushered her in the direction of the barn. "I'm going to kill you, and you're going to let me. Got that?"

Laura's eyes widened in fear, but she squashed the paralyzing emotion. She wracked her brain to remember what might be in the barn that could help her.

"Got that?" he demanded, the gun boring into her skull.

Laura nodded jerkily.

"Good," he acknowledged.

The scent of hay and stored fuels filled Laura's lungs as they entered the big double doors of the barn which stood partially open. No one ever bothered to close them, she remembered as if it mattered now. The albino made a half-hearted attempt at closing them. That effort would be to no avail Laura knew, the doors would only drift open again. They always did. But who would notice tonight?

Nick. Tears streamed down Laura's cheeks. She suddenly found herself praying that he didn't wake up and come to her rescue. Maybe if he stayed in the house, this bastard would just leave after he did what James Ed had paid him to do. Laura trembled. She didn't want to die. She wanted to be with her son, and she wanted to be with Nick.

But her life meant nothing if either of them was hurt by this. Laura closed her eyes against the painful possibility. Her captor flipped a switch and a long fluorescent light blinked to life overhead. Laura blinked quickly, her frantic gaze searched for anything that might aid her escape. The light's dim glow lit the center of the spacious barn, but the stalls remained in shadow. At one time, when she was a child, she remembered abruptly, there had been horses in this barn. But not anymore. Not in a long time. James Ed had gotten rid of what he had called an unnecessary nuisance.

The albino shoved her to the floor. "Don't move," he warned as he surveyed their surroundings. A smile lifted one side of his grim mouth when his gaze lit on something in particular. Laura shifted to see what it was that had captured his attention.

"Perfect," he muttered. Keeping the rifle aimed at her chest and his gaze trained on Laura, he walked to the row of hooks lining one wall and took down a sturdy-looking rope coiled there. Rope in hand, he moved back to tower over her. Laura committed every detail of his appearance to memory. Ghostly white hair and skin, and those eerie pink eyes. He wasn't very tall, but was solidly built. And strong, Laura remembered well. If she got away this time, she fully intended to be able to describe him to Nick.

"One peep out of you and I'll kill you now," he warned as he fiddled with the rope. "Then I'll kill lover boy just for the hell of it."

Not allowing his threat to frighten her further, Laura concentrated on his actions. Was he going to tie her up? She ordered the hysteria rising inside her to retreat, and her mind to focus. She had to escape. He was going to kill her this time, that was certain. The finality of that realization was oddly calming. Laura scanned her immediate surroundings for a weapon of some sort. A pitchfork stood on the wall farthest from her. She chewed her lip as she considered the distance. She would never be able to reach it before he shot her.

This was hopeless. There was nothing she could do.

Laura felt weak with regret. The thought that she would never see Nick or Robby again was a bone-deep ache.

No! she told herself. She had to do something. She couldn't just let him do this. She needed to get the albino talking. She had to stall him. At least it was some sort of plan. Maybe if she distracted him he would screw up somehow.

"Why did you have to kill Doc?" she demanded, her voice harsher than she had intended.

He cut his evil gaze to her and grinned. It was then that Laura noted the one thing about him that wasn't white—his teeth. They were a hideous yellow. She shivered.

"The old man was lucky once," he informed her haughtily. "When I came for him, he had left town. He had himself a sudden personal emergency." He laughed as if relishing Doc's troubles. "His only living relative, a sister out in Arkansas, had herself a heart attack and died."

"How do you know that?" Laura asked sharply, annoyed that he derived pleasure from Doc's loss.

"I was there at the clinic. One of the patients leaving that morning told me," he retorted. "If he hadn't left so quickly I would have taken care of him then and there." He shook his head with feigned regret. "But then he showed up this morning. Bad timing, too. I was taking your file." He frowned, his hands stilled on the rope. "Pissed me off that I couldn't get it the day he disappeared, but there were too many witnesses who saw me in his yard. I couldn't risk doing anything suspicious. So I left." That sick smile lifted his lips again. "People aren't likely to forget how I look."

Laura shivered. That was the truth if she had ever heard it. "You killed Doc just because he helped me?"

"I killed Doc because he knew too much."

Same difference, Laura thought with growing disgust.

"What about Mrs. Leeton, did you kill her, too, or was she working with you?" Laura clenched her teeth at the thought that the woman had betrayed her. Had helped someone steal her son. Laura's lips quivered with as much anger as fear.

"Not yet," he said casually. "The old bag disappeared. But I'll find her."

"Where's my son?" Laura held her breath. She feared the answer, but she had to know. Please, God, she prayed, don't let him have hurt my baby.

"You're not going to be needing him," he suggested as he tightened the strange knot in the rope. "Unless you want him buried with you."

Laura jumped to her feet, fury shot through her. "If you've hurt my son," she threatened.

"Don't worry, princess, he's worth too much alive." The albino recoiled the rope. "But you," he allowed that evil gaze to travel over her, "you're worth a whole lot more dead. And I'm tired of playing with you now. It's time to get down to business."

NICK ROUSED slowly to a piercing pain that knifed right through his skull. He touched his forehead and blood darkened his fingertips.

"What the hell happened?" he muttered.

He sat up, groaning with the pain pounding inside his head. He pushed to his feet and the room spun around him. Nick closed his eyes and fought the vertigo threatening his vertical position. He took a step and something crushed under his boot. Wiping the blood from his face, Nick stared down at the broken lamp and overturned table. The events that had taken place slammed into him with such force that he staggered.

"Laura." Nick scanned the room, then rushed into the hall. The front door stood open. The cold November wind had blown leaves into the hall. They skittered this way and that across the shiny hardwood like lost souls.

Nick hurried out onto the porch, his step still unsteady. The rental car was in the driveway where he had left it. He looked from left to right. Which way would the son of a bitch have taken her?

A shriek cut through the dark fabric of the night. Nick whirled in the direction of the sound. The barn. The barest glow of light filtered past the half-open doors. Nick ran like hell. He clenched his jaw against the resulting pain twisting in his knee and then shooting up his right thigh. He ignored the fierce throb still hammering inside his head. He had to get to her. Nick pushed harder despite the grinding pain and the vertigo still pulling at him. He stumbled, barely catching himself before he hit the ground. Nick swore and propelled himself toward the barn. He skidded to a stop near one wide door. Commanding his respiration to slow, he inched toward the crack where the door hinged to the doorway. He leaned forward and peered through the narrow opening.

Nick jerked back at what he saw. Laura was standing on a small stepladder. A length of rope had been strung over a rafter, its noose snug around her neck. Nick swallowed the terror that climbed into his throat. He carefully stepped back up to the narrow slit and forced himself to look again. The albino stood near her, talking to her, the barrel of his weapon jabbed into her stomach. Absolute fear held Laura's every feature captive. She clutched frantically at the rope as if it were too tight already.

A crimson rage engulfed Nick. The son of a bitch was a dead man. Nick remembered to breathe, breathe deeply and slowly. He needed to focus. He couldn't risk Laura getting hurt. But the albino was *dead*.

Nick moved soundlessly toward the open doorway. He needed to get as close as possible without being detected. Taking one last deep breath, Nick stepped into the reaching fingers of light and began the slow, careful journey toward his target. He moved to the far right, toward the shadows near the stalls. If he could circle around and come up directly behind the bastard, Nick would hopefully prevent any sudden or unexpected moves when he took him down.

"Go ahead," the albino sneered. "Don't be a wimp. Scream all you want. Nobody's going to hear you. Lover boy is out cold." He moved closer to Laura. "Sound effects always add to the pleasure."

"Just tell me where my son is," Laura demanded hoarsely.

"Now this isn't going to be so bad." The albino gestured

toward her precarious position with the barrel of his high-powered rifle. "It'll take about four minutes, depending on how long you can hold your breath, for you to pass out, and then it'll all be over. And everyone will live happily ever after. They'll all say, poor Laura, we did everything we could for her but she still committed suicide in the end."

"Swear to me that my son is safe," Laura spat vehemently.

Nick blocked the emotion that crowded his thinking at the sound of her desperation. She wasn't afraid to die, she was only afraid for her child. His throat constricted. The child no one had believed in, including him at first. Nick's lips compressed into a thin line, he barely restrained the roar of rage filling him now.

"Don't you worry about that baby boy of yours," the albino taunted. "He's going to make someone very happy. Happy enough to pay me all the money I'll ever need," he added in a sickeningly cocky voice.

Laura stiffened, the old, rickety stepladder rocked precariously beneath her.

"Don't move, princess," he warned. "I wouldn't want you to actually kill yourself." He stepped closer to her. "I want the pleasure of giving you that final little push myself. Then I'm going in the house and finish off your friend."

"You promised if I did what you said that you would leave Nick alone," she challenged.

The albino made a sound of approval in his throat. "I love it when you talk back."

Laura turned her face away from him. Nick stopped dead in his tracks when her terrified gaze flickered back to him. He shook his head but it was too late. Recognition and relief flared in her expression. Seeing the change, the albino whirled toward Nick. Nick took a bead right between his pink eyes.

"Drop it," Nick ordered.

The albino smiled. "Well, what do you know. That head of yours must be harder than I thought."

"Cut her down," Nick growled savagely. "Or you die where you stand."

The bastard stroked his cheek with his free hand, his weapon trained on Laura's face now. Nick tightened his grip on his Beretta in anticipation of the right opportunity to take this son of a bitch down.

"See here, wise guy," he smirked, "this is my little party and you weren't invited. Don't you know that two's company and three's a crowd?"

"Cut her down," Nick repeated coldly, the thought of killing the man making him feel decidedly calm. "And I'll let you live."

"What's to keep me from shooting her first?"

Nick heard the uncertainty in the albino's voice then. "Just one thing," Nick paused for effect, "the closed-casket funeral required since I'm about to take the top of your head off." Nick snugged his finger on the trigger.

"Wouldn't want that, now would we?" the albino relented.

His gaze locked with Nick's, the albino slowly began to lower his weapon. Nick took a step forward. And then everything lapsed into slow motion. The albino kicked his right foot outward. The stepladder clattered to the floor. A startled scream shattered the still air. Nick's horrified gaze riveted to Laura. Her arms stretched over her head, she struggled to grasp the rope and keep her weight from pulling her downward. Her legs dangled in thin air. Her face contorted with fear and desperation.

The albino kept his weapon trained on Laura as he

backed toward the door. Uncertainty flashed again in those strange eyes. ''Are you going to waste precious seconds trying to decide if you can put a bullet in me before she asphyxiates? How long do you think she can hold her breath?'' he added with a twisted smile.

Instantly, Nick found himself beneath Laura, supporting her weight to keep life-giving air flowing in and out of her lungs. His heart slammed mercilessly against his rib cage.

''Can you get the noose off?'' he asked hoarsely. Nick felt himself tremble with delayed reaction. The vision of Laura dangling from the end of that damned rope swept through his brain.

Gasping for breath between sobs, Laura didn't answer for a while. ''I think so,'' she rasped, then coughed.

Nick's gaze shot to the barn doors. The albino was gone.

But Laura was alive. Nick closed his eyes and held her lower body more tightly in his arms.

At the moment, nothing else mattered.

Chapter Eleven

"My baby's alive," Laura whispered. "He told me my baby was alive. I..." She shuddered. "You're still bleeding. I have to get you to a hospital."

"Shhh," Nick soothed. "I'm fine. The bullet didn't do as much damage as that damned table."

Laura caressed his cheek with trembling fingers, her worried gaze examining him closely. "But there's so much blood."

"I'm fine." He pressed a kiss to her forehead, then pulled her close against his chest. "Just let me hold you a minute." Nick sat on the cold dirt floor and held Laura in his arms. She trembled and he held her closer. He almost lost her tonight. He should have anticipated that the bastard would make a move after killing Doc. He was growing impatient.

Laura had been through so much already. Her missing child. Her son. Ray's words echoed inside Nick's head, *"A baby, maybe a year or so old."*

Laura's child.

Ray had seen her with the child. Ian would no doubt confirm tomorrow that the clinic Nick and Laura had visited had, indeed, registered the birth of a Robert Forester with the registrar's office in Montgomery. That would be more hard evidence. Laura had a child, and by noon tomorrow Nick would be able to prove it.

James Ed had lied. Nick couldn't believe he had been that wrong about the man. He had seemed genuinely overjoyed to have Laura back home. To know that she was alive and unharmed.

And Sandra. She might not even know her mother was alive. Her adoptive parents may have told her that the woman died years ago. What would Sandra stand to gain from Laura's death? Nothing, as far as Nick could see. It wasn't as if she and James Ed had needed the money that desperately. Of course, once it was available, they had apparently taken advantage of it. But Sandra wasn't in control of the money, James Ed was. All evidence pointed to James Ed.

Just like Laura said.

Nick frowned. Still, something about that scenario didn't quite fit. Didn't sit right with him. He blew out a disgusted breath. Nick closed his eyes and cursed himself for not believing her in the first place. He should have followed his instincts instead of allowing the past and his pride to get in the way. His eyes burned with regret. It shouldn't have taken him so long to come around.

He was a fool twice over.

Nick placed a soft kiss against Laura's hair. "Let me get you inside," he murmured. "We'll talk then."

"Okay," she said weakly. She stared into his eyes, her own bright with tears. "But first I want to get that wound cleaned up."

Nick nodded and they stood together. His grasp on her arms tightened to steady her when she swayed. She glanced around the dimly lit barn, her eyes wide with fear. Her body tensed as he slid his right arm around her waist.

"It's all right, honey, he's gone. I don't think he'll be

back,'' Nick assured her. He couldn't bear the fear in her eyes. If the bastard did come back he was a dead man.

Taking his time so as not to rush her, Nick ushered Laura in the direction of the house. Her skin felt as cold as ice. He had to get her inside and warmed up. He shuddered inwardly again at the thought of how close he had come to losing her tonight. Shock was a definite threat at the moment. A warm bath and hot coffee or cocoa would do the trick. He would call Ian and then Nick and Laura would talk. He wasn't sure she could tolerate any more surprises, good or bad right now. When she was up to it, he would tell Laura that she didn't have to worry anymore.

One way or another Nick would find her child. If he had to beat the truth out of James Ed with his bare hands.

Half an hour later Laura had cleaned and bandaged the wound on his forehead where the bullet had grazed him. Nick had a hell of a lump where the table had gotten in his way, but there was nothing to be done about that. Nick had settled Laura in the wide garden tub and then he'd put in a call to Ian while warming some milk for cocoa. Tracking down the identity of the albino probably wouldn't be difficult, Nick considered as he carried the steaming cocoa to the bathroom.

He paused inside the bathroom door just to look at Laura. Mounds of frothy bubbles enveloped her, hiding that exquisite feminine body. She had bundled all that silky blond hair atop her head in the sexiest heap Nick had ever seen. He loved every sweet, perfect thing about her. A fierce stab of desire sliced through him, making his groin tighten. How he wanted to touch her. But not tonight, he reminded the hungry beast inside him. Laura needed to rest tonight.

Relaxed within the warm depths, her eyes closed, Nick couldn't read what Laura's emotional state was now that the day's events had had time to absorb fully. His throat constricted at the thought of just how much she had endured over the past two years. Running for her life, and with a baby. How had he ever doubted her? If James Ed were behind all this—Nick shook his head slowly, resolutely—he would pay. He forced a deep, calming breath. Going off half-cocked wouldn't help, but there would definitely be a day of reckoning.

Nick's errant gaze moved back to Laura's face, then traveled down one soft cheek, past her delicate jaw, and over the fragile column of her throat. Anger unfurled inside him when his gaze traced the offensive marks caused by the rope. The abrasions, already shadowed with a purplish tinge, were stark against her creamy skin. The albino had better hope Nick didn't find him.

Adopting a calm he didn't feel, Nick crossed the quiet room and sat down on the edge of the luxurious tub. Laura's lids slowly fluttered open revealing those soft blue eyes. Nick smiled, then placed her cocoa near the elaborate gold faucet.

"It's warm," he told her. "You should drink it before it cools."

Laura moistened those full, pink lips. "I suppose it's safe to say that you believe me about James Ed now," she suggested with just a hint of bitterness.

Nick nodded. He deserved a good swift kick in the ass. "It would be safe to say that, yes. All the evidence seems to point to him."

Her expression solemn, those sweet lips trembled. "We have enough evidence to prove my son exists, too?"

Nick's gaze remained locked with hers for a long moment as he considered whether to tell her about the call to Ray. No, he decided, she'd had enough for one night. She needed to relax, not get all worked up again. "Yes. We can prove your child is real.'' He didn't want to think about another man touching Laura. She belonged to him....

Laura blinked away the moisture shining in those huge blue orbs. ''You'll make James Ed tell the truth?''

Nick smiled then. It didn't matter who the father was. Nick would find Laura's child. ''Absolutely.''

''He said that someone is going to pay him a lot of money for my baby.'' She swallowed, then pulled her lower lip between her teeth as she composed herself. ''I can't believe my own brother would sell my baby.''

''We'll get him back, Laura.''

Her arms folded over her breasts, Laura sat bolt upright. ''I want you to take me to James Ed. I want you to take me right now, Nick,'' she demanded. ''I don't want to waste any more time.''

For a moment Nick couldn't speak. Suds slipped over her satiny shoulders and down her slender arms. Laura was a wonderful mother. The kind any child would want, he realized suddenly. The kind of mother he wanted for his own children. She was sweet and beautiful and kind. And all that sass buried beneath her worry for her child pulled at him like nothing else ever had. She was everything he wanted.

''First thing in the morning,'' he countered finally, a restless feeling stirring deep inside him. ''We'll head for Jackson then.''

She pressed Nick with her solemn gaze. ''And you'll do whatever it takes to get the truth out of my brother?''

''You can count on it.'' He would have the truth out of James Ed...or else.

''Swear it, Nick,'' she insisted. ''Swear to me that you'll do whatever it takes.''

''I swear,'' he replied softly.

Laura nodded her satisfaction. Several tendrils of that

golden silk fell around her face, and clung to that soft neck. "That's all I can ask of you." A frown wrinkled her pretty forehead. "Does your head hurt much?"

"Not much," he whispered. The need to touch her overwhelmed all else. Slowly, while maintaining that intense eye contact, Nick allowed his fingertips to glide over one smooth cheek. Want gripped him with such ferocity that for a long moment he couldn't breathe. "You can ask anything you want of me," he murmured.

Laura took his hand in hers and pressed a soft kiss to his palm, her gaze never leaving his. "And would you give me anything I ask, Nick?" she whispered. A hot flash of desire kindled in her eyes.

He nodded, no longer capable of articulation.

"You're sure you're up to it?" she teased, a smile playing about the corners of her full mouth.

Nick hoped the grunt he uttered was sufficient response.

When Laura slid his hand down to her breast he knew it was. He squeezed. Her head lolled back and her eyes closed in sweet ecstasy. Nick watched as Laura guided his hand to all the places she wanted him to touch. Her other breast, then lower to her flat stomach, then lower still.

Nick groaned when she parted her thighs and opened for him. He slipped his middle finger inside her hot, moist body. A shudder wracked him as an instant climax threatened. Nick clenched his jaw and grabbed back control. Laura was the only woman who ever made him want to come with nothing more than a touch. Nick gripped the edge of the tub with his free hand as he moved that small part of himself rhythmically inside her. Her moans of pleasure urged him on. Her lips parted slightly as her breathing became labored. Nick used the pad of his thumb to massage her tiny nub of desire until it swelled beneath his touch. She reared back, thrusting her firm white breasts upward, as if begging for his attention. Determined to watch, Nick resisted the urge to taste her. Water and bubbles slipped over her smooth breasts. Her dusky nipples tightened and budded right before his eyes. Nick licked his lips. His arousal throbbed insistently, and he jerked with restraint.

Laura's fingers splayed on the sides of the tub, providing leverage as she arched against his hand. Nick growled with need when he felt the first tremors of her release. He moved more quickly, propelling her toward that peek. Laura cried out as her inner muscles tightened around Nick's finger. His own need for release roared inside him. Nick leaned forward and covered Laura's mouth with his own. She took him hungrily, sucking his tongue into her mouth. Nick groaned. His arms plunged into the water and around her. He pulled her to him savagely, his body needing to feel hers against him.

"I need to be inside you," he breathed against her lips.

"Now, Nick," she murmured greedily. "Hurry."

Holding her firmly against him, Nick lifted Laura from the tub. Water sloshed over the side. Wet heat and suds from her damp skin soaked into his shirtfront. Laura's legs wrapped instinctively around his waist. Nick stumbled toward the door, his mouth still plundering hers. Hot and sweet. She tasted so good. He had to get her to the bed. He couldn't hold out much longer. Nick backed into a wall, cursed—the word lost in the kiss—and groped for the door with one hand.

"No," Laura protested between kisses. "Here," she demanded.

Nick pivoted and pressed her back against the wall. His hips ground into her softness. Nick groaned deep in his throat. Squeezing Laura's thigh with one hand, he wrenched his jeans open.

Laura arched against him, her fingers dug into his shoulders. "Hurry, Nick," she moaned. "Hurry." Her breath came in fierce little spurts. She needed him as much as he needed her. The thought sent another jolt of desire raging through him, almost snapping his control.

Laura screamed at the first nudge of his arousal. Nick grunted, intent on plunging deep inside her. Breathtaking, gut-wrenching sensations washed over him when he finally pushed fully into Laura's hot, tight body. He sagged against her for the space of one beat as the powerful tide of pleasure almost took him over the edge. His heart pounded hard in time with Laura's. He gulped a much-needed breath.

Her arms tightened around his neck and she pulled him closer. "Nick," she murmured as her eyes closed in an expression of pleasure-pain. "Oh, Nick."

Capturing her sweet lips with his own, Nick began the slow, shallow thrusting that would bring Laura to the brink of release once more. He clenched his jaw and resisted the urge to swiftly drive into his own release. Her thighs tightened on his waist, urging him into a faster rhythm. The air raged in and out of Nick's lungs as he pushed ever closer to climax. The case and all its ugliness faded into insignificance, leaving only Laura behind. Her taste, her scent filled him, mind and body. The final, tense seconds before climax brought complete clarity to Nick's tortured soul.

And he knew in that crystal clear moment that his life would never be the same. He loved her. He had always loved her. She was part of him. She completed him.

The rocking explosion that followed left him weak-kneed and feeling totally helpless in her arms. Nick's gaze moved to hers, she smiled, and something near his heart shifted.

NICK'S NAKED FLESH felt hot against hers. Laura snuggled closer, then smiled. She wanted to feel all of him. To hold him closer still.

For as long as it lasted.

Laura's smile melted. She swallowed back the fear that crowded into her throat. The bandage on his forehead served as a reminder of just how close she had come to losing him tonight. Laura couldn't protect Nick anymore than she had protected Robby. Hurt twisted inside her.

And, dear God, what would Nick do when he discovered the truth? There would be no denying Robby's parentage when they found him. He looked so much like Nick. And Nick had promised her that they would definitely find her baby.

Blinking back the uncertainty, Laura redirected her focus to Nick's long, lean body pressed so intimately to hers. He had said they would talk. But he seemed content for the moment to simply lie next to her without words or questions of any sort. The cool sheets draped their heated skin. She glanced at the clock on the bedside table, 9:00 p.m. What was Robby doing now? she wondered. Her heart squeezed painfully. Was he sleeping soundly in a bed somewhere safe? If someone intended to pay a great deal of money for him, surely they were treating him well. Laura shivered at the thought of someone else cuddling and loving her sweet baby. The idea that he might call someone else mommy tore at her heart. She had to find him.

"You cold?" Nick asked, the words rumbling from his chest.

"I'm fine," Laura said quickly. She immediately regretted the shortness of her response.

Nick shifted onto one elbow and peered down at her. He frowned. The white bandage stark against his dark coloring. "We'll find him, Laura," he assured her. "Don't doubt that."

She essayed a faint smile. "I know." Nick was the kindest, most honorable man she knew. He deserved so much more than she had to give him.

Nick's frown deepened and he fell silent for a few moments. Laura's heart skipped into an erratic staccato. She recognized the precise instant that realization dawned. The air evacuated her lungs.

"You told the receptionist at the clinic that Robby was born on August sixth," he said slowly, thoughtfully.

Laura licked her lips. Ice rushed through her veins. "That's right."

Three seconds later the mental calculations were complete. Nick's gaze landed fully onto hers. "Forester. You used the name Forester."

Laura nodded. Speech wasn't an option.

Suspicion crept into his wary green eyes. "Robert?"

"Robert," she managed to agree.

"Robert what?" His tone held no inflection, his eyes were openly accusing now.

Laura drew in a deep breath. She met that accusing gaze. "Robert Nicholas Forester."

There was no way to describe the expression that claimed Nick's features then. Something between rage and wonder battled for control, but, in the end, the rage proved victorious.

Nick sat up, putting distance between them. "He's my son."

Laura knew it wasn't a question. She also knew with complete certainty that Nick would never forgive her for keeping his son from him.

"Yes," she said finally. Had it not been for the fierceness of his piercing gaze, uttering that solitary word would almost have been a relief. But there was no way to garner any good feelings from what she saw in Nick's eyes.

Nick shot out of bed. His back turned to her, he pulled

on his jeans. Laura sat up. She hugged the sheet to her chest and willed the emotions threatening to consume her to retreat.

He shifted back to face her, then raked those long, tanned fingers through his uncharacteristically mussed hair. A muscle flexed rhythmically in his tense jaw. "Why didn't you tell me?" His hands fisted at his sides. "Why didn't you come to me as soon as you knew you were pregnant?"

"You were one of them," she said quietly, defeatedly.

Slowly, but surely every nuance of emotion disappeared from Nick's eyes and expression. That cold, hard, unfeeling mask slipped firmly into place like the slamming of a door. His broad, muscled chest heaved with the rage no doubt building inside him.

"I was never one of them," he said coldly.

Tears stung her eyes, but Laura refused to cry. "You worked for James Ed. I couldn't be sure that I could trust you." She met his gaze with hope in hers. "When you first found me this time you didn't believe anything I told you. Then, later, I was going to tell you but so much happened."

"Believing you and trusting you are two entirely different things," he snapped. "Don't mistake the two."

Laura struggled to her feet, dragging the tangled sheet with her. They were back to the trust issue. "I couldn't tell you," she told him with as much force as she could summon. "I was afraid for my life, Nick! Don't you get it? James Ed was trying to kill me."

"What did that have to do with trusting me?" he demanded, his tone low and lethal.

Laura shook her head at his inability to see the obvious. "James Ed hired you. Your loyalty was to him."

"We made love, Laura," he ground out. "That didn't spell anything out for you?"

"I was afraid," she said wearily.

"You kept my son from me all this time and all you've got to say is that you were afraid?" Contempt edged his voice.

"I had to protect my child," Laura argued. The starch seeped out of her spine and standing proved difficult.

"Well you did a hell of a job, didn't you?"

The tears would not be contained then. The humiliating liquid emotion slipped down her cheeks. "I did the best I could considering the circumstances."

Nick stepped closer, his body rigid with fury. "But that wasn't good enough, was it? And it never once occurred to you to call on me for help?"

Anger surged, steeling her resolve. "Forget all that. The important thing now is finding him," Laura countered, her tone as lethal as his.

"I will find him," Nick promised. "And when I do, I'll make sure nothing like this ever happens to him again."

Stunned, Laura could only stare into those cold, emotionless eyes. This was her worst nightmare come true. Not only had she lost her son, but if she did find him he would still be lost even then. Nick's cell phone splintered the ensuing silence. His gaze still riveted to hers, he snatched the phone from the bedside table and snapped his greeting.

Blocking out all other thought, Nick listened carefully as Ian relayed his latest findings.

"The albino is a Rodney Canton, a dirty P.I. with a most impressive rap sheet. Kidnapping, assault with a deadly weapon, and worse."

Nick shifted his weight from his throbbing right knee. "Is there any connection between him and the Proctors?"

"No, not directly. But he worked with a Brock Redmond who owned and operated a P.I. office in Natchez for years. Funny thing is," Ian continued, "this Redmond fellow disappeared suddenly about two years ago. No one has seen him since.''

Nick frowned. "Do you have a physical description?"

"Oh yes. He fits perfectly the description Laura provided of the man who shot you.''

Anticipation nudged at Nick. "Any connection to James Ed?"

Ian laughed. "A long and productive connection. James Ed hired Redmond on several occasions to provide the low-down on potential staff members.''

"Do you have anything that will stand up in a court of law to back that up?"

"I'm looking at the man's files.''

Nick shook his head. "I'm not sure I want to know how you managed that.''

"It would seem that Redmond stiffed his secretary out of two months pay when he disappeared.'' Amusement colored Ian's tone. "So she confiscated his files. She has been most helpful.''

"Nothing else on Sandra?"

"The jury is still out on the first lady,'' Ian told him. "But the evidence against James Ed is undeniable. If Redmond is the man who shot you, and he appears to be, then James Ed is in this up to his politically incorrect neck.''

"Good work, Ian. I'll touch base with you tomorrow.''

Ian hesitated. "You sound a little strange, Nick. Is there anything you're not telling me?"

"I'll fill you in tomorrow.'' Nick flipped the phone closed before Ian could say anything else.

Nick had a son.

And James Ed Proctor was about to discover that Nick was more than just a man of his word. He was a man of action. Only Nick wasn't sure James Ed was going to like the action Nick had in mind. He intended to find his son if he had to wring the child's location one syllable at a time out of James Ed's scrawny neck. Nick would not stop until he found his son.

Nick shot Laura a withering look. "Get dressed. We're going to Jackson.

A NARROW SLIT of moonlight sliced through the darkness of the room from the gap between the heavily lined drapes. Propelled by her dreams, Elsa tossed restlessly beneath the thick covers. A cold sweat dampened her skin, making her nightgown stick to her in all the uncomfortable places.

It was wrong, it was wrong, her mind chanted.

Elsa sat up with a start. She blinked, then pushed her disheveled hair from her sweat-dampened face. She looked at the clock. Almost midnight. It seemed so much later. Elsa blew out a breath of weariness. The dreams. Oh, the dreams were so disturbing. She shook herself. But they were only dreams.

Soon it would be a new day.

The day.

Today the little boy's new family would come to take him away to their home. Elsa passed a hand over her face and tried to reconcile herself to that fact. She shook her head. It wasn't right. Deep inside, past all the indifference and looking the other way, she knew it wasn't right.

She swallowed. She had to do something.

Yes. A sense of calmness settled over her.

She had to do something.

Chapter Twelve

Uneasiness crawled up Nick's spine the moment he parked behind the Governor's home. The second floor of the house stood in darkness, a few lights glowed downstairs. Nick found it particularly odd that security had not already approached the car. He knew from experience how difficult it was to outmaneuver those guys.

"What are we waiting for?"

Nick shifted his attention to the woman seated next to him. It was the first time she had spoken since they left Bay Break. Renewed anger flooded Nick when he met her hesitant gaze. She had lied to him. Kept his son from him. Nick's fingers tightened on the steering wheel. No matter what her reasons, and no matter what that more foolish part of him wanted to feel, Nick wasn't sure he could ever forgive her for that.

"Something isn't right," Nick told her, emotion making his voice harsh in the hushed darkness that shrouded them.

"I don't care," Laura said with a shake of her head. "I have to find Robby."

Nick snagged her left arm. "You'll do exactly as I say, Laura," he ground out. "I'm going in and you're staying right here."

"No way," she argued. "I'm going in, too. You can't

stop me.'' The warning in her voice was that of a desperate mother's.

He blew out an impatient breath. ''All right, but stay right behind me. No wandering off on your own.''

Laura nodded her understanding.

Nick emerged from the car. He scanned the dark yard as he repositioned the Beretta beneath his jacket at the small of his back. Every instinct warned Nick that trouble awaited them inside. Finding his son and keeping Laura safe, no matter what she had done, were top priority. Laura climbed out behind him. They walked straight up to the back of the house without encountering anyone.

Where the hell was security? Nick wondered grimly. James Ed was too cautious a man to be caught with his pants down like this. Nick reached out and grasped Laura's arm as they stepped up to the verandah. No sense risking her making any sudden moves. Laura stalled at the French door leading to the rear entry hall.

''Promise me you won't let him talk his way out of this, Nick,'' she urged. ''No matter what James Ed says, you have to believe me. He tried to kill me and he took away my son.''

Nick met her fearful gaze in the darkness. ''No one is talking their way out of anything,'' he said pointedly. Including you, he didn't add. Nick set his jaw hard and reached for the doorbell. He paused. Maybe he didn't want to announce their arrival.

He turned back to Laura. ''Stay right behind me,'' he ordered tersely. When she nodded he reached for the brass handle on one French door and opened it. An eerie silence greeted them as they entered the dimly lit hall. Nick felt Laura move closer. He scanned the long, empty corridor with mounting tension. Something was definitely wrong. Very wrong.

The long hall extended the width of the house from back-door to front, with two ninety-degree turns in between. Nick paused and surveyed each room they passed. No Governor. No First Lady. No staff or security.

Every nerve ending had gone on full-scale alert by the time they reached the parlor. To Nick's relief, James Ed sat on the sofa, his head bowed over what appeared to be a photo album. Other photo albums were scattered on the sofa table. Wearing a robe and pajamas, James Ed appeared deeply involved in the pictures.

"Governor," Nick said, announcing their presence.

James Ed looked up, then quickly removed his glasses. "Nick?" He frowned. Something that resembled regret stole across his features when his gaze landed on his sister. "Laura?" James Ed pushed to his feet. "You're here."

Ignoring his comment, Nick crossed the room. Laura remained near the door. "There are a few questions I need to ask you," Nick told him quietly.

James Ed's gaze lingered on Laura. "You look as if you're feeling much better, Laura," he remarked with a sad smile.

Again, Nick couldn't shake the feeling that James Ed was serious in his concern for his much younger sister.

"Where's my son?" Laura demanded.

James Ed's expression turned distant. "I don't understand all this," he said, his tone remote.

"Laura does have a child," Nick ground out. It took every ounce of willpower he possessed not to grab the Governor by the throat. "I'm about to give you one last opportunity to redeem yourself here, James Ed. Why did you hire someone to kill Laura and where is the baby?"

"I would never do anything to hurt you, Laura," James Ed insisted. "You must believe that." His sincere gaze turned to Nick's. "I love her too much."

"Tell me about your associate, Brock Redmond," Nick suggested coolly.

Denial flickered across the Governor's features. "I didn't hire him to do this."

"So you admit that you do know him," Nick pressed.

James Ed hesitated, his expression distracted now. "What?"

"It's over, James Ed. We know what you did."

James Ed shook his head slowly. "I...I don't want to talk now. I'm not feeling well. Please go away."

"Redmond is the man who shot me, and left me for dead. He," Nick added bitterly, "is the man who tried to kill Laura on the riverbank that same night. And you hired him."

"You're wrong," James Ed argued wearily. "Brock Redmond is—"

"Was," Nick cut in. "He's dead."

James Ed seemed to shrink right before Nick's eyes. "I didn't know," he murmured. "I didn't know...."

Laura couldn't stand idly by and do nothing a moment longer. She had to find Robby. While Nick and James Ed were caught up in their discussion, Laura used the moment to slip back into the hall. They had already checked the downstairs rooms. Laura glanced at the wide staircase that flowed up to the second floor. He had to be upstairs. She frowned at the thought that Sandra was probably watching him. Why would Sandra go along with James Ed? She had never mentioned to Laura that she even wanted a child. Being the perfect political wife had always appeared to be enough for her.

Pushing the disturbing question aside, Laura rushed up the seemingly endless stairs. Once on the second-story landing she paused to listen. Laura strained with the effort to hear even the slightest noise. Something, some indistinguishable sound touched her ears. She turned to her right and followed the soft sound to the far end of the corridor. The room was on the right and across the hall from James Ed and Sandra's bedroom.

The closer Laura came to the door the louder and clearer the sound became. Music, she realized.

A lullaby.

Laura stopped dead in her tracks. A chill raced up her spine and spread across her scalp.

"Robby," she murmured. Laura ran the last few feet and burst into the room. She smoothed her hand over the wall until she found a light switch. A soft golden glow filled the bedroom when she flipped it to the on position. Blue walls embellished with white clouds, gold stars and moons wrapped the space in warmth. Beautiful cherry wood furniture, including a large rocking chair, filled the room. A lavish crib, adorned with a coverlet bearing those same moons, stars, and clouds stood near the open French doors. Blue, gauzy curtains fluttered in the cool night air. A wind-up mobile slowly turned, playing the familiar tune.

Her heart rising in her throat, Laura blindly walked the few steps that separated her from the crib. She braced her hands on the side rails and peered down at the fluffy coverlet and matching pillow and bumper pads.

The crib was empty save for linens.

No Robby.

Laura gasped, a pained, choking sort of half-sob sound.

"I've been expecting you."

Tears streaming down her cheeks, Laura turned slowly to face the cold, emotionless voice.

Sandra.

"Why?" The word struggled past the lump constricting Laura's throat. How could Sandra do this? Laura had trusted Sandra, loved her even. Had thought that Sandra loved her. How could this be?

Sandra laughed. She waved the gun Laura had only just noticed in the air. "Why not?"

"Where is my son?" Laura demanded more sharply.

"I wasn't finished with the first question," Sandra snapped. "In the beginning it was simply the money," she said boldly. She fixed Laura with an evil look. "It should have been mine anyway. If your meddling grandfather hadn't stepped in, my mother would have had the life she deserved. *I* would have had the life I deserved—your life."

Laura shook her head in confusion. "What are you talking about?"

Sandra smiled. "Oh, that's right you wouldn't know, would you?" She stepped closer to Laura, the gun pointed at her chest. "Your dear father was once in love with my mother. But she wasn't good enough for that blue blood that ran through his veins. So, your loving grandfather took care of the situation. He sent your father off to Harvard where he met your sweet, equally blue-blooded mother."

"What does this have to do with anything?" Laura didn't care about the past. The only thing she wanted was to find her son.

"Everything, my dear, everything." She used the barrel of the weapon to turn Laura's chin when she would have looked away. "You see, after your father deserted her, my mother married my sorry-excuse-for-a-father. He was a drunk and beat us both every chance he got."

Laura shook her head, fear and sympathy warred inside her. "I'm sorry, but what does that have to do with my son?" she murmured.

"I'm getting to that," Sandra snapped, her eyes sparkled with hatred. "Be patient. Not a day went by that my mother didn't remind me of what should have been ours." She poked Laura in the chest with the muzzle of the gun. "Money, position, power. Instead, we lived in poverty. Finally my mother had to be hospitalized and I was sent away."

Despite what Sandra had done, Laura's heart went out to the little girl who had suffered such injustices. Unlike James Ed, who was driven by greed, Sandra's evilness grew out of a horrible childhood. "But your adopted parents were good to you," Laura countered. "You told me so yourself."

"You can't make up for the past, Laura. What's done is done. And one way or another I intended to have what was mine." Another sinister smile spread across her face. "Of course I might never have been born had my mother not married the drunk who sired me. But, fate finally smiled on me. Your parents got themselves killed in that car accident and James Ed was all alone with a little sister to raise." Sandra drew in a pleased breath. "By then I was all grown-up, had a different name, and lived with parents who were socially acceptable."

Laura searched her mind for some way to get away from Sandra. The woman was deranged. Laura had to get to Nick and tell him about this room—she surveyed the beautiful nursery—and Sandra's crazy story.

"You like my baby's nursery?"

Laura blinked. Her gaze collided with Sandra's once more. "But you can't have children," she said before she thought.

Sandra's expression grew fierce. "Yes, well, that crazy old lady Leeton saw to that."

"What?" This just kept getting more confusing, more bizarre. Laura gripped the side rail more tightly. What did Mrs. Leeton have to do with Sandra's past? Mrs. Leeton had been Doc's nurse in Bay Break for as long as Laura could remember.

"I wanted to make sure I had James Ed right where I wanted him, so I got pregnant to seal our fate. But he didn't want children," she added with disgust. "He claimed he needed to get his political career off the ground and get you raised before he had children of his own." She sneered at Laura. "So I had to take care of that before he found out." She frowned. "Something went wrong. The stupid old nurse kept telling me that it wasn't her fault, that she had done the best she could. But I knew better. I could have killed her," Sandra said coldly. "But I decided I might need her in the future." She laughed then. "Guess I was right."

"Where is Robby?" Laura demanded, her anger suddenly overriding any misplaced sympathy she had felt.

"Why do you keep asking me that?" Sandra said haughtily. "You've been in a hospital for the past eighteen months. You have no proof that Robby even exists. I've seen to that. Who would ever believe you?"

"Nick believes me," Laura bit out.

Sandra shrugged. "Big deal. I can take care of Nick." Her lips compressed into a grim line. "I thought I had him out of the way once before. But Redmond screwed up. Oh well," she added with amusement. "He got his, didn't he, princess?"

Ice formed in Laura's stomach. "*You* sent Redmond to kill me?"

"Well, of course," she retorted unapologetically. "You didn't think James Ed had the balls to do it, did you?"

Laura shook her head. "I didn't have anything to do with what happened to your mother. How could you hate me so much?"

"I already told you," she intoned. "You had my life.

And now I intend to have it all. Everything that should have been mine all along. The name, the money, everything."

"Where's my son?" Laura stepped nearer, putting herself nose to nose with Sandra.

Sandra pressed the muzzle of her gun into Laura's stomach as a reminder of who was in charge. "I knew you didn't die in that river with Redmond." Her eyes narrowed. "I knew it. So I sent Redmond's partner to look for you. It took him almost a year, but he found you." Sandra's eyes lit with a glow that was not sane. "And lo and behold what did he discover? You'd had yourself a baby."

"Where's my son?" Laura demanded again.

"With my dark hair and hazel eyes, he was perfect," Sandra continued as if Laura had said nothing. "But, of course, with James Ed's career to consider, I had to make it all look legal. That wasn't so hard. Over the years I've gotten to know the hospital administrator at Serenity Sanitarium pretty well—" she smiled that evil smile again "—very well, in fact. So that part was easy. Canton, of course, was willing to do anything for enough money. Killing you and making it look like a suicide sounded like fun to him. All he had to do was find you." Sandra breathed a relieved sigh. "When you showed up in Bay Break, it was like a gift from God. Doc had no way of knowing that his former nurse owed me such a huge favor. She called me the instant you showed up at her house."

Rage rushed through Laura's veins. "You had Doc murdered."

"Unfortunately it was a necessary step in the process. He had a long and prosperous life, what's the big deal?"

"I want my son back," Laura said dangerously. At the moment she was prepared to kill Sandra with her bare hands if necessary.

"Enough," Sandra announced savagely. She gestured to the French doors. "Let's go onto the balcony. I wouldn't want to sully *my* son's new room."

She jabbed Laura with the gun when she hesitated. "I said move," she ordered.

Laura took one last look at the crib, then walked through the open doors. The barrel of the gun urging her forward, she walked straight across the wide balcony to the ornate railing. Laura stared into the darkness searching for some avenue of escape.

"Now jump."

Startled by her demand, Laura pivoted to face Sandra. "What?" She had expected the woman to simply shoot her.

Sandra stepped to the railing. "I said jump. I have to keep this on the up-and-up." She rolled her eyes. "Poor unstable Laura, she threw herself off the balcony after killing her lover and trying to kill her own brother. Not to mention poor old Doc."

Nick. Oh God. Frantic to stall her, Laura asked, "What makes you think James Ed will go along with you killing Nick?"

"James Ed will do whatever I tell him to." Sandra's smile widened. "Or else he'll have an accident, too." Her smile disappeared just as quickly. "Now jump."

Remembering her lesson in the barn well, Laura flicked a glance toward the open doors as if she had heard or seen something. Sandra followed her gaze. In that moment of distraction, Laura knocked Sandra's arm upward. The gun fired, momentarily deafening Laura. Laura kicked her in the shin and drove her fist into Sandra's wrist with all her strength. The gun flew from her grasp and slid across the floor.

"Die, damn you," Sandra hissed as she grabbed Laura

by the throat and slammed into her with her full body weight.

Laura stumbled back upon impact. She struggled to breathe and to pull Sandra's hands free of her throat. Laura pivoted, trying to shake Sandra loose, and lost her balance. Laura fell backwards. The rail cut into her back, breaking Laura's fall. Sandra leaned over her, her fingers cutting off the air to Laura's lungs. Determination contorted Sandra's features as she clamped down harder on Laura's throat.

"Die," Sandra shrieked.

Laura arched upward to throw her off. Sandra twisted, then went over the rail, pulling Laura with her.

THE LOUD REPORT of a weapon jerked Nick from the useless argument with James Ed. He turned to the door. Laura was gone. Damn. Nick ran into the hall.

"Laura!"

Nick took the stairs two at a time. He raced toward the one open door where light glowed. The room was empty. He frowned when his brain assimilated the visual assessment that it was a nursery. A shriek drew his gaze to the open balcony doors. Nick sprinted across the room and onto the balcony just in time to see Sandra and Laura go over the edge of the railing.

Outright panic slammed into him. Fear clawed at his chest as he rushed to the railing. Sandra lay on the concrete walk below. Laura was hanging on to one spindle. His heart hammering with fear, Nick leaned over the rail and reached for her.

"Give me your hand, Laura," he said quickly.

Straining with the effort to hang on, Laura reached one shaky hand toward his. The spindle she clung to snapped and Nick barely snagged her hand before she fell. Slowly, his hold on her slipping more than once, he pulled a trembling Laura over the rail and into his arms.

"Sandra stole my baby," Laura cried.

"It's okay," Nick assured her. "You're safe now."

"She sent security away, you know," James Ed remarked behind them as if nothing out of the ordinary had happened.

Nick turned to him, sensing a change in his tone. James Ed picked up the weapon on the floor, then stared at it a moment before lifting his gaze to Nick and Laura. His grip tightened around the weapon and Nick tensed for battle.

"I suppose it was for the best," he added.

"Put the gun down, James Ed," Nick told him calmly. He moved Laura behind him, but didn't reach for his own weapon. He didn't want to scare James Ed into doing something stupid. The man had just had his whole world turned upside down. He was obviously in shock.

"This is really all my fault," James Ed continued in a voice totally void of emotion. He shrugged halfheartedly. "I needed money to keep up appearances. I'm sure Sandra only thought she was helping me. She didn't mean to hurt anyone. I'm certain of that."

Nick felt Laura go rigid behind him.

James Ed shook his head in defeat. "I believed everything Sandra told me. I trusted her unconditionally."

Nick held Laura back when she would have rushed toward her brother. She wanted answers, now. Nick glanced over his shoulder and told her with his eyes to stay put. He took one cautious step toward James Ed. James Ed's gaze flickered to him.

"You do believe me, don't you?" James Ed looked past Nick and searched Laura's face as if looking for some sign of forgiveness. "I didn't know. You were so wild and unhappy it seemed. That's why I tried to marry you off to

Rafe. I hoped that he could do a better job of making you happy. I had so many responsibilities already. I just couldn't give you what you needed.''

Nick moved one more step closer. "So you didn't know about Sandra's scheme to kill Laura."

James Ed's expression filled with remorse. "I almost lost my mind when Laura disappeared." He waved the gun in frustration. "I had no idea that Sandra had hired Redmond behind my back," James Ed insisted. He shrugged wearily. "I truly thought Laura was unstable. Sandra had me convinced. Then Laura disappeared and I thought she was dead. Eventually I used the trust fund, but not until I felt sure Laura wasn't coming back," he added quickly. "I didn't want to but Sandra insisted that Laura would have wanted me to have the money.''

"But Sandra wasn't convinced that Laura was gone for good," Nick suggested. "She kept looking." More space disappeared between them.

James Ed nodded. "Apparently. I didn't know until tonight what she had done." He pressed Nick with his gaze, searching for understanding, beseeching him to believe. "That other man, Redmond's partner, showed up a few hours ago and told Sandra what happened." James Ed dropped his head in defeat. "I couldn't believe she had done it." A sob cracked his voice. "I couldn't believe that I had been so blind. I thought Laura was imagining the episodes, that she truly was unstable." His shoulders sagged in defeat. "I loved Sandra. I trusted her."

"Give me the gun, James Ed," Nick told him again.

James Ed stared at the weapon for a long moment as if it held the answers to all his worries. "I don't deserve to live after what I've allowed to happen."

Nick grabbed James Ed's arm when he would have lifted

the weapon. "That's not the issue right now," Nick argued. "Right now *we* have to find Laura's son."

James Ed relinquished the weapon. His gaze moved to Laura. "Can you ever forgive me, Laura? I'd give anything if this hadn't happened."

Laura was next to Nick then. She lifted her chin and glared at her brother with little or no sympathy. "Where is my son?" she demanded.

He shook his head slowly. "I'd give my life right now to be able to tell you. But, I swear, I don't know where your child is, Laura. We—" James Ed glanced at the room beyond the open doors, then at the balcony railing over which Sandra had disappeared. He winced. "—we were going to adopt a child. Sandra had made all the necessary arrangements. We were supposed to bring him home tomorrow."

"Him?" Nick echoed.

James Ed nodded. "A little boy just over a year old."

"Where is he?" Laura pressed.

"At the orphanage in Louisiana." James Ed looked thoughtful for a moment. "Sandra was there for a while when she was a child, and someone rescued her. She thought it only fitting..." His voice trailed off.

Laura tugged at Nick's sleeve. "Let's go!"

Nick pulled his cell phone from his pocket. "We have to get the police out here first." He glanced at James Ed who had wandered to a nearby chair and dropped into it. "We can't leave him like this."

"I'm not waiting," she argued.

Nick grasped her arm when she would have rushed away. "You will wait."

"I have to find my son," she cried, desperation in her voice.

Nick saw the pain and worry in her eyes, he hardened his heart to what he wanted to feel. "He's my son, too."

Chapter Thirteen

Laura awoke with a start. Shops, sidewalks and pedestrians lined the street. It was daylight now. Eight o'clock, according to the digital clock on the dash. Traffic moved at a snail's pace, morning rush hour apparently. Laura rubbed the back of her hand over her jaw, then massaged her stiff neck as she sat up straighter in the car seat. She wondered if this place was Careytown. She glanced at the driver's grim profile. Nick's beard-shadowed face was chiseled in stone, the white bandage stark against his dark skin and hair. He hadn't spoken a word to her since they left her brother's house. It had been almost four o'clock in the morning before the police had allowed them to leave.

A banner announcing Careytown's fifth annual Thanksgiving Festival draped from crossing light to crossing light over the busy street. Laura's heart skittered into overdrive. She was almost there. Very soon, possibly in just a few short minutes, she would be able to hold her son in her arms once more.

Laura closed her eyes briefly and summoned the memory of Robby's sweet baby scent. Her arms ached to hold him. But what kind of court battle lay before her? Laura blinked. Her gaze darted back to Nick's granite-like features. He was never going to forgive her for keeping Robby a secret.

In his opinion, she should have turned to him for help in the first place. But she just couldn't take the chance that he wouldn't turn her over to James Ed.

James Ed.

Regret trickled through Laura. She had blamed James Ed for everything all this time, when it had been Sandra all along. Laura still couldn't believe that Sandra had harbored such ill will toward her all those years. Had wanted her dead. Had wanted to steal her son.

Laura shook off the disturbing thoughts. Sandra was dead. She would never be able to harm Robby or Laura again. Canton was still at large, but hopefully the police would find him soon. She and James Ed would work things out eventually, she supposed. After all, he was her brother. The only thing that mattered now, Laura resolved, was getting her son back. She glanced at Nick again. She would just have to deal with his demands when the time came. No judge in his right mind would take her son away from her. But Nick was a good man....

Joint custody.

The phrase tore at Laura's heart. How would she be able to survive days or weeks without her son? Even if she knew he was safe in Nick's care. And what if Nick married someone else? Fear and hurt gripped Laura with such intensity that she thought she might be sick at her stomach. There could even be someone in his life right now. Nick was a very good-looking man.

But he had made love to her just last night. Laura swallowed tightly. It wasn't uncommon for people to cling to each other during or after near-death encounters. It had happened two years ago. Last night was probably no different. The time she had spent in Nick's arms obviously hadn't affected him as it had her. She loved him with all her heart. She would give most anything if they could be a family.

Laura closed her eyes and fought the tears brimming. She would not cry. She was about to be reunited with her child. If any tears were shed today, they would be tears of joy.

"This is it," Nick said quietly.

Laura jerked to attention. He guided the car into the parking lot of an old, but well-maintained two-story building. The parking lot wasn't large, but Laura could see a huge fenced-in play yard behind the building. Multi-colored playground equipment and numerous trees, bare for the winter, claimed the play yard landscape. The exterior of the building wasn't particularly bright, but it was clean and neat. If the staff took such good care of the property, surely they cared equally well for the children.

Nick was out of the car and opening her door before Laura realized they had parked. She shook off the distraction and emerged into the cool November morning.

Just a few more moments, she told herself. The first genuine smile in too many days to recall lifted her lips. *Thank you, God,* she prayed. Laura folded her arms over her chest and ignored the biting wind. Her son was in there somewhere and she was about to find him.

"Are you all right?" Nick's voice was gentle, laced with concern.

Laura looked up at him and mentally acknowledged the mistake she had made. She should have told Nick. She should have gone to him for help long ago. He was the father of her child. He was a good man. She should have trusted him. But she hadn't. And now she would pay dearly for that mistake.

The cost would be Nick's trust. If he had ever even considered trusting her, he wouldn't now. And there was no way he would ever love her the way she loved him.

"I'm fine," she managed past the lump in her throat. It

was a lie, she wanted to scream. She would never be fine again.

"Then let's go get our son."

Our son. The words echoed through her soul.

Nick's long fingers curled around Laura's elbow as he guided her up the long walk and through the double doors leading into the Careytown Home for Children. A wide, tiled corridor rolled out before them. Doors lined both walls. A sign proclaimed one as the main office.

A few moments later they entered the cheery office. A sunny yellow, the walls displayed hundreds of framed photographs. On closer inspection, Laura realized the pictures were of children of all ages. An older lady wearing a cartoon character T-shirt greeted them.

"May I help you?" She smiled kindly.

"I'm Nick Foster and this is Laura Proctor. I believe someone called to let you know we were coming."

The woman's smile immediately crumpled. "Yes. Our director received a call at home a couple of hours ago." She attempted another smile, which proved decidedly less enthusiastic than her previous one. She stood. "Follow me, please."

Uneasiness slid over Laura. Something was wrong. Her heart bumped into an erratic rhythm as a dozen possibilities flashed through her mind. They were too close now. Things just couldn't go wrong. Laura followed Nick and the receptionist into an inner office. Laura moistened her lips and squared her shoulders. Robby was safe. He was here and when Laura left, she would have her baby in her arms.

A woman of about forty waited for them inside the small office. Her hair was pulled back in a tight bun, revealing her attractive features. At present, those features were cluttered with what could only be labeled worry.

"Ms. Proctor. Mr. Foster." She shook first Laura's hand,

then Nick's. "I'm Mary Flannigan, the director. Please have a seat," she offered nervously.

"I'm sure you can understand that we're in somewhat of a hurry," Nick told her candidly.

With obvious effort, she produced a smile. "Of course." Mrs. Flannigan retrieved a file from her desk. "Before we go any further, I'll need you to identify the child."

Laura moved closer to the woman's desk. "Identify?"

Mrs. Flannigan opened the file. "We photograph all our children for our records."

The woman opened the folder and Laura's gaze latched onto the pictures of Robby. He smiled at the camera, those mischievous green eyes bright with happiness. "It's him," Laura breathed the words. Her fingers went instinctively to the photographs to caress her son's image. Tears rolled down her cheeks. "That's my baby," she murmured, awe in her voice.

Nick touched one of the pictures, his fingers tracing the image of his son. Laura watched the myriad emotions move across his handsome face.

"He's beautiful, isn't he?" Laura said softly.

Nick nodded. Laura knew that he couldn't possibly speak right now. He had just gotten the first glimpse of his son. A son he couldn't have denied even if he had been so inclined. Robby looked so very much like him.

Laura released the breath she had been holding and shifted her attention to Mrs. Flannigan. Maybe the lady was simply nervous over the mistake. She had placed a stolen child into adoption proceedings, unknowingly, of course.

"I'd like you to bring my son to me now," Laura said as calmly as she could.

Mrs. Flannigan looked first at Laura, then at Nick. As if somehow sensing that Nick would take the news better than Laura, she directed her words to him. "I am so sorry that this has happened." She shook her head. "I've been the director at this home for ten years and nothing like this has ever happened. Our staff is thoroughly screened."

"Get to the point, Mrs. Flannigan. Where is Robby?" Nick insisted.

"I don't know."

Laura's heart dropped to her feet. Her muscles went limp and passing out seemed a distinct possibility. "What?"

"When I arrived this morning, the night nurse was in a panic. Your child—" she moistened her lips "—was missing. When the midnight rounds were made he was there, but at seven this morning he was gone."

"Gone?" Nick leaned forward slightly, his intimidating frame looming over the woman's desk. "Don't you have security here?"

Mrs. Flannigan nodded. "Excellent security. No one gets in or out without a key after hours. We believe that one of our staff members took your son."

"No." Laura shook her head in denial. This couldn't be. She had only just found this place. He couldn't be gone.

"I thought you said you screen your staff," Nick countered hotly.

"We do, Mr. Foster. Elsa Benning is an excellent employee. I can't imagine why she has done this. She has worked here for more than twenty years. It doesn't make sense."

"How do you know it was her?" Nick demanded.

Mrs. Flannigan smoothed a hand over her hair. "She hasn't reported for duty this morning. In twenty years she hasn't missed a day." The director blinked beneath Nick's ruthless gaze. "She is the only employee who holds a key and who is unaccounted for this morning."

"No." Laura backed away from the reality. "No, this can't be."

"I am so terribly sorry. The Louisiana State Police have issued an APB."

"Laura." Nick moved toward her.

"No." Laura shook her head adamantly. "He has to be here."

"Ms. Proctor." The director stepped to Nick's side. "If it's any consolation to you at all, Elsa is a good woman. I don't believe she would hurt your baby."

NICK SETTLED an almost catatonic Laura into the passenger seat. He reached across her and buckled her seat belt. He had put a call into Ian to bring him up to speed. Nick closed the door and braced his hands on the top of the rented car. He squeezed his eyes shut and called the image of his son to mind. Dark hair, green eyes, chubby cheeks. Nick clenched his teeth to hold back the rage that wanted to burst from him.

Okay, he told himself. *Pull it together, man. You can't lose it now. Not here. Not in front of Laura.* His whole body ached at the look of pain and defeat sucking the life out of her. Nick straightened. By God he was going to find his son. One way or another. As much as Nick wanted his son, he wanted even more to reunite him with his mother. He couldn't bear to watch Laura suffer a minute longer. He skirted the hood and jerked his own door open. Nick dropped behind the wheel and snapped his seat belt into place. Laura had been through enough. Robby had been through enough.

And someone was going to pay.

Nick slammed his fist against the steering wheel again and again until the pain finally penetrated the layers of anger and frustration consuming him. Laura only looked at him, too grief stricken to react.

The cell phone in his jacket pocket rang insistently. Nick

blew out a heavy breath. He reached inside his jacket and retrieved the damned thing. He couldn't ignore it, it might be Ian.

"Foster," he said tautly. He had to get back in control.

"Nick, it's Ray."

Nick frowned. Why would Ray be calling him? The murder investigation. Damn. Nick massaged his forehead. He didn't want to do this right now. "Yeah, Ray, what's up?"

"I called James Ed's house and a policeman told me to call this number."

Nick impatiently plowed his fingers through his hair. "What can I do for you?"

"I'm not sure. But you mentioned that Laura's baby was missing." Ray exhaled mightily. "Maybe it's nothing, but a woman showed up here first thing this morning with a baby that looks the right age and the hair color's right. I remember all that black hair. She says she thinks the kid was stolen or something. We're running a check on her now."

Adrenaline pumped through Nick's veins. "What's her name?"

"One Elsa Benning."

"We're on our way." Nick started the car, then frowned. "Ray," he said before disconnecting, "do me one favor."

"Sure, buddy, anything."

"Don't let that woman and child out of your sight."

TIRES SQUEALING, Nick turned the wheel sharply, guiding the car into the precinct parking lot. Laura jerked forward when he braked to an abrupt halt. They had made the trip to Natchez in record time. She was out of the car right behind Nick. Her son was in that police station.

Laura rushed up the walk and into the building, Nick right on her heels.

"Detective Ingle," Nick said to the first officer they met in the corridor.

"Down the hall, fifth door on the left."

Laura was on her way before Nick could thank the man. Her heart pounding, her skin stinging with adrenaline, she burst through the door the officer had indicated. A half dozen desks filled the large room. Laura scanned each one. Her gaze locked on the back of a gray-haired lady. She sat in a chair, facing a desk. A tall man stood behind it shuffling through files. Ignoring all else, Laura rushed to the woman. Her heart pounding so hard in her chest that she felt certain it would burst from her rib cage, Laura stepped around the woman's chair.

Robby sat in her lap, pulling at the large ornate buttons on her jacket. Relief so profound swamped her, that Laura thought she might die of it. She dropped to her knees at the stranger's side. Laura held out her arms. "How's mommy's baby?" she murmured softly.

Robby reacted instantly. He flung his chubby little arms and bounced in the woman's lap. The woman, Elsa, smiled down at Laura and shifted Robby into Laura's arms.

Laura held Robby close. She inhaled deeply of his sweet baby scent. "Oh, my baby," she whispered into his soft hair. Emotions flooded her being so quickly and with such force that Laura could not think clearly.

The old woman nodded knowingly, capturing Laura's overwhelmed attention. "I knew this was no abandoned baby. Today they were going to give him to the adoptive couple." She shook her head. "I knew it wasn't right. So I brought him back to the police station in the city where they said he had been found."

"Thank you," Laura choked out. Robby tugged at her hair and made baby sounds as if nothing had ever been amiss. "I know you took good care of him."

"I did at that," Elsa agreed. "That's my job."

Laura smiled at the woman, then struggled to her feet. She turned to Ray Ingle, Nick's detective friend. "Thank you, Detective Ingle."

His lopsided smile warmed her. "Just doing my job, ma'am."

Taking a deep breath for courage, Laura turned to Nick. She manufactured a watery smile. "This is your son, Robby."

Total and complete awe claimed Nick's features. He touched Robby's hand. Instinctively Robby curled chubby little fingers around Nick's finger. The smile on Nick's face made Laura weak in the knees. She wanted so to offer Nick the opportunity to hold his son, but she couldn't bring herself to let go of him just yet.

"Hey, man," Ray exclaimed. "You've been holding out on me."

Nick just grinned at Ray, his eyes barely leaving Robby for a second.

"Canton is still at large," Ray mentioned quietly.

Laura turned to him, then looked at Nick.

"That's not good. Laura and Robby aren't safe as long as he's on the street," Nick returned, his gaze still riveted on his son.

Laura's arms tightened around her baby. "What will we do?"

"Do you have some place you can lay low until he's caught?" Ray asked Laura.

She glanced at Nick, then back to Ray and shook her head. "I couldn't possibly go to my brother's house, or the house in Bay Break." Laura had no money she could access without lengthy legalities. For one fleeting second fear slipped back into her heart. She snuggled her baby's head. None of that mattered.

She had Robby now.

"Laura, you can stay—" Nick began.

She shook her head, cutting him off. "That's not a good idea right now."

"Ma'am," Ray interrupted. "You and your little boy are welcome to stay with me and my wife until you figure this thing out."

Laura kissed Robby's satiny forehead. "Oh, I couldn't impose like that. I'm sure we can find some place."

"Why you'd be doing us a favor." Ray smiled widely. "You see, we're about to have our first child. My wife was an only child and has never had to care for a little one. She could use the practice." Ray blushed to the roots of his hair. "That is if you wouldn't mind."

Relief bolstered Laura's sagging resolve. "Thank you, Detective, that would be wonderful."

"I'll call my wife," he suggested quickly.

"You take good care of that fine little boy," Elsa said quietly.

Laura's gaze connected with the dark brown eyes of the older woman who had brought Robby here. "Thank you. I'll do my best." Belatedly, Laura shifted her attention back to Detective Ingle. "Is she going to be in trouble?"

"Don't you worry none about me," Elsa argued.

Ray shot Elsa a smile then turned back to Laura. "Apparently since her instincts were on the money, no charges will be pressed. And she won't lose her job," he added quickly. "But she will be on probation with Mrs. Flannigan for a while."

Elsa poohed Ray's comment. "Mary Flannigan will consider herself lucky I'm back. She couldn't get along without me."

Laura smiled down at Elsa. "I'm sure she couldn't."

Knowing she couldn't avoid the inevitable any longer,

Laura turned back to Nick. She steeled herself. It was impossible to read what he was thinking at the moment. "I've been on the run for a long time, Nick. So much has happened." She hugged Robby to her heart. "I need some time to pull myself together, before you take any legal steps to share custody." When he hesitated, Laura added quickly, "I'm not asking for forever, just a few weeks to figure out what happens next in my life."

Nick's gaze was intent on hers for several seconds before he answered. "All right. I can live with that as long as you keep me posted of exactly where you are and how—" his gaze moved to Robby "—and how my son is doing."

Laura stiffly nodded her agreement.

It was over.

She had gotten Robby back safe and sound.

She was safe.

But she had lost Nick.

Chapter Fourteen

Two weeks had passed. Nick had not tried to see Robby or taken any legal action, giving selflessly the time Laura had requested. She knew it was difficult for him. He called every day. Each time he asked the same question, how was his son? And then, how was she? Did he really care? Laura wondered. The way she did about him. She couldn't blame him if he didn't. And she certainly couldn't expect him to put off being with his son much longer. She could hear the growing anticipation in his voice with each call. Laura gazed forlornly at the salad on her plate. Though she felt more rested than she had in years, she had no appetite. Laura looked at her baby seated happily in the Ingles' brand new high chair, where he played with his food. His smiles and excited baby words let her know that Robby, too, was happy and rested. Laura's gaze shifted to her very pregnant hostess. Joy Ingle watched every move that Robby made with glowing anticipation.

Ray had been right. This time with Robby had done his wife a world of good, and greatly boosted her caregiving confidence. Laura was glad she had come. If only she could find that kind of happiness in her own life.

The doorbell chimed.

Joy frowned. ''Who can that be? It's too early for Ray

to be home for lunch,'' she said, glancing at the clock on the wall.

"I'll get it." Laura pushed to her feet. "I'm through anyway."

Joy smiled. "Thank you. I'll just bask in your son's eating antics."

Laura returned her smile, then headed for the front door. She breathed a sigh of satisfaction as she moved through the Ingle home. Ray and Joy were so much in love. When their baby came, he would lack for nothing in that department. Laura lifted a skeptical brow. Or any other department for that matter. She only wished Robby were going to grow up in a home filled with love and both his mother and father. How on earth would they ever manage sharing him? And if Nick married someone else?

Laura pushed the disturbing thoughts aside and paused in front of the door. Still cautious, she peered through the viewfinder. She didn't recognize the man waiting outside the door. Tall and handsome, he had dark hair and wore an impeccable black business suit.

Laura opened the door a crack, leaving the security chain in place. "May I help you?"

"Laura Proctor?"

Laura studied his steady gray gaze. "Yes."

"My name is Ian Michaels. I'm an associate of Nick's at the Colby Agency." The European accent, coupled with his dark good looks reminded Laura of James Bond.

She shook off the silly notion. Laura remembered the name. Nick had called him frequently, but she had never met the man. "Do you have any ID?"

"Of course." With practiced grace, Mr. Michaels removed the case containing his picture ID and held it up for Laura's inspection. "I have some news regarding your case."

Laura frowned. "Why didn't Nick come?"

"He thought you would be more comfortable if I took care of the final details."

Laura moistened her lips instead of allowing the frown tugging at her mouth to surface. Nick didn't want to come. He didn't want to see her. She supposed she really couldn't blame him. Laura had done a lot of thinking in the past two weeks. She had made a serious error in judgment. She should have trusted Nick. It was wrong for her to keep his son from him. Now she would face the consequences.

She removed the chain and opened the door. "Come in, Mr. Michaels."

He smiled. "Call me Ian."

Laura nodded and closed the door. She led the way to the living room and sat down on the sofa. Ian settled into a chair facing her.

"Laura, is everything all right?"

Joy hovered near the door, her expression wary.

"Yes," Laura assured her. "This is Ian Michaels, a friend of Nick's."

Ian stood. "It's a pleasure to meet you, Mrs. Ingle."

Laura watched the wariness melt from Joy's expression, only to be replaced by pure feminine appreciation. James Bond, all right, Laura decided.

Joy backed away from the door. "I'll just get back to Robby." She smiled. "Nice to meet you, Mr. Michaels."

Ian nodded. After Joy had gone, he sat down again. He settled his gaze back on Laura. "Canton has been caught," he said quietly. "He's being held by the authorities in Georgia awaiting extradition to Mississippi to face murder charges related to Dr. Holland's death."

Relief rushed through Laura. "Good. I'll breathe a lot easier knowing he's behind bars." Canton represented the last hurdle to a normal life.

"Nick has taken the liberty of upgrading security at your family home near Bay Break. You may return there whenever you're ready. He also suggested that you acquire a dog. A large dog," Ian added with a slight smile.

Laura couldn't help the answering smile. "Robby would love a dog."

"Good," Ian said with obvious relief. "Because Nick has already taken that liberty as well. A Mr. Rutherford is caring for the animal until you return."

Laura's smile widened at the thought of Mr. Rutherford. She hadn't seen him in ages. The day he had stopped by and talked to Nick she had been sleeping. Maybe it was time to go home. She swallowed tightly. Of course, it would never be the same. Doc was gone. And she still wasn't sure if she could forgive James Ed. He had called twice to check on her through Ray. With all that had taken place, James Ed had resigned as governor. According to Ray, James Ed had decided to return to practicing law.

"Detective Ingle tells me that James Ed has been cleared of all suspicion."

"That's correct," Ian confirmed.

Laura nodded. "I guess we'll work things out someday." For the first time in her life, Laura felt truly alone. She forced the thought away. She had Robby. She didn't need anyone else. Nick's image sifted through her mind, making a liar out of her.

"Mrs. Leeton has also been located. She has confessed to her part in your son's kidnapping."

Laura blinked back the moisture. "That's good." How could people she had known and trusted all of her life be so evil?

"It appears that James Ed and Sandra did not go through your entire trust fund. There is some money left."

Laura frowned. "I assumed he used all the money."

"Most of it," Ian explained. "But he has insisted on putting back all that he could. In fact, he plans to sell his private estate to add to that amount."

"I'm glad that some of the money is still there," Laura said with relief. Though she had her education, the idea of leaving her son with anyone after all they had been through was unthinkable, though she knew mothers did so everyday. After losing him once, Laura wasn't sure she could take the chance of leaving him in anyone else's care. "But I'd rather he didn't sell his home for me. If you would see that he gets that message I would appreciate it."

"Certainly," Ian offered. He paused for a moment. "Laura, the situation between you and Nick is none of my business, but I think you're both making a serious mistake."

Laura lifted her chin and leveled her gaze on this handsome stranger who seemed to read her entirely too well. "I don't know what else I can do. Nick doesn't appear to be interested in working anything out. Whenever he calls to check on Robby he never asks if I would like to talk about my plans. I have no idea what he wants. And, frankly, I'm tired of worrying about it."

Ian considered her words for a time. "Nick is suffering, too. He wants to do the right thing for his son. He's convinced that there is no hope for a relationship between the two of you, but he doesn't want to hurt you by taking legal steps."

Laura sat very still. "Did he tell you that?"

"Not in so many words. But I know him. He won't risk hurting you. But each day that passes knowing he can't be with his son, destroys another small part of him."

Laura shot to her feet. "Thank you very much, Mr. Michaels, for making me the bad guy." Suddenly restless, she paced back and forth in front of him.

Ian stood. "That's not my intent. I only wanted you to know that Nick—"

"Look." Laura's hands went to her hips. "I know I made a mistake, okay? I admit that. But it's done. I can't undo it. If Nick can't get past this, then what am I supposed to do?"

"You could start by telling him what you just told me," Ian suggested. "Nick doesn't want to take a wrong step where you and Robby are concerned. He's waiting for you to make the first move. He cares a great deal for you."

Laura's gaze connected with his. "And if you're wrong?"

Ian smiled, a lethal combination of confidence and masculinity. "I'm rarely wrong."

And somehow Laura knew he was right.

Laura locked the door behind Ian when he left. She sagged against it and heaved a beleaguered sigh. The first move. A knowing smile tilted Laura's lips. She had learned her lesson about not going out on a limb to trust the people she cared about. She would make a move all right.

All Nick Foster had to do was react.

NICK SHOVED the completed files into the out basket on his desk. Hell, it was Friday. If Mildred came up with any more paperwork for him today, her long-standing position at the Colby Agency would be in serious jeopardy. Nick smiled. The surface gesture felt strange on his lips after so long with nothing to smile about. The agency wouldn't be able to function without Mildred. She kept everyone straight, including Victoria.

Nick closed his eyes and allowed the images that usually haunted him free rein. Hell, it was late, he was tired. Why not add insult to injury? The memory of making love to Laura always surfaced first. Nick's fists clenched in reaction. The feel of her soft body beneath his. Her taste, her sweet smell. How would he live the rest of his life without being with her that way again? How would he live without her?

But he had ruined any chance of that with his arrogant pride. Nick had slowly, but surely come to terms with Laura's actions. She had been protecting her baby. Fear had kept her from coming to him. It still stung that she hadn't trusted him. But Nick had to remember that Laura had only been twenty-two at the time. Too young to make all the right decisions. Hell, he was thirty-four and he still screwed up regularly. Case in point, his handling of the situation with Laura.

Robby's chubby cheeks loomed as big as life in Nick's mind. His son. It still humbled him to think that he had a son. A son that wouldn't even know him at this rate. Nick had to do something. But what?

Laura apparently had no intention of ever speaking to him regarding her personal plans. He had given her every opportunity by always asking how she was when he called to check on Robby. What was he supposed to do? If he took steps to gain visitation rights he would only be making bad matters worse. How could he take Robby from his mother and bring him all the way to Chicago for weeks at a time? Nick knew he couldn't do that to Laura. There had to be a solution.

There had to be one, he repeated, as if the answer would come to him from his sheer determination.

But he had probably blown it with his unforgiving attitude.

A soft knock sounded at Nick's door. He looked up to find the subject of his reverie standing in his doorway. Stunned, Nick pushed to his feet.

"Laura." His first thought was that something was wrong.

"Hello, Nick." She smiled, Nick's breath caught. "May we come in?" She shifted Robby to her other hip.

The little boy looked as if he had grown considerably in the past two weeks. How could Nick allow one more day to go by without having his son in his life? He was not above begging at this point. But he wouldn't hurt Laura. The decision to work something out had to be hers. Her entire life had been spent with people manipulating her and telling her what to do. Nick wouldn't do that. He couldn't, no matter what it cost him personally.

Nick jerked himself to attention. "Yes, please, come in." He moved around to the front of his desk, his gaze riveted to the squirming baby in Laura's arms. A colorful diaper bag hung over one shoulder. Between the bulky coat, the diaper bag, and the baby, Laura was barely visible.

"Have a seat," Nick offered belatedly.

"No." Laura shook her head. "I need to say this right now before I lose my courage."

Nick's gaze connected with hers. Confusion formed a worry line between his brows. She had come all this way without calling first. "Is something wrong?"

Laura met his gaze head-on. "I've done a lot of thinking, Nick. And you're right. It was a mistake for me to keep Robby from you. I should have trusted you. I was wrong." She looked away for a moment. "But it's done and I can't take it back."

"Laura, I—"

She held up her free hand, halting his words. "Let me finish, please."

Nick relented with a nod. Anticipation stabbed at his chest. Could Laura possibly want to try again? Would she give him a second chance to prove that he loved her? And he did love her—with all his heart. He loved his son, too.

"I've decided that Robby needs to get to know his father. Enough time has been wasted already." Laura blinked, but not before Nick saw the uncertainty in her eyes.

She took the two steps that separated them and dropped the diaper bag at his feet. She thrust Robby at him. Surprised by her action, Nick put his arms around his son with the same uncertainty that he had seen in Laura's eyes. All else ceased to matter when Robby clung to Nick's chest. His little hands fisted in Nick's shirt. A foreign sensation seized Nick's heart. Nothing had ever felt like this before.

This was his child.

"So," Laura said, drawing Nick's awestruck attention back to her. "Here he is." She blinked again and backed toward the door a step. "Instructions are in the bag regarding what he likes to eat, and what he's allowed to drink. I'm at the Sheraton. Call me if you need anything, otherwise I'll pick Robby up on Monday." Moisture shining in her eyes, Laura whirled toward the door and started in that direction.

She was leaving.

Panic seized Nick. She couldn't do this—he didn't know the first thing about taking care of a baby. "Laura," Nick called to her swiftly retreating back. And, besides, he wanted her to stay. "Don't go," he added quietly. Robby bounced in Nick's arms, as if adding his agreement.

She paused at the door, then turned slowly to face him. Tears trekked down her cheeks. "Everything he needs is in the bag. You don't need me," she said, her voice quaking.

Nick swallowed with extreme difficulty. His arms tightened instinctively around the little boy in his arms. "Yes, I do. We do," he amended quickly. "I was wrong. You were afraid. You did what you thought was right. And I can't hold that against you.''

Laura crossed her arms over her chest. She swiped at the moisture dampening her cheeks. ''None of that matters. I just want to do what's right for Robby now.''

''So do I.'' Nick took a step in her direction. ''But I want us to do it together.''

Hope flashed in Laura's surprised gaze. ''You do?''

He smiled. ''I thought I made that pretty obvious a couple of times while we were in Bay Break.''

Laura pushed her hair back, her hand trembling visibly. ''I was afraid that it hadn't meant as much to you as it did to me. I can't be sure if you feel the same way I do.''

Nick reached out and touched one soft cheek. ''It meant the world to me—*you* mean the world to me.'' His heart ached at the worry etched across her beautiful face. ''It's been hell giving you the time and space you asked for. But this had to be your decision.''

Her expression grew suddenly solemn. ''I love you, Nick.''

''Could you put up with me for the rest of your life?'' he suggested softly.

''Are you asking me to marry you?'' Her eyes widened with anticipation.

''Absolutely.'' Nick leaned down and kissed those sweet lips. Her arms flew around his neck and she kissed him back. ''Is that a yes?'' he murmured when he could bear to break from her sweet kiss.

''Yes,'' she whispered.

Robby added his two cents worth in baby talk. Nick and Laura laughed. Nick stroked her cheek with the pad of his thumb. His fingers curled around her neck and pulled her closer. ''I love you so much, Laura,'' he told her softly.

"I've loved you since the day I first laid eyes on you."
Robby squirmed between them. "And I love our son."

Nick gazed lovingly at his son.

Laura's child.

His gaze moved back to the woman he loved with all
his heart. A frown creased Nick's brow. "You weren't really going to leave Robby here and me with no clue as to
how to take care of him, were you?"

She grinned. "Are you kidding? If you hadn't stopped
me before I got out the door, I was going to turn around
and demand that you marry me."

"I suppose it's only right that you make an honest man
out of me."

"It'll be my pleasure," Laura murmured, before kissing
Nick soundly on the lips.

Nick held his child and the woman he loved against his
heart as he planned to do for the rest of his life.

Epilogue

Victoria looked up from her desk when a knock sounded at her door. She smiled. "Ian, come in."

Ian Michaels crossed the room and paused before her desk. "You wanted to see me, Victoria?"

"Yes, have a seat, please."

Ian settled his tall frame into one of the chairs in front of her desk. As always, the man looked impeccable. Dressed in an expensive black suit, he presented himself in a manner very becoming to the Agency. His job performance remained at a superior level no matter how tough the assignment. He displayed numerous characteristics that Victoria admired. "I wanted to compliment you on your work here," she said finally. "You've done an outstanding job, Ian. The Colby Agency is very fortunate to have you."

"Thank you," he replied noncommittally.

Victoria almost smiled. Ian wasn't one to discuss his attributes, and he had many. He and Nick shared that particular characteristic. With Nick most likely not coming back, she needed to fill his position. Victoria had never seen Nick happier, and she couldn't be happier for him. Laura and Robby were just what he needed...what he deserved. But his absence left Victoria with a dilemma that required immediate action. Directing her attention back to the matter at hand, Victoria leveled her gaze on Ian's. "I'm sure you know that Nick has taken an indefinite leave of absence to be with his wife and child."

"Yes." That gray gaze remained steady on hers.

"That leaves me without a second in charge."

"There are several top investigators on staff. I'm sure you'll be able to find a proper temporary replacement."

Victoria did smile this time. "I already have."

"What can I do to assist in the transition?" he offered politely.

"You can direct Mildred to issue a memo announcing your promotion, effective immediately."

A hint of a smile touched Ian's lips. "Of course." He stood. "Is there anything else?"

"One more thing," Victoria said as she rose to match his stance. "I'd like you to personally handle this inquiry." She passed a thin red folder to Ian.

"Any specific instructions?" Ian glanced only briefly at the folder before meeting Victoria's gaze.

"The contact is Lucas Camp. He's a close personal friend. You have complete authority to handle whatever he needs."

"I'll keep you informed of my progress."

"That would have been my next request."

Ian smiled fully then, giving Victoria a tiny glimpse of just how much charm the man commanded. Without another word, he turned and walked to the door.

"Ian." Victoria halted his exit.

He turned back. "Yes."

"Don't let Lucas give you any flack. He can be a bit pushy at times."

Ian lifted one dark brow. "We'll get along fine."

"I'm sure you will."

Victoria watched with satisfaction as Ian Michaels walked away. She had made a wise choice.

0805/46 V2

❤ SILHOUETTE®
INTRIGUE™

SITUATION: OUT OF CONTROL
Debra Webb

Colby Agency: Internal Affairs

It was Colby agent Heath Murphy's sworn duty to bring Jayne
Stephens's father to justice...and protect her at all costs. Secluded
in the Colorado mountains, their forbidden passion hit him like an
avalanche. But who would be left standing once the dawn broke...?

MUMMY UNDER COVER Delores Fossen

Top Secret Babies

Infiltrating a fertility clinic suspected of manipulating DNA to
produce designer babies meant agents Riley McDade and Tessa
Abbott had to go undercover—as husband and wife wanting to start
a family. But as the danger intensified, their attraction—and their
baby—became all too real...

HIJACKED HONEYMOON Susan Kearney

Heroes, Inc.

After investigator Web Garfield had kidnapped Kendall Davis...
for her own protection, he wasn't prepared for the desire he felt
for his emerald-eyed captive. She'd been on the verge of a shotgun
wedding to a madman, but with her former fiancé on their trail,
would they succumb to temptation?

A ROSE AT MIDNIGHT Sylvie Kurtz

Eclipse

Nine years ago, Christiane Lawrence surrendered her innocence to
the mysterious Daniel Moreau. After making a deal with the devil
to keep his beloved safe, Daniel left without warning. Now back to
reclaim his woman—and the child he'd never known—could Daniel
banish the shadowy spectre of a madman bent on destruction?

Don't miss out! All these thrilling books
are on sale from 19th August 2005

*Available at most branches of WHSmith, Tesco, ASDA,
Borders, Eason, Sainsbury's and most bookshops*

Visit our website at www.silhouette.co.uk

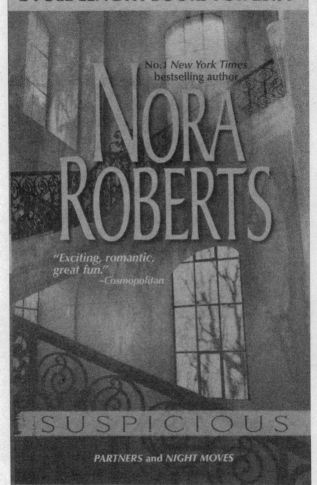

ANN HAVEN
PEGGY NICHOLSON

Homeward Bound

Because when baby's on the way
there's no place like home...

On sale 19th August 2005

Available at most branches of WHSmith, Tesco, ASDA,
Borders, Eason, Sainsbury's and most bookshops.

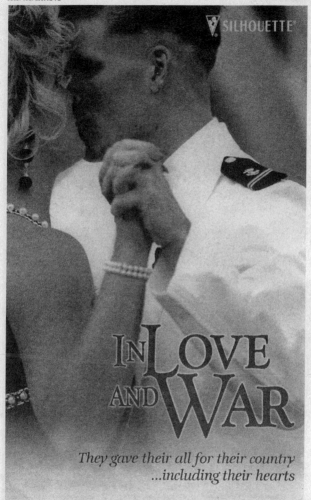

Desert
Heat

Susan Mallery
Alexandra Sellers

On sale 19th August 2005

Available at most branches of WHSmith, Tesco, ASDA, Martins,
Borders, Eason, Sainsbury's and all good paperback bookshops.

0805/51 V2

▼ SILHOUETTE®

Desire™ 2 in 1

Dynasties: The Danforths

THE ENEMY'S DAUGHTER Anne Marie Winston

The only woman who tempted Adam Danforth was the daughter of his father's most venomous rival. But when the media unexpectedly exposed their affair, he began to wonder...

THE LAWS OF PASSION Linda Conrad

Marc Danforth was going to have to get away from his sexy bodyguard. FBI agent Dana Aldrich was supposed to save him from doing anything stupid, like trying to clear his name, and she tempted him beyond all reason.

The Millionaire's Club

REMEMBERING ONE WILD NIGHT Kathie DeNosky

On New Year's Eve, Travis Whelan came home and found himself face-to-face with Natalie Perez, the one woman he couldn't forget...and the baby he hadn't known about.

BREATHLESS FOR THE BACHELOR Cindy Gerard

With her creamy skin, sultry eyes and luscious mouth, Carrie Whelan was ripe for the plucking, and Ry Evans was starving for a taste of her! Still, he wasn't about to ravish his best friend's *virginal* sister.

LONETREE RANCHERS: MORGAN Kathie DeNosky

Morgan didn't know a thing about delivering babies, until he came across a stranded woman in labour. He didn't anticipate the urgent, primitive stirrings the breathtaking beauty would arouse.

HOLD ME TIGHT Cait London

Alexi Stepanov was a powerful, dangerous male, everything that experience had taught Jessica Sterling to fear and mistrust, but Alexi warmed her world with his large, loving family...and a heat he alone stirred.

On sale from 19th August 2005

Available at most branches of WHSmith, Tesco, ASDA, Borders, Eason, Sainsbury's and most bookshops

Visit our website at www.silhouette.co.uk

Narrated with the simplicity and unabashed honesty of a child's perspective, *Me & Emma* is a vivid portrayal of the heartbreaking loss of innocence, an indomitable spirit and incredible courage.

ISBN 0-7783-0084-6

In many ways, Carrie Parker is like any other eight-year-old—playing make-believe, dreading school, dreaming of faraway places. But even her naively hopeful mind can't shut out the terrible realities of home or help her to protect her younger sister, Emma. Carrie is determined to keep Emma safe from a life of neglect and abuse at the hands of their drunken stepfather, Richard—abuse their momma can't seem to see, let alone stop.

On sale 15th July 2005

▼ SILHOUETTE

Passionate and thrilling
romantic adventures

Sensation

NIGHT
WATCH

Suzanne Brockmann

▼SILHOUETTE

Life, love and family.

SPECIAL EDITION

THE ONE
& ONLY
Laurie Paige

▼ SILHOUETTE

Super*ROMANCE*

Right place, wrong time

Judith Arnold

Enjoy the drama, explore the emotions, experience the relationship.

∇ SILHOUETTE

INTRIGUE™

Breathtaking romantic suspense.

His mysterious ways

Amanda Stevens